ARIZONA!

The twenty-first riveting adventure
in the WAGONS WEST series—
a showdown between the forces of good and evil,
where the destiny of a nation lies in the stark courage
of men and women strong in their passions
and unflinching in the face of death . . . or desire

★ ★

WAGONS WEST

ARIZONA!

FROM THE MOUNTAINS TO THE RIVERS, AMERICA WAS CASCADING TOWARD A CRISIS . . . A CONFRONTATION OF MIGHT AND RIGHT THAT WOULD DECIDE A NATION'S DESTINY

TOBY HOLT—
A man who has known triumph and tragedy, this valiant frontiersman is wary of the young girl who has won his heart . . . and blind to the enemy sworn to destroy him.

ALEXANDRA WOODLING—
A dazzling Kentucky beauty as fearless on horseback as she is bold in Toby's arms, only one thing can break her . . . the death of the man she loves.

CARL SYKES—
A Machiavelli of malice, he harbors a grudge against Toby Holt that can only be settled by a diabolical plan to capture him . . . and kill him.

REED KERR—
One of those fine young soldiers so brave a nation must never forget them, so willing to lay down their lives a nation can never repay them.

★ ★

★ ★

CINDY HOLT—
Victim of a broken heart, this loveliest of Western belles has rebounded into the wrong man's arms . . . and into an ambush on the cruel Arizona sands.

CAPTAIN HENRY BLAKE—
Honor is his talisman, yet deceit is what he must practice at his nation's request as he takes on a new assignment deep in the dark heart of international intrigue.

BARONESS GISELA VON KIRCHBERG—
One of the world's great beauties, she lives for the total abandoned love she gives to Henry Blake . . . as time runs out for a lady doomed by fate.

HERMANN BLUECHER—
His appetite rages for every extreme in gluttony and desire, as the crafty mind of this head of Germany's secret police schemes to expose the American he hates.

DOÑA ALLEGRA CHRISTINA Y MORENO—
Behind the venal mask of an ambitious woman, beats a heart so evil, so depraved, that a ring of poison is her chosen path to power.

JANESSA HOLT—
Still a spunky child in body, her daring fight against disease and death will transform her into a woman . . . but it may demand her innocence as the price of survival.

★ ★

Bantam Books by Dana Fuller Ross
Ask your bookseller for the books you have missed

WAGONS WEST ★ TWENTY FIRST IN A SERIES

ARIZONA!

DANA FULLER ROSS

 Created by the producers of
**White Indian, Stagecoach,
Children of the Lion,** and
America 2040.

Book Creations Inc., Canaan, NY · Lyle Kenyon Engel, Founder

BANTAM BOOKS
TORONTO · NEW YORK · LONDON · SYDNEY · AUCKLAND

ARIZONA!

A Bantam Book / March 1988

Produced by Book Creations, Inc.
Lyle Kenyon Engel, Founder

ISBN 0-553-27065-6

Published simultaneously in the United States and Canada

Bantam Books are published by Bantam Books, a division of Bantam Doubleday Dell Publishing Group, Inc. Its trademark, consisting of the words "Bantam Books" and the portrayal of a rooster, is Registered in U.S. Patent and Trademark Office and in other countries. Marca Registrada. Bantam Books, 666 Fifth Avenue, New York, New York 10103.

PRINTED IN THE UNITED STATES OF AMERICA

O   0 9 8 7 6 5 4 3 2 1

★ ARIZONA! ★

Virginia City

Nevada

San Francisco

California

Los Angeles

Pacific Ocean

San Diego

Yuma

Colorado River

Mexico

Fort Yuma

© BOOK CREATIONS INC. 1987

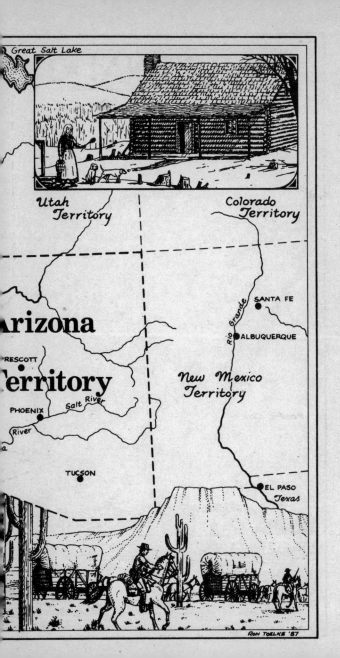

Great Salt Lake

Utah
Territory

Colorado
Territory

Arizona

PRESCOTT

Territory

PHOENIX

Salt River

River

TUCSON

Santa Fe

Rio Grande

ALBUQUERQUE

New Mexico
Territory

EL PASO

Texas

RON TOELKE '87

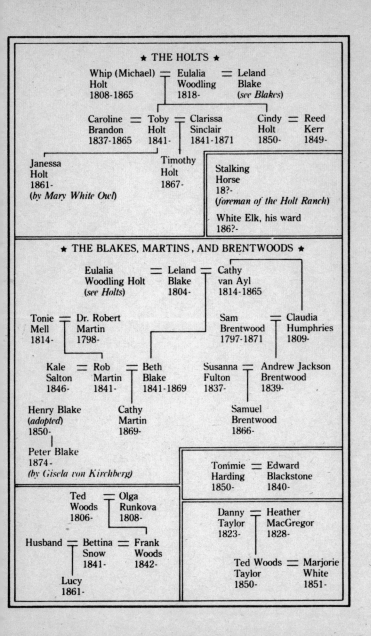

★ THE HOLTS ★

Whip (Michael) Holt 1808-1865 = Eulalia Woodling 1818- = Leland Blake (see Blakes)

Caroline Brandon 1837-1865 = Toby Holt 1841- = Clarissa Sinclair 1841-1871   Cindy Holt 1850- = Reed Kerr 1849-

Janessa Holt 1861- (by Mary White Owl)   Timothy Holt 1867-

Stalking Horse 18?- (foreman of the Holt Ranch)

White Elk, his ward 186?-

★ THE BLAKES, MARTINS, AND BRENTWOODS ★

Eulalia Woodling Holt (see Holts) = Leland Blake 1804- = Cathy van Ayl 1814-1865

Tonie Mell 1814- = Dr. Robert Martin 1798-

Sam Brentwood 1797-1871 = Claudia Humphries 1809-

Kale Salton 1846- = Rob Martin 1841- = Beth Blake 1841-1869   Susanna Fulton 1837- = Andrew Jackson Brentwood 1839-

Henry Blake (adopted) 1850-   Cathy Martin 1869-   Samuel Brentwood 1866-

Peter Blake 1874- (by Gisela von Kirchberg)

Tommie Harding 1850- = Edward Blackstone 1840-

Ted Woods 1806- = Olga Runkova 1808-

Danny Taylor 1823- = Heather MacGregor 1828-

Husband = Bettina Snow 1841- = Frank Woods 1842-

Ted Woods Taylor 1850- = Marjorie White 1851-

Lucy 1861-

ARIZONA!

I

Wind stirred the sparse, dry clumps of brush dotting the desert landscape as Luke Fergus rode toward a gaunt, boulder-strewn mountain in the distance. It was a mild day for this part of the Arizona Territory, with the torrid summer heat starting to give way to the cooler temperatures of autumn, but sweat streamed down Fergus's face.

A drifter who found occasional jobs here and there, Fergus was not a brave man, but before him lay an ordeal that would try the courage of the most dauntless hero. The scourge of northern Mexico, as well as of Arizona Territory now that most of the U.S. Cavalry had been withdrawn from the region, were the comancheros. Consisting of motley bands of renegade Indians, Mexicans, and outlaws from north of the border, they were more savage than the most warlike Indian tribes. And Fergus was on his way to meet the leader of the largest and most feared band of comancheros anywhere—a man known as Calusa Jim.

Three vultures circled lazily in the cloudless sky over the mountain, and Fergus eyed them with the uneasy feeling that they might be an omen of what awaited him. The promise of money that had drawn him here now seemed much less alluring. As he neared the base of the mountain, he turned his horse toward the mouth of a narrow ravine.

Two men with rifles at the ready suddenly stepped into view from behind boulders, startling Fergus. One looked like a Mexican, and the other was fair-haired, but both were ragged and filthy. Fergus reined up and swabbed sweat from his face with a sleeve. "Howdy," he greeted the men, trying to sound cheerful. "It ain't as hot today as it has been, is it?"

The two sentries merely stared at him, and at last one of them motioned him on with a wave of the rifle barrel. Fergus cleared his throat nervously as he entered the ravine. After a while it opened out into a wide arroyo that was crowded with some eighty men lounging around fires after their midday meal, their horses picketed nearby. Movement and conversation ceased as everyone stared at Fergus. He felt like a rabbit that had stumbled into a coyote den.

A mixture of Indians and whites, the men were as grimy as the two sentries, and just as threatening. Numb with fear, Fergus looked around and finally picked out the Mexican he had met outside Yuma. At first the man ignored him, then silently pointed to a big, heavyset, bearded fellow sitting a little apart from the others. Fergus dismounted and, leading his horse, walked over to the man he assumed was Calusa Jim.

Conspicuously neat and clean compared with the others, the bearded man wore a blue coat with red cuffs and collar that looked like a foreign military tunic. He glanced up at Fergus with eyes that were as hard as flint, then proceeded to pick his teeth with a long, gleaming knife.

"Are you Mr. Calusa Jim, sir?" Fergus asked, hat in hand.

"I am Calusa Jim," the man replied with a heavy French accent. "You have some information for me?"

Fergus nodded eagerly and related what he had heard two soldiers discussing in a Yuma saloon: Several heavy crates had recently been received at the fort and stored in a warehouse, and although they had been covered with canvas to conceal the markings on them, one of the soldiers had peeked under the cloth and seen that the crates contained the new model Winchester rifles. "The soldiers guessed the rifles must be going to Fort Peck," Fergus concluded.

"Yes, they must be." Calusa Jim pointed the knife toward Fergus. "I want to know when they will be sent there. When you find out, leave something under the tree where you met Mendoza. He will see it and wait for you there the following night."

"Yes, sir," Fergus said. "What do you want me to put under the tree?"

The man smiled menacingly as he took a twenty-dollar gold piece from his pocket and tossed it at Fergus's feet. "Put a wooden cross under the tree," he replied. "We shall find a good use for it if your information is wrong."

The comancheros nearby laughed in cold, ruthless amusement at the remark, and Fergus could still hear their laughter echoing well after he had snatched up the money, mounted his horse, and ridden rapidly back out of the camp.

Elmer Sewell walked along a quiet side street in San Francisco toward a sprawling, four-story Victorian house. The windows were dark, covered by heavy drapes, but a dim red light beside the front door announced the nature of the establishment and the fact that it was open for business. Sewell climbed the steps and went inside.

A hulking bouncer was sitting in the entry hall, and the stony expression on his scarred face changed to a servile grin as he jumped up to greet Sewell, who was a key member of the organization that owned the bordello. Nodding perfunctorily, Sewell handed the man his coat and hat.

"Why, it's Mr. Sewell!" The madam, a fleshy woman of forty wearing a garish dressing gown, stood in the drape-covered doorway to the parlor beyond. In the dim light, her cosmetics almost succeeded in softening her coarse features. "Are you looking for entertainment to-night, Elmer dear?"

"No, I have business upstairs," Sewell grumbled.

The woman gave a disappointed pout. "Well, when you're through, maybe."

Sewell nodded curtly and stepped past her into the large, candle-lit parlor. The air was thick with incense and perfume, and scantily clad women lolled on couches with well-dressed men and discussed terms, their voices almost drowned by a jangling music box in a corner. The few unoccupied women smiled at Sewell provocatively.

Usually Sewell would have responded to their un-voiced invitations, but tonight he was racked with anxiety. He was to meet with Carl Sykes, his employer and the head of the ruling criminal organization on the West Coast, to discuss a task he had been assigned but had failed to accomplish. And Sykes was ruthlessly unforgiving of failure.

A few months before, wanting to extend his organiza-tion eastward, Sykes had sent Sewell to Kentucky to es-tablish a presence in the horse-racing circuits there. Sewell had found a perfect location for a base of operations, a large horse farm near Lexington that was owned by a debt-ridden old man named Alexander Woodling.

Once in Kentucky, however, Sewell had met with nothing but obstacles. Far from achieving what he had been sent to do, he had not even managed to secure ownership of the farm, and two of his best men had been wounded in a gun battle. In the end he had returned to San Francisco in defeat.

Slowly climbing the stairs, Sewell thought in growing apprehension of what Sykes might do to him. The sounds from the bordello on the first and second floors had faded when he reached the top landing, where a guard sat outside the entrance to an apartment that occupied the entire floor. The guard stood up and knocked on the door, and a moment later a servant opened it and bowed as Sewell stepped inside.

Sewell followed the man along a wide, rosewood-paneled hallway with deep, costly carpeting underfoot. The servant tapped on a door, opened it, and quietly announced Sewell, then stood aside. Sewell stepped in, and the door closed behind him.

In the center of the room, a small, balding man was seated behind a desk, studying columns of numbers on a sheet of paper, and at first he ignored Sewell's greeting. With his rimless glasses, the man looked like an accountant or a bank clerk, but his thin, bloodless lips hinted at a cruel nature, and his eyes were devoid of life.

After nearly a full minute, Sykes sat back and stared at Sewell. His ominous silence and the fixed gaze of his strange, blank eyes made Sewell increasingly nervous. Knowing that a single quiet word from this man could bring death, Sewell shifted from foot to foot, feeling sweat breaking out on his brow.

Sykes finally spoke, his voice soft and almost effeminate. "So you had two men wounded, Sewell," he said. "Wounded by a girl with a rifle. You let a girl drive you back here with your tail between your legs."

"No, sir," Sewell replied. "A girl sneaked up on us with a shotgun loaded with buckshot, and she did wound two of my men. But that wasn't the reason I came back, Mr. Sykes."

"Then what was the reason?" Sykes asked patiently.

"That family is related to Toby Holt," Sewell said glumly. "I found out that the girl sent him a telegram, asking him to come there. And with him involved . . ." He left the sentence unfinished and shrugged helplessly.

Sykes nodded toward a chair beside his desk. "Sit down," he said.

The invitation surprised Sewell, particularly under the circumstances, because Sykes usually made his underlings stand when he talked to them. Sewell sat down, and after a moment Sykes spoke again. "What do you think we should do now?"

"Well, sir, before I left Kentucky, I did find a likely candidate to run the operation there—someone who knows all about horses. His name's Waldo Crowley, and he used to fix races back in New Jersey."

Sykes's reaction was unreadable. "And this Crowley, is he still in Lexington?" he asked.

"Yes, sir," Sewell responded.

"Is he wanted by the police?"

"He might be back east, but not in Kentucky, sir. Still," Sewell added nervously, "with Holt involved, maybe we'd better find another way of going about things. Everybody knows about him and what happens to anyone who goes up against him."

"Yes, everyone knows about him," Sykes agreed calmly. "But what would happen if we got rid of him? Everyone would be grateful to us, and they would fear us. No one would try to move in on us in Kentucky."

"Get rid of Toby Holt?" Sewell shook his head. "That's been tried before, Mr. Sykes. Like I said, anybody who goes up against that man always winds up—"

"Shut up and think for a moment!" Sykes snapped impatiently, finally revealing his anger. "When people hear a rattlesnake rattle, they're automatically afraid. The same thing happpens when people hear Toby Holt's name. Now, isn't that what happened to you?"

Sewell hesitated, recalling his first meeting with Toby Holt, and he realized that Sykes was at least partly right. Certainly he was wary of the man. "Yes, I suppose so," he confessed.

"Very well," Sykes said. "Let's look at the situation logically. Toby Holt is a difficult man to deal with, but he's still a man. He can be killed by a bullet, just like anyone else. How many men have you killed, Sewell? A dozen or more, haven't you? And several of them were men who were very difficult to deal with, weren't they?"

"Yes, sir," Sewell replied, understanding where the

conversation was leading. "With some of them I had to do a lot of planning, and I had plenty of men to help me. But Toby Holt is different, because he—"

"Now, wait just a minute," Sykes interrupted. "You're still letting that name scare you. To take care of Toby Holt, you might need a better plan and more men than just this Crowley fellow, but you would have them." His tone became confidential. "Look, you know it would be of great benefit to us if we got rid of Holt permanently. But it would also be of personal benefit to you, because it would make you a rich man. I would put *you* in charge of the operation in Kentucky, with a share of the profits."

Suddenly the entire matter was set in a different perspective for Sewell. Sykes was absolutely right: Toby Holt was a formidable enemy, but still he was only a man, and a man could be killed. "All right, I'll do it, Mr. Sykes," he said. "I'll deal with him, then set up the operation in Kentucky."

Sykes smiled in satisfaction. "I knew all along that you could do it, if you only made up your mind to it. I'll tell you what—I'll think of some ways to go about taking care of Holt, and we'll discuss them tomorrow. Maybe this Crowley fellow will be of use. For now, you just go downstairs and enjoy yourself."

"Yes, *sir*!" Sewell felt confident, and his nervousness had vanished. "It'll take a good plan and several men, but I know I can manage it. Right now, Toby Holt is living on borrowed time."

A crisp chill was in the air at the teeming port city of Bremerhaven, Germany, as Captain Henry Blake of the United States Army boarded a waiting train. He had arrived on a fast steamer from New York only an hour earlier and had hurried through customs and then across town to the station, yet even now he was impatient for the train to depart.

Oddly enough, this very station had been the scene of an attempt on Henry's life six months before, when he had been en route back to the United States from his duty assignment in Germany; but that scarcely entered his thoughts now. Instead, he was filled with anxiety over the condition of the woman around whom his entire life revolved—his mistress, the Baroness Gisela von Kirchberg. When the train finally began pulling out of the station, Henry dug into his coat pocket and took out the telegram that had brought him rushing back across the Atlantic.

Tattered from the innumerable times he had read it during his long journey, the sheet of paper contained a cryptic message, all of it except the last two sentences garbled from poor transmission on the transatlantic cable. The first legible sentence stated that a Dr. Ian MacAlister had been summoned to attend to Gisela. The other was a request for Henry to return to Germany as soon as possible.

He had lost little time, barely more than two weeks having passed since he received the telegram in Hartford, Connecticut. Dr. MacAlister, the staff physician at the British embassy in Berlin, was the doctor who, two years earlier, had diagnosed the recurring illness that troubled Gisela. He had called it a perityphlitic abscess—a condition somehow connected with the appendix—and it was eventually and invariably fatal.

When the white-jacketed porter announced dinner was being served, Henry was still staring blankly at the telegram, not knowing whether or not Gisela was yet alive. He put the telegram away and went to the dining car, where he picked listlessly at his food. At nightfall he went to his sleeping berth and lay staring into the darkness, worrying about Gisela as the train sped through the night.

The next day, the train was deep into the central provinces of Germany, where summer still lingered. Towns among the vast vineyards in the river valleys were decked with colorful pennants in the bright sunshine, indicating that the grape harvest was in and wine festivals were in progress. Henry thought about the festivals he had attended with Gisela and wondered if they would ever go to another one together.

The train pulled into Frankfurt-am-Main during late afternoon, and Henry had to wait an hour for a local train to Grevenburg, the village at the foot of the hill upon which Gisela's palatial mansion of Grevenhof stood. His agony of suspense was near its end, for people in the village would know about Gisela; yet that awareness only made the wait seem endless to him. Finally the local train arrived, and Henry stepped aboard.

The sun dipped below the mountains bordering the lush valley of the Main River, and the train chuffed along the tracks, stopping at every village. When it reached Grevenburg, Henry hurried down the steps. A porter was standing next to the baggage car, and the old stationmaster was there, too. Recognizing Henry, the man smiled and called to him.

"Welcome home, sir. The carriage from Grevenhof is not here, so they must not have known you were coming."

"I sent a telegram," Henry said tersely in fluent German, striding up to the man. "But I wasn't sure of my arrival time. How is the baroness?"

"I have not seen her, but I understand that she is well," the old stationmaster replied. "I was told she has resumed working."

For a moment Henry felt numb, unable to believe what he had heard. Then, with a physical impact, relief flooded through him. After weeks of frantic worry he was emotionally exhausted, and it took him a long moment to collect himself, listening as the stationmaster continued talking. The man had noticed the new insignia on Henry's epaulets and was congratulating him on his promotion. "Thank you," Henry managed. "And you are quite certain the baroness is well?"

"Absolutely, sir," the man replied cheerfully. "Instead of waiting for a carriage, would you like to use my horse to ride up to Grevenhof? You would get there more quickly, and you could return it when the carriage comes to fetch your baggage."

"Yes, I would like that very much."

"My pleasure, sir," the stationmaster said. "I'll send a boy to saddle it for you."

Henry thanked the man again and walked toward the stables to wait.

The boy seemed to take forever, and Henry, impatient after his months of separation from Gisela, himself lent a hand, then mounted and quickly rode past the village. Dusk had fallen, and the road leading up through the vineyards was dark and deserted. Near the top of the hill, Henry could see the lights of Mainz, at the junction of the Main and Rhine rivers, and a short while later the road curved into a wide, tree-lined avenue that led back through acres of formal gardens to Grevenhof, a palatial mansion of some one hundred rooms. Only a few windows were lighted.

Henry dismounted in front of the mansion and ran up the steps and inside. The butler emerged from a room at one side of the vast, dim entry and looked at him in astonishment. "Welcome home, sir," he said, after a quick bow. "I apologize for not having the carriage at the station for you, but we didn't know—"

"That's quite all right," Henry cut him off. "I borrowed the stationmaster's horse. Is the baroness upstairs?"

The butler seemed puzzled by Henry's words. "Yes, sir," he said. "Shall I send to the station for your baggage?"

But the question fell on deaf ears, for Henry was already halfway up the staircase in his eagerness to see Gisela. He reached the landing with long strides and went into the sitting room between their bedrooms.

He found her reclining on a couch and reading business papers through her pince-nez. She looked somewhat wan, he thought, as she often did after an attack of her illness, but otherwise she was as lovely as always—perhaps even more so. As Gisela looked up and saw him standing in the doorway, her pince-nez toppled from her nose. Her blue eyes were wide with surprise, and a delighted smile transformed her countenance. Her pale features suddenly glowed with the radiance of her love for him, and tossing the papers aside, she started to get up from the couch to come to him.

Henry rushed to her side and guided her back down. "No, you must rest," he said. "Let me look at you, Gisela."

"And let me look at you, Heinrich," she whispered, her eyes filling with tears as she caressed his face. "My heart has been gone for so long that I cannot believe it has finally been restored to me."

Savoring the sound of her deep, melodious voice and the scent of her perfume, Henry took her in his arms and kissed her. When she finally pulled back, she touched the insignia on his shoulder. "I am so pleased for you, loved one," she said. "You certainly more than deserve to be a captain." Abruptly her smile faded. "When I heard about that man who tried to kill you in Bremerhaven, I was terrified."

"You couldn't have been more worried than I was when I heard about your illness," he replied. "How long did it last this time?"

"Illness?" she echoed, then gave a puzzled laugh. "One would hardly call it an illness. Why do you use that term?"

His confusion more than matching hers, Henry took out the telegram and showed it to her. Gisela put on her pince-nez and looked at it, frowning over the garbled sentences and reading the two that were legible. Suddenly she began laughing merrily. Taking his hand, she stood up. "Come, I have something to show you, Heinrich."

Utterly mystified now, he followed her to the door. "If you haven't been ill," he questioned, "what was that telegram about?"

"You will see, loved one."

Henry walked down the wide, dark hallway with her. Outside the door at the end of the hall, Gisela put a finger to her lips for silence, then quietly turned the knob.

The room, dimly lighted by a single candle, was equipped as a nursery. A woman with a huge bosom, whom Henry recognized as one of the cook's helpers, was sitting on a chair by a large, ornate cradle. She stood up, curtsied, and moved her chair aside as Henry and Gisela stepped to the cradle.

Looking down at the sleeping baby, Henry was speechless for a moment, as something that had been bothering him for months was suddenly explained. Before he had left for the United States, he had sensed that Gisela was not altogether regretful over his approaching departure. That had seemed uncharacteristic, but now he realized that she was pregnant at the time.

When he looked back at her, Gisela nodded to his unvoiced question. "If we had to be separated, that was the best time," she said softly, so as not to wake the baby. "I would not have been a good companion for you while I was heavily pregnant. And besides, my business affairs needed attention." Her smile revealed a trace of anxiety. "It is a boy. Are you pleased? Do you like him, loved one?"

Henry laughed aloud as he reached into the cradle. "Nothing could please me more!"

Gasping in alarm, Gisela tried to stop him from touching the baby, but Henry was already tucking the blanket around the infant to pick him up. Gisela sighed in resignation, stepping back as the baby stirred and began bawling lustily. Henry beamed and spoke loudly over the wailing.

"He's very healthy, isn't he? He cries as strongly as any I've ever heard."

"Yes, it could serve excellently as a foghorn," Gisela replied with a frown.

Henry looked at her in surprise. "Does the crying bother you so much?"

"Yes," she replied bluntly. "I am not and never have been fond of children, Heinrich. Actually, Dr. MacAlister said it was slightly premature, but it's quite normal."

"He delivered the child?" Henry asked. "How long did he remain here?"

"Too long. He was here for a week after the baby was born, prodding at me and interrogating me daily. I finally sent him away when he began hinting that he would be more than willing to conclude his affairs in Berlin and become a household physician here."

"That wouldn't be a bad idea," Henry returned. "Many estates much smaller than this one have a household physician. I worry constantly about your illness, and—"

"No, Heinrich," Gisela said firmly. "The staff can see a doctor in Mainz, and I will not have that officious Scotsman hovering over me constantly. I don't need pampering. I am not a weak woman."

"No one would suggest that you are," Henry replied. "But I'd be much happier if there were a doctor here for you, as well as for the baby. Please do this for me, Gisela."

She started to refuse again, then hesitated. Henry rarely asked her for anything, and she was reluctant to turn down any request he made. "Very well, Heinrich," she said. "If you insist."

"I do." Henry handed the baby to the nurse, and Gisela took his arm as they walked back to the sitting room.

The butler came in a little later with a bottle of wine and a light supper, and as they ate, they discussed what to name the child. Gisela said that Richard was a traditional name in her family, but it was her nephew's name, and she also liked Henry's name. Henry, wanting the baby to have a name that was spelled the same both in English and in German, favored her first choice; but then an obvious alternative occurred to him.

"How about Peter?" he suggested. "It's the same in both our languages, and it was my father's name." Henry never talked about his natural father, a onetime gunfighter by the name of Peter Purcell who had been murdered by outlaws when Henry was only sixteen. Henry had subsequently been adopted by General Leland Blake—now the commander of the Army of the West—and, prospering in his new life, had repressed the memory of his real father.

Lately, however, Henry had not been on the best of terms with his adoptive parents, who had expected him to marry Cindy Holt, the general's stepdaughter. Cindy had since married another army officer.

Gisela did not fail to notice Henry's determined expression. "Then Peter it is, loved one," she said. "It is a fine old name. And your name will make a good second name, and my family name a third."

Henry smiled. "Peter Heinrich von Kirchberg Blake," he pronounced. "It has an impressive sound.

Over breakfast the next morning, Gisela again brought up a subject that Henry had successfully avoided the previous evening.

"The police in Bremerhaven," she said, "came to the conclusion that the man who tried to kill you last spring was an anarchist. To me that sounds unlikely, but I haven't been able to think of a better explanation. Do you have any idea of who the man was?"

As he had the previous evening, Henry made a noncommittal reply and changed the subject. In addition to the attempt upon his life in Bremerhaven, there had been a second attack, on board ship, which Gisela did not know about. It had come even closer to succeeding than the first attack, and Henry had good reason to suspect that the same man was behind both attempts.

The man was the head of internal security of German military intelligence, an enigmatic, obscure figure named Hermann Bluecher. He was rarely seen in public, but Henry had gleaned a few facts about him from a friend in British intelligence. An enormously fat man, Bluecher was zealously patriotic and independently wealthy, and he had many influential friends in German industry who shared his extreme, nationalistic views. Certainly the fact that Henry was posted as a foreign observer—purportedly to study procurement procedures—at the strategic Mauser Arms Works was not a mark in his favor. Gisela had used her considerable influence in Berlin to get him the post, and Henry had been sending back valuable information to Washington.

Gisela, sensing his mood, did not press him for further information, but Henry had barely finished breakfast when his peace of mind was once more snatched from him. A silver tray with two envelopes on it was brought to him by the butler.

"A courier from the American embassy in Berlin just delivered these, sir," he announced. "I took the liberty of showing him to the kitchen for breakfast while he awaits your reply." The butler bowed and turned away, and Henry glanced at the envelopes, then at Gisela, before opening them.

The first message was from John Simpson, Henry's project officer in Washington. It stated that a high State Department official had requested that Henry be temporarily assigned to work with a department employee in Europe on a matter of crucial importance. Accordingly, Henry was officially detached from active duty to work with the man, who would contact him.

The man, Henry knew, could only be Clifford Anderson, whom he had met and become friendly with during his last trip home. Anderson was a State Department employee only in a general sense; more to the point, he was an intelligence agent working with the British on a plan to end the civil strife in Spain and install a friendly government there. The plan involved assisting Alphonse Ferdinand, the young son of the deposed Queen Isabella II, to become the next ruler of Spain.

The other message was from Anderson. In obscure terms that had meaning only between Anderson and Henry, it indicated that the plan for Alphonse Ferdinand to announce his claim to the Spanish throne was ready to be set into motion. However, evidence had surfaced of a plot to assassinate the young royal heir upon his arrival in Spain. The message ended with an urgent request for Henry to come to England as soon as possible to assist in countering the threat to Alphonse's life.

Glancing over the messages again, Henry frowned. The vital interests of his nation were closely involved, because Alphonse Ferdinand had a high regard for the United States and would guide policies in Madrid accordingly. But the threat against the young Spaniard also worried Henry from a personal standpoint.

Alphonse Ferdinand was attending Sandhurst, the British military college, where Henry had met him a little over a year before. On that occassion, Henry had been fortunate enough to forestall an assassination attempt against the young Spaniard, and as a result the two men had become good friends.

Putting the messages in his pocket, Henry took Gisela's hand and broke the news to her as gently as he could.

When he had finished, she spoke. "I had hoped we would have some time together, but I suppose it was not to be. Very well—I will make the best of it. While you are gone, I will go to the mineral baths at Bad Kreuznach, to lose weight and fully recover from having the baby. After that, perhaps your duties will permit us to be together." She got up, put her arms around him, and kissed him invitingly. "But we still have today, loved one. And who knows?" she added, as the sound of the baby crying could be heard echoing from upstairs. "Perhaps by then our darling Peter will not cry constantly."

Lying on his back in his luxurious bedroom in Berlin, with his favorite courtesan performing expertly on top of him, Hermann Bluecher also knew that Alphonse Ferdinand would soon announce his claim to the throne of Spain.

In fact, Bluecher had long ago concluded that Alphonse would assert his claim as soon as he had the support of the army—and he now had that support, Bluecher's Spanish agents had reported. For various reasons, Bluecher urgently wanted the rival Carlist faction to rule Spain, but how to prevent Alphonse from taking the throne was a problem with no easy solution.

As always when he had an intractable problem, Bluecher was plunging into sensual excess to satiate himself and cleanse his mind of everything but the cold, unemotional logic needed to make the best decision. Adela Ronsard, a lissome, dark-eyed beauty who was the illegitimate offspring of an Egyptian woman and a French soldier, was a supremely skilled practitioner of her profession. Working atop him with a determination equal to her skill, she sweated and panted until she had finally achieved success, then climbed off him and lay exhausted on the huge bed that had been specially constructed to accommodate his three-hundred-pound bulk.

After catching her breath, Adela addressed him in the syrupy tones Bluecher knew she reserved for her wealthiest clients. "Did I please you, Hermann dearest?" she asked. "I hope I did, because I enjoy coming here. I grow so lonely for you between the times that you send for me."

Bluecher ignored her and lurched off the bed. Not bothering to conceal his gross nakedness, he went to a cabinet, opened a drawer, and tossed a handful of coins on the floor. "That is in addition to what the butler will give you," he said. Adela exclaimed in delight and scrambled after the money, and as she gathered it up, Bluecher put on his robe and slippers and left.

Before he reached the bottom of the stairs, the butler stepped from a doorway and silently waited for instructions. "Pay the woman and send her back in the carriage," he directed. "But first bring a repast to me in my study."

Bluecher proceeded along the hall to his study, where he sat down behind his desk and glanced over the papers awaiting his attention. One was confirmation from an agent that the American who had been a thorn in Bluecher's side, Captain Henry Blake, had returned to Germany. Bluecher glanced at it and put it aside.

The American had proved either lucky or far more capable than Bluecher had anticipated. A few months before, he had bested two of Bluecher's most reliable agents under circumstances few could have survived. He was, Bluecher mused, a dangerous threat. But in comparison with other matters at hand, he was no more than an annoyance that could be dealt with when an opportunity arose.

All the other papers and correspondence on the desk pertained to Alphonse Ferdinand and the civil war in Spain. As Bluecher scanned the messages and reviewed the facts, the butler carried in a tray bearing a deep custard pie and a tall, steaming tankard of cocoa.

The butler laid the tray on the desk and went back out. Using a soupspoon, Bluecher began pushing huge chunks of pie into his mouth, washing them down with gulps of the thick, sweet cocoa. As he pondered the problem facing him, he ate and drank faster and faster, the creamy custard and warm, sticky cocoa trickling down his mounded double chins.

Although the German government viewed Alphonse Ferdinand's prospects favorably, Bluecher himself preferred the Carlist faction, which was at odds with Great Britain. His superiors simply did not have the intelligence to see what was so clear to him: that if the Carlists succeeded, it could lead to war between Spain and Britain— and while those two powers were fully occupied, Germany could build a colonial empire.

The year before, Bluecher had provided weapons for Carlist agents to assassinate Alphonse Ferdinand at Sandhurst. The Carlists had failed miserably, which made him wary of assisting them again, but there was only one other serious alternative candidate to the throne—one that he did not even wish to contemplate.

Doña Allegra Christina y Moreno was a lineal descendant of Ferdinand VII, the ruler prior to Isabella II, who was Alphonse's mother. Doña Allegra had a twenty-year-old son, a young army officer who had virtually as legitimate a claim to the throne as did Alphonse.

The woman frequented all the courts in Europe, including Berlin, and Bluecher had accumulated a full dossier on her. While she would undoubtedly be willing to plot against Alphonse Ferdinand in favor of her own son, she was extremely headstrong and lacked intelligence, which would make her difficult to control.

Having finished the pie and cocoa, Bluecher picked up a bell from his desk and rang it. The butler opened the door and admitted a servant with a basin of water and towels, who proceeded to wash the custard and cocoa off his employer's face. As Bluecher sat there patiently, he decided to help the Carlists again.

The assistance, he reflected, would once more have to be through indirect channels. Certainly his own superiors must not learn about it, for their plodding minds would never understand. No, the only way to ensure complete success was to assign one of his most capable private agents.

As soon as the servant had finished his task, Bluecher summoned the butler and reached for pen and paper. He wrote a brief message, addressing it to Josef Mueller, one of his best agents, and directing him to return to Berlin at once.

Bluecher folded the message and handed it to the butler. "Take that to the telegraph office immediately," he ordered. Then, belching cavernously, he again picked up the report on Captain Henry Blake.

II

The fairgrounds on the outskirts of Lexington, Kentucky, were alive with activity as Toby Holt edged his buggy through the crowd toward the racecourse stables. Shouting vendors hawking refreshments trundled their carts around the crowded grandstands, and everywhere people were milling about, waiting for the day's main event to begin.

In the distance the trees were in autumn hues, a riot of color in the bright sunshine after days of rain. Toby smiled fondly at the small, slender woman on the seat beside him.

Alexandra Woodling, Toby's distant cousin, was strikingly attractive in a bright green dress, hat, and cape that complemented her auburn hair and sparkling hazel eyes—and, as was frequently the case these days, she seemed almost to read Toby's thoughts. "It's a perfect day for a race," she observed. "The course will be a bit muddy, but nothing I can't handle."

Toby's pride that Alexandra would be riding in the race today, and that her friends and neighbors respected her enough to allow her to compete with the men, was written clearly on his face. At thirty-two years of age and with rugged good looks, Toby was an experienced man of the world who had already been married twice and had two children back home in Portland, Oregon. He felt both protective and attracted toward Alexandra, who, he had to admit, acted much older than her eighteen years. As she smiled confidently at him from under her wide hat, her charming, mischievous features had the inner glow that came only from a first love, and while there had been other women in Toby's life, none had affected him quite the way Alexandra did. He foresaw problems between them, mainly owing to their difference in age, but Toby, too, was in love, and he could no longer envision life without this young woman.

Alexandra's eyes danced with the same excitement that gripped the crowd, for it was the day of the Lexington Cup, the major cross-county event of the year. The previous day, Toby had accompanied her to Lexington to bring a horse to the stables and to examine the course. It had looked formidable to him—a perilous, grueling test for both horse and rider—but Alexandra had been filled with eager anticipation as she paced off the approaches to the obstacles and planned her tactics for the race.

They had almost reached the stables when Alexandra gripped his arm and pointed. "There's the colonel, Toby."

Toby turned the buggy and brought it to a halt. Colonel Basil Claibourne, a tall, dignified older man whom Toby had met during his first visit to Kentucky, was master of the Fairfield Hunt, which Alexandra had been a member of for several years. Today he was also serving as secretary of the race committee, as was clear from his top hat and official's ribbon on the sleeve of his cutaway coat. He greeted the couple warmly as they stepped out of the buggy, then asked Alexandra about her father, who had been shot in the shoulder several weeks earlier, in an incident at his nearby horse farm, Fair Oaks. News of the trouble had brought Toby rushing to Kentucky.

"He's healing well," Alexandra replied. "But he regrets missing the Cup, of course. Our man Jonah is staying with him. When I brought my horse here yesterday,

Colonel, your head groom was kind enough to offer to look after him for me. I do hope you don't mind."

"On the contrary, I was delighted when Jubal told me about it. I noticed that you're riding a chestnut instead of your black stallion."

"Yes, Turco has a tender shoulder from a spill we took last week, so I decided to use Oberon. I'm still a bit stiff myself."

"Well, he's certainly a magnificent animal," the colonel said, "and he should do just fine. We have a total of sixty-three entries, so you'll be riding with a good field. But this may be the last year of open competition."

"Oh?" Alexandra's startled expression belied her calm reply.

The colonel nodded toward a man standing a dozen yards away. "That fellow in the traveling salesman's suit is the reason. His name is Crowley, and he's hired a commercial jockey to ride a horse he entered. He's also been betting heavily, and not simply sporting wagers, I'm afraid. We can't have professional gambling, so the entries next year will probably be limited to members of organized hunts."

Alexandra craned her neck to see Crowley through the crowd. He appeared to be about forty years old, with a considerable paunch beneath his flashy, checked, wool suit. He was talking loudly with another man and jabbing a cigar to emphasize a point.

Toby could understand Claibourne's disapproval. To the bluegrass aristocrats of Kentucky, horses were a way of life, and the competition in their hunts, races, and other events was fierce. But it was also governed by standards of conduct, dress, and sportsmanship that were as rigidly defined as the rules of chess. In this setting, Crowley stuck out like a sore thumb.

"The hunt master of Stone Ridge filed a protest about Crowley's using a commercial jockey," Claibourne continued, "and so did some other people, but I talked them into withdrawing them. At this point it would only hold up the race."

"I agree." Alexandra released Toby's arm. "Well, I'd better change into my riding clothes, or I'll be the one to hold up the race."

"I'll get Jubal to saddle your horse," the colonel volunteered, looking around. He called out and beckoned to his head groom, a short, aged black man in a neat suit and hat. "Mr. Holt," Claibourne said, turning back to Toby, "why don't you join me at the officials' stand after you park your buggy?"

"I appreciate that, Colonel." Toby got back into the buggy and handed Alexandra the bag containing her riding clothes. "I understand the governor will be here to see the race. I'd like to meet him, if possible, and have a word about who I think was behind the trouble at Fair Oaks. Has he arrived yet?"

"Yes, he has," Claibourne replied. "I'll be glad to introduce you."

Toby thanked the man again, wished Alexandra good luck, and drove off. Jubal Simmons, modestly hanging back, smiled affectionately as Alexandra greeted him. He was a gray-headed, wrinkled man, and like most others connected with the horse and hunting circuit in the region, he had known Alexandra since she was a child.

He took the bag containing her riding clothes as they walked to the stables. "That Oberon looks like he has plenty of speed and bottom, Miss Alexandra," he commented. "Between the way you ride and that horse, it'll sure surprise me if you don't collect a ribbon for at least second or third place today."

"Oberon can stay with the field," Alexandra agreed, "but he's only four, and he hasn't been in many competitions." As they entered the stable, the huge, muscular hunter recognized her, whinnied softly, and moved toward her. He bobbed his head and lashed his tail as Alexandra stroked his muzzle and talked to him, but he was excited rather than nervous, sensing the atmosphere outside. Alexandra took the bag from Jubal, went into the adjoining storeroom, and closed the door behind her.

As she undressed, Alexandra talked with Jubal through the partition. The man had examined the course as closely as she had, and they discussed the obstacles and their approaches. She had pulled on her tight white riding trousers, tucked in her shirt, and struggled into her knee boots by the time Jubal got around to mentioning Crowley, as she knew he would. "I expect the colonel told you about him," he said.

She took her black ribbon and black cravat from the bag and stepped to a small mirror on the wall. "Yes, he did," she replied, pulling back her hair and tying it with the ribbon. "He said several protests were filed against him."

"That's right. Everybody is mighty mad about how that man's been acting. Did the colonel tell you about the jockey he hired?"

"No, he didn't."

"Well, the colonel probably doesn't know anything about him, but I've heard some talk. His name is Durgin, and he'll do anything it takes to win. He's riding a bay. You'd better keep your eye on him, Miss Alexandra. Do you want me to put boots on your horse? Those banks might be slick today."

Tying her cravat, Alexandra weighed what to do. Leather boots on a horse's forelegs interfered with its stride to an extent. On the other hand, a horse sliding down a steep, muddy bank could catch a foreleg with a rear shoe. "Yes, boot him, please," she said.

The buckles on the boots rattled as Jubal began putting them on the horse, talking to it quietly. Alexandra took her small black derby and black riding coat from the bag, donned them, then stepped back to the mirror. As she was dusting her coat and smoothing the wrinkles from it, a thought occurred to her. "Jubal, do you know how long Crowley has been here and where he's from?"

"No, I don't—not exactly. I believe he showed up here a few months ago and decided to stay, and I've heard rumors he's from somewhere in the East. But I'm not sure. Do you want me to find out for you?"

"No, it isn't important. Thank you anyway, Jubal."

They fell silent, Jubal moving about on the other side of the partition and Alexandra thinking about Elmer Sewell, the man behind the recent attempt to drive her father off his farm.

Sewell evidently wanted the farm for some purpose to do with racing, yet it was obvious from her encounters with him that he knew nothing about horses. Even owners who never touched a brush or currycomb still had to know *something* about horses, if only to see that they were being properly cared for.

Crowley, on the other hand, was experienced with horses. He had apparently come onto the scene in Lexington at about the same time as Sewell, then had stayed. Alexandra wondered if he was the answer to how Sewell intended to manage a horse farm.

The overflow crowd had congregated around the racecourse when Alexandra left the stables. As she rode Oberon to the rear of the stands, where the other contestants were gathering, a rider who could only be Durgin crossed the dirt path in front of her.

The man was angular and wiry, with a dour expression. He was riding a bay, as Jubal had described, but Alexandra would have known him in any event. He was improperly dressed for the occasion, without a cravat and wearing a cap and jacket. With hunters and show horses, controlling the animal with undetectable signals was a measure of the rider's skill, but Durgin was reining his horse about as if it were a carriage hack.

Ignoring the glares of disapproval, he rode up to the other contestants. Alexandra, knowing virtually all of them, touched her riding crop to her hat in acknowledgment of their greetings. Durgin turned to her. "Well, lookee what we have here," he commented sarcastically.

"Yes, a lady, and one of the best riders in the state," a man named Tom Marshal replied heatedly. "Her presence makes up in large measure for the less desirable elements among us."

Others remarked in agreement, and Durgin's face flushed with anger. Another rider asked Alexandra why she was riding the chestnut instead of her stallion, and as she explained, she shifted in her saddle, uncomfortably aware that her right thigh was still sore from the fall.

But the main topic of conversation among the riders was the course. Portions of the fence enclosing the track had been removed for the cross-county race, a course of some eight miles across broken terrain to the east. The race began and ended at the stands. Always a difficult challenge, the course was changed each year.

A race steward made his appearance and began sending the riders out to the starting line at intervals of a few seconds, and the crowd broke into waves of applause as the finely trained horses moved along the track in front of the stands.

The applause became mixed with catcalls and boos, however, as Durgin rode out onto the track, reining his bay roughly. The steward frowned and glanced at the stands, then hastily sent out another group of riders, beckoning first to Alexandra.

Knowing what had to be done, Alexandra signaled her mount with a touch of her toes, and Oberon, immediately responding, broke into a graceful parade trot, arching his neck and lifting his hooves high. Out on the track, she guided the horse with her feet and calves, moving him along the front of the stands in a zigzag from one rail to the other.

The fancy gait, which was always pleasing to the spectators, was bone-jarring to the rider. Alexandra's bruised thigh throbbed, but the crowd's attention was turned from Durgin, and the applause was renewed, louder than ever.

In front of the dignitaries' boxes, Alexandra signaled again with her feet and calves, and Oberon spun and faced the stands, trotting sideward as Alexandra doffed her hat.

Colonel Claibourne, the governor, and the others tipped their hats in return, and Toby, who was also sitting in the governor's box, clapped as loudly as anyone. Alexandra had to look away from him to maintain her solemn demeanor. She signaled the horse, turning him, and replaced her derby as she rode on to the starting line.

The riders at the starting line were also watching her, and as she reined up, Tom Marshal called to her, "That chestnut can certainly show, Miss Alexandra, but can he run and jump?"

"Get a good look at his head, Mr. Marshal," she called in reply. "After the race begins, you'll see only his nether end."

Marshal laughed appreciatively, and presently the entire field was gathered behind the rope across the starting line. Colonel Claibourne came down from the stands, and a man with him gripped the lever attached to the rope. As the crowd became hushed, the colonel lifted an arm, waited for a moment, then dropped it quickly, the man jerked the lever and the rope fell.

The horses surged into motion. Oberon tried to break into a run, but Alexandra held him back to a gallop in the center of the field of straining, pounding animals. As they left the track itself, she concentrated on the perils of the course that lay ahead.

Some four or five abreast, the horses streamed across a meadow toward the first obstacle, a split-rail fence. It was a "natural," not having been created especially for the course, and as the riders came up to it, there was the inevitable milling confusion caused by the less-experienced contestants. Some horses refused the jump, running into each other as they turned from side to side, and the two judges stationed at the obstacle shouted at them to clear the path.

Concentrating on finding an unobstructed route, Alexandra let Oberon set his own approach and take the obstacle. Excited and still trying to run, he overreached extravagantly, soaring over the rails in a huge leap that would have cleared a triple fence. On the other side, Alexandra pulled him back to a gallop again.

The next obstacle was also a natural, a large fallen tree, and Alexandra held Oberon back firmly as he tried to expend his energy recklessly in his eagerness to jump it. Not until the final approach did she shift her weight forward, letting the horse surge ahead and build up momentum for the jump.

When she was in midair, a young rider who was vigorously using his riding crop passed and fouled her. The horses bumped as they landed, squeezing Alexandra's left leg between them, and she called out angrily. The young man shouted an apology, however, and one of the judges at the obstacle bellowed a warning to the man.

The course turned onto a narrow, wooded lane, and the first difficult obstacle loomed ahead. It was a high barricade, with a muddy brook on the other side of it. Alexandra knew from studying the course that those who crossed toward the left side would land in knee-high water, while from the center to the right the brook was considerably deeper.

Several riders had already made the jump, and the two judges, surveying the confusion on the far side, seemed disconcerted. One shouted in warning to the approaching riders, while the other was busy trying to clear up the confusion on the other side, in order to prevent serious injuries. Heedless of the judge's warnings, riders began bunching toward the left, and horses were bumping together as they leaped the barricade.

Alexandra, deciding against the moderate approach she had planned, gambled on the advantage of her lighter weight on a large, agile horse. She broke to the right side of the lane in a long, fast approach. At the barricade she leaned over the saddle, and Oberon lifted into a powerful jump. The obstacle passed below her, and she glimpsed the tangle of horses and riders flailing about in the muddy water.

Oberon cleared the deepest part of the brook, his rear hooves sinking into mud at the edge of it. Then out of nowhere a riderless horse cut in front of them, its eyes wide with panic. Oberon collided heavily with it, but Alexandra clung to the saddle, her sore thigh pinched tightly between the two horses as Oberon stumbled and almost fell. He regained his footing after a moment and galloped on along the lane.

The field was thinning rapidly. Only some fifteen riders were in front of Alexandra now, and the hoofbeats behind her were faint. She glimpsed Durgin ahead, beating his horse mercilessly to stay up with the leaders. As the lane curved out of the trees, angry shouts rose ahead, and Alexandra saw Durgin bumping his horse through others to get to the inside of the curve.

The course led into a meadow and across two barricades of logs and brush, both of which Oberon took easily; then a steep mound lay ahead. As the leaders went up the embankment, Durgin and others who stayed to the right side ascended it with normal difficulty, their horses struggling and sliding. But for some reason the left side was much more slippery, and the first horses that attempted it lost their riders as they tumbled back down the slope.

A judge at the top of the mound shouted and waved riders to the right side of the path. He also seemed surprised, and indeed, some difficulties on the course were starting to look like sabotage to Alexandra. A more immediate problem was at hand, however. Two horses were sprawled across the trail, blocking her path, and as one of them climbed to its feet, she swerved Oberon just in time for him to make the jump over the other horse. Oberon climbed the right side of the slope, mud flying into the air as his heavy hooves churned. Going down the other side of the mound, Alexandra felt Oberon's rear hooves slide into his forelegs, and she was relieved that Jubal had suggested the boots.

Another mound, even steeper, loomed ahead, and Oberon slowed to a walk as he struggled up it. On the other side, he planted his forefeet stiffly to slide down the slope on his rear legs. Again Alexandra felt his rear hooves hit his forelegs, this time knocking them from under him. She kicked out of the stirrups, ready to jump free if he tumbled.

For a breathless instant he teetered on the verge of rolling; then he turned onto his side and slid. Alexandra held on to the saddle, slipping down the muddy bank with him. A riderless horse rolled past, one of its flailing hooves coming within an inch of her face, but Oberon reached the bottom of the slope safely, and Alexandra pulled herself back into the saddle as he scrambled to his feet and galloped on.

The course followed a narrow road through trees again, in a gradual curve that led back toward the fairgrounds. The field was well spread out now, with some riders having fallen far behind and others saving their horses for the finish. More than a few had resigned from the race and were resting their horses before riding back to the fairgrounds.

Oberon was still galloping strongly, Alexandra having held him back from the start, and she began overtaking riders one by one. Presently she saw Durgin ahead. He had stopped whipping his horse, apparently saving its strength for a hard finish. The distance between them slowly closed.

When Alexandra was a few yards away, Durgin glanced over his shoulder. Then, as she started to pass, he reined his horse sharply toward hers. Oberon veered and slowed, falling behind again as he almost stumbled over a log beside the road. "That was a deliberate foul!" Alexandra shouted angrily.

The man's only reply was an oath snarled over his shoulder, and Alexandra, keeping her distance behind him, glanced around. She knew he would swerve toward her again if she started to pass, and while Oberon was hundreds of pounds heavier than the bay and more than a match in a bumping contest, no other riders were in view behind her to serve as witnesses if Durgin fouled her again.

The road curved slightly, and far ahead Alexandra saw and recognized a dismounted rider, his horse apparently lame. He was a man named Hamilton, a longtime member of the Exmoor Hunt. She eased the pressure on the reins, letting Oberon close the distance, then braced herself for a heavy collision between the two horses.

But this time Durgin used another tactic and slashed at Oberon's head with his crop. Alexandra jerked the reins back just in time, the horse slowing and flinching as the crop hissed past his eyes. Ahead she saw Hamilton looking on in angry astonishment, but her concern over having a witness was forgotten in the sudden, boiling rage that seized her.

The butt end of her riding crop consisted of an eight-ounce lead ball wrapped in leather, and she slipped her hand from the wrist strap and held the crop by the other end as she urged Oberon forward again. The two horses streaked past a shouting Hamilton, but Durgin ignored him and lifted his crop to slash at her horse's head again.

As he began to swing, Alexandra touched her spurs to Oberon's flanks. The horse surged forward, and the crop missed his head. Alexandra took the stinging blow across her stomach, but she was already swinging her own crop. Durgin's sour smile abruptly disappeared as he saw what was hissing through the air toward him. He tried to dodge, but the lead ball struck him solidly in the mouth.

It was as if he had run into an invisible barrier. His horse galloped out from under him, and he slammed down onto the road and rolled across it. Hamilton rushed toward him.

Alexandra reined up and turned back, ready to hit him again if he rose to his feet, but the man was sprawled limply, groaning, his face streaked with blood. "He deliberately fouled me and tried to hit my horse with his crop!"

she panted to Hamilton. "Will you back me if he protests?"

"I doubt if he can now, Miss Alexandra," the man replied, breaking into a smile. "But I'll stick up for you. Hurry and be on your way now—and good luck!"

Wasting no more time, Alexandra reined Oberon around. She knew the delay had cost her precious seconds, allowing the leaders to pull far in front of her. Long minutes passed before she saw other horses ahead, but then Oberon, as if sensing her burning desire to win, began catching up with them and passing them.

The last difficult obstacle was a steep hill with a barricade just beyond the crest. She climbed it, and from the top she could see that five riders were in front of her, the leaders some hundred yards away. A rider had been stopped by the barricade, and he waved and wished her good luck as Oberon cleared the height in good form.

The horse was tiring, however, and he lost his footing going down the steep slope. As he began to stumble, Alexandra kicked out of the stirrups and jumped clear. She tumbled and slid down the slope behind Oberon, pain stabbing her right thigh. At the bottom, she picked up her muddy hat and put it back on as the horse struggled to his feet.

The rider and judges atop the hill looked to see if she or the horse was injured. More vital seconds passed as Alexandra felt Oberon's sides and examined his legs and hooves. Satisfied, she sprang onto the saddle and rode on.

The remainder of the course stretched across rolling meadows, leaving the five riders ahead of her in clear view. Like her, they showed the evidence of the grueling course. Two of the men were without hats, one had the back of his coat torn open, and all of them and their mounts were spattered with mud.

Oberon was breathing heavily, his lips flecked with foam as he continued to overtake the other horses. The fifth rider reined to one side of the course to make room as Alexandra passed him and began closing on the next leader. The split-rail fence was ahead, and the other rider took the right side of the course as Alexandra guided Oberon to the left. The horses galloped neck-and-neck toward the fence and jumped it simultaneously. The other horse faltered in regaining his balance on the other side, however, and Oberon pulled into fourth place.

Tom Marshal was in the lead, Alexandra could now see, with the second-place rider some ten yards behind. Ten yards behind him and twenty ahead of Alexandra was a third-place ribbon, and Alexandra bent low in the saddle as Oberon steadily closed the distance.

The stands came into view ahead, and Alexandra could hear the distant cheering over the pounding of the horses' hooves. The third-place rider glanced back and began smacking his horse with his crop. The distance had shortened to ten yards but remained there as the horse ahead lengthened its stride.

Alexandra's heart was pounding, for she knew the moment of truth was at hand. Oberon had never before been tested to the limits of his endurance, and now she would find if he had the vital edge of will that made a magnificent horse a champion. She tapped his shoulder with her crop and touched spurs to his flanks, and his response sent her spirits soaring.

He *was* a champion, somehow finding the strength to increase his stride. Alexandra passed the rider in third place and began closing on the first two. Pandemonium broke out in the stands, the cheering a deafening roar as the horses pounded toward the finish line, less than a length separating them. Alexandra saw Colonel Claibourne standing in a tense half-crouch, shading his eyes with his hand to make certain of the order of finish, and then she was past him, knowing that she had not won, but feeling satisfied nonetheless.

Tom Marshal had finished first, the other man second. The applause and cheering from the stands continued unabated as Alexandra sat up on her saddle, letting Oberon slow and then stop. She shook hands with the two men, who, like her, were speechless with exhaustion, and Colonel Claibourne came along the track and congratulated all three of them.

In the aftermath of the race, Alexandra became aware of her aches and pains, but it was anything but a new experience, and she endured the discomfort stoically. As she walked Oberon back and forth at the stables to cool him down, she took firm steps and tried to keep herself from limping.

"I understand you had some trouble with Crowley's rider." Toby came up to join her, his smile indicating that someone had told him about Durgin. "I also understand that you attended to it—but if you don't think it's been dealt with completely, I'll go see him."

Alexandra put an arm around his waist and hugged him in appreciation. "I don't think that will be necessary," she said.

"I also hear that someone apparently made the course much worse than it was supposed to be. Crowley must have been behind that."

Alexandra had heard similar talk from the other riders, confirming her own suspicions. "Yes, I agree, but that isn't evidence, is it? It also occurred to me that he's just the sort of man Sewell would hire as a manager for a horse farm."

"We're thinking along the same lines," Toby said. While they talked, he kept glancing down toward her legs. "How do you feel?" he said.

"I'm fine."

"Uh-huh." Toby sounded unconvinced, but he did not press the point. "I wish," he said after a moment, "that I was a poet. Then maybe I could find the words to tell you how I felt when I watched you cross that finish line. As it is, all I can say is that I love you and you're truly the most amazing woman I've ever met."

Alexandra flushed, and with uncharacteristic shyness she turned away and busied herself stroking Oberon's muzzle. "I'd better get cleaned up now, or they might give my ribbon to someone else."

"They'd better not try. I'll see you in a few minutes."

Back in the stable, Jubal Simmons took the horse. Brushes, sponges, and buckets of water were in readiness, and Alexandra took off her coat and hat as Jubal began washing the mud off the horse.

"If you was a man," Jubal said, "I'd offer you a drink. But I suppose it's improper to offer a young lady a drink."

"It can be our secret," Alexandra suggested. "What do you have?"

"Well, it's supposed to be bourbon," Jubal muttered, taking a flask from its hiding place in the hay and handing it to her, "but it tastes more like plain old popskull. The man I bought it from charged me twenty cents, and I think he cheated me out of a dime. What do you think?"

Alexandra took a swig and blinked as the raw, harsh whiskey burned her throat. "More like fifteen cents, I reckon," she said, returning the flask. "Do you have any liniment?"

Jubal chuckled and handed her a brown bottle. In the storeroom, Alexandra pulled down her riding trousers and rubbed the liquid over her bruised thigh, which had turned a nasty shade of purple. A little later, after she had sponged most of the mud from her clothes, she thanked Jubal and led the horse back out.

At the side of the stands, she saw Crowley arguing with Colonel Claibourne and several of the judges. Toby was standing nearby listening, his expression stony. Crowley was blustering loudly, his face red with anger, and he pointed to Alexandra as she led her horse around the stands.

"That's her right there, and I had to send him to a doctor!"

"Your man," Claiborne returned icily, "deliberately fouled the young lady's horse and assaulted her personally. She merely defended herself."

Crowley shook his head violently. "My man said it

35

wasn't that way at all. But that's not the point. What I want is a no-winner declared for the race, and then both sides can present their cases."

"So you won't have to pay the wagers you made?" Claibourne added bluntly. "I'll do no such thing. You gambled on using a commercial jockey in a cross-county race, and you lost, sir. But maybe it wasn't gambling, considering there were unexpected pitfalls on the course that would have been of great advantage to a rider who knew where they were."

"Don't you accuse me of anything!" Crowley snapped indignantly. "If you do, you'll either prove it or be sued for slander. Now, I'm formally protesting the race, and I want a no-winner declared."

The colonel started to reply, but Toby, apparently tired of listening to the argument, interrupted him. "But there *was* a winner," he said, stepping closer to Crowley. "More than one, in fact. You're a winner also, Crowley, because you're still on your feet. I'm not accusing you of anything, but you know what you did, and so do I. So you'd better shut up and leave it at that."

Seconds passed, no one speaking or moving. The flush drained from Crowley's face, replaced by a blanch of fear; then he turned and stalked off. Claibourne politely thanked Toby for ending the pointless argument, and the other judges chimed their agreement. But as she watched Crowley stride away, Alexandra was not so sure they had heard the last of him.

Darkness had fallen when Toby and Alexandra turned off the road south of Lexington and onto the lane leading to the Woodling horse farm. Oberon, his ribbon pinned to his halter, was tethered to the rear of the buggy.

The lane, lined with towering trees that gave Fair Oaks its name, led back to an antebellum mansion that had seen better days. A lantern cast a pool of yellow light on the veranda where Alexandra's father and Jonah Venable, the farm's foreman, were sitting. The buggy pulled to a stop in front of the mansion, and Jonah came down the steps.

A small, wiry man in his sixties, Jonah was more like a family member than a hired hand. Munching a chew of tobacco, he took the reins to lead the horses to the barn and asked Alexandra how she had done in the race. He nodded in satisfaction at her reply. "A third in that race is a big win," he said. "I'm glad Oberon did so well for you."

"He'll win the next time," Alexandra called to him as she went up the steps. "I guarantee it."

Alex Woodling, a burly man of sixty, was almost as tall as Toby. He had a white beard and unruly white hair, and his left arm was in a sling. Smiling at his daughter's pluck, he shook his head as she chided him for being out in the cool evening air. "A breath of air won't hurt me, honey. And don't you be peevish. A third place in that race, with no broken bones, is nothing to be disappointed about. Did you talk to the governor, Toby?"

"Yes, I did," Toby replied. "I'll tell you all about it over dinner."

They went through the front door and along a wide, dark hall toward the rear of the house, their footsteps stirring echoes in the dusty, empty rooms on either side. During the years when Alex had been in the depths of despair over the death of his wife, he had turned to drink and neglected the farm, and all the employees except Jonah had left. After finally swearing off the bottle, Alex had managed to bring the farm back to a sound financial condition, but then the Panic of 1873 had struck.

With few buyers for hunters and show horses, Fair Oaks had verged on bankruptcy until Toby and his family had extended Alex a loan. The signs of the close brush with disaster were on every side, and only a few rooms at the rear of the house—the kitchen and the former servants' quarters—were furnished and still in use.

The kitchen, which now served as dining and sitting room as well, had originally been built and equipped to provide banquets for the lavish social events once hosted in the mansion. Soon a roaring fire was going in the stove, and the warmth, combined with the soft lamplight, made the room cozy on the cool evening. Household tasks were shared, with Jonah doing most of the cooking, and soon after he returned from the barn, plates of leftover stew were dished up, and they all sat down.

Alexandra gave a detailed account of the race, and the two older men chuckled over what she had done to Durgin. "It serves him right," Alex declared. "Men like that shouldn't be involved in the race in the first place, trying to turn a sporting event into a means of ill-gotten gain."

"Alexandra and I discussed the possibility that Crowley could be involved with Sewell," Toby informed him. "That would answer the question of how Sewell intended to manage a horse farm. But I don't think Crowley himself is a direct danger to us. The man is too cowardly."

Alex lifted his eyebrows. "Well, that's good to hear. What did the governor have to say?"

"He's very concerned that a criminal organization could be trying to move into Kentucky, of course. That hasn't been a problem here, and he offered to help. But until we have some concrete evidence to act on, there's little he can do."

"I figured as much," Alex said. "But maybe we have all the help right here that we'll need. Ezekiel Quint came over today, asking what he and his boys can do. I told him that you would talk to him."

Toby brightened at this good news. Quint, a brawling riverman turned minister, ran a boys' orphanage adjacent to Fair Oaks. In addition to being always ready to help, Quint was grateful to Alex for allowing him to use Fair Oaks's land on which to grow crops for his orphanage, and Toby had donated to the orphanage a sizable sum of money he had earned serving as a temporary federal marshal during the past months.

"In that case I'll go see him tomorrow," Toby said.

Later, when everybody else had gone to bed, Toby sat alone at the table with a cup of coffee. The old house was quiet and peaceful, but he was unable to enjoy the calm atmosphere. The threat that hung over the farm darkened and disturbed his thoughts, and he would not be able to rest until the peaceful security that Fair Oaks had once enjoyed was completely restored.

III

After breakfast the next morning, while Jonah ran some errands in Lexington, Alexandra and Toby saddled horses and set out to visit the Reverend Quint.

The weather was unseasonably warm, and with the trees a blaze of autumn color, the short ride was exceedingly pleasant. Fair Oaks was located in the center of Kentucky's bluegrass region, an immense, fertile plateau famous for its thoroughbred horses. North and west lay undulating hills and farmland, and to the east and south were the remote, still sparsely settled mountains through which Daniel Boone had cut his Wilderness Road a century earlier.

After a leisurely ride, they came in sight of the fields where Alexandra's father allowed Quint to raise crops for the orphanage. Toby spotted the minister and several of the boys hard at work among the rows of corn.

Quint was the most unlikely-looking minister Toby had ever met. A hulking, brawny man, he had a rugged face scarred from countless fights, with a crooked, flattened nose, and ears that were thick and shapeless. A longtime boatman on the Ohio, Quint had changed his ways when he had married, and to the amazement of his former friends, he had in quick succession sworn off heavy drinking, taken up the cloth, and then opened an orphanage for homeless boys.

His tiny, birdlike wife, Mathilda, who had been largely responsible for his remarkable turnaround, mothered the boys, while Quint himself administered a primitive but effective discipline. Toby and Alexandra observed an example of this as they rode up.

A large, muscular youth, howling in pain and brushing at an arm, burst out of the rows of tall corn, apparently having been bitten by one of the caterpillars that infested the plants. Quint, frowning impatiently, emerged from the corn nearby. "Jim, you stop acting like a crybaby!" he barked. "Get back in there and get to work!"

"I ain't going back in that corn, Preacher Quint!" the youth protested. "I've been stung by packsaddles four times this morning!"

"Then open your eyes and keep away from them!" Quint advised. Seizing the youth's shirt, he put a hamlike fist under his nose. "If you don't get back to work, you'll get stung by this!"

The youth was about six feet tall and well built, but his eyes widened in alarm, and he quickly retreated into the corn. Quint's frown disappeared as he turned to Toby and Alexandra. Taking off his hat, he greeted them politely and congratulated Alexandra on how she had done in the race.

After they had exchanged a few pleasantries, Toby got around to the purpose of the visit. Quint listened, his frown returning. "And you say this fellow's name is Crowley?" he commented. "It appears to me that Lexington would be a lot better off without the likes of him."

"It would, Reverend," Toby agreed. "Especially since we think it's possible that he's connected with Sewell. In any event, the reason I came to see you, sir, is to accept your offer of help in dealing with the threat to Fair Oaks."

"Well, I'm mighty pleased to hear that," Quint replied with conviction. "The Lord knows, there'd be nothing but hungry bellies at my orphanage if Mr. Woodling didn't let me use this land. And the money you donated, Mr. Holt, will buy winter clothes and boots for all my boys. Just tell me what you want me to do."

"I understand that two of your boys sell newspapers at the train station in Lexington," Toby said. "I'd like for them to be on the lookout for Sewell, or any group of suspicious-looking men. Also, I'd like to pick out some places along the south border of Fair Oaks and have you post a few of your older boys there at night to watch for intruders."

"That sounds fine to me," Quint said. "When Tod and Whitey get home from the station tonight, I'll send them over so you can give them Sewell's description. And you just decide where you want the older boys posted, and I'll put them there. So you think that trouble is more likely to come from the south?"

Toby nodded and explained that the land to the south was easily accessible from the Lexington road, and that unlike the other approaches, it offered numerous brushy creeklines and patches of forest as cover for anyone who wanted to get from the road to the farm without being seen.

Quint agreed, and after discussing a few more details with him, Toby and Alexandra left him to his work and rode back via the south boundary, keeping an eye out for prominent but sheltered places to post the boys on guard.

It was almost noon when they got back to the house. Jonah had returned from Lexington, and when Toby and Alexandra joined him in the kitchen for lunch, he handed Toby the mail he had picked up in town. A large, thick envelope had arrived from Chicago, from the manager of Toby's lumber mill and ironworks there, Dieter Schumann, and Toby sat down and opened it as Alexandra dished up the food.

The envelope contained a note from Dieter, as well as three sealed letters from Toby's hometown in Oregon. Toby exchanged occasional letters with his mother, Eulalia, his sister Cindy, and the foreman of his horse ranch, but his most frequent correspondent these days was his twelve-year-old daughter Janessa—and indeed all three of the letters were from her.

The note from Dieter was brief; there were papers he needed signed, it read, and he would himself bring them to Fair Oaks as soon as possible and inform Toby about the details of the business at that time. Toby put the note aside and began opening the letters from Janessa.

Her letters were always chatty, in marked contrast to the girl's quiet disposition. Trained by her Cherokee mother in herbal medicine, Janessa was mature far beyond her years and had few friends her own age. For two years now, since her mother had died of consumption, the girl had been studying medicine with Dr. Robert Martin, a semiretired physician in Portland who had taken a keen interest in her and encouraged her ambition to become a medical doctor.

On Toby's last trip to Portland—and over his mother's objections—he had given Janessa permission to work with Dr. Martin in the Portland Charity Hospital. He smiled as he read a wry comment about Eulalia's still-unbending attitude on the matter.

Scanning the second letter, he frowned as he read about his sister and her husband, Lieutenant Reed Kerr.

A few weeks before, Toby recalled, with the Indian raids in Arizona Territory having abated, the army units in that area had been shifted north to Council Bluffs to deal with unrest among the Plains Indians. Almost immediately afterward, bands of comancheros, consisting of outlaw whites and renegade Indians, had started raiding across the border from Mexico. In order to protect the area, a new outpost, Fort Peck, had been built in the badlands near the border and garrisoned with two companies of cavalry. And now Reed, who had been stationed across the river from Portland at Fort Vancouver, had been ordered to report to Fort Peck.

Toby reread the paragraph describing Reed's new posting. It would be dangerous duty, he knew, and although Reed had long wanted a cavalry assignment, the news that Cindy planned to join him shortly at Fort Peck was, to say the least, unsettling.

While he could understand why Cindy wanted to be with her husband, Toby wished that she would wait for a time. Until the comancheros were subdued, even traveling through Arizona Territory would be extremely dangerous.

The concern over Cindy's safety was shared by her husband. As he led twenty men in a patrol of the arid wastelands near the Mexican border, Reed Kerr was thinking about his last letter from Cindy, in which she had repeated that she would be joining him shortly.

He had mixed feelings on the matter. Nothing was more important to Reed than Cindy's safety, but life had meaning to him only when she was present. His love for his wife was the very foundation of his happiness, and he yearned for her to join him. And even though the journey itself would be dangerous, she would be safe once she arrived at Fort Peck.

In any case, Reed had no choice. Clearly Cindy felt it was her duty to join him, and a Holt who had determined on a course of action could not be swayed. And Cindy was certainly a Holt.

Yet Reed could not allow thoughts of his wife to distract him from his mission this morning. Leading the column of cavalry at a slow canter, he constantly scanned the landscape and listened for any sound of conversation from the men—an indication that they were not remaining alert for danger. Two weeks before, a ten-man patrol led by a sergeant had been wiped out to a man by what had to have been an unusually large band of comancheros in this very area.

Reed gazed ahead at the rocky, brushy hills studded with saguaro cactuses. This part of Arizona was dry, barren country, a place of snakes and scorpions, yet there was an austere, forbidding beauty to its vast spaces. Except for the ceaseless whisper of the desert wind, the land was silent, and the creaking of saddles and rattling of sabers sounded very loud to Reed.

The wind stirred the brush and the tall, thick clumps of dry grass, and the movements on all sides gave Reed a constant, uneasy feeling that someone was just on the edge of his vision. About a mile off to the west, he saw vultures circling—apparently the place where the patrol had been massacred. Lifting an arm in a signal to the column behind him, Reed turned toward the site of the ominous activity.

A few minutes later, the column breasted a low ridge and descended into a wide, sandy valley. Down the center of the valley ran a bare, scoured swath that was a warning to the knowledgeable that flash floods poured through here during thunderstorms. In the wiry brush and grass just beyond the swath, vultures were picking at scattered horse bones.

The large, angular birds lazily took to wing as the column approached. Reed lifted an arm, reined up, and turned to the sergeant behind him. "We'll rest the horses here, Sergeant Hoskins," he said.

The sergeant touched his hat brim and turned in his saddle. "Dismount and check your tack!" he shouted to the men. "And keep your eyes open!" The last order was hardly necessary, since everyone was fully aware that this was the place where their friends had been killed.

Reed rode a few yards away, looking around. With no survivors, and the wind having smoothed over the tracks before another patrol had located the scene of the disaster, the precise details of what had happened were unknown.

The captain who had led the mortuary detail to recover the men's bodies had made up the official report on the incident. It had simply stated that the sergeant and his men had been ambushed by a much larger force of comancheros. As Reed glanced at the scattered horse carcasses and inspected the terrain, he pondered that conclusion. Indeed, at one side of the scene of battle was a deep, brush-bordered swale where a large force of comancheros could have been hidden. However, it seemed highly unlikely that the comancheros could have taken that position ahead of a pursuing patrol without being detected. Reed had known the sergeant in command of the patrol, a man named Whittaker. A wily, resourceful veteran, he would not have charged headlong into a possible ambush.

Hoskins rode over to Reed. Like Whittaker had been, he was a seasoned veteran, with many decades in the cavalry. As the only second lieutenant at the fort, Reed realized it was not by accident that he was always accompanied on his patrols by a highly capable sergeant.

"Captain Sawyer concluded that the patrol was simply ambushed," Reed commented. "What do you think, Sergeant?"

Hoskins moved the wad of tobacco in his mouth, his weathered features reflecting dry humor. "I think," he replied, "that what the captain says is good enough for me. It ain't up to me to second-guess a captain."

"Nor to me," Reed agreed. "But I was thinking that Sergeant Whittaker would have been a very hard man to ambush."

Hoskins leaned over and spat tobacco juice. "Them horse bones ain't scattered over no more than a hundred feet, Lieutenant," he observed. "So whatever took place must have happened fast and sudden. It sure wasn't no running battle, and them comancheros could have hid right in this draw."

"Yes, I suppose so," Reed said. He tugged at his reins and turned his horse away. "We'll probably never know exactly what happened. Let's get the men mounted and ride on."

Hoskins touched his hat and rode back to the men to order them to mount. They formed into a column again, and Reed took his place at the head of it. As they rode away, the vultures circling overhead settled back toward the ground.

*   *   *

By early afternoon, Reed had covered his assigned patrol area. He was just about to head back toward the fort when the quiet was suddenly shattered by a burst of gunfire from the top of a distant rise. As bullets kicked up dirt around the column, Reed glanced back quickly to assess the effect of the gunfire. One man was wounded, clutching his shoulder and reeling sideways in his saddle.

Jabbing his horse with his spurs, Reed reined it around toward the low hill and shouted over his shoulder. "Left turn at the gallop, ho! Draw carbines, lock and load!"

The column broke into a full gallop, following Reed, and a metallic rattle sounded over the pounding hoofbeats as the troopers loaded their rifles. At the top of the rise, a half dozen men leaped up from hiding places in the brush. Brandishing rifles and whooping, they sprang onto horses and began riding away.

The six were comancheros, both Indians and white men among them, and one of the whites, wearing a military jacket, was large and heavyset, with a thick black mustache and beard. Watching their dust trails as the riders disappeared from view, Reed recalled that in his briefings upon arriving at Fort Peck, he had been told that one of the leaders of the comancheros was a large, bearded man called Calusa Jim, who habitually wore a foreign military tunic. It was believed he was a deserter from the French military forces that had been in Mexico during Maximilian's brief, troubled reign there. The man fit that description, but Calusa Jim's band of comancheros numbered some one hundred men, not six.

Skirting the rise so as not to run into a possible ambush, Reed led the column tearing through the brush. A large valley came into view. The comancheros, beating their horses mercilessly, were already crossing the open swath running down the center, where the vegetation had been scoured away by flash floods. As he rode down the slope in pursuit, Reed registered that the terrain here was very similar to the valley where Whittaker and his men had been killed.

In fact, the two valleys were almost identical. And while Whittaker had been too experienced to stumble into an ambush, Reed realized, he could have been lured into one by two or three comancheros. The valley wall was steeper on the far side, and the intervening brush was thick, obscuring the possible presence of swales similar to the one Reed had noticed earlier.

The comancheros disappeared from view into the brushy lower ground on the opposite side of the valley, and to Reed the place looked more and more like a trap. As he approached the bare, sandy swath in the center of the valley, he quickly came to a decision. Lifting an arm and reining his horse sharply to the left, he shouted over his shoulder. "Left turn, ho!"

The hoofbeats behind him became broken, some of the men hesitating in surprise. Hoskins bellowed a stream of profanity at them, and the hoofbeats again became a roar, dust boiling up around the column as the horses raced eastward along the bare strip. Hoskins spurred his horse and caught up with Reed.

With his hatbrim pushed back by the wind and his mustache fluttering, he glanced over at Reed. "Do you aim to circle around ahead of them and jump them from hiding, Lieutenant Kerr?" he called, half joking, half angry at apparently having given up the chase.

Reed shouted a reply over the hoofbeats. "I think there could be an ambush waiting on the other side of the valley. That could be what happened to Whittaker and his men."

Hoskins looked at the far side of the valley and back at Reed. "By gum, you might be right!" he exclaimed.

"If there *are* comancheros waiting in ambush over there," Reed called out, "a fire ought to flush them out. When I turn back south, spread the men out at hundred-foot intervals to set fires."

The sergeant nodded and dropped back to resume his place. A minute or so later, Reed lifted an arm and shouted the command to turn. The column left the sandy swath and cut into the brush, parallel to and upwind of the route the comancheros had taken. Reed glanced back to see his men slowing and spreading out, as he had directed.

When he drew near to the valley wall, Reed reined up and took out his matches. The men behind him were already striking matches and tossing them into the tinder-dry brush. Reed struck a match and dropped it into a clump of grass, which burst into flame. Wasting no time, he spurred his horse and doubled back toward the center of the valley, the men forming into a column behind him.

The horses were beginning to tire, and they panted heavily as Reed led the column back along the sandy swath toward the place where the comancheros had disappeared. Meanwhile, the steady wind had driven the patches of fire together into a wall of flame that was sweeping down the south side of the valley, with dense clouds of smoke billowing through the brush ahead of it.

When the column had drawn well ahead of the fire, Reed saw the first reaction to it. Dozens of horses that had been tethered in the concealing brush had broken loose at the smell of smoke and were racing to the west to escape the fire. At the point where the comancheros had crossed the valley, Reed slowed his mount to a walk and called out to the men to form a single file.

The order was rapidly executed, and Reed lifted his arm again. "At the walk," he shouted, "left flank, ho! Fire at will! Sergeant Hoskins, take the other end of the flank!"

The sergeant rode to the opposite end of the line. As the men advanced abreast into the brush, Reed took out his pistol and cocked it, and the men raised their rifles. Almost immediately, comancheros came into view some hundred feet ahead.

They were riding in panic toward the bare, open center of the valley to escape the flames. Suddenly facing a long line of cavalry, they reined up in consternation. At the same instant, Reed's men fired a volley, sending gunpowder smoke billowing up along the line.

Comancheros tumbled from horses as the hail of lead

swept through them. Others turned back, shooting over their shoulders as they fled, but their aim was poor and their fire ineffective. Reed's men kept up a steady, deadly accurate fire, and the remainder of the comancheros fell.

Moments later, more comancheros began coming through the brush. Many had lost their horses and were riding double. The soldiers picked off most of them, but a few got close enough for Reed to use his pistol. By now smoke had begun swirling around Reed and his men, but they continued to advance in the path of the fire to a point where they could see the main body of comancheros.

Some forty to fifty were fleeing to the west along the side of the valley, many riding double, while a few others were scaling the steep far hill. Reed shouted and pointed, ordering his men to shoot at the front of the larger group. As the rifles fired, the outlaws in the lead began falling.

Disorganized and panicked, the comancheros fired back, and bullets thudded into the ground and clipped through the brush around Reed and his men. Two of the soldiers weaved in their saddles, wounded, but the comancheros leading the retreat were dropping left and right as the soldiers kept up a blistering fire. Seeing their escape route cut off, the other comancheros turned back into the clouds of smoke or tried to scale the valley wall.

Then, for a few minutes, it turned into a turkey shoot. Through the thickening smoke, loose horses and comancheros headed in all directions, trying to escape the approaching flames. Reed aimed his pistol at the closer ones and fired, while the rifles did their deadly work and the soldiers whooped as outlaws fell. Finally, when the flames were drawing near and the horses were growing too jittery to control in the dense smoke, Reed shouted to the men and led them back to the center of the valley.

Riding out of the smoke and into the sandy wash, Reed blinked his stinging eyes and counted the soldiers to make sure all of them were present. Satisfied, he shouted an order to dismount, and the men quickly obeyed, holding their horses and calming them as the wall of fire passed and the wind began clearing away the smoke.

When the smoke had thinned, the men began talking and laughing, exuberant over the lopsided victory. Leading his horse, Reed stepped over to where Hoskins and others were attending to the three wounded men. To his relief, none of the wounds appeared serious.

After giving a few words of encouragement, Reed turned to Hoskins. "Let's get the horses picketed, Sergeant. As soon as the ground cools off enough, I'll take some of the men with me and get started on a body count."

"You're going to have plenty of counting to do, Lieutenant," the sergeant said with a chuckle. He took Reed's horse and walked it away, pointing to men and giving orders. Reed collected a squad of men and, a few minutes later, led them as they spread out and looked for bodies. The ground was still hot through their boots as they picked their way between smoldering clumps of brush.

At each body, Reed made notes of its physical description, the clothing, and the weapons the man had been using. Then he searched the body for jewelry, letters, a wallet, or other items that might be used to identify the man or help determine where he had been recruited.

The sun was low in the sky when Reed and his men finished, having counted twenty-six bodies. As the patrol saddled up in preparation to leave, Reed talked with the sergeant, who was in an unusually good mood.

"Ten is the most that any other patrol got in one fracas with them," Hoskins said, punctuating the sentence by spitting tobacco juice. "And I reckon we found out what happened to Whittaker." The sergeant paused. "He must have rode right into them, and I would have done the same, Lieutenant Kerr."

"You'd better watch what you're saying, Sergeant," Reed returned jokingly. "You might have to own up that a second lieutenant can do something right once in a while."

"By gum, I *will* own up to it!" Hoskins replied. "I'll

own up to it gladly. Besides, I figure it ain't going to be long before you're a first lieutenant, sir."

Reed laughed, and he and Hoskins mounted up. As the patrol resumed its journey back to the fort, Reed felt deeply gratified. However, his satisfaction would have been more complete if one of the bodies had been that of a large, bearded man. Calusa Jim remained alive, still a danger. His band of comancheros had taken a severe beating, but they could recruit other outlaws and recover from the defeat.

Once again, Reed thought about Cindy's intention to join him shortly. In the aftermath of the battle, his reservations about having her travel through the perilous region to Fort Peck were stronger than ever. He could only hope and pray that she arrived safely.

Ezekiel Quint frowned skeptically over a pair of boots. Twelve of the boys from his orphanage were gathered around him, and they and the shoemaker on the other side of the counter silently watched Quint examining the seams and feeling the leather. Finally he placed the pair on the counter. "They're good boots," he said grudgingly. "But the price is mighty high, considering I'm getting all of my boys shod here."

"I'm allowing for that, Reverend," the shoemaker replied meekly. "I'm also allowing for the fact they're orphanage boys. Quite frankly, I'm asking about half what I would charge somebody else."

Quint knew the man was telling the truth, but he had hoped to get the price even lower. "All right, then. Fit these boys here, and I'll bring the rest of them in tomorrow. I'll settle up with you for all of them tomorrow."

The shoemaker smiled in relief, glanced over the boys' feet, then began taking pairs of boots off the shelves. "Just have your lads line up at the fitting chair there, and I'll see to them."

"You heard him," Quint barked. "Line up, and keep quiet while you wait your turn. When you say your prayers tonight, remember that it was Mr. Toby Holt who gave us the money to have you shod." He frowned, and his voice filled the store as he made his next pronouncement: "And take good care of them boots! Pick up your feet when you walk!"

The boys eagerly fell into a line at the fitting chair, happy that their worn, tattered footwear was going to be replaced by brand new boots instead of the usual hand-me-downs. Quint, if anything even happier than the boys, stepped to the front of the shop and looked out the window. Money was scarce during the depression, and until a few days before he had been at a complete loss as to where he would find the means to clothe the boys for the winter. Then, out of the blue, Toby Holt had given him a generous donation, more than the boys could earn in years at their odd jobs. As he had done countless times since then, Quint took off his hat, closed his eyes, and silently prayed in fervent thanksgiving. His religious views were simple and straightforward, and he was of the opinion that future windfalls would be withheld if he failed to demonstrate gratitude that was equivalent in scope to the gift he had received.

When he had finished praying, he opened his eyes and replaced his hat. One of his charges, a tall, thin boy of twelve named Warren, was standing beside him. Warren grinned as he pointed to his new boots, and Quint nodded in approval. "Them boots look good on you, boy. Now you be sure to take care of them, do you hear?"

"I sure will, Preacher Quint!"

"And when we get done here, we'll go see about getting some new coats and britches—"

The boy's wide grin at this additional good news suddenly faded as something outside caught his eye. "Preacher Quint, that man coming out of the post office is Waldo Crowley, the one who caused all that trouble for Miss Woodling at the race."

Quint frowned, his gaze locked on the stranger. "Are you sure, Warren?"

"I'm positive, because I seen him there. I worked at the fairgrounds that day, remember?"

Quint nodded absently. Crowley's flashy suit and manner stirred instinctive hostility within him, a prejudice that remained unchanged from his years as a boatman. His wariness of suspicious-looking strangers was a point of contention between him and his wife; Mathilda adopted a benevolent attitude toward all people, while Quint felt that human kindness was due only to those who deserved it. Indeed, what he viewed as one of the great inequities of life was that people like Crowley were free to do whatever they could get away with, while people like Toby Holt and the Woodlings were constrained by the law, which placed them at a disadvantage.

In general, Quint followed the Ten Commandments and the Old Testament as best he could, but turning the other cheek was a concept he had never quite been able to take to heart. Stroking his chin, he watched as Crowley paused on the post office steps across the street. "You, Tom!"

"Yes, sir?" replied the youth Quint had addressed.

"I need to go across the street, so I'm leaving you in charge. If any of the boys here misbehaves, I'm going to take him and you and knock your heads together. Understand?"

"Yes, sir. Ain't nobody going to misbehave, Preacher Quint."

"Good. If you get done before I get back, I'll be across the street." Quint went out the door and steered a course toward Crowley, who was putting an envelope into his coat pocket as he walked away from the post office. Light traffic moved along the street, and Quint weaved through it with single-minded determination. Crowley was crossing the head of an alley as Quint drew up beside him and touched his hat in greeting. "Good day, sir," he said. "I'm Preacher Ezekiel Quint, and I'd like to talk to you."

Crowley frowned in annoyance but then looked up at Quint in alarm as the taller man moved closer, crowding him into the alley. "What are you doing?" he demanded. "What do you want?"

"To talk to you, sir," Quint replied in a friendly voice, all the while stepping from side to side to keep Crowley from slipping around him. When they were mostly out of view from the street, Quint took hold of Crowley's shoulders and effortlessly pushed him farther back into the alley. "There, now we can talk in private, can't we?"

"Why are you pushing me around!" Crowley protested. "You say you're a preacher? Preachers aren't supposed to act like this!"

"Well, that may be," Quint replied, "but it seems to me you're about the last one who ought to try to tell a preacher what he should or shouldn't do. Now, let's commence our talk. I believe you hired a man named Durgin to ride in a race a few days ago—ain't that so?"

"That's none of your business!" Crowley barked, again trying to step around Quint. "You either leave me alone or I'll have the police put you in jail!"

Quint had a firm hold of the man's shoulder and pulled him back. "But there ain't no police here," he said. Deftly he flicked Crowley's nose with a thick forefinger. "Answer my question, sir."

Crowley howled in pain and clutched his face. "Yes, I hired him!" he replied. "It's none of your business, but I hired him!"

"Where is Durgin now, sir?"

Feeling his nose gently with the tips of his fingers, Crowley glared up at Quint. "Why do you want to know?"

Quint sighed patiently and pushed Crowley's hands down. He took the man's nose between his first two fingers, clamped it firmly, and lifted. "Where is Durgin now, sir?" he repeated.

Crowley squealed, his eyes bulging as he lifted to his toes and tugged at Quint's hand in a futile attempt to free himself. "He went to Louisville!" he shouted, his voice muffled by the tight pressure on his nose. "He went to Louisville the day after the race!"

"I'm mighty glad to hear that," Quint said amiably, releasing the man's nose. "If he's already left, that's one less I have to deal with. Now, where are you from, sir?"

"Where am I from?" Crowley echoed blankly, taking out his handkerchief and holding it to his nose. "I'm from New Jersey. What's it to you?" He looked at his handkerchief. "You made my nose bleed!"

"I'm very sorry for that, sir," Quint said in a sincere tone. "You see, you should have answered my questions to begin with. I hate it that your nose is bleeding, and I certainly ain't been acting out of anger."

"You haven't?" Crowley exclaimed. "Then what do you call it?"

"Just persuasion to get you to talk to me," Quint replied innocently. "You see how friendly I'm being? If I was acting out of anger, it would be sinful. But I'm being polite and just persuading you, ain't I? Now, where are you staying in town, sir?"

Crowley dabbed at his nose with his handkerchief and scowled. "At the Preston Hotel. Did somebody send you to push me around?"

"Oh, no," Quint answered. "In case you ain't noticed, I'm big enough to decide on my own what to do. And like I said, I've just been persuading you. Now I need for you to do me a favor."

"Do you a favor?"

"Yes, sir. I want to go with you to help you pack your things, and then we'll go to the train station to get you a train back to New Jersey. And you'll be doing me a favor, because if you don't leave, I might start acting out of anger toward you, which would be sinful."

Crowley was speechless with astonishment for a moment, then shook his head furiously. "I'm not going to!" he blurted. "I don't have to leave here for you or anyone else, and I'm not about to!"

"I was afraid of that," Quint sighed, bending to grasp

the man firmly by the front of the coat and a leg. "I want you to know," he continued, hoisting Crowley over his head, "that I still ain't acting in anger, sir."

Crowley shrieked in panic, his arms windmilling and his legs kicking wildy as Quint heaved him at the side of the building. He flew through the air, his shriek breaking off in a grunt as he crashed into the building, then fell to the ground. He lay sprawled there, dazed.

Quint picked him up, dusted him off, and straightened his coat. "Have you changed your mind yet, sir?" he inquired solicitously.

"No, and this is not right!" Crowley protested. "It's not right for you to just make someone leave a place!"

"No," Quint said, "you mean it ain't *legal*. And it ain't. At the same time, what you and Durgin did wasn't legal, was it? But you got away with that, and I'll get away with this. The difference is, this is right, and that was wrong. Have I persuaded you yet, sir?"

"I—I'll give you money," Crowley stammered quickly. "I have money, and I'll pay you to leave me alone. I'll give you—" He broke off, his eyes wide as Quint began picking him up again. "No, don't! Don't!"

Quint threw him at the wall again, and as Crowley slammed into the building, an envelope slipped from his coat pocket and fell to the ground. Quint picked it up, pulled Crowley to a sitting position, and started to put the envelope back into the man's pocket. Then he frowned, looking at the postmark.

"That's mine!" Crowley exclaimed frantically, reaching for the envelope. "Give it back to me! That's mine!"

Fending the man off with an elbow, Quint opened the envelope. The postmark on it was San Francisco, and it contained a bank check. Nothing else was in the envelope, but the check, in the amount of two thousand dollars, was signed by Elmer Sewell. It was all the evidence Quint needed. "So you're working for Sewell," he growled.

Crowley hesitated, trying to think up an explanation, then leaped forward in panic as Quint began tearing up the check and envelope. "You can't do that!" Crowley wailed in despair. "That's my money!"

"Not no more it ain't," Quint snarled, ripping the envelope and check into shreds. "It ain't yours no more, because you're through working for him." He threw down the last bits of paper and reached out and seized Crowley by the neck. His hand clamped tight, and he pulled Crowley up close and glared at him. "Now you'll be doing me a bigger favor by leaving town. You'll be keeping me from killing you, which would be a worser sin than acting in anger. Do you understand me clearly?"

"Yes!" Crowley gasped, tugging at Quint's hand.

"You might have in mind leaving for just a while and then coming back, but you'd better think twice. If I ever lay eyes on you again, I'll tear you into littler pieces than that there check. Do you hear me?"

"Yes, yes!" Crowley choked. "I won't come back."

Grunting in disgust, Quint shoved the man away. Crowley collapsed against the wall, holding his neck and gasping for breath. At the same moment, the boys, finished at the shoe store, came hurrying into the alley. Seeing the aftermath of the confrontation, they ranged themselves beside Quint.

"Is that fellow up to no good, Preacher Quint?" Tom asked.

"Not around here he ain't," Quint replied. "We're going to take him to get his things, then to catch a train. He's leaving town, and he ain't coming back." He turned to Crowley. "Are you?"

Between despairing sobs Crowley muttered in agreement, then rose to his feet and spat an oath. Tom flushed and the next moment stepped forward and slammed a fist into Crowley's paunch. The heavy blow doubled the man over.

"Tom," Quint growled in a warning tone, "did you smite that man in anger?"

"No, sir," Tom replied promptly. "He cussed at you, and he had an eye for an eye and a tooth for a tooth coming to him. But it would have been sinful for me to cuss back at him, so I smited him instead."

Quint stroked his chin, weighing the youth's logic, then nodded in approval. "Tom, I do believe that you're going to grow up to be a real fine man. I'm glad to see that my teaching has done you some good. All right, boys, let's get that varmint out of here and on his way. We've got more to do than spend all day on the likes of him."

IV

Eulalia Blake was sitting on the back porch of her house at Fort Vancouver, trying to persuade her daughter, Cindy, to defer going to Fort Peck until the region was safer. Cindy, however, was as stubborn as her mother and had adroitly changed the subject to one she knew Eulalia could not let pass without comment.

"Cindy," Eulalia said severely, "we were having a pleasant visit. Why on earth did you have to spoil it by mentioning that man?"

Cindy was unfazed by the accusation. Her parents' house—her stepfather, General Leland Blake, was commander of the Army of the West—overlooked the Columbia River, and Cindy was sketching a steamship approaching the Portland docks, a mile or so across the river. "Because," she replied, "I was told that his promotion was by special order and not on the regular promotion selection list. I thought you might not have heard of it."

"Of course I've heard of it," Eulalia sniffed. "Days ago, in fact. Lee ruined a very pleasant dinner by telling me about it."

Cindy smiled sadly, reflecting that her stepfather had undoubtedly regretted mentioning it. She did not pause in her sketching, however, and detailed the river scene with swift, sure strokes. "All of Henry's classmates at West Point are still second lieutenants, so his promotion to captain is, to say the least, extraordinary."

"It's astounding," Eulalia retorted bitterly. "Especially in view of the fact that he's still living with that . . . that German woman without benefit of wedlock. It would appear that Washington has lost all sense of propriety. For someone who is wallowing in moral turpitude to be promoted is unbelievable—not at all like the army used to be."

"Mama," Cindy sighed, "I was the one engaged to Henry, not you. If I can put the unpleasant fact that he broke our engagement behind me, then so should you."

"If you ever have a daughter, you'll understand how I feel," Eulalia said, dismissing the subject and looking at Cindy's sketch. "That is extremely good, child. I knew you could draw, but I never realized until recently how marvelously talented you are."

"Until the past few months, I've never really had the opportunity to work on it," Cindy admitted. "When I kept house for Toby, I was always very busy. I've had much more leisure time since Reed and I got married."

Mindful of another possible way to keep Cindy at a safe distance from Arizona, Eulalia promptly took advantage of the conversational opening. "Perhaps you should go to an art school for a few months, Cindy," she suggested. "Although you're already highly skilled, I'm sure professional advice would help you. And it isn't as though money is a problem." Eulalia was alluding to the trust fund Reed had inherited upon his marriage; it had made Cindy a wealthy woman, although neither she nor Reed seemed to care about the money.

"I'm not interested in attending art school," Cindy replied bluntly. "As you know, Mama, I'm as practical as a frying pan, and I'm simply not the artistic type. Besides, I'm more interested in doing etchings than anything else, and that's taught through apprenticeship more often than in schools."

"Then that shouldn't be a problem," Eulalia persisted. "Certainly there are etchers on the staffs of the bigger newspapers, and you should be able to find one who—" Her words cut off as Cindy looked at her, slowly shaking her head.

"Mama," Cindy said, getting directly to the point, "my place is with Reed. I intend to go to Fort Peck."

"Yes, and you should, child," Eulalia agreed. "But not right now. Wait a few months, until it's safer."

"Mama, no one is perfectly safe anywhere," Cindy said patiently. "But an army fort is safe enough for me, and my place is with Reed." Finished with the sketch, she began thumbing back through the pad. "When I was over at the ranch the other day, I made some sketches to take with me when I leave. Here's one of Clara Hemmings. She may not be there too much longer; Janessa thinks she may get married again, to a man in Portland."

Eulalia looked at the sketch. "It is a bit soon, but I suppose she's too young to remain a widow for long. After all, she's a very attractive woman, with three fine children and property in Boston."

"Yes, whoever marries her will be a lucky man." Cindy turned the pages of the sketch pad. "Toby will be hard pressed to find another woman as good as Clara to look after Janessa and Timmy. But perhaps he'll take your oft-repeated advice and get married again himself, Mama."

Eulalia frowned slightly, for the comment stirred a nagging worry. "In some of his letters," she said, "Toby has mentioned my cousin Alex's daughter, Alexandra. He seems to find her attractive."

"He does?" Cindy exclaimed, looking up from the sketch pad in quick interest. "Why haven't you told me about this before?"

"Because it's no more than supposition," Eulalia admitted. "He's only mentioned her in passing, and actually I know very little about her. But what I do know doesn't augur well. Her father raised her, which isn't promising, and apparently the only thing she knows how to do is ride horses. She's hardly more than a child herself, so I don't see how she could look after Janessa and Timmy. And a good mother for his children is what Toby needs."

"Well, if that's all he needs," Cindy commented in amusement, "then he should hire someone to look after them, not marry someone to do it. But I'm sure Toby will do what's best for everyone involved." She turned another page of the sketch pad. "Here's one of Calvin Rogers and Timmy working on that old road locomotive. You know, they may eventually get that thing repaired."

Unsmiling, Eulalia looked at the sketch. While she felt sorry for Rogers, a former hot-air balloonist who had been crippled in an aborted ascent, she considered him a bad influence on Timmy. And she did not share Cindy's nonchalance about the huge, dangerous road locomotive—"an unreliable steam engine mounted on three steel wheels" was how Lee had described it.

"If they do get that thing running, what's to keep Timmy from starting it up himself?" Eulalia asked.

"A big whistle," Cindy replied, turning the page. "Calvin installed a whistle on the boiler that blows constantly when there's a head of steam. You can hear it a mile away. Here's a sketch I really like, Mama. It's the best one I've ever done of Janessa."

This time Eulalia smiled warmly. The sketch portrayed Toby's daughter with photographic accuracy—but that was not all. The likeness also conveyed a sense of the girl's reserved but determined personality. Eulalia deeply loved her granddaughter, and she even managed to ignore the cigarette Cindy had realistically depicted between the fingers of the small right hand.

"It's absolutely lovely!" Eulalia exclaimed. "You've captured her perfectly. You must make me a copy of it."

"I will, Mama. I'm glad you like it." Somewhat surprised by her mother's response, Cindy reflected that although Eulalia and Janessa disagreed on some things, they had much in common. Certainly they were in total agreement on one point: their abiding resentment toward the general's and Eulalia's adopted son. Mere mention of Henry's name was enough to anger either of them, even though Cindy herself had forgiven Henry for his past behavior. She could hardly do otherwise, considering how she still felt about him.

"I do wish, though," Eulalia went on, "that Toby hadn't given his permission for her to work with Robert Martin at that awful charity hospital. After all, disreputable women are given treatment there, and seamen who have cut each other in drunken brawls, and every other sort of vagrant you can imagine."

"Those people are in need of help," Cindy defended.

"Yes, I know," Eulalia said with a sigh. "Of course they are. But it simply isn't proper surroundings for a young girl. And worse, Dr. Martin sometimes keeps her there until all hours of the night. I'm certain Toby didn't intend *that*, and no one can tell me otherwise!"

"Well, I don't know, Mama," Cindy said noncommittally, closing the sketch pad. She changed the subject. "Judging from Reed's description of the quarters at Fort Peck, many of our wedding presents and most of our furniture would just be in the way there. Papa said I could store things here, so I've been going through everything and making a list of what to take. I'd better get back to it."

"Very well, dear," Eulalia said in a resigned tone. "I would feel much better if I could talk you into delaying for a few months, but I see that you've made up your mind. Let me know if you need any help."

Cindy stood up and kissed her mother. "Thank you, Mama. I'll have your copy of the sketch of Janessa finished in a day or two, and I'll bring it over. Tell Papa I said hello."

As soon as Cindy was gone, Eulalia sat back and sighed heavily. While she loved her daughter deeply and enjoyed her company, on this particular occasion their conversation had touched upon every source of her own current discontent.

The infuriating promotion of her ungrateful adopted

son was completely beyond her control. And she could not keep Cindy from leaving for Fort Peck, or do anything about the mechanical monstrosity that Toby had bought for Timmy. And she could not prevent Janessa from working with Dr. Martin at the charity hospital.

But she could, she reflected, do something about Janessa's working there until all hours of the night. She could talk to Dr. Martin and remind him that Janessa was still a child, regardless of what he thought, and should be at home and in bed at the same hour as any other child.

At the Holt ranch that evening, Janessa took unusually small servings from the dishes as they were passed around the table. Clara Hemmings noticed and frowned in concern. "You must eat more than that, Janessa," she said. "Here, have another piece of chicken."

"No, thank you," Janessa answered quickly. "I'm not very hungry tonight."

"Are you feeling all right, dear?"

Janessa nodded. "Yes, I feel fine, Mrs. Hemmings. I'm just not hungry."

Still frowning in concern, Clara appeared inclined to pursue the point, but an outbreak of giggling and shoving between her two sons drew her attention, evoking a stern warning addressed in their direction. Timmy looked on innocently. Janessa suppressed a sigh of relief and began eating.

Actually, she was quite hungry, but this evening she wanted as little food as possible in her stomach. Never an active conversationalist, Janessa ate in silence and then laid her silverware neatly on her plate. "Dr. Martin is expecting me," she said. "I'm sorry I'll have to leave the dishes to you, Mrs. Hemmings, but I'll do the pots and pans."

"You'll do no such thing," Clara replied with her usual generosity. "My word, you have more than enough to do, what with your schoolwork and the hospital. Just try not to stay out too late, dear. You know your grandmother doesn't approve of the hours you've been keeping."

"Yes, I know." Janessa excused herself and carried her plate to the sink. She went to her room for her coat and hurried out the front door, where she had left her mare tethered at the hitching rail near the porch. After lighting a cigarette, she mounted up and set off on the road to Portland, the sun setting in front of her.

It didn't take her long to reach the well-kept house where Robert and Tonie Martin lived, and in ten minutes she had hitched up the doctor's horse to the buggy, climbed up into the seat, and driven to the front of the house.

Dr. Robert Martin, one of the travelers on the first wagon train to Oregon, was in his seventies and was white-haired, stooped, and shrunken with age. His wife, Tonie, nearing sixty, was an active, vivacious woman with snow-white hair and a warm, outgoing personality. She walked her husband out to the waiting buggy.

"Remember that Janessa has school tomorrow," Tonie said when the doctor had climbed up onto the seat. "Don't keep her up too late." She smiled at Janessa. "I baked your favorite oatmeal cookies today, my dear. Would you like to take some with you?"

Janessa, after some hesitation, politely declined. As soon as they began to drive off, Dr. Martin addressed his young pupil. "We don't have to do what we planned tonight, you know. We can let it go until another time, if you wish."

"No, sir. I'll be all right."

The doctor nodded and patted her shoulder. As the buggy moved along the now-dark streets toward the charity hospital, the old man talked much more than usual. Janessa knew he was trying to keep her mind off what lay ahead.

Since they had begun working at the charity hospital, Dr. Martin had been experimenting with a procedure developed during the past few years to prevent infection in wounds. It involved the use of diluted phenol as an antiseptic and so far had proved a resounding success. Patients who ordinarily would have required amputations or been hospitalized for weeks had been leaving completely healed within days.

"It seems strange to me," Janessa said, "that all doctors aren't using antisepsis. It's such an obvious improvement, and Dr. Lister's papers on it were published over five years ago."

"People are very slow to change, Janessa, and the best doctors are too busy to go digging around for new procedures. And as strange as it may seem, a medicine or procedure that produces the most fantastic results is often the one that will be trusted least."

"You mean the people who read about it will think it's quackery?"

"Exactly," the old doctor said. "And you know what can happen to a doctor who uses an unorthodox procedure on a patient who dies."

"Yes, sir. A lawsuit."

"That's right. Two unfortunate appendages to our profession are undertakers and lawyers. Try to stay clear of lawyers, and if an undertaker sends you a turkey for Christmas dinner, send it back. It'll hurt your reputation."

"Yes, sir."

"During the past few days," the doctor said, changing the subject, "I've been reading in the newspaper about an outbreak of cholera in Independence, Missouri. It's late in the year for such an outbreak—they usually occur in the summer—but it might become an epidemic nonetheless. If it does, I'll probably go there and do what I can to help. There won't be enough doctors to deal with it."

"If you go there, I want to go."

The old man smiled. "I'll welcome your company, needless to say, but we'll have to get permission from your family. That might be a problem. But we'll see what happens."

Janessa turned the buggy off the street and parked beside the hospital. The Portland Charity Hospital was obviously not one of the city's better-endowed institutions. A ramshackle, three-story structure of unpainted wood, it looked more like a run-down boardinghouse than a hospital. In the spartan waiting room, recuperating patients were mopping the floor under the supervision of a volunteer nurse. Dr. Anton Wizneuski, who devoted his spare time to serving as hospital director, emerged from his adjacent office to greet his visitors eagerly.

Nearing sixty, Dr. Wizneuski was a fat, balding man with a short white beard and rimless glasses. Rubbing his palms together, he was obviously impatient to get to work, and his keen glance at Janessa was meaningful. She nodded confidently, assuring him that she was ready.

He turned to Dr. Martin. "Everything is prepared," he said quietly. "I'll be downstairs in a few minutes."

"How many do we have?" Dr. Martin asked softly.

"Only one this time, but it should be very interesting."

Janessa took Dr. Martin's arm as they descended the basement steps. At the foot of the stairs, a dim lamp in a wall sconce illuminated a heavy door, which the doctor unlocked.

The basement room was dark, and Dr. Martin struck matches to light the lamp hanging in the center of the ceiling and one over the sink at one side. Janessa selected the two cleanest-looking rubber surgical aprons hanging on the wall and handed one to Dr. Martin. As she tied her own on, her gaze was drawn inexorably beyond the cabinets filled with shiny instruments and glass bottles to the far wall, where three long, narrow tables on wheels were parked. On one was a form covered with a sheet.

Her surgical apron dragged on the floor as she helped Dr. Martin move a square white table to the center of the room, under the lamp. They took several of the shiny instruments from a cabinet and placed them on the table in a neat line, and as a precaution the doctor added a bottle of smelling salts.

The door opened, and Dr. Wizneuski came in. "Well, well, I see we're just about ready to proceed." He was grinning amiably as he went to the wall rack and took down an apron for himself. "I trust that you dined sparingly this evening, Miss Janessa?"

"Yes, sir."

"Good." When he had finished tying on his apron, he picked up a bucket from a corner and placed it beside the white table. "It won't hurt to have this here, just in case you need it," he said cheerfully. "And I see that the smelling salts are ready. Is there anything else you would like?"

"Yes, sir. I'd like to stop talking about it."

The doctor blinked in surprise. "Of course." Without further ado, Dr. Wizneuski went to the far wall and trundled the table with the sheet-covered form on it to the center of the room. He removed the sheet and put it aside. "The subject is an adult male," he said, automatically changing to a lecturing tone, "fifty-two years of age. And in poor physical condition, as you can see. He was admitted six days ago and expired during the forenoon today. The subject was suffering from acute perityphlitic abscess."

As she listened, Janessa's dread of the proceedings was suddenly overcome by perplexity. She knew that during the two to three days that it took for death to result from acute perityphlitic abscess—a severe internal inflammation—the lower abdomen became greatly distended and discolored. She had seen just such a case only a month ago. But the abdomen of this body appeared perfectly normal.

She remained silent, but Dr. Martin had no compunction about challenging his younger colleague's diagnosis. "Acute perityphlitic abscess?" he said skeptically, pointing to the abdomen. "Then explain that, Anton."

Dr. Wizneuski's smile returned. "I said it would be an interesting one, Robert. When the abscess became acute, resulting in the usual severe pain, the patient had a heart seizure and died within minutes."

Dr. Martin lifted his eyebrows. "You're right—that is

an interesting one. Well, let's have a look at what happened. Pass him a scalpel, Janessa."

Her trepidation returning, Janessa picked up a scalpel and handed it across the table. While she had seen corpses before, and had even been present at her own mother's death, nothing in her experience had prepared her for the grisly process of postmortem examination. Her stomach-turning horror was not helped by how Dr. Wizneuski went about the task, proceeding with the energetic nonchalance of a butcher slicing into a side of beef.

After opening the lower abdomen horizontally with a single firm stroke, Dr. Wizneuski laid the sides of the incision back. Janessa craned her neck, forcing herself to look. In a sense, it was the same as the pictures in the anatomy books she had studied—but only in a sense. She was unable to escape her awareness that the body had been a living human being only hours before.

Then, once again, her reactions as a twelve-year-old girl were overcome as she saw something she had not seen in the medical texts.

There was a theory that perityphlitic abscess originated in the veriform appendix, but it was only a theory. During the days that patients were dying in agony from the severe inflammation, the delicate tissues of their lower abdomen became so deteriorated that it was impossible to determine the origin of the inflammation through postmortem examination.

But this patient had died minutes after the condition had become acute. The appendix, swollen and inflamed, had ruptured. The tissue around it was a dark, angry red. To Janessa the evidence seemed indisputable, proving the theory about the disease.

"It's the appendix!" she exclaimed excitedly. "That proves the point of origin of perityphlitic abscess, doesn't it?"

Both of the doctors were more cautious, however. "What we have here," Dr. Wizneuski said, "is proof that the abscess originated in the veriform appendix in this particular instance. And that's all we have."

"And at best," Dr. Martin added, "we can conclude that the abscess originates in the veriform appendix in *some* instances. I would want to see more cases like this before I'd go any further than that. Unfortunately, that is hardly likely."

"But others have made this finding, haven't they?" Janessa asked. "Some doctors have even reported operating on a patient and removing the inflamed appendix."

The two doctors nodded, but both of them remained skeptical. "Such claims should always be taken with a grain of salt," Dr. Martin reminded her. "I've read reports about people who had their youth restored by those electrode machines, but you don't see me buying one, do you? Perhaps the inflammation has been excised through surgery, but I've never seen it done."

"Nor have I," Dr. Wizneuski added. "Besides, it's academic as far as the patient is concerned. After surgery on the abdomen, the mortality rate from infection is so near one hundred percent that it's futile to attempt it. But we're not saying that what we have here isn't an important finding, Janessa."

"Indeed we aren't," Dr. Martin agreed. "It is a significant finding, and we'll write a paper on it for the medical journals. We're just saying that you mustn't draw too many conclusions from a single case." He moved his gaze from the incision to the cadaver's chest. "You say that heart seizure was the immediate cause of death, Anton?"

"Yes, that's right," Dr. Wizneuski replied, and before Janessa realized what he was doing, he had cut a straight line up the center of the chest with a scalpel. "We'll verify that, then we'll be finished here. Janessa, if you'll pass that bone saw to me, I'll get this chest cavity opened up so we can take a look."

She handed him the saw. Dr. Wizneuski rolled his shirtsleeves up, and the muscles in his burly forearm knotted as he plied the saw vigorously. The blade cut through the center of the sternum, cracking the bone with a gruesome noise.

Janessa's knees suddenly felt unsteady, and the scene in front of her became dark and blurred. The sawing sound drifted far away, and the room began slowly revolving. Dr. Wizneuski stopped sawing and glanced at her. "Watch her, Robert!" he called sharply.

The older doctor grasped Janessa just as she swayed to one side. Putting an arm around her, he held her up and reached for the smelling salts on the table. "Take a deep breath," he said, holding the opened bottle under her nose.

The powerful fumes filled Janessa's nose and lungs, and her light-headed feeling quickly dissipated. She coughed and stood upright again. "I'm sorry," she said.

"No need to be sorry," Dr. Martin reassured her. "We certainly don't mind, do we, Anton?"

"No, not in the least," Dr. Wizneuski answered, sawing again. "You'll get used to it, Janessa. By the time you go to medical college, you'll be able to stand and eat a sandwich during dissection, while all your classmates will be chucking up their breakfasts." He put down the saw and reached into the chest cavity with the scalpel. "Let's get the pericardium out of the way. There, now you can take a look at the heart."

Peering into the chest cavity, Dr. Martin nodded. Janessa stepped closer to the table and forced herself to look. A muscular spasm had ruptured a wall of the heart—a classic heart seizure.

The postmortem was finished, and Dr. Wizneuski pushed the table back into the shadows of the far wall. Janessa walked a bit unsteadily to the sink and turned on the water. The three of them busied themselves washing the instruments and putting things away.

As they worked, the two doctors talked about the paper they intended to prepare on the postmortem, then began arguing good-naturedly about who should have primary credit for the examination. "You're the senior physician, Robert," Dr. Wizneuski said, "which is the main consideration. I'll put myself down as your assistant."

"That's absurd, Anton," Dr. Martin objected. "It was your patient. You are the director of this hospital, and you actually performed the postmortem. Do you call that assisting?"

Dr. Wizneuski started to reply, but hearing the doorknob rattle, he broke off abruptly. As the door opened, Janessa looked over her shoulder to see Eulalia Blake step into the room.

"Oh, there you are, Robert," Eulalia said. "I've been looking all over for you. Good evening, Anton, Janessa. Robert, I must talk with you about the late hours that Janessa is keeping. . . ." Her attention was wandering around the room, and she frowned. "And what *is* Janessa doing down here? She is supposed to attend only to women and children, and—" Her eyes suddenly opened wide as they took in the body on the table, its stomach and chest cavities open.

The color drained from her face, her eyelids fluttered, and her knees started folding. "Catch her, Anton!" Dr. Martin called.

The younger doctor stepped forward quickly and swept Eulalia up as she fell. He carried her toward one of the empty tables. "How on earth did she get down here, Robert?" he asked, gently laying her down.

Dr. Martin sighed in exasperation and stepped to the cabinet for the smelling salts. "I've long since stopped being surprised at anything that woman does. When she sets her mind to something, you'd better just get out of her way. Well, we'll just give her a whiff of Janessa's smelling salts, and—"

"No!" Janessa said in alarm, stepping in front of him. "I don't think it would be a good idea to revive her on that cadaver table, sir. And before you wake her up, we'd better decide what we're going to say. I don't think explanations will do any good, but she'll expect one."

*　　　*　　　*

The following evening, Janessa again ate very little for dinner, this time because anxiety robbed her of appetite. The Blakes were to visit the Martins that evening to "clear the air," as the doctor had put it, but Janessa was certain that no good would come of the meeting. It seemed inevitable that at least some restrictions would be placed on her.

After dinner, Janessa rode slowly into Portland to the doctor's house. She was in no hurry, and in fact she hoped to arrive after the discussion began, which would make her own part in it that much less. But as luck would have it, there was no carriage in the drive when she arrived at the house.

She had just finished putting her horse in the stable when a carriage from the fort turned into the drive. With a sense of relief, Janessa saw that Cindy was with Eulalia and Lee Blake. More like a sister than an aunt, Cindy was always quick to come to her defense.

The carriage stopped, and Lee stepped out of it. Tall and distinguished in his major general's uniform, he was nearly seventy years old but had the agility of a much younger man. He waved to Janessa, then helped his wife down.

The passing of a full day had done nothing to improve Eulalia's frame of mind. She nodded coldly at Janessa. "Good evening, dear," she said.

"Good evening, Grandmama," Janessa replied.

Cindy joined them, taking a place beside Janessa as they all walked to the house. Janessa could read her aunt's moods easily, and it was clear from Cindy's sparkling blue eyes that she was filled with amusement over her mother's having stumbled upon a postmortem. The general, too, she was relieved to see, had a twinkle in his eyes that indicated he was not unaware of the humorous aspects of the situation.

Janessa felt better when Tonie Martin, as warm and gracious as always, greeted them at the door and made a special effort to welcome Eulalia, embracing her warmly.

Everyone filed into the parlor, where Dr. Martin was waiting. As soon as Janessa looked at him, however, her misgivings returned. He was different from the night before, not at all regretful. An aged man with much he wanted to do before he died, he could be impatient with details and niceties when he had an objective in mind.

At the same time, his friendship with the Blakes reached back through many decades, and he greeted them with unfeigned friendliness. They all sat down, and the conversation was cordial enough at first, if somewhat strained. When Eulalia started getting to the point, however, Dr. Martin interrupted, objecting strongly to her choice of terms.

"Sneaking around?" he said, echoing a phrase she had used. "Eulalia, I don't sneak around in anything I do."

"Robert, you're picking at words," she defended. "You're well aware that I wasn't implying dishonesty on your part. But that room *is* tucked away in a far corner of the hospital, isn't it?"

"Yes, and for a very good reason. Live patients tend to find postmortems disturbing."

Suppressing a giggle, Cindy cleared her throat and looked up at a corner of the ceiling. Eulalia frowned at her, then turned back to the doctor. "Aside from that," she continued, "I'm sure you would have found an isolated place in any event, if only because Janessa was involved."

"We don't let people know what she does, if that's what you mean," he said. "Again, there's a good reason. She knows so much about medicine that it's simply hard for most people to believe, and I don't intend to start her out in her career with a reputation as some sort of quack child healer. I let people think that she's a nurse of sorts and that she helps me get around because I'm old and feeble."

"I believe there is a further reason," Eulalia persisted. "You were evading the conditions that Toby laid down for her working in that place. Toby clearly specified that Janessa was to attend only to women and children. The one on that table was a man."

The doctor was unfazed. "That's true, of course. But then again, she wasn't exactly 'attending' to him. No amount of attention by anyone would have done that fellow a bit of good."

"You're deliberately misunderstanding me!" Eulalia snapped. "You know full well that I'm referring to Janessa's being exposed to the sight of that man in his . . . his disgraceful state! He was . . ." She hesitated over the word, then finished the sentence: "*Nude!*"

Cindy coughed into her handkerchief, and her mother glared at her, then turned back to the doctor. "Toby's intention is perfectly clear," she said. "He doesn't want Janessa exposed to situations that are entirely inappropriate for a young girl. Also, I'm sure he wouldn't want her keeping late hours."

The doctor sighed wearily. "Well, we'll just have to work this out, Eulalia," he said. "Besides, something of much greater importance has come up since last night. There's been an outbreak of cholera in Independence, and I read in the newspaper today that it has grown to epidemic stage. They need more doctors. I'll have to go there and do what I can to help, and I want to take Janessa with me."

The last remark hit the room like a bombshell; even Tonie Martin looked surprised. Janessa cringed, thinking that the doctor's impatience had led him to broach the subject at the worst possible time. Cindy sat up, her amusement abruptly disappearing. Lee Blake pursed his lips and frowned. Nearly everyone began talking at once.

Eulalia, Lee, and Cindy variously cited Janessa's age, the danger of her contracting the disease, her having to miss school, and other reasons why she could not go to Independence. The doctor patiently waited for them to finish.

"Everything you say is quite true," he said when they had fallen silent. "And I can understand why you want to protect Janessa. However, all that misses the essential point."

"And what point is that, Robert?" Lee Blake asked.

"She possesses a unique skill," the doctor replied. "Like everything else in life, that skill is not free. It comes with responsibilities, and its price is duty to humanity. There are people in Independence who are dying for the lack of that skill, and she must go there."

Cindy's voice rose above her mother's, both of them quick to object. "Dr. Martin, the responsibilities you're talking about are adult responsibilities. Janessa is not yet an adult. And until she is, burdening her with such responsibilities is neither just nor fair."

Dr. Martin nodded. "You're right, of course, Cindy," he said. "But you know Janessa as well as I do, and probably better. And while she's only twelve, she isn't exactly a child, is she?"

"She certainly isn't an adult!" Eulalia snapped as Cindy hesitated. "This entire conversation is absolutely ridiculous, Robert. Janessa will not go to Independence with you, and there's an end to it!"

"If that's your last word, then I'll have to accept it," the doctor said, shrugging. "And as much as I dislike doing it, I'll have to try to have you overruled. Tomorrow I'll send a telegram to Toby explaining the situation and asking him for a decision. I hope that this won't create any lasting ill feeling between us, Eulalia. We've been friends for a long time, and I value your friendship highly."

A stiff silence was his answer, and it appeared to Janessa that the hopes the doctor had expressed were doomed.

A reply arrived from Toby only two days after the doctor sent a telegram to Lexington. When school finished that day, Janessa went straight to the doctor's house, as she always did. A horse with an army saddle on it was tethered in the drive, and General Blake was talking with the doctor on the front porch.

As soon as she was close enough to hear what the men were saying, Janessa knew that the expected telegram from her father had arrived. "I think it was appropriate," Dr. Martin was saying, "for Toby to address it to his mother. She's the one whose feelings were bruised in this affair."

"If that's the case, it certainly didn't make her feel much better," the general replied, his tone reflecting lingering resentment. "However, he is the girl's father, and the decision is his to make."

The two men turned to Janessa and exchanged greetings with her. She tried her best to conceal her mounting excitement when the general informed her that she had her father's permission to go to Independence, and she managed a restrained "That's good news, sir." It helped when Dr. Martin apologized for what he had felt compelled to do; the general seemed to accept the peace offering with good grace. Janessa knew that, like the doctor, she now had to soothe injured feelings as much as possible.

To this end, when the general turned to leave, Janessa asked him if she might accompany him back across the river. His eager reply revealed no annoyance at her personally, and Janessa hurried to the stable and saddled her horse.

When they had reached the ferry dock and were waiting for the next boat across, Janessa was painfully aware of her own ineloquence. She wanted to talk with the general and try to overcome his irritation toward the doctor, but she couldn't think of the right words. And he remained silent, lost in thought.

Not wanting to worsen matters, Janessa refrained from smoking. She yearned for a cigarette, but she knew that her smoking vexed her grandmother, and probably the general, too. After they boarded the ferry and were standing at the rail, however, Lee Blake suddenly broke the silence.

"It occurs to me," he said wryly, "that I haven't seen

you smoke a cigarette since you arrived at Robert's house. If you wish to, go ahead and light up."

His smile broke the ice. "No, thank you, sir," Janessa said. "I . . . I certainly regret what happened, Grandpa, and all the trouble it caused."

"Well, disagreements occasionally arise between people," he said philosophically. "With goodwill on both sides, though, they can be overcome in time. But I'm certainly not angry at you, my dear."

"Yes, I can see that, and I'm glad, sir. But I wish you wouldn't be angry at Dr. Martin, either."

The general hesitated before he answered. "I'm not angry at Dr. Martin. He did what he had to do. However, I don't like to see your grandmother's feelings hurt."

"I don't either, sir. Mrs. Martin will probably come over to visit her, and maybe she'll be able to patch things up."

"Yes, in time," the general mused. "But it will take time, because your grandmother is a very proud woman. That's one of the things I admire about her, but it also keeps her from forgiving and forgetting as quickly as some do. For example, I don't think she'll ever forgive our adopted son for breaking his engagement with Cindy. Time has passed, and Cindy is married now, but Eulalia still—"

He broke off, for Janessa had turned abruptly away. "I can understand how Grandmama feels about that, sir," she said quietly, "because I feel the same way."

The general sighed in resignation, reflecting that Eulalia was not the only one who was slow to forgive and forget.

As the ferry eased up to the pier on the other side of the river, he and Janessa went to fetch their horses on the lower deck. They mounted and rode up the slope toward the fort.

At the main gate, the general parted with Janessa to return to his office, and Janessa continued along the road to the quarters for senior married officers. She dismounted at the Blake home and tethered her horse to the rail, then walked up the path and, taking a deep breath, knocked several times. A moment later, Eulalia opened the door.

Janessa stood there as her grandmother looked down at her resentfully, tight-lipped and pale with anger. Seconds passed, but neither of them moved or spoke. Finally Janessa lifted her arms.

Responding instantly, Eulalia reached down and began weeping as she hugged the girl and kissed her. "Whatever that old fool tells you to do, you be careful," she sobbed. "Be careful and come back to me safely."

"I will, Grandmama," Janessa replied, holding her grandmother tightly. "I'll be careful, and I'll come back safely."

V

The lights of Aldershot, the city nearest the Royal Military College at Sandhurst, glowed dimly through the dense fog outside the carriage window. Gradually the city fell behind, and the wheels jolted over ruts in the road. Except for the faint gleam of the coach lamps, it was pitch dark outside.

After a while, a match flared inside the carriage, illuminating the planes of a thin, pale English face as a man lighted the oil lamp beside the window. "In this fog, we'll be an hour or longer reaching Sandhurst," Sir Charles Willoughby commented. "We might as well be able to see each other while we talk."

Clifford Anderson, sitting in the seat opposite Henry Blake, fished inside his coat pocket. "And we might as well have a cigar," Anderson suggested, taking out a leather case. "These are quite good, if I do say so myself."

"Well, not to be outdone in hospitality—" Willoughby produced a flask from his coat pocket. "—I'll offer a bit of brandy."

Henry smiled, reflecting that the exchange was the equivalent of lively repartee between the two men, both of whom were reserved by nature. Willoughby was a member of the British Foreign Office, and Anderson was

81

an American State Department employee, although Henry knew that both of them were in essence intelligence agents.

Puffing on their cigars and sharing brandy from the small silver flask-cap, the men broke the silence they had maintained from the station at Aldershot, where Willoughby had met the two Americans. During the train ride from London, Anderson had briefed Henry on the upcoming meeting at Sandhurst, but now he brought up a personal matter. In the closing stages of the recent Franco-Prussian War, a young American reporter, John Lawrence, the son of a deceased colleague of Anderson's, had been imprisoned in Germany on spy charges. Anderson had subsequently asked Henry to see if he could prevail upon his many contacts in Germany to obtain the man's release, which Henry had done, and Lawrence had arrived back in the United States a few weeks before. Anderson, amazed at how quickly Henry had arranged the release, related the incident to Willoughby.

"Yes, I heard about the young man," Willoughby said when Anderson had finished. "And I haven't forgotten, Clifford, that it was his father who once saved your life. Or did you neglect to tell Henry that?"

Anderson smiled. "I don't want to belittle what Lawrence did, but you were the one who saved my life, Sir Charles."

The story was new to Henry, and he listened with rapt attention.

"No, I merely rendered a bit of rather unskilled medical assistance," Willoughby returned. "I'm sure you would do the same for me, Clifford."

Turning to Henry, Anderson smiled and put a finger to his left eye, which Henry knew was false, made of glass. "We're referring to the time that this happened to me," he explained.

"You were with Lawrence's father and Sir Charles?" Henry prompted. Anderson had never told him how he had lost the eye, and Henry had never asked.

Anderson nodded. "It happened in Lisbon, many years

ago. We were in a café, and a man shot a pistol through the window at me. Lawrence saw him in time to push me out of the path of the bullet, but I got a shard of glass in my eye. Old Lawrence turned green around the gills when he saw the shape I was in, but Sir Charles, as cool as a cucumber, dealt with the man outside, then removed the glass for me."

Willoughby's blue eyes reflected amusement. "It *was* a rather ghastly situation, with blood all over and people screaming and running about."

Henry refrained from asking why Anderson had been shot in the first place.

"In any event," Anderson went on, "Sir Charles stuffed his handkerchief into my eye socket to stop the bleeding and poured liquor onto it."

"It was my aperitif, actually," Willoughby added. "Have you been to Portugal, Henry?"

"No, I haven't."

"Well, they make some excellent aperitifs, as well as the best port wine, of course."

Anderson expressed his agreement concerning the merit of Portuguese aperitifs, and as if that had broken the ice, the conversation quickly turned to their purpose in coming to Sandhurst.

"There is definitely an assassination plot afoot," Willoughby said. "General Moncaldo has been investigating it, and he'll go into all the details. We're to meet at Brigadier Halloway's house."

Henry nodded his understanding. He had met Moncaldo, a senior general in the Spanish Army, and Brigadier Halloway, the college's commanding officer, during a previous visit to Sandhurst. "Will Alphonse Ferdinand be with them?" he asked.

"Yes," Willoughby replied. "And looking forward with great anticipation to seeing you. I trust you have been well, with no more . . . untoward incidents?"

Henry reassured Willoughby there had been no further attempts on his life since his trip to the United States the previous spring. At that time he had secured the identification documents carried by one of his assailants and given them to Willoughby, who had taken them to London to be examined by specialists. They had proved to be excellent forgeries, and all the circumstantial evidence had pointed to the head of internal security for German military intelligence, Hermann Bluecher.

"It's pure speculation that he's involved," Willoughby had stated at the time. "But the pattern is consistent with what is known about Bluecher. He very vigorously pursues the interests of his nation as interpreted by his own, rather extreme, views. By those views, your presence at Mauser would be a distinct danger to Germany."

Observing that Willoughby still appeared concerned for his safety, Henry assured the Englishman that caution had become an established habit for him. Anderson, who had been listening absently, reminded his friends that the men who had tried to kill Alphonse Ferdinand the year before had used German weapons, specifically Mauser military model rifles.

"Yes, that is curious," Willoughby mused. "Germany keeps popping up, doesn't it? There's even a German involved in the current plot."

The news surprised Henry. "In what way, Sir Charles?"

"Possibly as an agent for a gun dealer. We're not sure, and under normal circumstances we would ask the Germans to investigate the man. But in view of what we've just discussed, I'd rather leave them out of it. And I see no reason to mention this at Sandhurst and involve the Spanish in our private concerns."

Henry and Anderson agreed with him. By the time the three of them had finished their cigars, the carriage was pulling to a stop at the entrance of the military college. A guard looked into the window, exchanged a salute with Henry, then waved the driver on. A few minutes later, the carriage drew up in front of the commandant's quarters, a large stone house with ivy-covered walls.

A military aide met them and ushered them inside,

where Brigadier Halloway greeted them. A beefy-looking man in a fastidiously neat uniform, he had a ruddy complexion and snow-white hair and mustache. After shaking hands all around, he congratulated Henry on his promotion to captain. "You're pressing ahead in grade very rapidly, aren't you?"

"Well, sir, I've been lucky enough to be in the right place at the right time," Henry said modestly.

The brigadier shook his head. "That may be, but you also happened to *do* the right thing instead of simply being there. Well, gentlemen, let's go into the study. General Moncaldo and His Highness are awaiting us."

He led the way down the hall and into a book-lined room, where a fire was blazing in the fireplace. The two men seated by the hearth stood up as the others entered. General Rafael Vincente Moncaldo was about fifty, a heavyset, swarthy man with dark hair. Although he wore civilian clothes, his bearing gave him a distinctly military appearance.

At seventeen, Alphonse Ferdinand was more a youth than a man, and he was wearing a British captain's uniform, as he had been the first time Henry met him. The friendship that had been established between them on that occasion was reflected in his evident delight as they greeted each other. At first Henry addressed him by the respectful form that the others used, but the slender, handsome youth immediately objected.

"No, no," he said firmly. "Do you not remember what I told you? Regardless of what position I achieve, you are always to address me as Captain Ferdinand. That will be the symbol of our friendship."

Henry smiled in recollection. "I'm sorry I forgot," he said. "But I do remember our conversations about firearms. Is your markmanship still improving?"

Alphonse smiled and nodded. A common interest in firearms had brought him and Henry together on their first meeting, at the Sandhurst firing range. Ferdinand practiced there frequently with weapons from his large private collection, and Henry's marksmanship had amazed and impressed him.

Although he was young, Alphonse had an air of total assurance and an already regal bearing. The conduct of the three older men in the room reflected their awareness that they were in the presence of one who would probably soon be a European monarch, for they waited with quiet patience while Alphonse chatted about his target practice.

Despite Alphonse Ferdinand's regal bearing, however, in some ways he remained a typical youth, and when everyone sat down and Anderson, as was his custom, made himself comfortable by removing his glass eye and replacing it with a black patch, Alphonse gaped at the American with boyish fascination.

The discussion began, with Moncaldo referring to a notebook and doing most of the talking. For the past years, with the secret advice and aid of friendly foreign governments, Moncaldo had solicited support for Alphonse Ferdinand among senior army officers in war-torn Spain. Agreement among them was now universal, and the army would align itself behind Alphonse Ferdinand when he formally announced his claim to the throne.

Moncaldo had also recruited agents throughout the country and among the various factions vying for political power. Most of the more influential groups now supported Alphonse, with the exception of the Carlists, who had already attempted to assassinate the young claimant to the throne. From an informant among them, Moncaldo had learned that they were planning another attempt.

"The leader of those involved in the plot," Moncaldo said, "is Emilio Garcia. You probably recall the man, Captain Blake."

Henry nodded; he had glimpsed Garcia on a train just before the previous attempt on Alphonse's life. The man had a knife scar on one side of his face, which had made him easy to identify.

Moncaldo went on, referring occasionally to his notebook. "Three days ago, Garcia was observed in Madrid with a German named Josef Mueller. That night, Carlos Chacon, one of Garcia's lieutenants, left Madrid with Mueller." He glanced over at Willoughby and Anderson. "Today I received a message from Madrid. Chacon sent a telegram to Garcia, which my man read. It consisted only of the address of a hotel in Darmstadt."

"That's good news, because it answers our questions," Willoughby said. "Chacon went to Germany to buy weapons, and the telegram is a signal that he arrived safely."

Alphonse Ferdinand looked puzzled, and Anderson, noting this, elaborated. "Darmstadt is the arms trading center of Germany. Apparently Chacon went there to buy weapons."

Moncaldo looked up from his notebook with a frown. "That still doesn't answer our questions about Mueller. We don't know enough about that man."

"I believe we do," Willoughby replied. "It seems clear that he's either an arms dealer or an agent for one. As before, Garcia wants weapons of foreign manufacture so that the Carlists can't be directly implicated. Mueller is his contact to obtain the weapons."

"Perhaps," Moncaldo said. "But we need to verify that."

Willoughby shook his head. "I disagree. What we have here is a minor side issue. The plot itself, and those at the center of it, are in Spain."

"Even so," the general insisted, "we need to know everything we can about the plot. I believe we should ask German intelligence to investigate Mueller, to watch him and Chacon."

Willoughby remained calm. "No, that would be a mistake. When His Highness assumes the throne, it is essential he do so in an atmosphere of universal support and goodwill. Knowledge about the plot against him must be kept to as few people as possible."

"But surely we can trust German intelligence to be discreet, Sir Charles. And if they investigated, perhaps they could tell us how many weapons Chacon buys. They could also tell us exactly when he leaves to return to Spain. These are things we need to know."

Willoughby again shook his head and pointed out that the same information could be obtained by closely monitoring the Carlists in Spain; Moncaldo countered that close surveillance over the Carlists raised the danger of alerting them.

As the two men debated the issue, Henry reflected that each had excellent reasons to support his viewpoint. Willoughby, however, was unable to reveal his strongest reason—that he wanted to avoid involving German intelligence because, in short, he did not trust it. Henry weighed what was involved and decided to resolve the argument himself.

"I'll go to Darmstadt," he said during a pause. "There are, as has been mentioned, many arms dealers there. I'll pass myself off as one, make contact with Mueller and Chacon, and find out what I can about them."

Silence fell, everyone looking at Henry. Moncaldo was first to object. "It's generous of you to volunteer to do this, Captain Blake," he said, "but how could you pose as a German arms dealer? Even if you speak fluent German, your American accent would reveal your subterfuge."

Anderson quickly came to Henry's defense. "Captain Blake doesn't have an American accent in German, General Moncaldo. He speaks the language like a native, with a Prussian accent."

Brigadier Halloway spoke for the first time. "Yes, but he's a soldier," he objected. "The moment he puts on civilian clothes, he places himself in jeopardy and could even be arrested as a spy. Regardless of how well you're established in Germany, Captain Blake, you could end up in a very nasty situation."

"That is a good point, Henry," Willoughby said. "I could provide you with suitable identification and other documents, of course. But you would be mixing with a very unsavory lot that is watched closely by the authorities, and we would be unable to protect you. If you became involved with the police, you would be a soldier out of uniform with forged identification. That would be an extremely embarrassing position."

"Yes, but I believe it's worth the risk," Henry said.

Moncaldo, Anderson, and Willoughby exchanged glances. Their silence indicated agreement.

"Very well. I'll make arrangements to have you provided with suitable clothing, documentation, and such," Willoughby declared. "Naturally, we're extremely grateful to you for doing this." His pale blue eyes were warm with gratitude. "Very grateful indeed, Henry."

Two days after the meeting at Sandhurst, Henry boarded a steam ferry at Dover to cross the English Channel. The weather was raw, with a gusty wind sweeping in from the North Sea, and the surf pounding at the foot of the chalk cliffs nearby made a rumbling background noise to the shrill cries of gulls swooping overhead.

As he gazed across the gray expanse of water to the distant French coast, Henry recalled Anderson's parting instructions.

"All we need to know is when Chacon leaves Darmstadt," the State Department agent had said. "General Moncaldo's men will be waiting at the Spanish border and can follow him to the others, and the weapons will be legal evidence of a plot. Above all, remember you'll be alone among a crowd of thugs. It is imperative that your true identity not be discovered."

Henry glanced down at his suit and coat. He had been well outfitted by Sir Charles's people. The cloth and cut were definitely German, yet the style spoke of a business traveler rather than of a wealthy gentleman of leisure. Gisela certainly would not approve of them.

Henry found a seat in an upper-deck lounge, and some three hours later, after a rough crossing that had made many of the passengers violently seasick, the ferry docked at Calais. The French customs officer glanced at Henry's passport, stamped it, and waved him past, and less than a half hour later he was on a train en route to Paris.

Rain trickled down the sooty windows of the railroad carriage as an early dusk turned into nightfall over the French countryside. The following morning, after spending the night in a Paris hotel, Henry crossed the German border at Saarbrücken. It had begun raining again, and owing to a series of delays, he did not arrive in Darmstadt until late afternoon.

The capital of the Grand Duchy of Hesse, Darmstadt was an ancient, graceful city flanked by districts of brash new construction housing chemical plants, ironworks, and other industries. When the factories had developed and expanded, a canal had been dug to connect them with the barge traffic on the Rhine, some fifteen kilometers to the east. The small hotel where Chacon and Mueller were staying, the Friedrichshof, was a short distance from the train station and fronted a cobblestone street, Nordkanalstrasse, running beside the canal. It was a neighborhood of dingy shops, noisy taverns, and small businesses that catered mostly to boatmen and transients, and the hotel fit well into its surroundings. The unkempt clerk in the ill-lit, dusty lobby asked for payment in advance, then handed Henry a key.

A few hours after he arrived, Henry saw Chacon and Mueller having dinner in a restaurant adjacent to the hotel. Chacon, matching the description Moncaldo had given him, was a swarthy, well-built man of about thirty who had come into conflict with others from time to time, as evidenced by a scar on his forehead and a nose askew from having been broken. Mueller, as Moncaldo had said, was a handsome man of medium height and build, some forty years old.

Limiting himself to a single look at the German as he went to a table in the restaurant, Henry quickly gauged him to be a formidable opponent. Mueller was quiet and watchful, his gray eyes missing nothing, and with his hard, craggy features he had a look of grim competence. Henry guessed that he was more than merely an agent for an arms dealer.

The waiter took his order and brought a small meal, and Henry finished eating as Mueller and Chacon were paying and putting on their coats. Leaving the restaurant shortly after they did, he followed them along the dark street at a safe distance, while a soft rain fell and fog drifted up from the canal.

The two men went into a tavern, a burst of loud, drunken singing and conversation carrying out through the open door. Henry delayed for a minute, giving them time to get settled, then followed them into the crowded, noisy establishment. Mueller and Chacon were at a table with a third man. Keeping out of Mueller's line of sight, Henry went to the bar and bought a mug of beer, then sat down where he could watch the three men.

The third man was stout and slovenly and was wearing a cheap, soiled suit that was too small for him. He had coarse features and an abrasive manner and waved a soggy cigar as he talked with Chacon. Mueller sat silently listening. As soon as Henry had assured himself that the third man was an arms dealer, he left the tavern and returned to his hotel.

His room was on the second floor, around the corner from the stairwell. An hour passed as Henry stood inside his room, beside the cracked-open door, waiting and listening. Finally his patience was rewarded. He heard Mueller and Chacon coming up the stairs, the Spaniard identifiable by his accent. The two men went into adjacent rooms down the hall.

Henry pondered what to do next. He was perfectly situated to watch Chacon and inform Anderson and Willoughby by telegram when the man left Darmstadt. That was what he had come to Darmstadt to do, and the prudent course of action was to do no more. However, he felt uneasy about Mueller and his role in the plot. For some reason Mueller was advising Chacon and escorting him about, which seemed to suggest a separate, unknown di-

ARIZONA!

mension to the plot against Alphonse Ferdinand. Troubled, Henry went to sleep still wondering about Mueller.

The next morning he decided to make personal contact with the men, regardless of the risks. After Mueller and Chacon had breakfast at a nearby café—Henry watched from a distance outside—they split up, the German going toward the center of the city while the Spaniard headed back to the hotel. Henry reached the hotel first and hurried upstairs. When he heard Chacon reach the landing, he stepped rapidly around the corner and jostled the man.

"Please excuse me, sir," Henry said apologetically, reaching out to steady Chacon. "That was clumsy of me."

Chacon gave a flustered nod and turned sideways to slip past, not wanting to draw attention to himself. "There is no need to apologize, sir," the man murmured. "Please excuse me."

"Ah, you are Spanish!" Henry exlaimed before the man could escape. "I recognize your accent. Not long ago, I sold some weapons to people from Spain. Or perhaps I should say Catalonia, as they prefer to call their homeland." He smiled slyly and shrugged. "Or perhaps I should say nothing at all, because one never knows when one is speaking with a government agent."

The reference to the rebellious Catalonians, who for centuries had agitated for autonomy from Spain, made Chacon hesitate. "No, I am not a government agent," he said. "What kind of weapons did you sell them?"

The blunt request almost caught Henry off-guard. "Oh, an assortment of Lebel, Berthier, and Fusil rifles and pistols acquired during the recent war with France," he replied. "They were not the best of weapons, mind you, but the men wanted as many weapons for as little money as possible. I provide what a customer wants, whether it be old foreign weapons or new Mausers."

Chacon's dark eyes widened with interest. "You have new Mausers?" he said. "Those are difficult to obtain, Herr . . ."

"Hoffmann," Henry supplied. "Friedrich Hoffmann.

Yes, they are difficult to obtain, but I can get Mausers in perfect condition." He glanced along the hall in both directions. "If you wish to discuss business, we should go somewhere more private. Come, my room is right here."

Without hesitation, Chacon followed Henry into the room. Inside, the Spaniard introduced himself, and they sat down and began discussing the proposition in general terms. Henry asked if Chacon had been talking with other arms dealers, and the man replied that he had, identifying the fat German he had been with the previous evening as Wenzel Krauss.

Chacon had been in the room only a few minutes before he admitted he wanted to buy six Mauser rifles. Henry quoted a price well below what Krauss would ask, and Chacon clearly was interested. "I would like my friend to meet you and talk with you," he said. "His name is Josef Mueller. Can you be at the restaurant next door at noon?"

"Yes. In fact, I intend to have lunch there," Henry replied. "But why wait until then? We can go and talk with him now."

"No, he went to the railroad station," Chacon said. "But he will return by noon, and we will be at the restaurant."

Henry agreed to meet them. Chacon went to his room, and Henry sat back in his chair and weighed the implications of what he had done. He thought about Mueller. It seemed likely that the German had gone to the train station to use the postal or telegraph facilities there to make a report on his activities. But to whom?

At noon, Henry went to the restaurant and joined Chacon and Mueller at a quiet corner table. He shook hands with the German as Chacon introduced them, and while they waited for their food they discussed the rainy weather and other innocuous subjects. Mueller's gray, watchful eyes studied Henry all the while.

Finally, as they began eating, Mueller brought up the subject of the rifles, asking Henry where he would obtain them. Henry countered by asking Mueller and Chacon where they would obtain their money.

The German smiled weakly. "You will be paid what you ask," he said. "Who provides the money is not your concern."

"That is true, Herr Mueller," Henry agreed. "Similarly, where I obtain the rifles is not your concern."

"My concern," Mueller said woodenly, "is safety. I like to know with whom I am dealing so I can be sure that no trouble will arise. Specifically, I must be certain that Herr Chacon doesn't end up in possession of stolen weapons that the police are looking for."

"You are dealing with Friedrich Hoffmann, from Trier," Henry replied. "I am dealing with Herr Mueller, who is from somewhere in Pomerania, judging by his accent. If I can assume that the money I receive will not be counterfeit, you can assume that the rifles you receive will be Mausers in good condition with serial numbers that cannot be traced."

Mueller was silent for a long moment. "Very well," he said. "When can you have one of the rifles to show us?"

Hesitating for a moment himself, Henry pondered the step he was taking, which would place both himself and another at great risk. He would have to obtain the rifles from his friend and Gisela's nephew, Captain Richard von Kirchberg; and an officer who mishandled military weapons could suffer severe penalties.

As for himself, not least among the risks was what the fat, arrogant Wenzel Krauss might do. Illegal arms dealers were notoriously unscrupulous, and Krauss appeared worse than most. It seemed unlikely that he would simply overlook the loss of a lucrative sale.

Coming to a decision, Henry took a sip of his beer, then replied. "I will have a rifle here to show you three days from now."

It was a rainy Sunday when Henry arrived in Kassel, a small city on the Fulda River in Hesse, near where the

Twelfth Dragoon Brigade was stationed. On a narrow street of old but well-kept half-timber residences, Henry stopped at a house and tapped the door knocker.

The curtain on the leaded front window stirred, someone peered out, and then the door opened a crack. An attractive young woman clutching a dressing gown around her stuck her head out and asked what he wanted. "Tell the master of the house that Heinrich is here," Henry said.

Hearing Henry from the front parlor, Richard Koehler whooped in delight and scrambled hastily about inside the house. The door was snatched wide open a moment later, and the tall, well-built Prussian dragoon officer stood there, shrugging into his uniform tunic. He pulled Henry inside.

Looking his friend up and down, Richard became puzzled. "Why are you in civilian clothes, Heinrich? And when did you return to Germany? I thought you were still in the United States—"

Henry lifted a hand, interrupting him. "I must talk with you in private, Richard," he said.

Richard, appearing a bit embarrassed, quickly turned to the young woman. "Heinrich, this is Malwine, my . . . maid. Malwine, please bring us a bottle of wine and something to eat. My good friend and I must talk."

The woman smiled and nonchalantly fastened her gown as she walked away. Richard, ebullient over seeing Henry again, led him into the front room. The chairs and tables were cluttered with newspapers, wineglasses, and other litter of a leisurely Sunday afternoon at home, and Richard cleared a place for Henry.

"And so, I have a new cousin!" Richard announced as they sat down. "Heinrich, you must be a man of astonishing virility. Everyone had presumed that the baroness was about as fertile as a slab of granite. You have my most sincere congratulations."

"Richard, I love your aunt," Henry said, refusing to be provoked. "I know that she can be less than cordial at times, but you would do well to heed her advice on some matters. For example, she commended Ulrica Fremmel to you as a good marriage prospect, and she was absolutely correct."

"She was indeed," Richard agreed readily. "I would be the last to deny that the baroness is extremely intelligent. Of course Ulrica is not the most beautiful woman in the world—but in fact I've taken the baroness's advice. Ulrica has consented to be my wife, and, more to the point, General Fremmel has consented to have me as a son-in-law."

"Then you're the one to be congratulated," Henry returned. "Let's just hope that Ulrica doesn't find out about your maid."

Richard looked amused. "Not to worry, Heinrich," he said. "Malwine served coffee when Ulrica called on me a few days ago, to present me with a box of cigars. Ulrica isn't jealous like the baroness. She wants only to be my wife and doesn't demand my very soul in return."

"Not yet." Henry chuckled, then, changing the subject, began telling Richard about the garbled telegram and the misunderstanding that had brought him rushing back from the United States. While they were laughing about the incident, the young maid brought in a tray laid out with bread, cheese, sausages, and a bottle of wine.

As they ate, Henry explained why he had come. "The reason I'm in civilian clothes is that I'm working on a very sensitive matter. I'm not allowed to talk about it in any detail, but it involves vital interests of my country and several others, including Germany."

"And there is a way in which I might help?" Richard asked.

"Yes, but I want you to feel entirely free to decline," Henry replied. "I need six Mauser rifles, one of them immediately. I realize that you would be endangering your career by taking them from your armory, and believe me, I wouldn't have come to you if I had another way of obtaining them."

Richard sipped his wine and shrugged in seeming

unconcern. "I have hundreds of Mausers in my armory," he said, "and if you need six of them, you will have them. When will you need the remaining five?"

Henry knew he would probably require some time to learn as much as he could from Chacon and Mueller. "In about a week," he replied. "But first, perhaps you should think about this, Richard. It entails a very serious risk to you."

"Yes, it does," Richard agreed. He emptied his wineglass and stood up. "But you are my friend above all others, Heinrich," he said quietly. "When you need anything, it will be done."

Henry stood up and offered his hand. "You've certainly proven that, Richard. I hope that sometime I'll have an opportunity to repay you. If this gets you in trouble, I promise I'll do my best to protect you."

The waggish sense of humor that always lurked in Richard's blue eyes surfaced. "If the armory is inventoried and I'm found out, I'll be beyond help. During my last supply inspection, I was short one stirrup on a spare saddle, and I'm still trying to explain that!"

Richard excused himself, promising to return in a few hours, and Henry picked up a stack of newspapers and made himself comfortable.

Dusk was falling when Richard returned, with a disassembled Mauser packed in a canvas bag. He walked with Henry to the train station and waited with him until his train arrived. Henry repeated his thanks, which Richard shrugged off, telling him that the remaining rifles would be waiting for him his next visit.

Another gray, rainy dawn was breaking when Henry reached Darmstadt, and the canal along Nordkanalstrasse was busy with Monday morning barge traffic. At the hotel, Henry assembled the Mauser in his room, laid it on the bed, then stepped down the hall and knocked on Chacon's door. When the Spaniard answered, Henry told him to come to his room and bring Mueller.

A few minutes later, the two men knocked on Henry's door. Chacon's face lit with glee as he saw the Mauser on the bed, but Mueller revealed no reaction.

The Spaniard picked up the rifle and examined it. "This weapon appears in excellent condition, Herr Hoffmann," he commented. "If the others are the same, I will be satisfied."

"I told you they would all be in good condition, and they will."

"When will you have the rest of them?" Mueller asked.

"Within the next ten days," Henry replied. "My business associate must get back to me. In the meantime, take that one with you."

"I will pay you for this one now," Chacon offered, tucking the rifle under his arm and taking out his wallet.

"No, no," Henry insisted, raising a hand. "We've made a bargain, and I trust you. Pay me when I deliver the remainder. I *am* ready for a good breakfast, however, and I'll see you in the restaurant, if you'll join me."

The two men agreed and stepped to the door. A few minutes later, they met downstairs in the restaurant. As on previous occasions, Mueller remained silent most of the time, speaking only in reply to questions. Chacon obliquely remarked that the "merchandise" would be used for the benefit of Spain, but Henry let the comment pass, intending to pursue it another time, to find out if Chacon knew any specifics about the plot against Alphonse Ferdinand.

After coffee, Mueller excused himself and left without a word of explanation. But he again headed in the direction of the train station—to send a report to his employer, Henry assumed. Later in the day, as Henry emerged from a café on the Nordkanalstrasse where he had gone to pass the time, he saw Wenzel Krauss.

The arms dealer had a chewed cigar in the side of his mouth, as usual. He was walking along with a large, muscular man who was shabbily dressed and had a surly expression. The two had been talking but fell silent as they passed Henry. Krauss glowered at him, and Henry knew he would have to stay on guard against the arms dealer.

During the following days, Henry glimpsed Krauss two other times, but the threat of trouble never progressed beyond glares. Henry used the pretext of messages from a fictitious business partner to stay in close contact with Chacon and Mueller so he could continue to talk with them and learn all he could. However, the German began missing some meals, remaining in his room and not going to the restaurant.

On the fourth day after Henry had supplied the first Mauser, Mueller missed breakfast and then lunch. At dinner, when he again failed to come to the restaurant, Henry asked Chacon about the man. The Spaniard said Mueller had left the previous evening by train.

"Did he say where he was going?" Henry asked in a conversational tone.

"No, he didn't," Chacon replied. "Herr Mueller says very little about himself, but I know that he will return. His room is paid for, and his baggage is still in it."

"What time did he leave?"

The Spaniard shrugged. "Sometime yesterday, but I'm not sure."

Henry decided not to press the subject; obviously it would be futile to find out where Mueller had gone by checking the train schedule. Cautious and secretive, the German had apparently foreseen just such a possibility and deliberately misled Chacon. It appeared likely that Mueller had gone to report in person to his employer, but beyond that, all Henry could do was guess, and that made him extremely uncomfortable.

In fact, Josef Mueller was in Berlin, experiencing a different kind of discomfort. He had heard rumors of the confinement and interrogation facility located in a deep vault under Bluecher's mansion, and on one occasion Bluecher had actually mentioned it to him. He had envisioned something darker and less specific, however, and had been unprepared for the stark reality.

Mueller's profession had hardened him to suffering in others, but still he regretted accepting Bluecher's invitation to come to observe while the man checked on a prisoner. The cells were tiny barred cages, as in a zoo, and the interrogation room was a well-lighted torture chamber.

The keeper of the place, a closemouthed fellow whom Bluecher referred to as Graben, seemed perfectly at home. Completely bald, he was pallid and sluglike and moved about with a shuffling gait to Bluecher's commands.

The prisoner, a young woman, was gagged and strapped naked to a table in the interrogation room. She was unconscious, and there were bruises and red marks all over her body. Bluecher had a bland smile on his face as he talked about her. Graben stood at the head of the table, his dull eyes glinting with furtive life as he touched her neck with his white, thick fingers. The scene was extremely offensive to Mueller.

"The art of interrogation, Josef," Bluecher confided in his soft, high-pitched voice, "is to know when the subject is telling the truth. This subject, for example, will now readily confess to anything." He wheezed a theatrical sigh. "But will the confession be true? That is where interrogation becomes an art."

"Who is she, and what did she do?" Mueller asked.

"Oh, a clerk in my department at the ministry," Bluecher replied. "Naturally, all employees there are warned never to discuss their work with anyone, and particularly never to take anything out of the office. She was caught taking home a folder of secret documents."

"To sell them?"

Bluecher smiled boyishly. "I'm not sure yet. But I will know before she dies."

"Won't there be questions about her from her family and friends?"

Bluecher shrugged his sloping shoulders. "People disappear every day, for no apparent reason. It is regretful, but we must have perfect security in my department." He walked over and tapped Graben's shoulder, to draw his attention from the woman. "When she comes to, put her in a cell," Bluecher said. "And give her food. I will be back tonight."

Mueller followed with relief as Bluecher left the room and made his way along the narrow passageway to the stone staircase. Grasping the iron handrail, Bluecher stopped every few steps to catch his breath. During one of his pauses, while he was panting heavily, he took out his watch and commented that dinner should soon be ready.

Food was the last thing Mueller desired, particularly while in Bluecher's company, but when the two of them reached the ground floor of the mansion and emerged into the hallway, the butler was waiting to tell Bluecher dinner was ready.

In the large, luxurious dining room, Mueller picked at his slices of roast veal. At least it was no longer necessary for him to converse with Bluecher, for the monstrously overweight man devoted his full attention to his food.

Watching his host eat stirred Mueller's boyhood memories of an old boar on his father's farm in Pomerania. The largest of the swine and rolling in fat, the boar had stood at its trough and gobbled its food in the same way that Bluecher ate. Smacking its mouth as it grunted and sighed in enjoyment, it had chewed and gulped down each bite quickly in its hurry to take another mouthful.

The servants deftly kept Bluecher's plate filled so that his eating would not be interrupted. The man devoured the bulk of the roast, as well as heaping bowls of potatoes and vegetables and a platter of rolls. His murmurs of satisfaction were punctuated by occasional loud belches.

After gorging on an entire pie, Bluecher sat back while a servant wiped the sauce and gravy from his face with a damp towel; then another servant helped him to his feet and brushed crumbs from his waistcoat. Mueller stood up and followed as Bluecher waddled out of the room and along the hall to the study.

The butler brought cigars and glasses of brandy as Bluecher installed himself in the oversize chair behind his desk and waved Mueller to a seat. When the cigars were lighted and the butler had left, Bluecher spoke for the first time in an hour. He said only two words: "Friedrich Hoffmann."

Mueller put down his cigar and began explaining what had happened, only to be interrupted.

"Josef, I know all that," Bluecher said. "It was in your reports. Tell me about the man, about your impressions of him."

"Well, he's young," Mueller said. "No more than twenty-five. And he's taller than average. From his looks, he would have no difficulty securing female companionship, although he's shown no interest in women at Darmstadt. Apparently he's been in the army, because he has a military bearing; and his manner is assured, like that of an older man."

Bluecher was silent a moment. "In one of your reports," he said, "you mention that he became acquainted with Chacon through talking with him in the hotel hall. Yet you say that Chacon was following orders and not talking with strangers?"

"Yes, sir. This Hoffmann is determined as well as intelligent—a Prussian in every respect. I would guess that he saw us talking with Krauss and inferred that Chacon wanted to buy weapons. Then he planned a way of meeting Chacon and drawing his interest."

Bluecher tapped his cigar ash as he spoke again. "Could the man be an impostor?"

"An impostor?" Mueller was puzzled. "He says he is a Prussian from Trier and an arms dealer. His accent and manner are certainly Prussian, and he has weapons to sell. I'm not sure of your meaning, sir."

Bluecher gave a cryptic smile. "Krauss must be very

angry," he continued, "and there undoubtedly will be one fewer Prussian in Germany before this matter is ended."

"There will probably be trouble between Krauss and Hoffmann," Mueller agreed cautiously.

"Let me know what happens," Bluecher said. "Submit your final report after Chacon leaves for Spain. Then return to Leipzig and wait there until I have another assignment for you."

Mueller, realizing he had been dismissed, stood up, bowed, and left. A moment later, the butler came into the room. "The carriage has arrived with the woman, sir," he said. "She is waiting in your bedroom."

Bluecher nodded as he puffed on his cigar. The butler picked up Mueller's glass and ashtray and went back out. After swallowing some brandy, Bluecher rubbed the padded leather arm of his chair and contemplated the fact that Adela Ronsard was upstairs. Ecstasy and gratification of his every whim awaited him, for the dusky, exotic courtesan was always ready with an endless variety of fascinating techniques to please him. Still, a nagging, undefined worry would not let him rest.

As he reviewed in his mind the developments in Darmstadt, Bluecher knew there was every reason for him to feel confident rather than uneasy. He had wanted the Carlists to obtain arms, and by a means that had as little connection with him as possible. That goal had been virtually achieved, and instead of dealing through Krauss, who had been contacted by Mueller, Chacon was being supplied by a third party with no connection whatsoever to Bluecher. Still, he mused, something about Hoffmann bothered him.

Boosting himself from his chair, Bluecher forced all thoughts of Adela Ronsard from his mind and decided first to complete his unfinished business downstairs.

VI

Dieter Schumann, a muscular, heavyset man in his late forties, backed quickly away from the barn door as Toby Holt led a saddled gelding outside. The thoroughbred hunter was a large, high-spirited animal, and its heavy hooves came too close to Dieter for comfort as it stamped and pranced from side to side.

Toby managed to calm the horse, then mounted it. "Are you sure you don't want to go riding with us?" he asked.

"No, I'm not that much of a horseman, Toby," Dieter said quickly. "I'm not even sure I could stay on one of those hunters."

"They can be a handful," Toby admitted with a smile. "In any event, you aren't quite dressed for riding. You do look very dapper, Dieter."

Dieter glanced down at his expensive, conservative business suit. "Well, considering how our business is thriving, I feel obliged to look at least a bit successful."

"You certainly deserve it," Toby said sincerely. "I'm particularly pleased that you've raised the men's wages back to what they were before the depression, and from what I hear, you've worked harder than anyone else. You're probably not being paid enough, if anything."

Dieter shook his head firmly. "You gave me this job and a new chance in life, and I consider what I'm making now generous. I'm more than satisfied."

"Well, I'll be glad to make another agreement with you anytime you want," Toby offered. "Alexandra and I will probably be back by noon, and we can talk again before you have to catch your train."

"Take your time, Toby. I'll find something to occupy myself."

Toby reined his horse to one side as Alexandra led her stallion out of the barn. While the gelding had kicked up something of a fuss upon leaving its stall, the stallion was seething with excess energy, as if ready to explode.

Alexandra looked tiny in comparison with the huge animal as it snorted and stamped, its teeth bared and its ears laid back. It looked vicious and wild, and for a fleeting second Dieter expected Toby to hurry to his young friend's assistance.

But then he saw that Alexandra was unruffled and that she had a firm grip on the reins. Toby smiled in admiration as he watched her control the unruly horse, and Jonah Venable, working on a stock pen nearby, chuckled as he watched.

When the horse was in the yard, Alexandra vaulted lightly onto the small saddle and turned the stallion's head toward the stock pen. The animal lunged into a run and effortlessly leaped the fence. It went straight through the pen, jumped the opposite fence, and Toby, after waving good-bye to Dieter, urged his gelding around the pen to catch up with Alexandra.

As the couple rode away across the rolling pastures, Dieter walked over to where Jonah was replacing broken rails in the fence. Unable to stand idly by and watch another work, Dieter took off his coat and put it aside. Jonah, who was in overalls, looked at him skeptically. "This here is pretty dirty work," he warned.

"I've had my hands dirty before," Dieter replied, picking up an adz. "And I've repaired fences before." He began trimming the end of a rail, sending chips flying. "That Alexandra is a remarkable young woman," he said between chops with the heavy blade. "I've never seen a woman who could handle horses and ride like her."

Jonah shifted the chew of tobacco in his mouth and watched until he was assured that Dieter wasn't going to trim one of his own feet instead of the rail. Then he resumed working. "I ain't neither, and I've spent most of my life around horses. Turco is extra lively because he ain't been rode much lately. Ain't many men could handle him when he's like that, but Miss Alexandra does it without even trying."

"Has she ever been injured?" Dieter asked.

"Plenty of times," Jonah replied. "But she always bounces back." He chuckled to himself. "What's more, she can down her stirrup cup as neat as the hardest-drinking man in the hunt."

Dieter was not surprised. "Yes, after dinner last night I noticed that a nip of bourbon didn't give her any trouble. I also noticed that Alex didn't take a drink."

Jonah nodded. "Wasn't always like that. When his wife died, he began making reg'lar trips to the bourbon cellar. In fact, he stayed sozzled most of the time for several years. Then, when he begun pulling hisself together again, he gave liquor up altogether."

Dieter had not failed to notice the effect on the farm from years of neglect. Still, it remained a beautiful, restful place, far from the soot and the scurry of the cities. The setting was particularly bucolic on this sunny autumn day. In the garden patch, cornstalks had been gathered into shocks, with pumpkins scattered around them, and the oak trees lining the drive were arrayed in brilliant yellows and oranges. Smoke curled from the chimney atop the smokehouse, where winter pork was curing, and it gave a tangy scent to the fresh, cool air.

Dieter finished a rail, and he and Jonah lifted it into place. Then Dieter immediately began working on another rail. "For a city fellow," Jonah observed, "you're pretty good with your hands."

Dieter replied without pausing in his work. "Not so long ago I was working on the docks in Milwaukee."

"But I bet you didn't always," Jonah pressed. "I had an idea that you're one of them businessmen who lost everything in the depression."

"Not everything. I did once own several lumber mills in Milwaukee, and I lost all of my property, but I still had the important things—my wife, my children, and my good health."

"Yes, them's the important things," Jonah agreed. "Was you in the lumber business when you met Mr. Holt?"

Dieter nodded, pausing to reflect. It seemed like a lifetime ago when he had first met Toby Holt, and indeed he had since become a different man. Back then he had been enormously wealthy, but he had also been hard and unscrupulous in his dealings with others. Meeting Toby had completely changed his priorities in life, and he no longer valued the things that had once blinded him to the beauty around him.

Jonah spat tobacco juice to one side. "Well, we're sure lucky that he's here, because it's certain that them scalawags will be back. With Mr. Alex still not all healed, me and him could never handle them by ourselves."

"Yes, Toby's a good man to have around when there's trouble."

"No doubt about that," Jonah agreed. "From all them papers you brought with you, he must have a big business in Chicago."

"Yes, he owns a lumber company in the city and a logging camp up the lake in Wisconsin. Much of our trade these days is with farmers, who exchange produce for lumber, and we sell the produce in a store in Chicago. Last year we began selling packaged materials for houses, and we bought up a bankrupt ironworks to get the necessary hardware from their inventory. And now we're putting the ironworks back into operation."

"That *is* big business," Jonah commented, impressed. "I get the idea that he don't spend much time on it hisself, though."

Dieter smiled, for he considered the remark a compliment. "You saw how long it took him last night to go through all those papers and sign them. Well, that's the way it always is. Toby is interested in his employees and wants to know how things are going, but he trusts me with the details."

Jonah nodded, and as they continued working, he asked other, probing questions about the business in Chicago, leading Dieter to suspect that he had a hidden motive. Not wanting to offend the man by telling him to get to the point, Dieter let Jonah take his time in working up to what he wanted to say. At length Jonah began talking about a deceased friend.

"His name was Frank Seeley," Jonah said. "He was the best friend I ever had, besides the Woodlings, and I've been sort of looking after his widow ever since he died. Her name is Mabel."

Anticipating that Jonah wanted to find a job for the woman, Dieter attempted a shortcut. "Has Mrs. Seeley ever worked at any sort of trade, Jonah?" he asked.

"Yes, she's a seamstress," Jonah replied, "and a mighty good one. She's been making Miss Alexandra's clothes for years, and she has plenty of other customers in Lexington."

Concluding he had been mistaken about the point toward which Jonah was rambling, Dieter fell silent again. As Jonah continued, however, Dieter discovered that his original suspicion had not been far from the truth. Evidently Mabel had a much younger brother—actually a half brother—who sponged off her.

"His name is Luther Bingham," Jonah said. "He was little when his folks died, and Mabel raised him. But he's like a colt who won't be weaned, and Mabel is too good-

hearted to throw him out. Worrying over him helped put
Frank into an early grave."

"I see. Would you like me to give him a job?"

Jonah hesitated and spat tobacco juice. "I'd like for
you to give him a job, but I don't want to ask you to do it.
What I mean to say is, I wouldn't recommend Luther
Bingham to nobody. Besides that, he probably wouldn't
take a job if you offered it to him."

"That's certainly straightforward enough," Dieter said.
"What sort of work can he do?"

"He ought to be able to do might near anything,"
Jonah answered, in evident disgust. "Luther is plenty
smart, and he went to college for a while. He worked as a
teacher in a town near Louisville, but he got run off. It
seems he was learning some older girls a few things their
folks didn't want them to know. Other than that, he's just
loafed around."

"Has he had any trouble with the police?"

"Some, because he gets in with a rough crowd now
and then. But nothing serious. It seems to me that Luther
is like a train trying to climb a steep grade in a snowstorm,
with no sand to sprinkle on the rails. If'n he could once
get started, he might be all right."

Dieter pondered a moment. "What about this: When
you take me to the train station this afternoon, we'll leave
early. You can show me where Mrs. Seeley lives, and I'll
talk with her brother. As you said, he might not accept a
job, but at least I'll make the offer."

"You will?" Jonah exclaimed, clearly surprised. "After
what I told you about him? Why would you do that?"

"Because you want me to," Dieter replied, smiling.
"Things may or may not work out, but I'm willing to try."

"Well, whether or not things work out," Jonah said
gratefully, "I sure do appreciate it. There ain't many who
would be as obliging as you."

Dieter shrugged off the compliment and resumed
working. "I like to think that I'm willing to help others,"

he said, between chops, "but I haven't always been that way. It's something I learned from Toby Holt."

Jonah gazed at Dieter with new respect, then helped the businessman lift the finished rail into place on the fence.

That afternoon, Dieter completed his business with Toby, and Jonah took him to Lexington in the buggy. Mabel Seeley lived a short distance from the depot, on a street of small, decrepit wooden houses.

Dieter preferred to talk to Bingham in private, so Jonah stopped the buggy and let him off, promising to check his baggage at the station. Dieter dismissed the man's thanks once again, shook hands with him, then walked up to the house and knocked on the door.

The house showed far more care than others on the street. There were curtains in the windows, and the yard was well tended. The woman who opened the door was similarly tidy, in a freshly ironed if somewhat faded dress, with graying hair pinned in a neat bun. Mabel Seeley was about fifty years old, with blue eyes and a good-natured face, and from what Jonah had told him, Dieter suspected that people took advantage of her.

Dieter introduced himself, and when he explained that he knew Jonah, Mabel smiled radiantly and immediately ushered him in. The parlor was her workroom, and dress forms lined an entire wall. There was a workbench by the window, and shelves were filled with bolts of cloth, racks of spooled thread, and other sewing articles.

Dieter had a train to catch, so he wasted no time. "Actually, I've come here to make a proposition to your brother, Mrs. Seeley. Is he in?"

"Why, yes, he is." The woman seemed perplexed for an instant; then understanding dawned on her. There could be only one reason Jonah would send a stranger to talk to Luther. "Is it about a job?" she asked, reddening slightly.

Dieter nodded.

A worried look came over her. "I—I'll take you to him, Mr. Schumann."

Wanting to spare her any anxiety, Dieter raised a hand. "If you don't mind, I'll introduce myself. Which room is his?"

The woman pointed toward it, and Dieter crossed to the door and knocked. Inside, a man murmured something, and Dieter went in and closed the door behind him. Luther Bingham, who appeared to be about twenty-five, was lying on the bed amid a clutter of books. He had features somewhat resembling his sister's, but he was unshaven and rumpled and looked as indolent as she did industrious.

He smiled sourly as Dieter introduced himself and began explaining the purpose of his visit.

"So old Jonah sent you, did he?" Luther interrupted rudely. "He's getting to be such a gossipy, nosy old biddy that he should start wearing an apron and bonnet."

"Let me begin over, Mr. Bingham," Dieter said, restraining his temper and keeping his voice calm. "Jonah Venable is a friend of mine. I won't listen to sarcasm or criticism about him from you, and if you say another word along that line, I'll remove you from that bed and box your ears. Have I made myself clear?"

Bingham flushed with resentment and sat up to reply hotly. But taking a closer look at Dieter's muscular shoulders and arms, he changed his mind and lay back on the pillow. "Jonah's all right, I guess," he grumbled. "I just wish he would stop trying to mind my business for me, that's all."

"Jonah is concerned about your sister, not you. But as I was saying, I'm the manager of a lumber company and a produce store in Chicago. I'm also reopening a bankrupt ironworks that will soon begin making barbed wire as the first in a line of metal goods. In return for honest work, I'll provide fair wages and steady promotions as deserved."

Bingham had begun shaking his head even before

Dieter had finished. "Barbed wire?" he scoffed. "You'll never be able to sell it. Barbed wire is the most useless—"

"This is a different kind," Dieter cut him short. "The man who patented it came to me a few weeks ago, and I looked into everything involved before I struck a bargain with him. Other barbed wire breaks easily and loses its barbs because it's a single strand of wire with the barbs soldered or crimped onto it. This is two-strand wire, with the barbs woven into the twists. I showed a sample to livery stable owners and farmers, and they all said that they would use it."

Bingham looked skeptical but didn't say anything at first. "It's patented, you say?"

"Yes, and once on the market it will revolutionize farming in this country. Countless millions of acres now lie fallow because crops can't be grown on land that isn't fenced against livestock. And as even you could probably figure out, fences of stone, wood, or hedge aren't practical on the prairies. This will be a turning point in the history of our nation, and you could have a hand in it."

The young man, obviously sharp-minded and well educated, seemed to grasp the full implications while Dieter was still explaining. For a moment interest shone in his eyes; then he shook his head. "I don't want to go to Chicago. I'll stay here in Lexington."

"To continue leeching off your sister?" Dieter's patience was wearing thin. "I'm giving you an opportunity to make something of yourself."

"Well, I didn't ask you to," Luther replied with unconcealed resentment. "You have no right to come here and talk to me like this."

"On the contrary, I have every right," Dieter returned hotly. "I'm here with the permission of the head and wage-earner of the house." Controlling his temper once again, he lowered his voice. "Listen, I'll pay your way to Chicago and see that you have lodgings in a boardinghouse while you start to work. Try it for a month, and I'm sure you'll be very happy that you did."

"No, I'll stay here," Luther said. "I'm looking around,

and I'll find something here." He picked up a book from the bed and turned away as he opened it. Fuming, Dieter left the room, but his anger quickly faded as he saw Mabel Seeley once more.

The woman was sewing at her workbench, but clearly she had overheard the conversation, for her fingers were trembling as she plied her needle, and she was almost in tears. Dieter judged that she would persevere and continue to support her brother, however, just as his own wife, Abigail, had remained loyal to him when he least deserved it. The sterling qualities that were taken for granted in many women had made him feel humble and grateful ever since.

Putting down her sewing, Mabel forced a smile and tried to stammer an apology. Dieter waved it aside and tried to say something to ease the tension of the moment, but he succeeded only partially. A stiff silence prevailed as Mabel accompanied him to the door.

On a shelf near the door Dieter noticed a display of handkerchiefs. Intending to buy a small present to take back to Abigail, he looked more closely. "Are these for sale, Mrs. Seeley?"

"Well, in a manner of speaking," Mabel answered shyly. "They're something I tack together in spare moments and keep on hand for customers who have a need for them."

As she handed one of them to him, Dieter saw that her description had been ridiculously inadequate. Made of smooth muslin, the handkerchiefs were edged with fine lace and expertly embroidered in intricate rose patterns. As a finishing touch, they had been cleverly folded and ironed into triangular creases that unfolded like a fan.

"Jonah said you were a skilled seamstress, and now I see what he meant. How many of these do you have, and what would you sell them for?"

"I keep a dozen on hand, Mr. Schumann, and I usually sell them one or two at a time for about a dime each. Would a dollar for the dozen be too much?"

"On the contrary, it would be far too little," Dieter declared. "I'll pay you five dollars for them."

The woman shook her head quickly. "No, I couldn't take that much. A dollar will be fine."

Dieter fished in his pocket. "I'd like to have these for my wife, because I know they would please her. However, I insist on paying you five dollars for them."

Mabel hesitated, but Dieter pressed a five-dollar gold piece into her hand. She thanked him politely and found a piece of brown paper to wrap the handkerchiefs in.

At the door, Dieter tried to leave with encouraging words, telling Mabel that her brother might find a way to sort himself out. Mabel forced a smile, but it was clear that she, too, did not consider it a likely prospect. Dieter waved a good-bye and walked along the street to the train station.

His failure to help Jonah, combined with his pity for Mabel and anger toward Luther, made Dieter feel moody. Then he smiled to himself, suddenly amused by his reactions. Not too long ago, his sole and driving objective in life had been amassing wealth. Compared to that obsession, his newfound sense of responsibility toward others was anything but a burden. It was more like the solid weight of his healthy young sons when he lifted them in his arms.

Shrugging off his glum mood, Dieter walked with a lighter step. It was a glorious autumn day, and the handkerchiefs would bring a smile of delight to his wife's face. He had done his best to help Jonah and Mabel, and now he eagerly looked forward to returning home to his wife and sons.

That evening, while Toby and the others were preparing dinner at Fair Oaks, there was a knock on the kitchen door. Alexandra went to answer it.

"Why, come in, Whitey," she said in surprise. "My goodness, have you run all the way from the city?"

It was one of the orphanage boys who sold newspapers

at the train station. A tall, gangling lad of twelve, he stepped gratefully into the warm kitchen.

"Might near, ma'am," he panted, his face flushed with exertion and excitement. He turned to Toby. "Sir, I seen that man Sewell get off a train that come in from the west."

"Are you sure it was Sewell?" Toby asked.

The boy nodded rapidly and repeated almost word for word the description that Toby had given him. Then, digging in his pocket, he pulled out a crumpled baggage ticket and handed it to Toby. "There was two men with him, and one of 'em threw that on the floor, sir. I followed 'em from the train station, and they went to that big hotel on Elm Street."

Toby looked at the ticket. Its station of origin was San Francisco. "I appreciate your coming right away to tell me, son," he said. "I'll make sure Reverend Quint knows what a fine job you did."

Alexandra, cutting a thick slice from a cake on the counter, had caught the boy's attention. "Here, you can have a piece, Whitey," she said.

"Thankee, Miss Alexandra!" the boy exclaimed. "We don't never get no sweets, and Preacher Quint tells us just to be glad we've got vittles between our belt buckle and backbone. I'm much obliged."

"You're more than welcome," Alexandra said, handing the boy the slice of cake. "Be careful and don't drop it. I'll hold the door for you."

The boy went out with the large slice of cake in both hands, his eyes wide. Alexandra closed the door behind him.

"Well," Alex said, when no one else spoke, "the boy could have seen someone who looked like Sewell."

"That's possible," Toby agreed. "I'll ride to Lexington tomorrow morning and look around."

The others resumed preparing dinner. The atmosphere in the kitchen had changed completely, however, the cheerful conversation and laughter replaced by a somber silence. During the meal the conversation was desultory, and everyone went to bed early.

The next morning, Toby was up before daylight. Carrying a lantern, he went to the corral and put a halter on the gelding he was accustomed to riding. He was leading the horse back out of the barn after saddling it when he saw Alexandra. Her white nightgown was a lighter shadow in the darkness on the back porch.

"You don't intend to confront them, do you, Toby?" she asked when he approached.

"No, that wouldn't accomplish anything," he replied. "Except make them more careful. If I can get a look at them without being seen myself, that's what I'll do."

"Are you armed?"

Toby nodded, patting the Colt in his shoulder holster. Alexandra stepped off the porch, heedless of the frost-covered grass, and Toby took her in his arms and kissed her. Her lips were urgent as he held her tightly against him, and her body was soft and pliant through her nightgown. Abruptly he lifted her back onto the porch, then mounted the horse and rode away.

Dawn was breaking as he passed the outskirts of the city. When he reached the downtown, the sun had risen and a few people were stirring. Toby tethered his horse up the street from the hotel, then walked to the front entrance and went into the lobby.

The dining room off to one side was half filled with people having breakfast. Positioning himself where he could not be seen, Toby scanned the tables. Sure enough, he glimpsed Sewell, seated with two other men, at the far side of the room. Toby turned and left the hotel.

As he rode back to Fair Oaks, he thought of the various preparations he could make to defend the farm. Sewell would want to get settled and organized first, he felt certain, and that would give him a few days' respite. But Toby also knew that his wait for the anticipated trouble was now drawing to an end.

*   *   *

After arriving in Independence, Dr. Martin and Janessa had stopped at the Brentwood house only long enough to announce their presence and drop off their baggage before proceeding to the main city hospital downtown.

Earlier, the scene that had greeted them at the railroad station had not been reassuring, to say the least. The platform and waiting room had been virtually deserted, even though it was a weekday afternoon, and during the ride to the Brentwood house their hired carriage had passed a wagon bearing three coffins—practically the only traffic on the road. Red quarantine flags tacked onto front doors were everywhere in evidence, although there were relatively few in the uncrowded neighborhood where the Brentwoods lived.

At the imposing Victorian residence, Claudia Brentwood and her daughter-in-law Susanna had greeted them eagerly, obviously overjoyed to see Dr. Martin and Janessa, but both women's joy had been tempered by their reluctance to have someone of Janessa's age working with the sick. Dr. Martin had given them little time to protest, however, asking Claudia a few pointed questions about her family's shipping business and the availability of empty warehouses, then hustling Janessa back into the carriage. Now the clopping of the horse's hooves and the rumble of the wheels on paving stones echoed along the eerily quiet streets as they drew near the center of the city. The carriage pulled to a halt in front of a towering Gothic brick building, which a sign over the doorway identified as the Metropolitan Hospital. As Janessa helped the doctor from the carriage, the driver jumped down to assist her.

To their surprise, the man refused payment. "Seeing as you've come here to help, that's payment enough," he said, boosting himself back to his seat. "God bless you and the young lady, and good luck to you." He snapped the reins and drove off.

The doctor and Janessa climbed the steps and entered the hospital. After the quiet of the streets, the chaos inside seemed overwhelming. Scores of people stricken by cholera lay on blankets in the vestibule, with relatives hovering around them and looking imploringly at the doctor and Janessa as they passed by. In the main lobby the scene was even worse.

People on pallets, moaning in pain as they tossed and turned, took up almost all the available floor space. Tearful relatives added to the confusion, and an older, harried-looking man, apparently in charge of admissions, was moving about trying to take down names as visitors shouted and pulled at him.

The man's harassed frown changed to a smile of relief as the doctor introduced himself over the uproar. After extricating himself from a knot of petitioners, the man explained that he was the head clerk, and he led the doctor and Janessa into a side hall, where the hospital director was making the rounds of even more patients. A rumpled, hefty man who looked as if he had not slept for days, the director was almost tearful with gratitude as he shook hands with Dr. Martin and was introduced to Janessa.

"I'm Jim Harbin," he said, taking the old doctor's arm and ushering him and Janessa into a nearby office. "And words can't express how grateful I am for your help." The clerk shut the door behind them so that they would have relative quiet. "The city has organized to deal with this crisis," Dr. Harbin continued, pulling up chairs for his visitors, "and medical supplies are pouring in from all parts of the country. But as you can see, we're mighty short of space. Most of all, though, we're short of doctors. Scores of people are dying for lack of proper attention."

"Well, I may be able to help on the shortage of space," Dr. Martin said. "Claudia Brentwood, a friend of mine, has an empty warehouse she can spare. If I can get equipment and a staff, I'll take the overflow from the halls and lobby here."

Harbin beamed at the suggestion. "You'll have no argument from me. In fact, we have a growing corps of volunteer nurses and orderlies, and more donated equipment and supplies than we'll ever use." He turned to the

118

clerk. "Let's put one of your assistants with Dr. Martin to help him get set up."

"I'll fetch Markham, sir," the man said, halfway out the door already. "He's just the one for the job."

While Janessa sat patiently listening, the hospital director and Dr. Martin discussed the situation in Independence and what staff would be needed at the warehouse. After ten minutes or so the clerk returned with Markham, a small, redheaded man with an intense manner and seemingly bursting with energy.

Markham immediately took charge of organizing what had to be done, and Dr. Martin and Janessa followed him to the supply rooms at the rear of the hospital. Janessa was astonished to see row upon row of tall shelves crammed with cartons of medicines and equipment. Markham disappeared through a doorway and called out a stream of instructions, and in a matter of minutes he had a small brigade of men carrying the cartons he indicated to the loading dock. As the men worked, Markham consulted Dr. Martin. "On the medicines, you'll need opium, tannin, and calomel, won't you, sir?"

"Yes, as much as you can spare," Dr. Martin replied. "Also plenty of nux vomica, lactopeptine, zinc sulphocarbolate, and subnitrate of bismuth. How is your supply of phenol?"

"We have barrels of it, sir."

"That's the quantity I use it in, because I believe in antisepsis. Have the men take out half a dozen barrels."

"Yes, sir." Markham made a few notes. "Extra cots and bedding are stored in another building, and I'll have them loaded into wagons as soon as I finish here. And I'll consult with Dr. Harbin on precisely who the staff will be."

"I'll need a good head nurse," the doctor said. "And capable cooks. If any of the staff catches cholera, chances are it'll come from the food we eat. Pick good people, and when we set up at the warehouse, keep an eye on their sanitary procedures."

"Yes, sir!" Markham clearly was pleased by Dr. Martin's decisive manner, and Janessa took an instinctive liking to the efficient little man. By late afternoon several wagons had been loaded and dispatched to the Brentwood warehouse on the outskirts of the city, and Dr. Martin and Janessa took their leave of Dr. Harbin and rode with the next wagon.

The air took on a fresh, damp feel as the city was left behind and the broad surface of the Missouri River came into view in the distance. Two riverboats were forging upriver toward Kansas City, smoke streaming from their tall black funnels, but the normally bustling warehouse district on the overland route was as quiet as the center of the city had been.

The first sign of life was at one of the Brentwood Shipping Company warehouses, where two men were vigorously sweeping debris out the wide doors opening onto the loading dock. Other eager hands began unloading the wagon, and Janessa followed Dr. Martin inside.

The warehouse was huge, with two main bays that would serve conveniently as separate wards for men and women, and there were empty offices along the far side. Picking the largest of these, which was equipped with a stove, the doctor called to the men and told them to put the kitchen equipment in it. Another room, which was lined with shelves, was designated the storeroom. Janessa took off her coat and set to work, opening the cartons and placing the bottles of medicine on the shelves.

Markham arrived with the wagons filled with cots and bedding, and he called out orders to the workers. By the time dusk had settled and lanterns had been lighted and hung, the first of the staff began arriving, to add to the confusion. Their leader, a tall, formidable-looking woman of about forty in an immaculate nurse's uniform, surveyed the scene with a frown, then marched rather than walked across the warehouse to the doctor and Janessa.

"Dr. Martin?" she said in a rough, contralto voice. "I'm Eleanor Granby, your head nurse."

The doctor peered over his spectacles, his eyes reflecting immediate satisfaction with what he saw. "Pleased to meet you, Nurse Granby," he said. "I'd like to have the floor washed down and all the cots and bedding sprinkled with a ten percent solution of phenol. Put your staff to work on that, and then we'll discuss how things will be done."

The other nurses and the orderlies, who had trailed behind their leader, apparently were unfamiliar with antiseptic procedures, for they exchanged puzzled glances and murmurs. Nurse Granby's cold gray eyes also reflected a degree of skepticism, but she obeyed instantly. "If you want to learn why things are done," she turned and announced to them acidly, "then go to a medical college. In the meantime, we're here to work, not to learn. Come along."

She marched away, and the others followed. Dr. Martin allowed himself a smile as he and Janessa resumed opening cartons. A few minutes later the staff was busily at work, and Nurse Granby returned. Dr. Martin instructed her on the work routine that would be followed, then with a nod he indicated Janessa.

"This is Janessa Holt," he said, "and she will be addressed as Miss Holt. Her mother was an herbal healer and trained her from when she was very small, and I've been working with her for about two years. She'll be a medical doctor someday, and right now she knows more about medicine than some who are. For obvious reasons, I don't want it talked around that she's treating patients; but she's my assistant in every respect."

The tall woman nodded in understanding, and her frosty eyes thawed a degree as she looked down at Janessa and put out a large hand. "I'm pleased to meet you, Miss Holt," she said.

"Pleased to meet you, Nurse Granby," Janessa replied, shaking hands in a businesslike fashion.

"That more or less covers things," the doctor concluded. "Problems will arise, as they always do, but I'm sure we can find ways to deal with them."

Janessa turned back to her work, and by the time she had unpacked the last of the cartons, the confusion had settled into an orderly bustle of preparations to receive patients. She was pleased to see that the building had already taken on the appearance of a hospital, with the lanterns hanging at intervals around the walls shining down on cots in neat rows. There was also the unmistakable astringent smell she now associated with hospitals, as the orderlies finished swabbing diluted phenol across the floor.

Walking out to the loading dock, Janessa shivered in the cool night air and realized that she was ravenously hungry. She glanced down the street to see if there was a place nearby to eat, but the sight that greeted her banished all thought of food from her mind. A line of wagons was approaching, with lanterns hanging on their brake levers to serve as coach lamps. The line was long, reaching to a distant corner, and there was no end in sight. And every wagon was filled with patients.

VII

"I'm well enough to shift for myself now, Doctor," the woman said, standing up from her cot. "See? I could go home now."

Dr. Martin frowned doubtfully. "You're doing fine, but you'd better stay with us another day. If you start moving about too soon, it could take you much longer to fully recuperate."

The woman looked unconvinced, but she obediently lay back down on her cot. With their morning rounds finished, Janessa and the doctor walked toward the room they used as an office. The past days were a confused blur in Janessa's memory, a time of brief periods of sleep between endless hours of monitoring temperatures, deliberating over medications to administer, and trudging from cot to cot with the doctor.

However, the grueling work had been more than amply rewarded. Sixteen patients had already been sent home, and dozens more were recovering rapidly enough to be sent home within two or three days. The few who had died had been in hopeless condition when they arrived, but even some who had seemed hopeless were beginning to rally against the disease.

The unusual, and indeed unexpected, rate of recovery among the patients made the atmosphere cheerful as the old doctor and Janessa went into the office with the head nurse and Markham. Consulting one of his countless lists, Markham talked about the patients who were replacing those who had been sent home. He mentioned that the news about the high recovery rate at the warehouse hospital had spread quickly throughout the city.

"It seems we've gained an excellent reputation in a short time," he said. "Dr. Harbin expected to send us more patients when we had empty cots, but I had to notify him that patients are being brought here directly by their relatives. However, we do have a few cots in those empty rooms that we could use."

"No, let's keep them empty for now," Dr. Martin said. "We may get some patients who are ill with something besides cholera, and they'll have to be kept separated from the others."

"Yes, sir." Markham made a note. "Our supplies are diminishing, so I'll replenish them today. If you can think of anything else we need, I'll get it at the same time."

The doctor shook his head and looked at Janessa questioningly.

"I *am* almost out of cigarettes," she volunteered.

Markham, without blinking an eye, added them to his list, although Nurse Granby looked less than approving. The doctor reached in his pocket for money, but Markham shook his head. "The hospital has a petty cash fund," he said, "for just such contingencies."

When Markham left, Nurse Granby made her daily report, which was always blunt and concise. "Some of the patients are complaining about the cold when all the doors are opened every morning," she said. "And we're still getting complaints from patients and relatives about the strong fumes from the floor and bedding."

"If they're well enough to complain," Dr. Martin replied unperturbed, "they're not dying. I think the fresh air and phenol are the major factors contributing to our recovery rate. We're using the same medications I've always used, but the patients are recovering better."

The head nurse did not argue, and when she left, the doctor and Janessa began reviewing the patient charts stacked on the desk and discussing the medications. A few minutes later, however, Dr. Martin rose to his feet in delighted surprise when a tall, dark-haired military man in his mid-thirties stepped into the room. Janessa immediately recognized Andrew Brentwood, who had been expected home on leave. Handsome in his colonel's uniform, he was deeply tanned from his months in Arizona. After shaking the doctor's hand, he bowed to Janessa, greeting her as he would an adult. He broke into a smile as the doctor began explaining her presence.

"As you may imagine," Andrew offered in return, "I got an earful on the subject from my mother. However, I feel much the same about it as Susanna. I'm sure it was far from an easy decision for Toby to make, but knowing him as I do, I'm not particularly surprised."

"Yes," the doctor agreed, "with the Holts, duty comes first. Susanna told us she was expecting you. When did you get home?"

"Only a few hours ago," Andrew replied. "I'm on indefinite leave, awaiting my next assignment. By the way, when I arrived, Susanna and I heard people at the depot talking about what you're doing here. Everyone agrees that a patient has a better chance here than at any other hospital in the city."

Dr. Martin brushed aside the compliment. "Susanna had no business meeting you at the train station. I told her she should avoid public places and stay at home."

Andrew shrugged in resignation. "You know how it is, Dr. Martin. It's been a while since we've seen each other, and she has a mind of her own."

"She also has a young child to think about," the doctor said, referring to her and Andrew's son, Samuel. "And this is far from the best place in the world for you to be, Andy, while we're on the subject."

The colonel did not protest as Dr. Martin and Janessa escorted him to the door. Before they parted, Dr. Martin expressed appreciation for the use of the warehouse.

"It's the least we could do," Andy said. "We certainly couldn't make much use of it with the condition our business is in now, and I was very pleased when I heard you were using it. But you be careful and don't overwork yourself—you're not a young man anymore."

Andrew mounted his horse, waved, and rode away, and Janessa followed the doctor back inside. The concern that Andy had expressed had been her own greatest worry, but the past few days had actually set her mind at ease on that account. Indeed, Dr. Martin looked younger and more fit than he usually did, the crisis seeming to have infused him with new strength and vitality.

Later in the day, Markham returned from the city hospital with a wagonload of supplies, including two cartons of cigarettes. While the wagon was being unloaded, Janessa noticed Markham talking with a stranger on the loading dock. A moment later, the little red-haired man led the visitor inside. Janessa followed them to the front office.

"Dr. Martin," Markham said, "this is Mr. John Lawrence. He's a reporter for the *Express Courier* of New York."

The doctor frowned as he looked up from the papers on his desk. "The people at the mayor's office will give you all the information you need about the epidemic," he said curtly.

Lawrence, a well-built man in his late twenties, was wearing a neat, stylish suit and had an imperviously cheerful manner. "I've been there, sir," he said. "As well as to all the hospitals in the city." He turned his affable smile toward Janessa. "And you must be Janessa Holt."

The man, obviously failing to meet with the doctor's approval, brought out Janessa's taciturn nature in full. She ignored him and busied herself measuring out medicine at a worktable. Lawrence turned back to the doctor.

"Dr. Martin, it's common knowledge all over the city that more patients are recovering here than at any of the other hospitals. They're also recovering faster. To what do you attribute that?"

"To a good staff and being left alone to do my work," the doctor replied gruffly. "There's nothing here of interest to you."

"I beg to disagree, sir," Lawrence said, undeterred. "There is much here to interest me and my readers. I could smell the phenol being used in here when I was a hundred yards away. This is the most successful medical facility in the city, and it's being run by a doctor who has a young lady for his assistant. What are Miss Holt's duties?"

The doctor glanced at Markham, who, standing behind Lawrence, shook his head to indicate he had said nothing. The doctor turned his attention back to Lawrence. "As you can plainly see," he said, "I'm an old man. Miss Holt is the daughter of a close friend of mine. She helps me get about and assists me as she is doing now."

Lawrence's smile was skeptical. "I've talked with a couple of people who were patients here," he offered. "They seemed to believe that she does more than that."

"I can't help what people say," the doctor replied irately. "Now, I'd appreciate it if you would leave me to my work, young man."

Still smiling, Lawrence lifted his hat, bowed to the doctor and to Janessa, and walked out the door. Markham began apologizing to Dr. Martin, but the old man dismissed the incident with a wave, and Markham hurried away to escort the visitor out.

"One percent of what reporters write," the doctor explained to Janessa, "is true. The other ninety-nine percent is dressing to make that daub of truth interesting. If we're not careful, the newspapers will be plastered with stories about a girl named Janessa Holt who cures cholera by touching people. And when you go to medical college, you'll be laughed right back out the door. You say nothing at all to that fellow."

"I hadn't intended to," Janessa replied.

The doctor nodded, satisfied. Later, however, Janessa noticed that Lawrence was still in evidence, loitering outside the door. When she looked again, however, twenty minutes later, he was gone.

He returned at daybreak. Dr. Martin and Janessa were sitting at a table in the room reserved for the hospital workers, having their morning coffee. Lawrence stuck his head in the door and spotted them, and he appeared somewhat surprised to see Janessa with a cigarette. She exhaled smoke through her nose and looked at him woodenly, but he seemed determined to be good-natured. He approached with a smiling "good morning" and told Dr. Martin that he was desperate for a cup of coffee but was afraid to drink coffee anywhere in the city. The doctor looked annoyed but pointed to the coffee urn.

Lawrence served himself and chatted politely with the nurses and orderlies. Once the daily routine of work began, he stayed well out of the way, but Janessa noticed him outside on the loading dock, and later she saw him talking with the cooks.

While Janessa and the doctor were reviewing the patient charts, Susanna Brentwood burst into the office with an attractive, expensively dressed young woman at her heels. Both of them looked distraught.

"Dr. Martin, this is my friend, Amelia Whiting," Susanna said, before Dr. Martin could object to their presence. "Her husband, Simon, is outside in a carriage. He's very ill, but I'm sure he doesn't have cholera."

The doctor frowned, but his voice remained calm. "Susanna, I told you not to come here. Mrs. Whiting could have found her way without your help. And where is Andy?"

"He went up to Plattsburg, to see about some horses." Susanna was almost in tears. "Dr. Martin, Amelia and Simon are family friends. Will you please see what you can do for him?"

The doctor sighed heavily and motioned the two women ahead of him as he went out of the office. Following, Janessa beckoned to Markham, who in turn summoned two orderlies. Outside, a large, luxurious carriage was parked, and a young man was lying on the back seat.

Dr. Martin briefly questioned the man, then directed the orderlies to carry him to one of the empty rooms. As Amelia Whiting followed the little procession back inside, Dr. Martin took Susanna's arm and held her back.

"Susanna," he said, "I told you to stay at home. Now you get in that carriage, go home, and stay there." He shook his head and interrupted her as she started to object. "No, the only thing you can do here is catch cholera. Now get in the carriage."

She finally drove off, and Dr. Martin went back inside. Markham was talking with Amelia Whiting and making up a patient chart, and Janessa joined Dr. Martin as he washed his hands. A few minutes later Nurse Granby appeared with the chart and said the patient was ready.

Watching while the doctor examined Simon Whiting and talked with him, Janessa soon identified the illness. She concealed her regret, for the young couple were obviously very much in love, and Simon Whiting's symptoms offered little if any hope.

"You say you've had pains like this before?" the doctor questioned, writing on the chart.

"Yes, sir," Simon replied in a whisper. His face was flushed with fever. "Several times, but never this bad."

Dr. Martin handed Janessa the chart. "Nurse Granby, ask Mrs. Whiting to come in now."

The tall, stern woman opened the door, and Amelia hurried in, heading straight to the cot and taking Simon's hand.

"I'm going to be perfectly honest with both of you," Dr. Martin said, taking off his glasses. "Mr. Whiting, you have a perityphlitic abscess. That's an extremely serious inflammation of the lower abdomen, and there's no accepted treatment for it. The only thing we can do is give you something for the pain and keep you on light food in the hopes that it will subside."

The unspoken conclusion was clear, and the young couple gazed at each other in despair. Clutching her husband's hand and struggling to hold back her tears, Amelia turned to the doctor. "May I stay here with Simon?" she asked in a trembling voice.

Dr. Martin hesitated, then nodded. "I suppose you can have your meals with the staff. But you must remain in this room as much as possible, because you'll be in constant danger of catching cholera."

Amelia tried to express her gratitude as she fought back tears. The doctor turned to Nurse Granby and told her the dosage of laudanum to administer, then left the room.

Joining him back in their office, Janessa at first said nothing, for clearly the doctor was deep in thought. Finally, when she could stand the silence no longer, she brought up the subject of the postmortem in Portland.

The doctor's quick answer indicated that he, too, had been thinking about it. "We don't know that the abscess is always centered in the veriform appendix," he said. "But we do know the fatality rate from infection following abdominal surgery."

"Yes, sir. But we also know that man will die in dreadful pain, unless he's extremely lucky. And we know that diluted phenol kills infection."

"Most of it most of the time, but not all of it all the time," the doctor countered. He lifted a hand as she started to say something else. "Let's finish going through these charts. We have scores of patients with cholera, and that's a disease we *can* do something about."

The subject was dropped, but Janessa could tell that the doctor was still thinking about it. When they finished with the charts and went to check once again on the newer patients, she noted with some annoyance that John Lawrence had already ingratiated himself with the Whitings.

Apparently he had made a trip to their house for Amelia, since he was bringing in books and other things.

In spite of her distrust for Lawrence, Janessa had to admit he was a likable enough fellow; at least she viewed him with less distaste than before. She also sensed that Dr. Martin was beginning to respect the man, if not his profession.

A short time later, however, her improving opinion of Lawrence was severely tested. Having finished lunch, she was relaxing with coffee and a cigarette while Dr. Martin puffed on a cigar. Lawrence came in, poured himself a cup of coffee, and stepped over to their table.

"Do you mind if I join you?" he said, sitting down. "And I hope you don't mind my helping myself to more of the coffee here, Dr. Martin."

"Not at all," the doctor replied. "But every minute you're here, you take a chance on catching cholera—I'm sure you know that."

Lawrence smiled and shrugged. "Taking risks is part of my job. Not to make myself out a hero or anything, but I've been in tight spots before. Only a few months ago, I was in prison in Germany, charged with being a spy."

The doctor lifted his eyebrows as he puffed on his cigar, and Lawrence began telling him what had happened. Janessa listened absently, still thinking about Simon Whiting and not finding the story particularly interesting.

"My release was finally obtained by an American army officer," Lawrence went on. "He was stationed in Germany and apparently had more influence with the Germans than our own State Department did. I've never met the man, but someday I hope to thank him personally, for he certainly went out of his way to help me. He's a captain by the name of Blake."

Janessa, her attention jolted, put her cigarette in an ashtray. "Captain *Henry* Blake?" she echoed.

Lawrence looked at her in surprise. "Yes, that's his name. Do you know him?"

"Yes, I know him!" Janessa retorted angrily, standing up. "And before you go see him, I hope you catch cholera first and give it to him!"

Silence fell, and everyone turned to look as Lawrence sat there in shock and Janessa stamped out of the room. She returned to the doctor's office and threw herself into a chair, lit another cigarette, and puffed on it furiously.

A few minutes later, Dr. Martin came in. "Janessa," he said mildly, "I know how you feel about Henry Blake. But you're going to be a doctor someday, and keeping that in mind, what you said to that man was completely out of line." Seeing that his words had had little effect, the doctor cleared his throat and sat down at the desk. "Well, let's make the afternoon rounds."

In one part of her mind, Janessa did indeed realize that what she had said to Lawrence was unwarranted; other people certainly had every right to their own views of Henry Blake, even if they were totally mistaken. But she was not about to forget the pain and distress her beloved aunt had suffered on account of Henry Blake.

No more was said of the incident, but Dr. Martin had apparently made some explanation to Lawrence, because later in the day he approached Janessa with words of apology. Although her sense of fairness told her that she should be the one to apologize, Janessa still could manage only a cold nod in reply. As the day wore on, however, her preoccupation with the incident was replaced by another concern.

The laudanum that Simon Whiting had been given only partially deadened his severe abdominal pain, and his condition grew steadily worse. That evening he was unable to eat even the broth that his wife took to him, and the next morning his temperature was higher than it had been when he arrived. Janessa could tell that Dr. Martin was still pondering the possibility of surgery and waiting to see if the man's condition would improve.

By midafternoon, with the disease approaching the acute stage, Dr. Martin made up his mind. After a brief examination of the patient, he called Amelia back into the room and broached the possibility of surgery.

The couple seized upon it eagerly. "Then there *is* a cure for it," Amelia said happily.

"No, not an accepted cure," Dr. Martin replied. "I consider this a last resort."

"But others have had surgery on their stomachs and healed up properly afterward, haven't they?" Amelia persisted.

The doctor nodded. "Yes, a doctor in Kentucky named McDowell performed abdominal surgery in 1809. The patient lived to a ripe old age—and there have been others. But not many."

Simon, his eyes glazed with fever, patted his wife's hand and spoke in a hoarse whisper: "But it's our only hope, doctor, isn't it?"

"Yes, if the disease fails to subside. But I want both of you to understand the dangers involved, and the fact that it is a desperate measure."

Simon and Amelia looked at each other and nodded in silent agreement.

"Good. I will examine you again in an hour," the doctor said.

He went back out of the room, and Janessa followed him. "We must make every effort to prevent inflammation," he said, determination in his voice now that his course of action was clear. "We'll use one of the empty rooms, and the walls and floors will have to be washed down with disinfectant. The instruments and swabs that we use, our hands, everything else must be rinsed in basins of phenol."

Janessa, her heart suddenly pounding, hurried off to find Markham and the head nurse.

Little more than an hour later, after Simon Whiting had been examined and shown no improvement, everything was in readiness. The orderlies had moved Simon to a table in the lantern-lit surgery room, and Janessa followed the doctor and head nurse in and closed the door. Her eyes were immediately stung by the thick, pungent fumes from the disinfected floor and walls. Nurse Granby dripped chloroform onto the gauze cone over the patient's mouth and nose as Dr. Martin dipped his hands into a basin of phenol and then stepped to the operating table.

The instruments in the basins of phenol gleamed in the lantern light. Janessa dipped her hands into the basin and shook them off to dry. After a minute, Nurse Granby thumbed back one of the patient's eyelids. "He's asleep," she said.

Dr. Martin nodded to Janessa. "Dampen the surgical area with phenol and then hand me a small scalpel."

Janessa did as instructed. Dr. Martin leaned over the patient and drew the scalpel in a diagonal, four-inch line across the lower right abdomen.

As blood began flowing, Janessa wiped it away with swabs and dropped them into a bucket on the floor. The old doctor blinked several times and adjusted his spectacles with a knuckle, then after a moment stood up straight, complaining that his vision was becoming blurred. "That looks like a lot of blood," he said, "but we shouldn't be into any veins or arteries yet."

"We aren't, sir. That's only capillary blood."

Dr. Martin handed her back the scalpel and asked for a larger one. To Janessa's consternation, as the doctor deepened the incision, the patient's body visibly flinched. Even worse, the doctor failed to notice.

Janessa waited for a moment, then glanced at Nurse Granby. "Twenty more drops of chloroform, please," she said.

As the nurse began dripping the chloroform onto the gauze mask, the doctor looked up. "Did he move, Janessa?"

"Yes, sir."

"Well, I'm having a little trouble seeing," he said. "This confounded phenol is hard on my old eyes."

The scalpel passed through small arteries and veins, and Janessa quickly clamped them. The doctor squinted, cutting more cautiously, then straightened up again. "I think we're through the abdominal wall."

Janessa could see the glistening sheath of the peritoneum through the incision. "Yes, sir, we are."

The doctor handed her the scalpel, then took off his spectacles and wiped his eyes with his sleeve. "You'll have to finish the surgery, Janessa," he said. "These eyes of mine have completely given up—I'm almost as blind as a bat. Go ahead and put retractors on the incision. I can see well enough to hold it open for you."

Janessa looked at him in shock, then glanced at Nurse Granby. The woman's stern face relaxed, and she nodded confidently. Feeling numb, Janessa poised the scalpel, hesitating a few seconds to gather her composure, then began cutting through the peritoneum.

To her relief, instead of being afflicted by the queasiness that she felt during postmortems, she was steadied by the same sense of urgency and purpose she always felt when helping the doctor with a sick or injured patient. The peritoneum opened cleanly, revealing almost precisely what she had expected. "The veriform appendix is the site of the abscess, sir. It's three or four times normal size and discolored with inflammation."

"Good!" the doctor exclaimed. "*Good!* Now put a ligature around it where it joins the cecum and remove it."

Taking the length of thread she had prepared earlier, Janessa cautiously probed at the thin membrane that enfolded the appendix, finding a path through the web of blood vessels. She pulled the ligature around the base of the organ and tied it, then reached in with the scalpel. She severed the organ at its base and lifted it out.

Swollen and taut, it burst as she dropped it into an empty basin. The doctor, stooping to eye it closely, shook his head. "I'm glad we didn't wait until tomorrow," he said. "Now suture the incision."

The suturing, a familiar process to Janessa—back in Oregon she had helped sew together dozens of wounds—

went quickly. Dr. Martin squinted and peered at the closely spaced stitches and nodded in approval. When it was finished, Janessa followed the doctor out, and Nurse Granby went for orderlies to clean up the room and return the patient to his cot.

In the office, reaction set in on Janessa, her knees becoming weak and her hands shaking as she washed them in a basin.

"It's easy for me to forget that you're so young," the doctor said. "That was hard on you, but I'm mighty proud of how you came through. Anton would be as well. Now we'll have to see if inflammation develops."

Janessa barely heard him. Later, to clear her head, she took a walk around the building, then went to the room where she had a cot. Gnawing worry about the operation filled her thoughts, but the day's tension had so exhausted her that she fell asleep almost immediately.

When nurses and orderlies began moving around before dawn the next morning, the commotion woke Janessa. The doctor was already up, and he sent her for a thermometer, then accompanied her to Simon's room. Amelia Whiting, her face drawn with anxiety and fatigue from being awake all night, was sitting beside her husband's cot. Simon appeared to be sleeping peacefully, Janessa observed with some surprise.

Dr. Martin leaned over the patient and woke him gently. Simon opened his eyes, licked dry lips, then winced. "I have a headache," he said. "And my stomach hurts really bad."

The doctor and Janessa exchanged a glance; the man's voice was stronger, and the feverish flush was gone from his face. "That's to be expected," the doctor replied. "Chloroform often causes a headache, and when your belly has been cut open, you can be certain that it's going to hurt. Let's check your temperature."

Janessa put the thermometer under his tongue. The doctor glanced at his watch, waited for a few minutes, then looked at it again and handed the thermometer to

Janessa. She took it and held it up to the light, turning it
so the doctor could see it. Simon's temperature had plummeted to little more than a degree above normal.

"Well, we'll have to keep a close watch for a day or
so," Dr. Martin said cautiously, "but there's no sign of
inflammation yet. Other than the headache and pain in
your abdomen, how do you feel?"

"I'm hungry, Doc," Simon replied promptly. "I've
never been so hungry in all my life."

"*That*'s certainly a good sign," Dr. Martin said dryly.
"All right, you can start catching up on the meals you've
missed—but stick to porridge and soup today."

Not until they were outside the room did Janessa and
Dr. Martin exchange a smile of satisfaction. And during
breakfast, they saw evidence that Simon had not been
exaggerating his appetite; Amelia returned to the kitchen
twice to refill his bowl with porridge.

At intervals through the day, Janessa checked Simon's
temperature, which remained stable. The following morning, with his temperature virtually normal and the threat
of infection past, it was evident that his strong, young
body was healing rapidly.

As she sat finishing breakfast with Dr. Martin, Janessa
felt immensely pleased with herself. At first her spirits
were not even dampened when John Lawrence came into
the room, helped himself to coffee, and took a seat across
the table from her.

After his usual amiable greeting, he launched directly
into what he had to say. "I've just been to see Simon
Whiting, and I'm very pleased that he's well on the road
to recovery. I'm also curious. You see, Dr. Martin, I've
done more than my share of articles on hospitals and such,
and I know quite a bit about medicine. For example, I
know that perityphlitic abscesses are widely believed to be
incurable."

"I'm glad to hear that you know quite a bit about
medicine," Dr. Martin replied with a straight face. "I have

a couple of patients who aren't responding as well as I'd like, so perhaps you'll take a look at them for me."

Lawrence laughed at the suggestion. "I know enough about medicine to write about it, but that's all. Getting back to the subject, though, I would like to know what happened with Simon. If you've found a way to cure perityphlitic abscess, it will be of wide interest to the public. Also, you have a responsibility to let others know, because—"

"I don't need you to tell me my responsibilities, Mr. Lawrence," the doctor said, his tone suddenly cold. "And if you know the first thing about medicine, you know that a doctor doesn't discuss his patients with strangers. As far as what happened is concerned, it will be reported in due time in a medical journal. But it won't be made the subject of a sensationalized story to confuse, mislead, and raise false hopes in people who don't know the difference between an esophagus and a rectum."

Lawrence heard the doctor out, then replied. "I'm sorry I offended you, sir, but let me be candid with you. I know that you performed abdominal surgery on Simon. And instead of having another doctor or a nurse assist you, I have a strong hunch you were helped by that young lady right there. In any event, that's how it's going to be reported. I like you and respect you, so I'm giving you a chance to tell your side of it." He smiled innocently. "Now, is that direct enough?"

"It certainly is," the doctor answered. "I like you as well, Mr. Lawrence, and I'd probably respect you, too, if you found a better way to earn a living. You were direct with me, so I'll be the same." He took a puff on his cigar, then continued. "I have many friends in Independence. If there's any mention of Janessa Holt in your newspaper, you'll be horsewhipped, tarred and feathered, and hauled out of this city on a rail. You have my word of honor on that, which I don't give lightly."

For a moment it looked as though Lawrence was going to lose his temper, but his reply, when it came, surprised Janessa. With a chuckle, he sat back in his chair. "Well, it's an interesting story, but it isn't worth that." Wisely, he changed the subject. "The temperature is still dropping, and it's chilly this morning."

"Yes, it is getting cooler," the doctor agreed, puffing on his cigar. "Winter must be in the offing, Mr. Lawrence."

The two men continued talking about general subjects, and after Lawrence left, Janessa made an appreciative comment about how the old doctor had handled the situation. He replied gravely that he would never tolerate anything that could be a threat to her future career in medicine.

The morning was indeed cool, and after the warehouse's daily airing, the orderlies built up the fires in the stoves. Cold was welcome, since it inhibited the spread of disease, and the drop in temperature during the past few days had already produced a change that Janessa noticed during morning rounds. For the first time, there were a few empty cots.

The doctor and Janessa had just finished their morning routine when Andrew Brentwood came into the warehouse. He crossed the ward with long, hurried strides. "Dr. Martin, Susanna is very ill this morning," he said. "I'm afraid it might be . . . Well, do you want to go to the house to see her, or should I bring her here?"

"No, we'll go there," the doctor replied. "We'll get our coats and my bag, and we'll be right with you, Andy."

Only minutes later, as the carriage moved along the road to town, Andrew described Susanna's symptoms. It sounded like cholera to Janessa, but the doctor withheld judgment, as she knew he would.

At the Brentwood home, Claudia was waiting at the front door. Janessa helped the doctor out of the carriage, up the steps, and inside, and Claudia and Andrew followed them up to a second-floor bedroom.

A maid was with little Samuel, who was seated well away from the bed as he talked with his mother. Claudia shooed them out, and the doctor began examining Susanna. Janessa tried to hide her mounting fear as she looked on, for the symptoms were unmistakable. Susanna, her fair features flushed and drawn, forced a smile. "I suppose I should have taken your advice, Dr. Martin," she whispered weakly.

"Well, you will now, young lady," he replied in a stern but fatherly tone. He glanced at Janessa and nodded toward his bag, then turned back to Susanna. "You'll do exactly as I say, because I'm going to stay close and make certain that you do."

Janessa, understanding the silent nod, picked up the bag and left the room. In the hallway, she reached into the bag for one of the red quarantine flags to hang on the front door. Susanna Brentwood had *cholera morbus*, the most virulent form of the disease.

VIII

The gaslights outside the Darmstadt *Bahnhof* cast a dim illumination along the street to a small park, where Henry Blake sat in a hired carriage with Carlos Chacon. Henry had arrived alone at the rendezvous at the appointed time, and Chacon had materialized out of the shadows to join him.

The smaller man appeared anxious in the dim light. "Do you have them, Herr Hoffmann?"

Henry tapped a small trunk on the opposite seat. "They are ready for you to take with you. Inspect them if you wish."

The Spaniard's eyes sparkled as he took the key Henry held out to him. He unlocked the trunk and, one by one, unwrapped and checked the disassembled Mausers. When he was satisfied, he nodded to Henry, who leaned out the window and told the driver to proceed to the station. As the carriage moved away, Chacon relocked the trunk, pocketed the key, and handed Henry an envelope of money. Henry counted the bills twice, for the sake of appearances.

"It has been a pleasure to do business with you, Herr Hoffmann," Chacon said, offering his hand.

Henry shook it. "It has been a pleasure for me as well. Perhaps we can do business again sometime."

At the station, a porter put the trunk and Chacon's hand baggage on a cart. As agreed to beforehand, Henry accompanied Chacon to the baggage counter—a precaution Chacon had insisted on in order to ensure that he got his precious cargo on board safely.

In the waiting room, newsboys were shouting out the headlines that had electrified all Europe that day: From exile in Britain, Alphonse Ferdinand had proclaimed himself rightful monarch of Spain. The Spanish Army had immediately affirmed its support and invited him to Madrid to assume the throne.

One of the boys approached Henry and Chacon at the baggage counter, but the Spaniard shook his head angrily. After the baggage had been checked with no problem, Henry went with Chacon to the platforms. Newsboys were also selling papers there, and Chacon glared sourly at the headlines.

"It appears," Henry commented, "that you will soon have a new king."

"Not for long," Chacon muttered.

Immediately changing the subject, the Spaniard began talking about how much he had enjoyed his trip to Germany. Hoping to extract a last bit of information, Henry feigned concern for the customs checks at the borders. "The French are usually lax toward those who are merely passing through the country," he said, "but I am not so sure about the Spanish authorities."

"I shall have no trouble if the trains are on time," Chacon replied confidently. "We are scheduled to reach Spain late tomorrow night, when everyone at the border crossing will be tired." He winked, rubbing a thumb and fingers together. "And a small sum will overcome any possible trouble."

Henry laughed, satisfied with what he had learned. A few minutes later, Chacon's train pulled into the station. The Spaniard shook hands again with Henry, then joined those boarding the train. After the last car moved out of the station, Henry went back to the waiting room.

At the telegraph company counter, he wrote out a telegram to Clifford Anderson, addressing it to a private London residence Willoughby used for confidential correspondence. Referring to a journey by a fictional relative, Henry listed the time Chacon's train had left Darmstadt and when it was expected to arrive in Spain. After paying for the telegram, he walked back toward his hotel.

With his mission in Germany completed, Henry had several days left before he would join Anderson and the others in Madrid. By now Gisela would have returned to Grevenhof from Bad Kreuznach, and he yearned to see her and his baby son. He also wanted to determine whether she would be free to accompany him to Madrid, for surely she would enjoy the social occasions connected with the coronation.

However, he also wanted to find out more about Josef Mueller. The man remained an enigma, and it seemed at least possible that he was the agent of some powerful figure who wanted Alphonse out of the way. Mueller had checked out of the hotel and disappeared as soon as Henry had confirmed the arrival of the remainder of the Mausers, but the man might still be in Darmstadt.

Pondering what to do, Henry turned onto Nordkanalstrasse. The wariness that previous attempts on his life had taught him was always in the back of his mind, but now, as if by instinct, that wariness suddenly became more acute, and he concentrated on his surroundings. He had left the center of town behind, and the street, a wide, cobblestone quay, was dark and deserted. Henry's footsteps echoed back from the quiet buildings facing the canal. Ahead there were long stretches between the dim lights in shop windows and over signs, and nothing moved on the barges moored along the edge of the canal.

The distant light over the sign for his hotel was brighter, like a beacon in the night, and Henry walked toward it. Then, when he was only a hundred feet from the hotel, he had a feeling of imminent danger. Ahead was a shadowed doorway, and Henry's previous instinct was reinforced by something he smelled. Wenzel Krauss, the obnoxious gun dealer who had been trying to sell weapons to Chacon, always had a soggy cigar in his mouth, and Henry, scenting the unmistakable odor of tobacco, took a long, quick step away from the buildings just before he reached the doorway.

The move saved his life. Two men lunged into the street, their knives gleaming in the dim light. The nearest, slashing at where he had expected Henry to be, snarled "Die, dog!"

Henry reacted instantly. Gripping the man's knife arm with both hands, he pulled him off balance and turned the knife back toward him. The man, too sure of himself and taken by surprise, gasped in shock and pain as the knife plunged deep into his chest.

The second man—Krauss, Henry saw—rushed in and stabbed at him. But Henry was already pulling the knife from his first assailant, whom he pushed between himself and Krauss. Krauss elbowed the staggering form aside and stabbed again before Henry could get a proper grip on the handle of the knife.

Henry twisted away from the thrust but was unable to avoid it completely. The razor-sharp blade sliced through his coat and slashed across his right shoulder, tracing a path of fiery pain. Finally palming the knife securely, Henry stepped back as Krauss's companion collapsed on the cobblestones.

Trying to keep the initiative, Krauss lunged again. But this time Henry was ready and, deftly dodging to one side, slashed with his own weapon. Krauss stumbled back with an oath, his right sleeve gaping open to reveal a deep cut on his forearm.

More wary now, Krauss feinted with his knife and searched for an opening as he taunted Henry. "You took my customer," he growled, "but I will take your life, Prussian dog."

"Your customer came to me," Henry answered, circling to get his back to the light from the hotel. "He told me that he was revolted by the smell of Hessian swine."

Krauss swore in rage and leaped at Henry. Trying to take advantage of his weight and bulk by closing and grappling, he clutched for Henry with his left hand as he thrust with his knife. Henry danced away from the blade and flicked his at his opponent's left hand. Krauss hissed and stepped back quickly, a deep cut across his palm.

Now Henry had his back to the hotel, so that the light was silhouetting him and shining on Krauss. He began taking control of the fight, moving his knife from hand to hand to confuse Krauss. "You said you were going to take my life," he goaded. "You must have changed your mind, because I still have it."

"Not for long!" Krauss hissed, squinting against the light and trying to watch Henry's knife. "I will take great pleasure in—"

He broke off, lifting his blade to parry as Henry feinted with his right hand. But the knife was in Henry's left, and now it swept up and jabbed into Krauss's forearm. Almost dropping his weapon, Krauss rapidly backed away. Henry followed him, pressing the attack.

By now the fat man's belligerent confidence had disappeared. His eyes were wide with fear, and sweat shone on his heavy jowls. "Wait, Hoffmann," he panted. "We have no reason to fight. There are plenty of customers for both of us, and we could do business together."

Henry ignored him, feinted, then thrust again.

Krauss whimpered in terror, dodging and retreating, glancing around for an opportunity to break away and flee. Henry kept moving his knife from hand to hand and feinting. Krauss, confused and fooled once again, lifted his knife toward Henry's empty left hand. Stepping in with a quick thrust, Henry sank his blade deep into the man's bulging stomach.

Krauss dropped his knife and clutched his stomach. He opened his mouth wide to scream, but a choked, gurgling sound was all that came out as Henry's next slash found its mark. Krauss reeled backward and fell heavily to the street, dead.

Henry looked around, but no one was in sight. He tossed his knife into the canal and then gingerly touched his shoulder, which was throbbing. Working quickly, he dragged the first man to the edge of the canal and tumbled him into the water.

Krauss, lying in a pool of blood, was harder to move, but Henry managed to pull the body across the cobblestones to the canal's edge. He bent over and felt the pockets. He found a small notebook, which he pocketed, and then shoved the body over the edge. After kicking Krauss's knife into the water, Henry walked to the hotel.

The clerk was dozing behind the registration desk. Henry closed the door quietly behind him and, with his right hand tucked into his coat pocket to avoid dripping blood on the floor, crossed the lobby and went up the stairs. In his room, he lit the lamp and took off his blood-soaked coat and shirt. Nearly every movement caused him to wince with pain.

The deep cut, reaching from the point of his shoulder to his chest, was bleeding heavily. With great difficulty, Henry tore strips from his shirt and bandaged himself as best he could to stop the bleeding, then opened his bag, took out a flask of brandy, and drank deeply. The tingling warmth of the spirits restored his strength somewhat. He sat down with the bottle and the book he had taken from Krauss's body.

Most of the notes in it were cryptic and meaningless to him, but meetings with a "J.M." were listed, which could refer to Josef Mueller. Henry started to close the notebook, then noticed what looked like a date. If the initials did refer to Josef Mueller, Krauss had met with him before Mueller had brought Chacon to Darmstadt.

Henry put the notebook in his bag, deciding to discuss it later with Anderson and Willoughby. He laid out clothes to replace his shirt and bloody coat and reflected wryly that the fight had settled at least one issue. He would have to go to Grevenhof now, to have his wound treated, and further information about Mueller would have to wait.

Crumbs spilled down the front of Hermann Bluecher's robe as he pushed an apple pastry into his mouth. Sitting at his desk in his study, he was reading a report written by Josef Mueller. It was a final report, for Mueller's assignment was now finished.

After emptying half of a tankard of thick, sweet cocoa, Bluecher crammed another pastry into his mouth. The filling in the pastries was made from juicy apples flavored with cinnamon and ginger and cooked to perfection. The crusts, glazed with honey, were light and flaky. Although the pastries were one of his favorite treats, they were tasteless to Bluecher as he pondered the report.

Mueller, with his customary efficiency, had done precisely what he had been ordered to do. The Carlist agent was en route to Spain with the rifles, and everything was proceeding as planned. The fact that Hoffmann had apparently killed Krauss and his employee was a matter of total indifference to Bluecher.

Still, a vague, uneasy discontent gnawed at him. Hoffmann was apparently so extremely capable that a difficult undertaking had been simple for him. He had appeared on the scene at the right moment, sold weapons to Krauss's customer, then gone quietly on his way. And the manner in which he had dealt with Krauss and his henchman—wily, experienced men in a violent business—had been perfunctory.

Who, Bluecher mused, was this man Hoffmann?

After pondering a few minutes, he came to a decision and reached for pen and paper. He wrote a brief note to an agent in Trier, ordering him to investigate Hoffmann thoroughly and prepare a full report on the man. He put the note into an envelope and addressed it, then put it aside to be mailed. If the report was favorable, which it promised to be, he would proceed to recruit Hoffmann as an agent.

Sitting back, Bluecher pushed another pastry into his mouth. It tasted delicious, and he sighed in satisfaction as he chewed.

A heavy knocking and a boy's voice at the kitchen door woke Toby Holt. His clothes were carefully arranged on the chair beside the bed so he could dress in the dark, and it took him only a few seconds to put them on. He pulled on his boots and buckled a pistol belt around his waist as he walked along the hall to the kitchen. He could hear Jonah, Alex, and Alexandra up and about in their own rooms.

He unlatched and opened the kitchen door, and a blast of cold air came in with the waiting boy. With a ragged blanket clutched around his coat for extra warmth, the boy looked flushed from the cold and was panting from a long run. "Three men, Mr. Holt," he gasped. "I seen three riders coming onto the farm from the south!"

Behind him, Alex was striking a match to light a lamp, and Toby saw Jonah and Alexandra come into the kitchen. "Alex, we don't want any lights showing in the house," he cautioned, closing the door. "Where were the men when you saw them, son?"

"They was coming out of them pine woods by the big bend in the creek," the boy replied. "It'll be a few minutes before they get here, Mr. Holt. They was riding slow, and I run as hard as I could."

Toby thought rapidly. The three might be innocent strangers, but that was unlikely. It was the same number as Sewell and his men, which made it unwise to delay. "Go back by the road and tell Reverend Quint," Toby directed the boy. "And have him send for the sheriff right away."

"Yes, sir!" The boy was back out the door at once.

Jonah said, "If that boy spotted three riders coming out of the pine woods, he's got good eyes."

ARIZONA!

"Yes," Toby said, "but it looks like a very bright night. All right, let's get rifles and get outside. Alexandra, you stay here in the kitchen. If any of them gets as far as the house, run for the root cellar."

Toby and the other two men went back into the hall and a few moments later reappeared, shrugging into heavy coats and tucking rifles under their arms. Outside, it was indeed a bright night, the moon high in the clear sky and thick frost crunching underfoot. Toby, Jonah, and Alex walked toward the barns, which were clearly visible in the moonlight. Looking up at the stars, Toby estimated that dawn was less than an hour away.

They took positions beside the last outbuilding, behind a corral fence that offered a view across the south pastures. Toby whispered instructions to the other two, who agreed that he should challenge the riders before anyone began shooting.

Within a few minutes, the cold had penetrated Toby's boots and coat. Then he saw a vague movement at the far range of his vision. The shadowy forms gradually became more visible, and he could make out three men on horseback.

Toby silently pointed. Alex and Jonah peered into the dim light, then checked their weapons. Toby eased the bolt back on his rifle to check the round in the chamber, then prepared himself. The three riders gradually drew closer.

They were well within rifle range by the time they turned their horses toward the main barn. Toby watched them until they reached the nearest point to him that their path would take, then lifted his rifle. Lining his sights on one of the men, he called in a loud voice, "Stop right there and state your business!"

Immediately the three men kicked their horses into a run, snatched out pistols, and opened fire. Alex and Jonah crouched and returned the fire at once, but Toby waited a few seconds, patiently tracking the man he had picked out until his sights were a fraction ahead of the dim form.

Alex shouted at Toby to get down. A bullet slapped into the fence rail in front of them, but Toby did not flinch as he squeezed his trigger. The man in his sights screamed and fell off his horse. The other two rode behind the barn.

As the two men began shooting from the corner of the barn, Toby knelt and rested his rifle across a fence rail. Alex fired, then glanced at Toby as he reloaded. "That was a good shot," he said. "But you almost got yourself shot in the process."

"They were on horseback and aiming blind," Toby replied. "It would have been pure luck if one had hit us." He fired and quickly reloaded. "Those men are right outside the stalls in that barn, which is the worst possible place they could get."

Alex could hear the horses neighing and kicking inside. "If Alexandra's Turco got shot, I'd certainly hate to face her."

"You and Jonah cover me," Toby directed. "I'll work my way around this corral. If I can get to the other side of it, I'll have a clear shot." Toby ran in a crouch along the fence. The two men behind the barn, realizing his intentions, began firing at him rapidly. Alex and Jonah fired back, keeping the men from taking accurate aim, but bullets struck the fence and hissed past Toby.

At the far corner of the corral, Toby stopped and knelt, looking toward the barn. Now at a much better angle, he could see the men clearly as they leaned around the corner to shoot.

Resting his rifle across a fence rail, he took careful aim. When a man leaned out, Toby fired. The man howled in pain and spun round. Toby reloaded and advanced toward the barn.

Before he could get far, two horses raced out from behind the barn. Toby stopped and lifted his rifle. One man was holding his arm, and both were leaning low in the saddle. The risk of hitting a horse was too great, and Toby lowered his rifle and watched the men ride away in the thin, first light of dawn. The one who was not wounded was Sewell.

Toby walked up to the man sprawled on the ground. He was dead. His horse had wandered off, its reins trailing. Alex and Jonah came around the corral, and Jonah, satisfying himself that the man was dead, trotted away to retrieve the horse.

"You sure lit a fire under their tails," Alex said, helping Toby search the body for identification. There was none. "Do you think they'll be back?"

"Yes. Sewell won't give up that easily." Toby stood up. "When the sheriff gets here, we can follow their trail and see if it gives any clues as to where they're hiding out."

Jonah reappeared, leading the horse, and he helped Toby lift the body over the saddle. As they all walked to the front of the barn, Alexandra came out of the house. She was bundled in her overcoat and had a shotgun under her arm. Alex told her what had happened.

"You should be more careful, Toby," she remarked, more annoyed than relieved. "Jonah, get that body off that poor horse, please. It looks like it hasn't eaten for a year."

Jonah shrugged at the others, then pushed the body from the saddle. It fell heavily to the ground, and Alexandra took the reins and led the horse into the barn.

Intending to saddle horses for themselves and Alex, Jonah and Toby followed her. They were still in the barn when Ezekiel Quint shouted a greeting and rode up from the direction of the road. He was on a mule and was carrying a shotgun.

He dismounted, glanced at the body, then doffed his hat to Alexandra as she came out of the barn. His scarred, rugged face lit up with a smile when Alex told him what had happened. Meanwhile, Toby and Jonah joined them with three saddled horses. Quint agreed to stay behind with Alexandra, and the other men were mounting up when the sheriff arrived on a lathered horse.

A lean, leathery, older man named Charlie Burnett,

the sheriff had already spoken several times with Toby and was familiar with his recent service as a federal marshal. Burnett inspected the body on the ground, listened to Toby's brief explanation, and agreed they should waste no more time and give chase.

The sun was rising as the four men rode south across the pasture. The frost was still thick on the ground, and the tracks the horses had made were clearly visible and indicated that Sewell and the wounded man had fled back along the same route by which the three had approached. At the pine woods near the bend of the creek, the tracks disappeared into the trees, and the four riders slowed to a walk to follow the trail.

In a field on the other side of the woods, the trail emerged again and cut across to the road that led south from Lexington. Toby and the others reined up on the road and inspected the tracks, which gradually disappeared on the hard, rutted surface. Sewell had come from somewhere to the south and had ridden back in the same direction.

The sheriff pointed to where the road breasted a hill in the distance. "The county line runs along that ridge," he said, "and so does the limit of my jurisdiction, Mr. Holt. It looks to me like Sewell and his men have been hiding out in the hills south of here so they won't draw the attention of the authorities in Lexington."

Toby was of the same opinion. "That explains why they haven't been seen in the city since they arrived," he said. "Well, if I'm going to scout around the countryside, I'd best do it alone, so that Fair Oaks won't be left undefended."

After some argument, the others were forced to agree, and they all turned their mounts and rode back to the farm, where Toby intended to outfit himself for an extended search. As they rode they talked about the area to the south. It was almost entirely rural, with only a few small farming communities in the foothills of the Appalachian Mountains. South of the foothills were wooded, remote mountains, where the settlements were even more widely scattered and most of the people lived in isolated hollows, following a way of life that had changed little during the past hundred years.

Back at the house, Alexandra was talking with a man in the barnyard. Toby recognized Colonel Claibourne.

"When I heard there had been shooting here," Claibourne said as Toby approached, "I thought I'd better ride right over. I had no doubt as to who would win, though, Mr. Holt."

"I appreciate your concern, Colonel," Toby replied. "It did turn out well, thanks to the help we had."

"And you have more of the same available, simply for the asking," the colonel offered. "I can muster twenty to thirty Fairfield Hunt men upon a few hours' notice. If there's any way at all in which we can help, you need only say the word."

Toby thanked the tall, white-haired man for the offer but declined. Meanwhile, the sheriff had loaded the body back onto a horse, intending to take it to the coroner. He declined Alexandra's offer of a hot toddy before he left.

"I'm much obliged," he said, "but it's a bit too early for me. Preacher Quint, do you want to pray over this body before I go?"

Quint shook his head. "It would be a waste of time, Sheriff," he answered. "That one is already sizzling in Satan's lair, and nothing can help him. Miss Alexandra, I wouldn't mind wetting *my* whistle with a sip of that bourbon neat, if it's handy."

After the sheriff rode away, accompanied by Colonel Claibourne, Toby went inside with the others.

Over coffee—and bourbon for Preacher Quint—the men discussed Toby's plan to track Sewell down and bring him to justice. Alex and Jonah objected to his going alone, but the most insistent opposition came from Alexandra. "It just doesn't make sense," she said. "I won't debate the point that Dad and Jonah should stay here to protect the farm, but that doesn't mean you have to go by yourself. Colonel Claibourne's offer wasn't empty words, you know."

"Yes, I know, Alexandra. But I've tracked men before, and I prefer to do it alone. A troop of horsemen would draw too much attention. I don't want to chase Sewell all through the Appalachians, and I'm fully capable of dealing with him and a wounded man by myself."

Alexandra did not look the least convinced. "I don't like this, Toby," she said. "I don't like it at all."

Toby tried another tack. "Alexandra, you'll just have to trust my judgment. Situations like this come up often for me, and I certainly hope I'm not going to have an argument from you every time I set out to do something."

The indirect reference to a shared future for them made Alexandra hesitate. This was the first time Toby had stated his intentions so clearly. Alex, Jonah, and Quint looked on with sudden interest.

"If you're traveling to the south," Alexandra said at last, "you'll not be finding any hotels. I'd better put together some cookware, supplies, and blankets for you. And I'll put in a bottle of our best bourbon."

"I'd appreciate that."

She forced a smile, but her eyes remained troubled.

It was noon when Toby set out on the main road south. The farms bordering the road gradually became smaller and more scattered, interspersed with stretches of rocky, overgrown hills where men could hide, but Toby felt certain that Sewell would be far to the south. During midafternoon, he stopped and talked with a man who was working on a fence. The man said he had seen two riders galloping along the road early that morning, and that one of them had appeared injured.

Toby camped in a copse of trees at nightfall, and he was deep into the Appalachian foothills by midmorning of the following day. During the afternoon, he came to a village named Richmond, consisting of a few houses clustered around a tavern, general store, and blacksmith shop.

It was a cold, windy day, and the only sign of life was smoke coming from the chimneys. Toby tied his horse in front of the general store and went inside.

The dim, cluttered interior had the usual mixture of odors from the hardware items, clothing, foodstuffs, and odds and ends hanging from the ceiling and filling the shelves along the narrow aisles. The stove in the center of the store glowed cherry red, and near it two old men were seated at either side of a barrel, pondering a checker game while a portly younger man stroked his chin and watched.

The onlooker turned to Toby. "Come in, neighbor, come in," he said. "It's right cold today, ain't it? Did you just come in to get warm, or you want to buy something?"

"I could use a few supplies."

The man picked up a canvas apron from the counter and tied it on, then began moving briskly back and forth as Toby asked for a large slab of bacon and cans of tomatoes and beans. He totaled up the prices and put the items into a gunnysack, and Toby counted out the money on the counter.

"Thank you, neighbor," the storekeeper said, gathering up the coins. "Just traveling through, are you?"

"That's right. Did you happen to see or hear tell of two strangers who passed through town late yesterday or early this morning?"

"Yes—Mr. Gibson mentioned two strangers." He turned to the two old men and raised his voice: "You said that you saw two strangers yesterday, didn't you, Mr. Gibson?"

The oldster named Gibson had lifted a hand to move a checker, and his opponent was leaning forward, watching intently. The shouted inquiry caused Gibson to lower his hand.

"I said that my cousin Lem seen them," the man drawled without looking away from the board. "Widow Starkey seen them too. They was city folk."

"When did they see the men, Mr. Gibson?" Toby asked.

The old man scrutinized Toby before he answered. "Late yesterday," he finally replied. "They was traveling fast to the south, one on a roan and t'other on a bay. The one on the roan was acting puny, like he had fell and hurt hisself."

Satisfied that the two were Sewell and the wounded man, Toby picked up the gunnysack, thanked the old man and the storekeeper, and went back outside. Although the information was what he had expected, it left him with a vague feeling of uneasiness. Sewell's trail was almost too easy to follow. It would have been simple enough for the men to ride around the town to avoid being seen. Toby thought about it for a moment, then mounted and rode on.

Twelve miles to the south, Elmer Sewell was sitting beside a small campfire in a thicket near the road, listening in satisfaction to one of his men, whose name was Jack Roberts. Roberts, who had caught up with Sewell only minutes before, was weary from having ridden many hours at a hard pace, with only brief stops for rest.

"Then you're sure he's following me?" Sewell questioned.

"I'm positive, Mr. Sewell," Roberts replied. "At the pace he's going, he should be passing through Richmond soon, if he hasn't already. Like you said, if people there saw you, they'll tell him. Everything is going just like you planned, ain't it?"

Sewell glanced at the wounded man lying on the other side of the fire. "Not exactly like I planned," he grumbled. "I meant to set fire to that barn to draw him out, and I didn't plan to get one man killed and another shot. He must have had a lookout posted." He shrugged the trouble off. "But at least the hard part is over now, and he's trailing me. The rest should be easy."

Roberts chuckled. "Just like you said, he probably found out when you and the boys arrived in Lexington. But he couldn't know about the rest of us."

Sewell smiled, his air of satisfaction returning. "You go on to the rendezvous and join up with the other fellows," he directed. "I'll keep moving along this road, staying just far enough ahead of him to keep him following. I'll join up with you day after tomorrow, then we'll all go to that place I picked out and put an end to this business."

"Good-bye to Toby Holt," Roberts said with a laugh, standing up and stepping to his horse.

As the man rode away, Sewell stared into the fire and pondered. Then, deciding it was time to leave, he gathered up the cooking utensils and other gear. "Come on, get up," he said impatiently to the other man. "We have to keep moving."

"I need a doctor, Mr. Sewell," the man whimpered, holding his arm as he struggled to his feet. "I've been shot bad."

"We'll get you a doctor," Sewell barked. "As soon as we have time. But right now we have to keep moving. So shut up about it!"

The man was silent as Sewell readied the horses. Sewell helped him onto his horse, and the two of them rode back onto the road.

As they continued south, Sewell thought about the plan he had devised. The deadly hail of gunfire back at the farm had been unsettling, to say the least, and he was keenly aware that he had escaped unscathed only through good fortune. He could easily have been the one killed or wounded.

Now, however, he reassured himself once more, the greatest danger was past. Toby Holt was a hard man to deal with, but no one could live through riding into an ambush with six men shooting at him.

The wounded man whimpered again, and Sewell gritted his teeth in annoyance. He had contemplated taking the man off the road somewhere and killing him but had decided against it, at least for the present. After all, there was still a useful purpose for him to fulfill.

The opportunity Sewell had foreseen presented itself only minutes later, when they approached a roadside house. It was the only house for miles around, Sewell knew, and he was certain Toby Holt would stop there to ask if strangers had passed by. Wanting to leave a good trail for him to follow, Sewell turned off the road to ask for aid for his wounded companion.

IX

The day of Susanna Brentwood's funeral was raw and cold, with an icy rain driven ahead of a gusty wind from the north. During the service, Janessa sat beside Dr. Martin on the bench behind the Brentwoods.

The epidemic was over, and the last few patients from the warehouse had been sent to the main hospital, but people were still avoiding crowds, and the gathering for the funeral was small. The handful of household servants and Brentwood employees who had clung to their jobs through the ebbing fortunes of the shipping company were there, along with a few friends.

Simon and Amelia Whiting were also present, sitting beside Janessa and Dr. Martin. The young man was holding a cane, and his chin was set at a determined angle against the pain from the healing incision when he moved about. Also present—and, at least as far as Janessa was concerned, not welcome—was John Lawrence.

With his usual imperturbability, Lawrence was seated among the employees. When the service was over, he stepped forward with the warehousemen to help with the coffin. The Brentwoods followed it out the side door of the church, little Samuel weeping and clinging to his grandmother as Andrew helped her down the steps, his tanned, rugged face drawn with grief.

The graveside service was simple and brief, but to Janessa it represented a shattering defeat. The rate of recovery among the patients at the warehouse had been nothing short of spectacular, and the mayor of Independence had met formally with Dr. Martin to express the gratitude of the city and to grant him an honorarium. Even the surgery on Simon Whiting appeared to be an unqualified success; but seeing the coffin being lowered into the grave left Janessa feeling drained and helpless.

When the service was over and the gathering broke up, Simon Whiting approached Dr. Martin to express his gratitude once again. John Lawrence, who was with the Whitings, hung back a few feet but listened closely, Janessa observed.

"We'll always remember you, sir," Whiting said, "and we intend to name our first son after you." He glanced at Lawrence. "John tells me that you and Miss Holt are leaving Independence this afternoon."

"Yes," Lawrence added hurriedly, "that's what I heard at the hospital downtown." He offered his hand to Dr. Martin. "It was a pleasure meeting you, sir, and I'm still curious about how you prevented infection after Simon's surgery."

The doctor smiled amiably as he shook hands. "Keep your eye on the medical journals, Mr. Lawrence, and you'll read about it sooner or later. I appreciate your not mentioning the surgery in your newspaper."

"As I recall," Lawrence replied, "I had little choice in the matter. However, I'll take your advice—though I've never been able to make heads or tails of articles in the medical journals." He offered his hand to Janessa. "I'm sorry that we got off on the wrong foot, Miss Holt."

Janessa did not respond to the gesture. "I doubt that you'll lose sleep over it," she returned curtly.

Lawrence seemed more amused than offended, and after he had left with the Whitings, Dr. Martin and Janessa once more offered their condolences to Andrew Brentwood. They would not be seeing him again for a long time, since he had received orders, just a few days before Susanna died, to report as the new military attaché at Bern, Switzerland. At least, as Dr. Martin had observed, the change of scene might help him recover from his recent tragedy. And Claudia could look after little Samuel in his father's absence. Andrew's only reservation was that his mother already had her hands full with the family business, which had not recovered from the economic depression. Janessa had even heard him mention the possibility of asking Henry Blake for financial help or advice—a subject Andrew had evidently been reluctant to discuss in her presence.

Markham was waiting in the carriage, and after Dr. Martin and Janessa had said good-bye to the Brentwoods, the short, redheaded man drove them to the train station. Despite the funeral, Markham was in a buoyant mood. The extraordinary success at the warehouse hospital had rubbed off on him to an extent, and in the past few days he had been offered positions at two other hospitals. "One was from Riverside," he said. "They asked me to be assistant to the administrator, at a very good salary, and I've accepted."

Dr. Martin leaned forward to offer his congratulations. "I'm very pleased to hear that, Mr. Markham. You thoroughly deserve it, of course, and any hospital that employs you will get more than it gives."

Not until they reached the station and were on the train, however, did Dr. Martin get around to examining his own and Janessa's reward for their services, in the form of the honorarium. He put on his spectacles, took out the envelope the mayor had given him, and opened it. His eyebrows rose in surprise, and he handed the bank check to Janessa—to whom the amount was meaningless, although she knew it was a lot of money. "You can order whatever you want when we go to the dining car," he announced cheerfully, putting the check back in his pocket. "Now we'll have steak instead of liver."

Expenses on the trip to Independence had been held to a minimum—largely a matter of indifference to Janessa, who before she had come to Portland had lived on the edge of poverty. "It's enough to pay for all our expenses, then?" she asked.

"Our expenses! My goodness, yes. Janessa, we can make a generous donation to the charity hospital in Portland and still have a few hundred left over. Part of it is yours, too. Heaven knows you worked hard enough for it."

"But I don't need to buy anything, sir. I was glad just to come here with you."

"You earned it, and it's yours," the doctor insisted. "Once I've paid our expenses, I'll write out a fat check for Anton, and the rest goes in the bank. When you want any of it, just let me know."

It sounded like a good enough plan to Janessa. When the train started moving, she opened her carpetbag and sighed in resignation as she took out a textbook. "I've missed a lot of school, so I'd better get to work on my mathematics. I don't like mathematics."

"Wait until you get to algebra and calculus," the doctor replied, in a good mood now. "Then you'll have something to really dislike. But it all has to be learned, because you must have a rounded education." He took out his notebook and pencil. "And while things are fresh in my mind, I'd better organize my notes on the journal articles I must write."

They fell silent, the doctor poring over his notes and Janessa concentrating on her textbook. Her attention soon wandered, however, and she found herself gazing out the window at the gray, dreary landscape and thinking of home.

Her only regret over coming to Independence was that Cindy had intended to leave within a short time to join her husband in Arizona. Janessa hoped that something had delayed her aunt and that Cindy would still be in Portland when she returned.

Cindy was already in San Francisco, however, having arrived there less than an hour earlier on the steam packet from Portland. As her hired carriage halted in front of the Golden Gate Hotel, the uniformed doorman summoned bellboys, then opened the door and helped her down.

Cindy went inside and across the luxurious lobby, with its plush velvet chairs and couches, gilt trim, and deep carpeting. Halfway to the desk she stopped, for she had spotted a familiar figure at the tobacco and newspaper counter. The dark dress, cape, and hat identified the woman beyond a doubt. "Marjorie!" Cindy exclaimed. "Marjorie White!"

Others in the crowded lobby looked up as Marjorie spun around, gasped in delight, and rushed across the room. "Cindy, you look wonderful! It's such a pleasure to see you again!" she said as they embraced. "And such a surprise!"

"I knew it was you," Cindy said, "even without your camera cases. What on earth are you doing in San Francisco?"

"Perishing from boredom!" Marjorie exclaimed. "But now you've come to my rescue. Let's get you settled in a room, and then I'll tell you all about it, and you can tell me why you're here."

Cindy went to the registration desk, and a few minutes later, after the bellboy had deposited the bags in the room, Marjorie explained what had brought her to San Francisco.

Her enthusiasm evident, she told Cindy she was on the brink of a great adventure. For nearly as long as she had been a professional photographist—earlier that year she had photographed Cindy's wedding—Marjorie had been trying without success to arrange passage for herself on a whaling ship, so that she could photograph its voyage, something that had never been done before. Time after time she had been turned down for no other reason than that women—other than captains' wives—were simply not allowed on board whalers. Finally, however, she had been successful. With the help of a friend, she had obtained a berth on a whaler that was now being refitted at its home port in Maine. It was an older ship, a sailing vessel, and its coming voyage would take it to the whaling grounds in the South Pacific. Because she might be gone for as long as two years, Marjorie had decided to break the news to her husband, Ted Taylor, in person. Both Marjorie and Ted had jobs that forced them to travel, but both seemed content with the arrangement.

"As you probably know," Marjorie went on, "Ted is now in charge of security at a gold mine in Virginia City, Nevada. When I got there, I found he was escorting a large shipment of gold to St. Louis, so I came here to wait until he returns. But what about you?"

"It can wait till dinner," Cindy said. Since she was only staying overnight, she had little to unpack, and linking her arm in Marjorie's, she led the way back downstairs. To Cindy, a whaling voyage sounded dangerous, but Marjorie assured her it was as safe as any railway journey.

When they were seated in the dining room, Marjorie repeated her question.

"I'm on my way to Arizona, to join Reed at Fort Peck," Cindy explained. "Tomorrow I continue south on a packet to San Diego, and from there I head east by coach across the desert."

Marjorie looked dumbfounded. "And you have the nerve to tell me what *I'm* planning is dangerous?" she exclaimed. "Cindy, the newspapers are full of stories about the atrocities of the comancheros in Arizona!"

"But I'll be at a fort," Cindy defended. "My goodness, if an army fort isn't safe, then we might as well let the comancheros have Arizona!"

"Yes, but you have to *get* to the fort, and on the way there—"

"On the way there," Cindy interrupted, "I'll have an army escort. Marjorie, I'll be perfectly safe."

Although obviously not convinced on this point, Marjorie dropped the subject. During the meal, the two women talked about Marjorie's prospective voyage and Cindy's family. Cindy was eager to hear about Alexandra, whom Marjorie had met when she visited Toby in Kentucky a few months before.

"She's about as far as anyone could get from a typical housewife," was Marjorie's conclusion. "But I believe she'd be a perfect mate for Toby."

"And she wears breeches," Cindy commented in amusement, "and doesn't cook? Mama was right, I guess, when she said Alexandra had been raised like a boy. If she does marry Toby, I'm afraid she'll have plenty of trouble from Mama."

"And your mother will have plenty in return," Marjorie ventured. "Alexandra is a very strong-minded young woman."

Changing the subject, Cindy asked why Marjorie had come to San Francisco instead of waiting in Virginia City for Ted. Marjorie had little good to say about the mining boom town, and after relating some amusing if somewhat unlikely stories about the rustic restaurants and hotels, she explained that the mountain under Virginia City was honeycombed with mine tunnels and that the abandoned ones sometimes collapsed. Consequently, any building in town could drop into a sinkhole in the middle of the night with no warning whatsoever.

Marjorie went on to describe the stamp mills that crushed ore and hammered with a deafening noise at all hours. "Listening to a two-shoe mill would make Job himself tear out his beard," she explained. "But they have six-shoe mills in that town! At least they have an ordinance regarding the location of the mills. They can't be any closer than two miles to a cemetery, because the dead people might jump out of their graves to get away from the noise."

"Marjorie!" Cindy scolded. "Now that's stretching it too far!"

Marjorie admitted it was an exaggeration. "However, it is true that the drinking water has arsenic in it. Some of the women like it, because it makes their cheeks rosy. Other people drink water brought in from the mountains, or just beer and liquor. Personally, I'd rather drink the water here in San Francisco."

Cindy agreed that coming to San Francisco had been a good idea. After an excellent dinner, the two young women went back upstairs to Cindy's room to continue their conversation. Among Cindy's baggage was a leather portfolio for her sketch pads, a parting gift from her mother. When Marjorie asked about it, Cindy opened it and showed her the sketches she had made on the steam packet. Marjorie looked at them in puzzled surprise. "These are as good as any professional's!" she exclaimed. "I didn't know you were an artist, Cindy."

"Well, it's only lately that I've begun to work at it seriously," Cindy explained, flattered by Marjorie's appraisal. "I still have a long way to go. Actually, I'd like to take up etching someday."

"That's an excellent idea," Marjorie agreed. "Drawings like these *should* be reproduced for public enjoyment, not hidden away in some portfolio." She hesitated a moment, thinking. "While I was in Maine, I introduced myself to Gilbert Paige, to photograph his studio. You've heard of him, haven't you?"

"Of course," Cindy replied. "He's one of the greatest American painters alive. But I thought he lived in Paris."

"He has a home there, as well as one in Maine. He told me he spends time here to preserve the American perspective in his work—but he's not at all a snob. I'm sure he'd be willing to advise you on how to develop your talent professionally, Cindy."

"Well, Maine is a long way from Arizona, and I don't—"

"You can write," Marjorie interrupted eagerly. "After I see Ted, I'm returning to Maine to make final arrangements to leave on that whaler next spring. I'd be happy to take a couple of your sketches to show to Mr. Paige, and I'll give you his address. The two of you can correspond."

Cindy was hesitant only because she disliked intruding upon another's privacy. Marjorie assured her that Paige viewed helping promising artists as a responsibility and he would be happy to assist her. Cindy looked through the sketches and selected two for her friend to take, and Marjorie wrote down Paige's address, which was near a small coastal village.

When that was done, Cindy protested that she didn't want to keep Marjorie from enjoying the sights that she had come to see.

"Then see them with me," Marjorie laughed. "There's a little café just down the street that stays open until all hours, and we can go there for a late snack and coffee."

Feeling adventurous, Cindy picked up her hat and coat and, arm and arm with her friend, went out the door.

The chill wind sweeping across the high plateau east of Madrid whistled around the Kirchberg private railcar as it approached the sprawling capital city. Henry Blake sat in a comfortable easy chair, reading a newspaper and occasionally looking out the curtained window. The butler was making morning coffee in the kitchenette at one end of the car, while Gisela finished dressing in a curtained enclosure at the other end.

Drawing the curtain aside, Gisela stepped out, dazzlingly beautiful in a blue brocade gown. Her gleaming black hair was arranged on top of her head, with strings of pearls worked through it that matched her earrings and necklace. Henry stood up and put down the paper.

"You're exceptionally lovely this morning," he commented, helping her to the chair across from his. "If we weren't almost in Madrid, I would insist upon returning to bed."

"You wouldn't have to insist," she replied without hesitation. "For you, my clothes always come off more quickly than they go on."

Henry smiled, relieved that Gisela was more or less back to her normal self. Since his return to Grevenhof, where his shoulder had been stitched back together by Dr. MacAlister, she had been understandably preoccupied with his safety, and Henry had been hard put to reassure her, for he did not want to reveal more than necessary about his work. Under the circumstances, she had been remarkably patient in accepting his explanations, and she had been almost eager to rearrange her schedule in order to accompany him to the coronation.

The butler placed a silver coffee service and a bowl of peeled fruit on the small table between the chairs. He poured the coffee and left, and Henry and Gisela sipped it and looked out the window.

The scene outside had changed from barren, windswept fields to a skyline of tile-roofed buildings and church spires in the near distance. The train clattered through switchyards and past suburban tenements, and soon the major thoroughfares and plazas of the city came into view. A festive atmosphere prevailed, with crowds everywhere and balconies gaily decorated with flags and bunting.

One thoroughfare was a solid river of people waving banners. Gisela observed Henry's reaction to the scene. "Those banners are the right colors, Heinrich," she commented. "The red and yellow of the royal house of Castile and Aragon."

Henry knew she was still thinking of his safety. "Yes, I don't see the opposition's colors anywhere."

"The Carlists are probably off skulking in the alleys," Gisela offered, again watching for his reaction.

"Let's hope that's all they do," Henry said.

The train was pulling into the station, and Gisela returned to the end of the car to put on her hat, coat, and gloves. Henry was wearing civilian clothes, and the butler brought him his coat and hat. Outside on the platform a small, dapper Spaniard was waiting to receive them, and as Henry helped Gisela down the steps, the man removed his hat with a flourish and bowed deeply to Gisela. He began speaking German in a strong Spanish accent, and Gisela interrupted long enough to introduce him to Henry as Francesco Alameda, her business agent in Spain. Alameda had already dispatched porters for the baggage, and he escorted Gisela and Henry to a waiting carriage.

As Alameda talked nonstop, filling in Gisela on various obscure business dealings, Henry sat back and looked out the window while the carriage wound through narrow cobblestone streets of stuccoed buildings with red tile roofs. At length they turned onto a wide, crowded thoroughfare leading toward the center of the city. Massive baroque churches and elegant palaces lined the route, with arched doorways and arabesque details lending an occasional Moorish touch.

Normal business activity appeared to be at a standstill, with everyone crowding into the streets in celebration and impromptu parades started on every side. The carriage slowed to a crawl as it weaved through the congestion in the Puerta del Sol, the vast, impressive square at the center of the city.

At last the crowd thinned and the carriage picked up speed. It passed the Hotel Santander, where Henry was to meet Anderson and Willoughby, then drew up in front of what looked like a large private residence. A doorman appeared at once to show them in.

Evidently Alameda had rented the entire building, for he beamed at his employer, confident that she would be satisfied. Indeed, Gisela looked pleased as she entered, for the residence was extravagantly luxurious in every detail, and a complete staff was lined up in the main hall to greet her.

As always, she wasted no time setting to work. An office had already been prepared for her in a drawing room, and she handed her hat and coat to a servant and, with Alameda standing at her shoulder, began flipping through the papers awaiting her on the desk. Henry excused himself, promising to be back in time for lunch.

Gisela looked up a bit guiltily. "Do you need me to accompany you, loved one?" she asked. "If you do, I will gladly put business aside. After all, this is our holiday, isn't it?"

Henry smiled and shook his head. "Gisela, you don't know what a holiday is. But I promise I won't be long."

A few minutes' brisk walk brought him to the Santander, where the clerk at the desk informed him that Anderson and Willoughby had adjoining rooms on the third floor.

Upstairs, the Englishman opened to Henry's knock, and his normally reserved expression relaxed into a warm smile. "Come in, Henry, come in! What a pleasure to see you again! Clifford, the man of the hour has finally arrived."

Anderson, his eye patch in place, crossed the room and offered his hand. "The man of the hour indeed," he affirmed. "What you did in Darmstadt was absolutely perfect. No one else could have done it as well."

"I had some invaluable help," Henry said, "in the form of six military Mausers supplied to me by Captain Richard Koehler. Have Chacon and the others been arrested yet?"

"No, but thanks to you General Moncaldo has the situation well in hand," Willoughby assured him. "He'll be here any minute, and I'll let him tell you all about it. Did you run into any trouble in Darmstadt?"

Henry could not help but laugh. "Well, the suit your people provided me with was ruined during a scuffle I had with another gun dealer."

"I trust there will be no . . . ah, repercussions as a result of that?" Willoughby suggested quietly.

"None." Henry took Krauss's notebook from his pocket

170

and handed it to Willoughby. "I relieved him of this afterward." Henry proceeded to give a short account of what had happened in Darmstadt, and he finished with a description of Mueller. "If those initials refer to him—and I believe they do—then he had meetings with Krauss *before* coming here and taking Chacon back to Germany."

"Yet Mueller allowed Chacon to buy weapons from you instead. Odd, to say the least. Evidently Mueller works for someone besides Krauss, which means we have a definite German connection in the plot."

"And if the Spanish find out about it," Henry added, "there could be trouble on an international scale."

Willoughby looked troubled. "Back at Sandhurst, I merely wanted to avoid involving German intelligence, but I didn't want to tell General Moncaldo that. Needless to say, Clifford and I appreciate your discretion, Henry. Whatever the German connection was, it's now ended. But I'd like to show this notebook to my people to see if they can draw more conclusions from it."

Henry agreed with the suggestion, and Anderson excused himself to get something from his room. A few moments later he returned with a rifle case, which he handed to Henry.

While back in London, Henry had ordered a presentation-grade Winchester rifle as a present for Alphonse Ferdinand's coronation and requested that it be sent to Anderson. Now he opened the case and inspected the rifle with satisfaction. The entire weapon, including the stock, was decorated with intricate patterns and hunting scenes, and Henry was certain that the young monarch-to-be would appreciate the gift. He was still admiring the rifle when a knock sounded at the door.

"That must be the general now," Willoughby said. He opened the door, and Rafael Vincente Moncaldo, an impressive figure in the full-dress uniform of the Spanish Army, entered the room.

On the previous occasions Henry had meet Moncaldo,

the man had always been attired in conservative business suits and seemed somewhat ill at ease. Now, in his dark blue tunic trimmed with gold braid and epaulets, and with a gold baldric across his chest and sword at his side, he seemed perfectly natural.

"Captain Blake!" he exclaimed, shaking Henry's hand. "I have been eagerly looking forward to the opportunity to express my appreciation for what you did in Germany. I am most grateful indeed."

"Sir Charles tells me that you have the situation well in hand," Henry replied. "I just arrived myself."

The general nodded confidently and began explaining. Acting on the telegram Henry had sent from Darmstadt, he had alerted his agents at the Spanish border. The agents had followed Chacon to the suburbs of Madrid, to a villa that served as the headquarters for the conspirators. Apparently planning to strike on the day of the coronation, the plotters had been gathering at the villa, which was now under close surveillance by plainclothes agents.

"Emilio Garcia, their leader, arrived with two others this morning," the general said. "There are now some forty men in the villa, and I am certain that all the important ones are there. Late tonight, I intend to take two full companies of soldiers to arrest them, if they will surrender. If they refuse . . ." He purposely left the sentence unfinished.

"I'd like to come along, if I may," Henry said, picking up the Winchester. "I ordered this as a coronation gift for His Highness, and I'm sure he wouldn't object if I tested it before I gave it to him."

The general smiled in appreciation. "I shall send my orderly for you before we leave, Captain Blake."

The sound of distant cheering rose from outside, and the general grew thoughtful as he looked toward the window. "The people of Spain have reason to celebrate," he observed. "After years of strife, my nation will finally have peace. But not until Alphonse Ferdinand is safely crowned king."

Willoughby and Anderson expressed their somber agreement. The coronation was yet two days away, and it might be weeks or even months before a stable government was in place. And other dangers as threatening as the Carlist plot could be lurking, as yet undetected amid the cheering throngs.

X

At a shallow creek beside the road, Toby Holt reined up to let his horse drink. He was deep in the Appalachian Mountains, and the dense trees that rose on steep slopes to either side were dusted with snow that had fallen during the early morning. The hoofprints Toby was following on the road were fresh, made within the past hour or two.

When the horse had finished drinking, Toby rode on at a walk. The gray sky threatened more snow, and the wind gusting through the valley was cold. Toby pulled his coat collar higher and reined up again to look closely at the hoofprints.

The tracks were identical to those he had found occasionally in damp spots on the road during the past days: One of the horses had a bent toe cleat on its right fore shoe, and the other an oddly narrow right rear shoe. In the new snow the tracks were easy to follow, yet at no point had the trail been difficult to follow.

Gazing ahead to where the narrow road disappeared around a fold in the hillside, Toby thought of how easy it had been to track Sewell through the warren of roads in the mountains. He had often wondered during the past days if he was being led into a trap. Each curve in the road was a potential ambush, where Sewell could be waiting in hiding.

He would not turn back now, though. The possibility of an ambush was a risk that had to be taken, because he had to track down the man. His only defense was to be as watchful and as cautious as possible.

The road began to leave the creek and curve up the hill. Here the trees broke the force of the gusty wind, and as Toby urged his horse to a canter, he remained aware of another danger—that Sewell might hear him approaching.

The man might have turned off the road to rest and warm himself, as he had done regularly over the past days. Sewell clearly was unaccustomed to the discomforts of life away from the city, and each time he stopped, even briefly, he built a fire. Riding along the road, Toby remained alert for the odor of wood smoke.

Up until two days ago, there had been an almost constant faint smell of smoke from cabins along the road; but it had been several hours now since Toby had seen even a deserted cabin. The air was fresh and clear, free of any scent but pine.

Farther up the mountain, the bare birches, ashes, and elms gradually gave way to evergreens, and suddenly Toby heard a clatter off to one side. He reined up, listening, and identified the sound as a deer running through the trees. He nudged his horse with his heels and continued on the road. Around the next curve, he saw the tracks of the deer, over those made by the two horses. Then the deer tracks veered off into the woods. He wondered if the deer could have been spooked by Sewell and his companions. Perhaps, for once, Sewell had turned off the road and stopped without building a fire. A dense pine thicket lay ahead, and Toby felt vaguely uneasy.

Once more he reined back to a walk. The wind had subsided, and a strange quiet had settled. Woods were always quieter during the colder months, when the birds and small animals found shelter from the cold. But there usually was at least some activity in the forest, except when something disturbed the wildlife.

To Toby, both the quiet and the behavior of the deer were ominous signs. The pines ahead provided a perfect setting for an ambush. As if to confirm these suspicions, Toby's horse lifted its head, cocking its ears and flaring its nostrils.

An instant later, Toby knew what had drawn the animal's attention: It was the smell of horses. An icy fear gripped him, and he jerked his pistol from its holster and jabbed his horse with his heels, turning it off the road toward the protection of the trees.

Abruptly the world exploded around him. The roar of gunfire battered his ears, and smoke from rifle blasts spewed from the pines. A bullet struck his head with a hammer impact, and another hit his chest a crushing blow, knocking the air from his lungs.

Toby felt himself falling from the saddle, as if in slow motion, while other bullets plucked at his coat and slapped the hat off his head. His horse was screaming, rearing, plunging into the trees at the side of the road.

Toby sensed he was in the air, then suddenly he slammed down into brush. His horse pounded away through the forest, its hoofbeats fading. Darkness and a heavy, irresistible lassitude closed over him. . . .

For a long time he seemed to be floating in darkness, detached from everything. Then faint sounds penetrated, as though from far away, and he heard horses and men approaching, the men talking and laughing in satisfaction.

Sewell's laughter echoed over the other voices. Someone commented that Toby had almost evaded the ambush, and Sewell answered. "Almost ain't good enough. He was smart, but not quite smart enough. Looks like we got him in the heart and the head, and even Toby Holt can't live through that."

The men laughed raucously. "Do you want us to run down his horse and catch it?" someone asked.

"No, forget it," Sewell replied. "No one's going to nab us for horse thieves. But I'll take his pistol, and you men can split what's in the wallet. From now on, I'm going to be known among all the gangs as the man who carries Toby Holt's pistol."

Footsteps approached, and Toby sensed his limp hand move as the pistol was jerked from it. Hands searched his pockets and removed his wallet. He was vaguely aware of the men discussing what to do next. One of them suggested building a fire and resting.

"No," Sewell said. "We're heading straight for Lexington. With him out of the way, it'll be easy to snatch that girl. We'll take her to the place at Frenchman's Creek and keep her there until the old man agrees to sell."

The words barely registered in Toby's mind. Horse hooves scuffled on the road, saddles creaked as men mounted, then the horses rode away. The silence of the woods once again enveloped Toby, his only sensation the pain in his head and chest.

Then even that began fading, consciousness slipping away from him. In a remote corner of his mind he felt an urgent need to do something, a refusal to give up. He struggled to cling to consciousness, but he was powerless to resist. The darkness closed in and became complete.

The cold, gusty wind made Henry Blake's overcoat feel thin as he walked along a road with General Moncaldo and two other Spanish officers. The night was cold but bright, a full moon shining down on the outlying Castellana district of Madrid. It was a neighborhood of expensive villas set on fenced grounds along wide avenues.

Squads of soldiers passed, running noisily, but the wind rushing through the trees along the road drowned the heavy footsteps and rattle of equipment. Ahead, Henry saw the large villa in the moonlight. It looked uncomfortably like a fortress to him, the angles of its tile roof barely peeking above a tall, thick wall surrounding it and the inner courtyard.

At the outer edge of the lawns ran another, much lower, stone wall, where the soldiers were taking up positions. The general talked quietly with the two aides, but he broke off as a shot rang out ahead. Exclaiming in anger, he ran forward, and Henry and the aides followed.

Other shots rang out, and rifle fire flashed along the top of the wall protecting the villa. At the opening in the low stone wall where the driveway emerged, a lieutenant stood behind the gateposts with a platoon of soldiers. He saluted the general and began explaining something in Spanish, but Henry had no need to understand the words in order to see what had happened: Sentries at the villa had spotted the soldiers moving into position.

The general cut off the explanation with an impatient gesture and pointed to a speaking trumpet on the ground. The lieutenant handed it to him, and the general put it to his mouth and shouted what sounded to Henry like an ultimatum to the defenders of the villa. The only reply was a burst of gunfire, sending bullets slapping into the ground and ricocheting off the stone wall. The general ducked behind the gatepost and reeled off a string of orders to his aides.

The two officers raced away around the wall, evidently to prepare the men for an assault. As the lieutenant assembled a squad to rush the courtyard's iron-grilled gateway some thirty yards up the drive, Henry loaded the Winchester and prepared to join them. The general put a cautioning hand on his arm.

"No, stay with me until after the first assault, Captain," he said. "You are in civilian clothes, and my soldiers might mistake you for one of the enemy."

It was a good point, and Henry agreed and knelt by the stone wall with the general. The soldiers in the platoon fixed their bayonets, and the lieutenant stood sword in hand, awaiting the general's signal. After a burst of fire from the walls, Moncaldo nodded, and the lieutenant lifted a whistle, blew it, and waved the soldiers forward with his sword.

Their bayonets gleaming in the moonlight, the men advanced at a run. Other whistles shrilled around the low wall, and soldiers piled over it in a wave, firing as they rushed the villa gate. The gunfire from the top of the inner wall increased, and Henry could see red flashes at intervals along its entire length.

Some soldiers stumbled and fell, but it appeared to Henry that the assault would succeed. General Moncaldo was following traditional tactics, sending a concentrated force against the strategic point, the grilled courtyard gate. Abruptly, however, the rapid cracking of rifles was drowned by the thunderous roar of a Gatling gun deployed somewhere in the courtyard, behind the gate.

The stream of lead from the gate passed through the squad on the drive, some of the bullets ricocheting from the iron bars. Several soldiers fell, and others lay prone or took cover behind low ornamental bushes. The soldiers converging from both sides also hesitated, not having expected heavy weapons. Then they began retreating to the outer wall, leaving wounded comrades scattered across the lawn.

The general was disconcerted, for his surveillance had not detected the Gatling gun. As he helplessly watched the lieutenant and the remaining soldiers dash back to the stone wall, Henry touched his arm and pointed to the trees bordering the road. "I could get up in one of those trees," he suggested. "I believe I can get high enough and at the proper angle to shoot through the gate at the men who are firing that Gatling gun."

Moncaldo glanced at the trees. "That is perhaps a good idea, Captain Blake," he said. "But you should not take the risk. I will put two of my soldiers up in those trees."

"Sir, I can empty the magazine in this Winchester before a soldier can fire one of those breech-loaders twice. With all due respect, it would be better—"

"When you start firing," Moncaldo interrupted impatiently, "the enemy will fire back at you. It will be better if I put my soldiers into the trees."

"Then the enemy will simply move the Gatling gun out of their line of fire," Henry argued. "With this Winchester, I can keep the gun crew pinned down. The soldiers can give me covering fire with another assault."

Moncaldo hesitated, clearly tempted by the plan. "If you are wounded," he warned, "His Highness will make me the oldest private in the army. But go ahead, Captain."

"May I borrow your baldric, sir?" Henry asked.

"My baldric?" Moncaldo looked at him uncomprehendingly.

"As a sling for the rifle," Henry explained. "I'll need two hands to climb."

"Of course." Moncaldo unbuckled the belt and handed it to Henry.

Henry thanked him and trotted away toward the trees. He had already picked out the one affording the best angle, and after pausing to fashion a sling so that the Winchester dangled behind his back, he began climbing, favoring his bad shoulder. The soldiers around the stone wall and the defenders inside the villa were keeping up a sporadic fire, and Henry reached his perch unobserved.

The tree swayed in the wind as Henry scanned the courtyard. Lighted windows cast dim beams onto the inner drive, and Henry could clearly see the Gatling gun, about ten yards behind the gateway. Four men were huddled around it, shadowy forms protected from gunfire by a hastily erected barrier of furniture.

Henry braced himself between a limb and the trunk, took aim, and began firing, working the lever rapidly. The four men leaped up, scattering quickly from the Gatling gun. Two were not quick enough and lay sprawled in the courtyard.

A bullet shattered the bark near Henry's head as he was reloading. He swung himself back around the trunk, and only seconds later a hail of bullets flew through the tree, shredding bark and branches around him. Whistles shrilled again, indicating that another assault was under way.

The bullets stopped striking the tree as the men in the villa redirected their fire at the onrushing soldiers. Henry peered around the trunk. A squad was nearing the gate, but more men were gathering around the Gatling gun. Henry braced himself, aimed, and began firing from behind the trunk.

Two more men fell before bullets again slammed into the tree trunk, the splinters stinging Henry's face. But the squad had rushed through the gate, and a roar of gunfire rose from the courtyard. Elsewhere around the inner wall, soldiers were boosting their comrades over, while others were throwing torches over the wall to illuminate the courtyard. The confusion of dark forms changed into a scene of furious struggle, with bayonets flashing and pistols and rifles firing. The Carlists fell back into the villa, leaving their dead and wounded behind. Moments later a half dozen soldiers broke through one of the side gates, but some fifteen Carlists ran out a door opposite the gate to counterattack and try to escape.

Henry began firing, and the Carlists at the front of the group fell. Their followers hesitated in confusion over the deadly gunfire from some unseen source, and the soldiers, reinforced by another squad, chased them back into the house.

General Moncaldo had joined his troops in the courtyard, and the Carlists had already been driven back from the doors and windows. Henry climbed down from the tree and trotted toward the villa. He could hear a muffled uproar of shouting voices and gunfire as the battle inside raged from room to room.

It was finished by the time he joined the officers in the front room. The place reeked of gunpowder smoke, furniture was scattered about, and the walls were riddled with bullet holes. Moncaldo turned to Henry. "Your plan saved many lives, Captain. We are indebted to you."

The other officers added comments in Spanish that Henry did not understand, but their grateful expressions needed no translation. "I'm pleased I was able to help," he said.

Moncaldo pointed to a familiar-looking crate at the side of the room. "My men found the Mausers. I am glad they were not used against us."

"So am I, needless to say." Henry was aware he would have to arrange their immediate return to Richard, but he was confident that General Moncaldo would cooperate in every way possible. "How many of the Carlists were taken prisoner, sir?"

"Very few," Moncaldo replied. "And only their hired killers, it seems. All of the leaders were killed or committed suicide." He nodded toward a door. "The men are collecting the bodies in there. Chacon and Garcia are among them."

Henry handed the general back his baldric, then went out the door to the courtyard for a breath of fresh air. The chain of events that had begun for him in a quiet room at Sandhurst had reached a successful, if bloody, conclusion, and he hoped that the coronation two days hence held no more surprises.

General Moncaldo was in an ebullient mood when he appeared the next day to escort Henry and Gisela to an audience with Alphonse Ferdinand. The general was in dress uniform, as was Henry, and Gisela was dazzling in a flowing silk gown embroidered with silver and gold thread. A state coach took them in style along the broad, crowded avenues to the royal palace on the Calle de Bailén.

Guards in colorful ceremonial uniforms and plumed helmets stood on the steps in front of the grandiose columned structure, built by the Bourbon dynasty in the eighteenth century. The guards stiffly presented arms as Henry and the general stepped from the coach. Henry tucked the Winchester in its case under his arm and assisted Gisela down.

As they went up the steps, Moncaldo told Henry that he had seen Alphonse Ferdinand that morning and had related to him the events of the previous night. Henry remarked that Alphonse must be very busy these days.

Moncaldo smiled wryly. "His Highness has been quickly learning about the obstacles, compromises, and difficult choices that face anyone who is in a position of authority," he said. "At present he is meeting with a delegation from the Cortes, our legislative body. Yesterday and earlier today he had meetings with advisers and prospective cabinet members. Countless people of influence are awaiting audiences with him, and his secretaries have been presenting a few of them between each meeting, to ease the toil for him. But seeing you, one of his best friends, will cheer him considerably."

They went down an echoing hallway and through a wide door into the main reception hall of the palace. It was a huge room, lavishly decorated, with a sprawling, colorful mural on the high ceiling. People hoping for an audience with Alphonse Ferdinand were standing about in groups and chatting, the women a scintillating display of sparkling, costly jewels and elaborate gowns.

Most of the men were Spanish nobles and business leaders, Henry assumed. A few he vaguely recalled meeting at some reception or other in Berlin, and Gisela was acquainted with many more of them. She exchanged greetings with people on either side as Moncaldo led them straight through the room to the door at the other end.

Henry recognized the Countess von Lautzenberg, a pleasant old woman he had met on board ship during his last journey to the United States. She smiled and waved to him, then peered appraisingly at Gisela through her bejeweled lorgnette. A woman nearer to Henry glared at him, obviously resentful that he and Gisela were being taken to see Alphonse Ferdinand ahead of the others. About forty-five years old, she was pale and fleshy and had an unpleasant, predatory face. Gisela, without turning her head, said to him in a low voice that she was Doña Allegra Christina y Moreno, a relative of the royal family.

The guards flanking the door at the end of the room presented arms, and Moncaldo informally returned the salute. Other guards were posted along the wide hallway on the other side of the door, and Moncaldo led the way past them to a large, sparsely furnished office.

Alphonse Ferdinand, his handsome young face reflecting weary frustration, was seated at a desk scanning a document, with a dozen older men gathered around him expectantly. As he looked up and saw Henry, an expression of delight replaced his frown, which seemed to be transferred to the men whose meeting had been interrupted.

Alphonse stood up and stepped to Henry, greeting him with boyish exuberance. "I'm delighted to see you again, Captain Blake, especially after General Moncaldo told me what you did last night."

Henry smilingly acknowledged the compliment and stood aside as he introduced Gisela. The young Spaniard bowed elegantly over her hand as she curtsied, and then Moncaldo introduced Henry to the assemblage, most of whom were future cabinet ministers.

When the introductions were finished, Henry opened the rifle case and took out the Winchester. "I've brought you a coronation present, Captain Ferdinand," he said— the form of address raising some eyebrows. "This is the new model of Winchester, with special decorations, as you can see."

Alphonse took the rifle and inspected it with obvious pleasure. "I have heard about the new Winchester, but this is the first one I've seen," he said. "It is beautiful, and I will treasure it for the rest of my life, Captain Blake."

"I can assure you it is in working condition," Henry added, "because I took it with me when I accompanied General Moncaldo last night."

Alphonse looked at the rifle again, then stepped to a sideboard. A sword as richly decorated as the Winchester was lying there, and Alphonse picked it up and put down the rifle. "I would like for you to have this in return," he said. "This sword is made of the finest Toledo steel, and it has been in my family for many generations. I meant to use it as a ceremonial sword, but I would rather you have it."

Seeing the royal arms of Castile and Aragon emblazoned on the scabbard in gold and jewels, Henry shook his head. "I cannot accept a family heirloom," he said. "Your friendship is the best gift I could ask from you, and—"

"No, I insist you take it," the young man said firmly. "Since I have been told that it would be ill-advised to decorate you in public for what you've done, at least you can take this to show others my great esteem and friendship for you."

Henry hesitated a moment longer, but seeing General Moncaldo nod encouragingly, he took the sword and expressed his deep thanks. Before Ferdinand Alphonse could say another word, however, the court chamberlain stepped to his side and pointed out that people had been waiting in the reception hall for hours. The young man's face fell, but then he seemed to think of something. "Will you and the baroness join me for dinner this evening?" he asked. "I have appointments before dinner, after dinner, and seemingly every moment that I am awake, but we can talk during dinner, can we not?"

"We certainly can, and I accept with thanks, Captain Ferdinand," Henry replied promptly.

"Good! I'll send a coach for you, then, at seven."

Back in the reception hall, Moncaldo paused to talk with some of the petitioners. Countess von Lautzenberg immediately fastened on to Gisela, interrogating her in German, and Henry stood by, amused by the aged woman's adroit probing and Gisela's equally expert evasions. Glancing around the room, Henry again noticed Doña Allegray y Moreno, who stood impatiently near the entrance door, obviously angry and frustrated.

"She looks formidable, doesn't she?" Gisela said, rejoining him. "His Highness would do well to avoid Doña Allegra, and we're fortunate he didn't invite *her* to have dinner with him."

"Why do you say that?"

"Because she is ambitious, and she is a lineal descendant of Ferdinand VII and has a son who would have a legitimate claim to the throne if something happened to Alphonse Ferdinand. If she had the opportunity, she would no doubt like to put something in his soup that would make him worse than ill."

Gisela's tone was joking, but the subject was not amusing to Henry after the events of the past weeks. As he and Gisela waited for General Moncaldo, Henry noticed that Doña Allegra was wearing a large, unusual-looking enamel ring on her left forefinger. It was vaguely reminiscent to him of another ring he had seen somewhere, but he was unable to recall where or when.

As he left the reception hall with Gisela and the general, Henry tried to dismiss his thoughts about the ring, but he was unable to. The image of a similar ring lurked just beyond his grasp, and for some reason it seemed to portend evil.

After what seemed like an eternity, Toby became aware of sensation again. He was choking, and he swallowed instinctively so that he could breathe. The shock of raw, harsh liquor burning a path down his throat brought him to full consciousness. Coughing, he opened his eyes, and gradually the blurred scene around him came into focus.

It was night, and he was on a pallet in front of a fireplace, evidently in a small cabin. He was wearing a coarse, unfamiliar nightshirt, and a girl of about sixteen was kneeling beside him, holding a gourd dipper that she had used to pour moonshine whiskey into his mouth. In a homespun dress, she was angular and slender, with blue eyes and bold, tanned features.

Five similarly lanky men, all bearded and in home-spun, sat on stools and benches around the room, gazing solemnly at him. The five were virtually identical, except that one of them had a white beard.

For a moment Toby wondered if he was dreaming. The watchers were motionless and silent, staring at him as though he were a curiosity; and two hounds lying beside the fireplace gazed at him with the same grave, thoughtful eyes as the people. Toby began to realize that he was among hill folk who had lived in isolation for generations and who had probably never ventured into the outside world. The four younger men must be brothers, he thought, and the older man their father.

A full minute passed, the only sound the crackling of the fire. Then the girl lifted the dipper and drank the remainder of the liquor in it, swallowing the powerful whiskey without blinking. "Them varmints," she observed, "come within a flea's whisker of sending him to his maker. But it looks like he might heal up."

Her strong dialect was barely intelligible to Toby in his weak, light-headed state. After several seconds, the white-bearded man grunted in agreement, then the others joined in a chorus of grunts. Silence fell again.

The entire family was certainly less than talkative. Toby licked his dry lips and spoke to the girl, who leaned over to listen closely to his weak voice. "Where . . . where am I?" he asked.

"Culley Hollow," she answered, sitting back up. "About fifteen miles from the road you was on." She indicated two of the men with her chin. "My brothers Zeke and Zeb, they found you and brung you here."

Moving slightly to look at the men, Toby felt a thick bandage around his head. "I appreciate that very much," he said.

The men seemed perplexed by his words, and all five of them exchanged puzzled glances. The girl laughed softly. " 'T'weren't no need to thank them," she said. "You would have died if they hadn't holpen you, so they couldn't leave you laying in the woods."

The backwoods code that dictated helping others in need sounded logical enough to Toby, and he nodded, for he had no strength to argue. Even the slight movement caused his temples to throb, making him wince. The girl frowned sympathetically, then told him he had a deep furrow over his left ear from a bullet. Another bullet had struck his left side over his heart, fortunately for him glancing off a rib and traveling along it under the skin all the way around to his back, where it was lodged.

"You've lost too much blood for me to see to fixin' them wounds now," she went on. "In two or three days, when you've gained some strength, I'll clean them out so they'll heal up good." She turned to her father. "He ought to sleep now, Pa. There'll be plenty of time for him to tell us about hisself."

After a few seconds, her father grunted in agreement and stood up. He went into another room, and the younger men stood up and also left the room. The girl put a log on the fire, then crossed the room to a trunk and returned with a quilt, which she spread over Toby. She reached to a shelf for a tin cup and put it beside the pallet.

"If you need anything in the night," she said, "knock this cup against the floor. I sleep light, and I'll hear it."

Toby thanked her—which again seemed to amuse her—and she left the room. The two hounds stood up, turned around, and settled themselves for the night. Toby closed his eyes and waited for sleep. He had never felt weaker or more exhausted, but a nagging worry in the back of his mind kept him awake.

His memory of what had happened on the road was clear enough. In his mind's eye, he could still see the gunpowder smoke billowing from the trees and feel the bullets striking him. He could also recall what had happened during the next moments, when he had fallen into the brush beside the road and Sewell and the other men had come up to him.

The rest was a blank. Sewell and the men had talked, but he could recall only the sound of voices. He knew that something they had said was vital, and he struggled to recall the words, but it was like the fleeting trace of a dream after waking, gone in every detail but leaving behind a strong impression that the meaning had been of transcendent importance.

XI

A bugle blowing reveille awakened Cindy Kerr; it was the same sound that had awakened her every morning since she had arrived in Yuma. The fort, a five-minute walk from where she was staying, was the dominating feature of the town on the edge of Arizona Territory.

Cindy had taken a room in a private home belonging to a family named Phelps. Mr. Phelps was a civilian employee at the fort commissary, and while Cindy was getting dressed, she heard his gruff voice down the hall in the kitchen. By now he would be finishing breakfast, and as she had the past few days, Cindy waited until she heard him leave for work, then went to the kitchen.

Anne Phelps, a stout, likable woman of forty-five, turned from the sink and smiled at her. "My, you always look so pretty first thing in the morning, Mrs. Kerr," she said. "If your husband knew you were here, he'd run all the way to Yuma on foot. I have two eggs and a nice piece of pork for your breakfast this morning."

Cindy sat down at the table. "I'm so grateful to be here instead of up at the fort, Mrs. Phelps. I couldn't in good conscience allow the colonel to evict one of his officers on my account."

"Well, there are some other officers' wives who

wouldn't give it a second thought," Anne said as she broke the eggs into the pan. "I wouldn't take in boarders as a regular thing, but I certainly don't mind having a proper young lady like you in my house. And you certainly couldn't stay in a hotel, could you?"

Cindy gave a short laugh; it had not taken her long to discover that the "hotels" in Yuma were notorious as bordellos for the soldiers. As Anne moved around the kitchen, the two women discussed the same subject that occupied them every morning: Cindy's prospects for joining Reed.

After she had reached Yuma by stage, and the cavalry escort had gone back with the return stage, Cindy's journey had come to a standstill. Lone travelers and small parties did not venture across the Colorado River on the roads leading east, and the telegraph lines to Fort Peck, sixty miles away, were down, presumably cut by the comancheros again. Cindy had been unable to continue on to Fort Peck or to contact Reed and let him know she was in Yuma.

The previous day, a squad of cavalry had left the fort to escort repairmen along the telegraph lines. The sergeant in charge, a gray-whiskered veteran named Burns, had refused even to consider taking her with him. He had regarded his squad as far too small to offer her protection, and they would be making stops along the way to repair the telegraph lines. Colonel Hatfield, Yuma's commanding officer, had ended discussion on the issue by firmly supporting the sergeant's viewpoint.

Fort Peck was garrisoned by two full companies of cavalry, a comparatively large force. The post was self-sufficient in most respects, but Fort Yuma served as its supply depot. The repairmen might take a week to put the telegraph lines back into operation—at which time Reed could be notified of her presence—or wagons might arrive from Fort Peck to pick up supplies before then.

As Cindy ate breakfast, her hostess concluded that she would be able to join Reed within the next week to ten days, at the most. Mrs. Phelps ventured the opinion that it might well be sooner, since she had heard from her husband about a shipment of priority freight for Fort Peck that had been warehoused at Fort Yuma for some time now, waiting to be picked up. It consisted of several wooden crates covered with canvas to conceal the markings on them.

Cindy had finished her breakfast and took a sip of her coffee. "What on earth could they be sending to Fort Peck that is so secret they cover it with canvas?"

"Oh, I haven't the slightest idea," Mrs. Phelps said. "But it's covered to keep the comancheros from finding out about it. You see, any loiterer in one of the saloons could be a comanchero, and all he'd have to do is listen to the soldiers talking."

The idea of comancheros possibly lurking in town alarmed Cindy. "I suppose the shipment could be Gatling guns, or maybe . . ." She was about to mention the new Winchester carbines she had heard about back at Fort Vancouver, but she thought better of it. Anne Phelps and her husband were generous, friendly people, but perhaps a trifle too talkative. And, as Mrs. Phelps had said, any loiterer in a saloon could be a comanchero. "Well, it could be anything. That was a delicious breakfast, Mrs. Phelps." Cindy rose from the table. "I'll help with these dishes."

"You will not," Mrs. Phelps said firmly. "You get yourself right over to that telegraph office and see if the lines are up yet."

Cindy gratefully took the advice, and after returning to her room for her hat, coat, and sketch pad, which she almost always carried with her these days, she went outside into the cold, bright morning.

The town of Yuma, formerly known as Arizona City and only recently renamed, had sprung to life as a river port and supply point for travelers to California during the gold rush, and most of the buildings, of clapboard or adobe, were huddled up under the fort, which commanded a promontory at a bend in the river. Despite the cold wind whipping in off the desert, Cindy was glad that it was winter, for summer temperatures here soared to legendary levels.

Since her arrival in Yuma, Cindy had learned a good deal about the Arizona Territory. Of course everyone spoke of the Grand Canyon, where the Colorado River had carved a breathtaking, mile-deep gorge. It was claimed to be the most spectacular natural wonder on the continent, and only some five years before, a man named John Wesley Powell had led the first party down the length of the canyon by boat. Cindy hoped she could visit the site someday, although it was hundreds of miles to the north.

At the opposite corner of the territory from Yuma was the Four Corners junction with Utah, Colorado, and New Mexico territories, the only point in the Union where four jurisdictions touched. In that region lay the land of the Navajo and the Hopi, and the fabled Painted Desert and the Petrified Forest. Cindy had also heard fascinating tales of ancient cliff dwellings—ghostly, deserted ruins that once had been home for thousands.

The territory was undeveloped, yet everyone in Yuma agreed that it had vast potential. Gold had been discovered years before near Prescott, a town adjacent to Fort Whipple, and evidence of gold and other valuable minerals had been found at various other places in the territory. But more important for sustained growth, settlers at Phoenix had found that the desert was fertile. The town, begun years before as a hay camp to supply fodder for cavalry horses, had drawn Mormons from Utah as well as settlers from the east. They had developed the settlement into a rich farming community by tapping the waters of the Salt River, just as the waters of the Colorado were now being used to irrigate fields on the outskirts of Yuma.

As Cindy made her way to the telegraph office, she passed the stagecoach depot, where a squad of cavalry was assembling to escort a departing stage. She paused across the street to make a quick sketch of the activity, and after the stage had left, she went into the telegraph office.

The wizened old clerk behind the counter looked up

from under his green eyeshade and shook his head apologetically, knowing what she was going to ask. "No, not yet, ma'am. When the comancheros cut the lines, they usually do it in several places. I expect it'll be at least another three or four days before we can get through to Fort Peck."

Downcast, Cindy thanked him, but as she went back outside, she heard a sound that made her spirits suddenly soar. It was the unmistakable rumble of a large cavalry column, approaching from the east. Others heard it, too, and were coming out of buildings and stopping along the street to look. Cindy watched and waited in breathless anticipation.

Rounding a corner, the officer at the front of the column came into view, with the sergeant and guidon bearer directly behind him, and Cindy felt momentarily disappointed that the officer was not Reed. Her disappointment changed to eager satisfaction, however, as she watched the rest of the column of soldiers wheeling onto the street, for now she knew that her waiting would soon be over.

In all, she counted a half company of cavalry—some forty men—and at the end of the column were two wagons, each drawn by three teams of mules. Cindy was puzzled by what amounted to a huge escort for only two wagons, but she quickly dismissed the thought; supply wagons had arrived, which was all that mattered to her.

The lieutenant lifted a gloved hand to his hat as he passed women on the street, and Cindy smiled and waved in response. She watched the column climb the hill leading to the fort and disappear through the wide gate. Lifting her chin and squaring her shoulders, she set off after them at a fast walk, determined to get a ride in one of the wagons when they returned to Fort Peck.

The guard at the gate touched his hat as she passed, and seeing the newly arrived lieutenant and Colonel Hatfield talking next to the wagons, Cindy walked right up to them.

The colonel greeted her politely and introduced her to the officer from Fort Peck, a Lieutenant Nolan. Nolan gallantly bowed over Cindy's hand. "Delighted to meet you, Mrs. Kerr. And I'm certain Reed will be even more delighted when I tell him you're here."

"Oh, you won't have to do that, Mr. Nolan," Cindy replied sweetly. "I see no reason why I can't go back to Fort Peck with you and your men."

Nolan glanced nervously at Colonel Hatfield and stammered apologetically. "I—I came here to pick up an important shipment of equipment, Mrs. Kerr. But the very moment I reach Fort Peck, I'll let Reed know you're here. I'm sure Major Fargo will immediately give him permission to set out with an escort to come get you."

Cindy glanced at the empty wagons, and an idea suddenly occurred to her. "What equipment are you talking about—the new Winchester rifles?"

It was only an educated guess, but both the lieutenant and the colonel looked startled. The colonel finally found his tongue. "How did you know that?" he demanded.

"Oh, I just guessed," Cindy said innocently. "Some arrived at Fort Vancouver before I left, and I noticed your men are still carrying Spencers, although all the cavalry are to be outfitted with the Winchesters. And what else would require such a large escort?"

The colonel sighed ruefully. "Well, it's supposed to be a secret, Mrs. Kerr, and I would appreciate it if you kept it that way. The comancheros would love to get hold of those rifles."

"You see now why I can't take you with me?" Nolan pleaded. "If the comancheros *have* found out about those new carbines, we're going to have plenty of trouble on the way back."

"I have total confidence in you and your men," Cindy assured him. She turned to the colonel. "Colonel Hatfield, you were absolutely correct that I shouldn't go to Fort Peck with Sergeant Burns and his men. But there's no reason at all why I can't go in one of these wagons, is there?"

The colonel seemed to waver. "Well, Lieutenant Nolan is actually in command of the escort," he temporized. "The decision is up to him. But to answer your question, I won't object to your going."

"There you are, Lieutenant," Cindy said. "Colonel Hatfield won't object, so I can go with you. What time should I be here tomorrow morning?"

Nolan put up a final struggle. "Mrs. Kerr, those rifles and ammunition are heavy, and you must have considerable baggage with you. I can't overload those wagons, and—"

"I'll leave my baggage here," Cindy said quickly, "and take only a bag containing a few necessities. The rest can be sent for later."

Having run out of objections, Nolan looked in vain to the colonel for assistance.

"I can't help you, son," he said. "Looks like we've met our match."

Nolan gave in as gracefully as he could. "Very well, Mrs. Kerr. Be here an hour before sunrise, if you would."

Not waiting for him to change his mind, Cindy thanked him and quickly left, eager to see the last of Yuma.

By the time the sun rose the next morning, the column to Fort Peck had crossed the Colorado River and was well east of Yuma, moving along a narrow, rutted dirt track. Cindy was seated next to the driver of the first wagon, a young private named Johnson, and the rest of the column rode in a defensive posture around the wagons, with a dozen men on each side and the remainder divided ahead and behind. The ride was bumpy, but the miles passed swiftly, with the column traveling at a canter part of the time, then slowing to a walk until the horses and mules caught their breath.

The arid landscape was almost deserted, with only an occasional ranch house, built like a tiny fort, set back in the hills from the road. There was a stark, austere beauty nevertheless, which Cindy tried to capture on her sketch pad whenever the column slowed to a walk.

Johnson was so awed by Cindy that he was silent at first, but gradually he became talkative, and his obvious desire to imitate his older colleagues by resolutely chewing a cheekful of tobacco—so much that it nearly gagged him—was comical to observe.

There was a brief stop at midday for a cold meal from tin cans, and then the journey resumed. Twilight thickened to darkness, but the column continued on, for Nolan wanted to set up camp farther ahead in a shallow arroyo that was easy to defend. Finally the wagons turned off the road and bumped over the uneven ground as they went into the arroyo.

Within a few minutes, the animals had been picketed, guards were posted, and fires blazed up. Coffee began boiling in large pots, its nutty scent blending with the appetizing smells of bacon frying and beans heating in pans. Cindy shared a fire with Nolan, his sergeant in command—a veteran named Hoskins—and several corporals.

While they were eating, Cindy found out that Sergeant Hoskins had been on numerous patrols with Reed and knew him well. The sergeant told her about one of the patrols and their clash with the comanchero leader Calusa Jim. Hoskins clearly was proud of Reed, giving him full credit for the heavy casualties inflicted upon the renegades.

"I would have rode straight into 'em," he admitted bluntly, mopping up bacon grease with a chunk of bread. "But Lieutenant Kerr outfoxed that Calusa Jim. Didn't he write to you about that, ma'am?"

"No," Cindy admitted. "This is the first I've heard about it, Sergeant."

"Well, it figures," Hoskins chuckled. "Your husband ain't one to blow his own horn—is he, Lieutenant?"

Nolan agreed emphatically. "And what's more, if that

197

patrol had been armed with these new Winchesters, those comancheros would've been cut up even worse."

Hoskins concurred, and over a second cup of coffee the men discussed the remainder of the journey to Fort Peck. The column had almost reached the halfway point, and they expected to arrive at their destination the following evening, unless a wagon broke down or some other mishap occurred.

The fires burned down, and the men around them wrapped themselves in their blankets and went to sleep. Hoskins and the corporals shifted the crates in one of the wagons to make a place for Cindy to sleep, and although she was weary from the long day, anticipation of seeing Reed and her new home kept her awake for a time. When she finally dozed off, it seemed only moments later that Hoskins was making the rounds to wake the camp.

After a hasty breakfast of leftover coffee and bread, the column formed up and moved out of the arroyo in the cold, early morning darkness. The sun was rising when they passed a cairn of stones marking the halfway point between the two forts. A few soldiers began cheering, but Hoskins quickly snapped at them to shut up and watch the hills.

Several miles farther along the road a huge butte loomed into view, and Johnson told Cindy it was called Sandstone Butte. It stood immediately to the right of the road, which threaded between it and a vast, brushy slope rising to a ridge opposite.

The butte was spectacularly beautiful, its layered colors like the rich, deep shades of a sunset. As the column reached it, Cindy took in the scene with wonder, pondering how to capture it in a sketch. The colors would be lost, but they were less important than the immense size of the butte, which made the column seem like a line of ants.

Her reverie was abruptly shattered by the sound of echoing gunfire. Halfway up the ridge opposite the butte, some twenty ragged-looking men leaped into view and, firing rifles and pistols, rushed down the slope toward the column.

For a moment, Cindy was frozen in shock. The soldiers on her left were already shooting back, and Sergeant Hoskins, his voice ringing out over the gunfire, led the rear guard forward to defend the wagons.

Private Johnson was also momentarily stunned, his young face pale and his eyes wide; but then a corporal rode by, waving a hat, and slapped a lead mule with it, bellowing at the private to get the wagon away from danger. Johnson snapped the reins and shouted at the mules—which was hardly necessary, for the frightened animals had already lurched into a run—and as the wagon careened along the road, with soldiers riding alongside it and firing, Cindy clutched the seat and gazed up at the men on the slope.

The column's alert return fire had already taken a devastating toll, and the charge had been stopped, with more than half the attackers sprawled on the ground. The remainder were fleeing back up the slope or taking cover behind brush and boulders.

Ominously, more puffs of gunpowder smoke began rising from higher up on the slope as Cindy watched, and as the crackle of gunfire increased, she realized that only a small contingent of the attackers had been positioned near the road. And apparently they had been concentrating their fire on the column's vanguard, where a few soldiers had been wounded; but now bullets began slamming into the wagon, and spouts of dust and dirt erupted from the road and its verges. Cindy saw a soldier tumble from his horse, and another horse racing by suddenly collapsed, it and its rider rolling along the ground. At almost the same instant, a bullet struck one of the lead mules, and its legs folded. The other mules stumbled and were dragged down screaming, and Cindy clung to the seat as the wagon swerved and veered wildly, tilting up on two wheels and almost rolling over before it finally slid to a stop.

Johnson sat there, dumbfounded, until Cindy grabbed

the reins from him. "Cut the injured mule loose and untangle them!" she shouted. "I'll try to hold them for you."

The young soldier sprang into action, leaping down to the wagon tongue and pulling out his knife. Cindy gripped the reins tightly, praying for him to hurry as bullets whizzed past her. To her relief, two other soldiers had dismounted to help, and the mules started to climb back to their feet.

The other wagon had not passed them, so Cindy knew that it had also stopped. She glanced over her shoulder to confirm this, and when she looked ahead again, she saw Johnson's hat fly off, a red streak growing where a bullet had pierced his skull.

Cindy gasped and watched in horror as another soldier pulled him over the mules and laid him on the ground, for he was dead. Meanwhile, no progress was being made unhitching the wounded mule, so Cindy forced herself into action. She jerked back the brake lever, wrapped the reins around it, and began climbing down to the wagon tongue to help the soldiers.

Just as she stepped down, another mule was hit by a bullet. Its screaming set the other animals rearing and kicking, and Cindy almost lost her footing as the wagon lurched under her. But Lieutenant Nolan had reined up beside her, and he reached for her. Cindy put her arms around his neck, and he lifted her over a plunging mule and put her safely down beside the wagon.

In the midst of the pandemonium, Nolan seemed as calm as could be, even though he was hatless and the shoulder of his tunic was stained with blood. "They've stopped us here, Mrs. Kerr," he said. "Stay behind the wagon, then get under it as soon as the team is unhitched."

Cindy crouched behind the wagon as Nolan rode away, shouting orders to soldiers. The mules had already been unhitched from the other wagon, and soldiers were pushing it forward. It bumped into the rear of Cindy's wagon, and then the soldiers went to free the first team. Cindy helped other soldiers carry and drag the injured behind the wagons, and the badly wounded mules and horses were being led to the exposed side of the wagon and shot, in order to create a barricade.

In a matter of minutes, all the soldiers were under or around the wagons. Those who had come through the hail of bullets unscathed or with only minor wounds took position behind the dead animals and fired up at the men on the slope, and Cindy crawled about and did what she could for the wounded. As she tied a strip of her petticoat around a trooper's blood-soaked arm, Nolan and Hoskins were a few feet away, discussing the situation.

The two agreed that the comancheros would be unable to encircle the wagons, since the butte offered no cover, and the road gave an open field of fire on both sides. However, Hoskins pointed out, it was also impossible to send for help, because there was no concealed escape route. The sergeant looked grim.

"This is Calusa Jim's bunch," he said. "I caught sight of him on the slope."

"Yes, it's hard to mistake that beard and coat," Nolan agreed. "I estimate there are over a hundred men on that slope."

"If they get those Winchesters, they'll be twice as dangerous," Hoskins said. "Way I figure it, we could either burn them, or use 'em ourselves."

"We still have time," Nolan answered after a pause. "We'll burn them if we have to, but not until we've fired every last round we have, by God. Have the men knock the floorboards out of the wagons, and get those Winchesters and ammunition passed out."

"Yes, sir!" Hoskins replied, and slid away. Only seconds later, soldiers were prying at the floorboards, and to Cindy's relief a medical kit was the first item to be pulled through the gap. Just then, a bullet from the slope knocked splinters from a board above her head, and looking up, she saw that the comancheros were now much closer. Bullets were hammering into the wagons in a steady, ominous drumming.

A trooper called out in triumph as the floorboards spread apart and a case of ammunition slipped down. Men under the other wagon were dragging the canvas-covered crates down, opening them, and passing out the rifles, while some of the wounded pitched in by loading the new weapons for their companions who were busy firing.

The comancheros kept moving closer, but now the men on the firing line were being handed the small, slender Winchesters. The whoops and jeers that had begun rising on the slope were drowned in the louder, sharper report of the Winchesters as two and then three of the weapons began firing.

Soon, as more rifles joined in, the sound rose to a deafening roar. Through the thick, acrid gunpowder smoke, Cindy glimpsed comancheros fleeing back up the slope and saw three of them fall. The firing gradually diminished, with the comancheros moving back to a safe distance.

Lieutenant Nolan moved among the men, positioning them better and reorganizing the defenses. All of the canteens and food were put in one place, boxes of ammunition were stacked along the firing line, and the wounded were moved to the edge of the wagons facing the butte. Cindy was rebandaging a corporal's head wound when Nolan approached. He had blood on a trouser leg as well as his shoulder.

"I'll take care of you next, Lieutenant," she said.

"They're just scratches," he said. "You're doing a good job, Mrs. Kerr, and the men appreciate it. As soon as we're overdue at the fort, they'll send out a patrol to look for us."

His tone lacked conviction, and Cindy noticed that he had an extra pistol under his belt. She moved closer to him and spoke in a low voice. "Exactly what are our chances, Lieutenant?"

He hesitated, then met her gaze squarely. "They could be much better, ma'am. I think you had better keep this with you."

Looking at the pistol, Cindy saw that it had but a

single bullet in it. She nodded her acknowledgment, pushed the pistol under the belt of her dress, and turned back to the wounded man she had been treating.

The light of another dull, overcast day was coming through the cabin windows when Toby Holt opened his eyes.

A headache was pounding in his temples, and a sharp pain stabbed the left side of his chest each time he breathed. When he tried to move he felt as weak as a child, and his arm seemed like an immense weight as he lifted a hand to push back his hair.

The cabin door slammed, the girl coming in with an armload of firewood. She was wearing a thick bearskin coat that hung down to the floor. She dumped the wood into a box beside the hearth, then smiled at him. "So you finally woke up."

"How long have I been here?"

"Two days," she replied, shrugging out of her coat and putting it aside. "But you've been so fevery that I 'spect you don't remember." She knelt beside him and put a cold hand on his forehead. "But it looks like you've got over it now, ain't you?"

"Yes. My name's Toby Holt."

"I know," she said. "You talked up a storm while you was fevery. My name is Eileen Culley, and my brothers are Zeke, Zach, Zeb, and Zadoc."

"What's your father's name?"

"Pa," she replied. She moved a kettle onto the coals of the fire. "But it would probably be better for you to call him Mr. Culley, like some do. Zeke shot a wild pig, and I've boiled its liver down to soup. I'm going to have to feed you up some and get them wounds cleaned out for you tonight. If I don't, you ain't never going to heal up good. I 'spect you want to get even with them varmints who shot you."

The last comment made Toby suddenly mindful of the danger facing Fair Oaks. He thought about the additional men of Sewell's that had unexpectedly appeared, and about his own inability to warn Alex and the others of the peril. In the back of his mind was an even greater threat, something he thought he recalled hearing Sewell and the other men discussing, but the memory continued to elude him. With growing anxiety, he wondered how long it would be before he would be able to return to Fair Oaks.

As if reading his mind, Eileen said that her brothers had found his horse in the forest and put it in the barn with the family mules. "Your saddle, rifle, and t'other things are in the storeroom," she added, nodding toward the door. "My brothers said that's a might pretty rifle you have."

It seemed possible to him that the last remark was a less than subtle hint as to how he might be able to repay the family for their help. "I'm not a poor man," he said. "I'll be more than glad to pay for what you and your family are doing for me."

The girl suddenly looked much older than her sixteen or so years. Her bold features, more handsome than pretty, flushed with anger, and her gaze became cold and hard. "We don't take no pay for helping them in need," she said.

Realizing he had misinterpreted her meaning, Toby apologized. Still angry, Eileen took a bowl off a shelf and stamped to the hearth. "City folk has got some odd ways," she murmured to herself. She turned toward Toby. "We may be poor, but we have enough money to get by, what with the furs that Pa and my brothers catch." Seeing Toby's discomfiture, she relented, her anger fading as quickly as it had appeared. "I expect that Alexandra is your sweetheart, ain't she?"

Toby was surprised to hear the name. "Yes," he admitted. "Did I talk about her while I was feverish?"

"No more than all the time," Eileen replied, her eyes twinkling. She fingered a string around her neck and pulled it out from under her collar to show him a thin gold band that hung on it. "I've got a beau, too, see? His name is Clem Siler, and he lives over in the next hollow. He already has a cabin built for us, and he's bought a team of mules."

"When do you intend to get married?"

Eileen sighed heavily as she filled the bowl from the kettle on the fire. "Whenever one of my brothers gets married, or Pa finds hisself another wife. I can't leave them here to shift for theirselves, can I? There's plenty of women about who would have them, but the men in this family are all as slow as Christmas molasses when it comes to courting."

Eileen placed the bowl on the hearth, gently helped Toby to a sitting position, then sat down on a stool and began spooning the rich, thick soup into his mouth. While liver was not one of Toby's favorite foods, the soup also contained onions, potatoes, and carrots and was well seasoned with pepper. Once he started eating, Toby found that he was ravenously hungry, and Eileen refilled the bowl several times. However, their fitful conversation while he was eating did nothing to improve his state of mind. He brought up the subject of when he might be able to leave, and Eileen was certain that it would be at least a week after she tended to his wounds.

The food made Toby irresistibly sleepy, and while Eileen washed the bowl and moved about at her chores, he dozed off. At midday, he woke again when Eileen's father and brothers came into the cabin.

The men put their rifles on a wooden rack inside the door, and Toby saw why his Sharps had stirred admiration among them. Their rifles were well oiled, clearly kept in good condition, but they were old, obsolete weapons. Toby greeted the men and received silent nods in reply. All of them listened with evident interest as Eileen talked about his condition, but they said nothing.

After taking off their coats, they sat down around a heavy, homemade table on the other side of the room. Their midday meal, served by Eileen, was cornbread and the liver soup, and the five men looked at their bowls in glum, silent dissatisfaction.

They ate slowly and with evident distaste, and the soup occasioned the first remark Toby had heard any of them make. "When I shot that pig," one of the brothers said, "there was plenty of pork around the liver. What happened to it, Eileen?"

"It's hanging in the smokehouse," she replied cheerfully, filling a bowl for Toby. "And a pan is hanging right there. You fry up all you want to, but you fetch your own firewood, and you be sure to wash that pan and put it back like you found it. And if you get in my road while I'm setting about supper, then I ain't going to fix none."

Silence fell again. Toby winced with pain as Eileen put an arm around his shoulders and lifted him to a sitting position. While he was eating, the five men finished their meal and left the cabin.

After washing the dishes, Eileen put on her bearskin coat and went out. She returned a few minutes later with a pork shoulder, which she put on a spit in the fireplace. As it began roasting, filling the cabin with a delicious aroma, Eileen took Toby's shirt off a peg in the corner. She had washed it, which had removed only part of the bloodstains, and there was a hole in it made by the bullet that had traveled along his ribs. Shaking her head and murmuring about the shame of ruining such an expensive garment, she sat down with a sewing basket to mend it. While she worked, Toby talked to her, trying to get a clear idea of where the cabin was in relation to the place where he had been ambushed. Eventually his eyelids became heavy again, and he dropped off to sleep. It was early evening when he woke, and for the first time he felt much stronger. With Eileen helping him, he moved to the side of the hearth and sat up against the wall. He was ravenously hungry again, his appetite whetted by the scent of the pork sizzling over the hot coals. A short time later the men returned, the two hounds preceding them into the cabin.

Mr. Culley nodded in satisfaction at seeing Toby sitting up, and they all seemed pleased at the dinner being prepared. Eileen dished up the food, then served Toby at the hearth. The food was delicious, and when dinner was finished, the five men filled corncob pipes and lit them as Eileen washed the dishes. When she was done, she heated another kettle of water, took out bandage rolls made from worn-out clothing, then sat at the table and sharpened a knife.

Her earlier remarks about attending to his wounds had suggested it would be an ordeal, and Toby steeled himself. She poured him a generous drink of moonshine whiskey, then helped herself to an equally large portion. She started with the wound on his temple, first cutting the hair away from it with the knife, then washing the area and rinsing the wound with whiskey.

It burned like fire, and Toby's head was throbbing unmercifully by the time she had finished and tied a fresh bandage in place. She urged him to drink more of the whiskey, then had him remove the nightshirt and started on his chest. An ugly purple welt of clotted blood under the skin marked where the bullet had traveled around his ribs and lodged itself. Eileen cut the entire length of the wound open, removed the bullet and washed the clotted blood out with hot water, then dabbed the whole with whiskey. When she had finished and wrapped a bandage around his chest, Toby was light-headed from the pain, and beads of sweat were trickling down his face.

The five men and the two hounds had watched the entire process, and the men refilled their pipes when it was over. Eileen helped Toby back into his nightshirt, then started asking him questions about himself. It was obviously for the benefit of her silent father and brothers, for she brought up matters that Toby had already discussed with her during the day.

He told them about himself and his family in Portland, then talked about the trouble at Fair Oaks, which he had not gone into previously. The story evoked another flash of anger from Eileen.

"City folk has got some odd ways," she remarked, not for the first time. "Why ain't somebody already shot that Sewell man for being the copperhead he is?"

"Well, there's such a thing as law and order," Toby said. "You can't go around—"

"There's such a thing as right and wrong," she shot back. "When a man don't do nothing but live off'n others like a bloodsucking leech, he belongs in the ground."

Her father and brothers murmured in agreement, but Toby shook his head. "The law and justice don't always coincide," he said, "but the law is the law. The only way for people to live together in harmony is through respect for the law."

"*You* ain't living in harmony," she pointed out. "Or else you are, but he ain't. What are you going to do when you find him?"

"I'll at least try to bring him in to be arrested," Toby said, letting his listeners draw their own conclusions.

Eileen seemed at least partly mollified by the reply. Presently the men nodded good night to Toby and went to their rooms, and Eileen sat down at the hearth with her sewing basket and mending. Watching her, Toby was touched by the tireless, dedicated way in which she went about everything, and he again thanked her for what she was doing for him.

"I don't mind seeing to you," she said. "Besides, it's good to have someone to talk to. It's almost like having a woman about."

Toby smiled, but he detected the wistful, lonely note in her voice. "I hope that Clem Siler talks to you more than your father and brothers do."

"Oh, he does," Eileen replied quickly. "Not as much as a woman, but he talks plenty. Clem is really nice to me—lookee here." She reached into her sewing basket, took out a tiny candy box, and opened it. Inside were a bright scarf and several colorful hair ribbons that were neatly folded. "He bought these for me the last time he sold some furs."

"They're very pretty," Toby said.

Eileen carefully closed the box. "Yes, they are, ain't they? He said he was going to get me something pretty for Christmas when he gets a chance to go to Frenchman's Creek again."

The name was remotely familiar to Toby—then suddenly he remembered: It was the place Sewell and the others had mentioned—the place where they meant to take Alexandra after they kidnapped her! Speechless with shock for a moment, Toby thought furiously as Eileen placidly began darning a sock. Finally he spoke.

"Where is Frenchman's Creek, Eileen?"

"Oh, a fair piece from here," she replied, glancing up. "You go back to the road where my brothers found you, turn right, then bear left at all the forks. On a middling good mule it's about a day's travel."

She resumed sewing, and Toby stared unseeing into the fire, thinking about the days that had passed since he had been shot, and the distance to Fair Oaks. Within the next day or two, the woman he loved was going to be kidnapped and taken to somewhere in the vicinity of the town that Eileen had described, and he was absolutely powerless to prevent it.

XII

Sergeant Jake Burns, in command of the telegraph repair detail from Fort Yuma, let his horse pick its way across the rocky, broken terrain as he checked the guard posts set out in a perimeter around his camp. A guard in a mesquite thicket emerged from the shadows of the trees and signaled that everything was quiet.

Burns waved to the man and turned his horse toward the next guard post. Escorting repairmen along the telegraph lines was a task he disliked, if only because a cavalry unit had to remain mobile in order to defend itself, and the repairmen were like an anchor. And this time progress had been maddeningly slow, for instead of simply cutting the lines, the comancheros had chopped down three adjacent poles and then burned them.

The next guard post was located in boulders halfway up a rocky hill. Burns exchanged waves with the guard and continued up the slope. Half his men were assigned to guard duty, and the other half were helping the repairmen, and from the hill he could observe the work in progress. One pole had already been replaced with a spliced-together spare, and a second and third were ready to be raised.

Burns was reflecting in satisfaction that the job would soon be completed, when he heard a whisper of sound in the distance that seemed to be gunfire. It was coming from the direction of the Fort Peck road, which paralleled the telegraph line, and he rode around the hill in order to hear better.

Reining up again, he took off his hat, put it behind an ear, and listened closely. When the wind subsided momentarily, he heard the distinct sound of many guns firing. A furious battle was raging somewhere in the vicinity of Sandstone Butte, several miles away.

He pondered for a moment, thinking about the troop of cavalry and two wagons he had spotted moving along the road to Fort Yuma two days before. It was possible that they could be returning to Fort Peck and had been ambushed by a large band of comancheros.

Burns spurred his horse and rode quickly back around the hill to the guard in the boulders. The man stepped into the open to see what was the matter.

Burns reined up to a skidding halt. "Go around the perimeter and tell all the guards to return to camp on the double," he ordered. "When you get to the camp, tell Corporal Kelly to take command and put the men into a defensive position until I get back."

The guard ran off, and Burns turned his horse toward the Fort Peck road. The animal picked its way down the hill, sliding in the loose dirt, then accelerated into a pounding run when they reached level ground.

Thirty minutes later, after he had ridden over several low hills, Sandstone Butte came into view ahead. The gunfire was loud now, yet Burns was puzzled, because he was certain that none of the rifles were Spencers. He rode up the next slope but halted and dismounted before he reached the top.

Carrying his binoculars, he climbed the rest of the way, being careful not to silhouette himself against the skyline. When the wagons and the brushy slope beyond the road came into view, he lay down and surveyed the scene through the binoculars. It didn't take him long to figure out why none of the rifles were Spencers.

211

He had heard rumors about the new Winchesters, and the wagons, he reflected, must have been making a trip to Yuma to pick them up. Either the comancheros had somehow found out about the rifles or had simply decided that the wagons were a tempting target.

Scanning the terrain with the binoculars, Burns estimated the number of comancheros and realized that the men at the wagons were in a hopeless position, outnumbered and pinned down. As he started to lower the binoculars, a bright spot of color among the blue uniforms caught his eye, and he focused again and saw that a woman was moving among the wounded. He immediately thought of the young officer's wife who had wanted to accompany his squad to Fort Peck. Cursing to himself, he hurried back down the hill to his horse.

Alternating between a run and a canter, he rode back to the camp as fast as he dared push his horse. The men were a line of rifles and hats along the edge of a low ridge, and when he reined up they gathered around him.

He motioned impatiently for silence and addressed the foreman of the repairmen: "Can you contact either Yuma or Peck on them telegraph lines?"

"No, I can't," the man replied. "Nobody told me to bring the transmitting equipment. What's wrong, Sergeant?"

"Nobody *told* you?" Burns muttered an oath to himself, then thought for a moment, weighing possible courses of action. Briefly he explained the situation. "They won't be able to hold out much longer," he concluded. "They're pinned down, with about twenty effectives left, and they're outnumbered three or four to one."

"It's well over twenty miles to Fort Peck," his corporal put in, looking up at the sky. "And there ain't that much daylight—"

Burns, however, was already pointing to a private, Thomas Lambert. Barely more than a youth and weighing little over a hundred pounds, Lambert was an excellent horseman. "You. Saddle a good horse and pick out two spares to lead. Move!" As the man ran toward the picketed horses, Burns pointed to the two laziest, most unreliable men in the detail. "You and you. Take these civilians up in them rocks over there. If nobody comes for you within two days, walk to Fort Peck."

"Only two men?" the foreman exclaimed. "Sergeant Burns, this squad was sent out here to protect us, and you can't—"

"I don't need you to tell me my job!" Burns cut him off angrily. "I was sent out to get them telegraph lines working, but now I've got a more important problem to deal with!" He turned to the corporal. "We'll get saddled up and go on over to Sandstone Butte, but there ain't no hurry, seeing as there ain't enough of us to scare them varmints off. As long as we get there by dark will be plenty of time."

"Yes, sir, Jake," the corporal acknowledged. "Are we going to join the men at the wagons?"

"If they can hold out, we'll wait for the relief from Peck," Burns said. "If they can't, then we'll join the fight. The main thing is to keep the comancheros from getting them new Winchesters."

Lambert rode up a little while later, leading two spare horses. He received instructions and advice from Sergeant Burns, then set off without further delay. At seventeen years of age, Lambert was a veteran of two years in the cavalry, and he had experienced many arduous rides during that time. None had ever approached this one in importance, however, and he looked forward to it with apprehension as well as with pride because he had been the one chosen.

As the horses cantered eastward, Lambert glanced up at the sun occasionally. When he estimated that an hour had passed, he reined up and moved his saddle to one of the spare horses. Everything seemed very quiet after he stopped, the panting of the horses the only sound, and he had an uncomfortable feeling of hostile eyes watching him, even though he was still a safe distance from the road.

After several hours, the unremitting pace had taken

its toll on all three of the horses. Foam dripped from their mouths and lather streaked their flanks. Lambert's own back and legs were aching. He began moving his saddle from horse to horse at shorter intervals, and he used his spurs to make the animals maintain a fast canter.

During late afternoon he cut over to the road, which he had been paralleling at a cautious distance. His heart sank as he heard a metallic clanking in the hoofbeats of one of the horses, and when he stopped to move his saddle again, he inspected the animals' feet and untethered the horse with the loose shoe. He hoped it would make its way along the road to the fort.

By sunset, Lambert and the two remaining horses were almost exhausted. He continued spurring the horses along the road until twilight thickened into impenetrable darkness; then he slowed to a walk, reclining in the saddle and waiting for the moon to rise and illumine the road.

An hour later, shortly after he had spurred the horse to a canter in the dim moonlight, he saw a dark spot on the road and started to pull the reins to one side, but he was too late. The horse stepped into the deep rut, fell heavily, and Lambert was suddenly tumbling through the air.

He jarred into the rock-strewn shoulder of the road, and sharp pain raced through his left arm and his head. For a moment he wavered on the verge of unconsciousness, but he forced himself to climb to his feet, and he staggered back onto the road. Blood was streaming into his eye from a deep cut on his forehead, and his left arm was unresponsive—probably broken, he decided.

The horse had climbed to its feet and was keeping its weight off its right foreleg. Feeling the foreleg with his good hand, Lambert found that it was sprained, not broken. He removed the saddle and bridle from the animal, and after hiding them in the brush, he pulled himself up onto the last horse.

Without stirrups to lift part of his weight, he bounced heavily as he urged the animal to a canter, and each jolt caused his injured arm to throb excruciatingly. The horse's breathing became labored after a short time, and Lambert was forced to use his spurs almost constantly.

The animal gave out suddenly and teetered to a stop, trembling on its legs and its sides heaving as it panted. Lambert slid down and patted the horse. In the moonlight, the flat terrain looked all the same, but he knew he had to be within a few miles of his goal. Gritting his teeth, he began running along the road.

The bouncing of his arm was almost unbearable, and as he ran he fashioned his neckerchief into a sling. Then the pain was less intense, but it still threatened to make him faint. His legs were already aching with fatigue, and his steps became heavy and sluggish.

The fear of failing, however, goaded him on, and time passed in a blur. Through a haze of exhaustion, he recognized the features of a shallow valley and knew he was within reach of the fort, which was on the next rise ahead. After what seemed an eternity, the road became wider, leading up a slope.

He could see the lights of the fort and the shadows of its walls in the moonlight. He tried to call out, but his voice was a hoarse, breathless whisper. He reached for his holster, and the pistol felt enormously heavy as he dragged it out and lifted it over his head. The shot rang out in the darkness, echoing back from the fort, and the reaction was immediate. Voices bellowed for the corporal of the guard, and the powerful carbide lamps above the gate flared to life, their reflectors casting a blinding glare along the road.

The gate rumbled open, and men ran out. Lambert ducked his head against the light, staggered and weaved along the road, and then arms were helping him, half carrying and half dragging him toward the gate.

They put him down against the wall and hovered over him in a babble of puzzled voices, asking him his unit and what he was doing at the fort. Lambert tried to reply, but he was unable to speak, his breath coming in hoarse gasps.

Then the men moved back as a stern voice rang out, and a lone figure knelt beside him with a canteen.

The officer of the day, Lieutenant Reed Kerr, had heard the pistol shot and seen the light of the carbide lamps through the orderly room windows. He had crossed the quadrangle toward the gate, to find the knot of soldiers gathered around the slumped private. He had ordered the men back and borrowed a corporal's canteen.

After a moment, the man drank, licked his lips, and identified himself in a weak whisper. Finding strength, he began relating what his sergeant had told him.

Reed had already suspected the worst, because he knew that Nolan had gone to bring back a full issue of new Winchesters. He gently questioned Lambert, finding out all he knew about the situation. His heart jumped when Lambert mentioned there was a woman with the wagons.

Fighting his growing panic, Reed spoke in the same quiet voice as before: "Did he have any idea of who she is?"

"He didn't say, sir, but I think she's an officer's wife. There was one who wanted to come here with us, but she couldn't."

There was no doubt at all in Reed's mind that the woman was Cindy. He stood up. "You did very well indeed, trooper. Corporal, have him taken to the dispensary—and wake up a bugler, on the double."

Reed walked rapidly back across the quadrangle. On the porch in front of the fort commander's quarters he saw the red glow of a cheroot, indicating that Major Marcus Fargo had been awakened by the activity at the gate.

The major had pulled his coat around his shoulders. An imperturbably calm man, he returned Reed's salute and puffed on his cheroot in silence as Reed repeated what he had learned. "The sergeant said there is a woman at the wagons," Reed added as he finished, "and I'm positive that it's Cindy."

The major shook his head in anger and regret. "Considering what's involved," he said, "the relief column should be a full company. Let's hope there's still time."

"I'd like permission to lead it, sir."

The major puffed on his cheroot, glanced at the bugler as the man ran up to the steps and stood at attention, then nodded. "Very well, Reed. Take Company A."

"Thank you, sir!" Reed saluted and turned to the bugler. "Sound Boots and Saddles."

The man raced away into the darkness as Reed hurried toward his quarters to get his saber. A moment later, from the flagpole in the center of the quadrangle, the penetrating notes of the bugle shattered the quiet of the fort. Lights began showing in the windows of the barracks as men scrambled from their cots and shouted at each other.

By the time Reed emerged from his quarters, fastening his saber onto his pistol belt, the fort had come alive. Sergeants and corporals bellowed orders, and men were shrugging into coats and buckling on pistol belts as they raced to the stables. Reed threaded his way through the bedlam to get his own horse.

Back on the parade ground, the company first sergeant was waiting for him. A tall man named Murphy, he listened intently as Reed explained the situation. They took their places at the head of the almost-assembled formation, and gradually the pandemonium faded into order, with saddles creaking and gear rattling as horses stamped impatiently, in two lines abreast.

Reed rode over to the commander's quarters, where the major was still standing on the porch, smoking his cheroot. "Company A is ready to move out, sir," he said.

"Then move out, Lieutenant," the major replied, returning his salute. "And I pray to God that everything turns out well for you, Reed."

The remark, Reed knew, was a reference to Cindy. "Thank you, sir," he said, and wheeled his horse back across the quadrangle. "First sergeant and guidon bearer, post!" he shouted. "Company, right turn! Forward at the canter, ho!"

With practiced precision, the ranks became a double column headed by the sergeant and guidon bearer. Reed led them at a canter out the gate and into the night.

As if sensing the excitement, Reed's horse fought the bit and tried to run. Reed, too, wanted to race headlong down the road, but he knew that the horses and the men had to be in condition to fight at the end of the ride. He held the reins tightly until his mount gradually warmed up in the cold night air and stopped fighting the bit.

As the troop moved along the road, Reed checked his watch to estimate when they would arrive at Sandstone Butte. He feared that Nolan and his men would be unable to hold out for very long the next morning, if indeed they had not been overrun already. But as the hours and the miles passed, with the horses fresh and making good time, it appeared that they would arrive shortly after sunrise.

Inexorably, Reed's thoughts kept returning to Cindy. For weeks he had been anticipating her arrival and making preparations for her. He had cleaned their quarters, scrubbing the rooms until they were spotless, and had even found a few pieces of pottery and bright rugs to decorate the otherwise spartan rooms.

During the months they had been apart, a vital force had been missing from his life. Reed deeply loved Cindy—had loved her for years before they had married—and to his mind she was a perfect wife. A few officers' wives had refused to come to the remote outpost of Fort Peck, but Cindy had been eager to join him. In every way possible, she had done as much as the most demanding husband could expect.

What made that particularly significant to Reed was that he knew Cindy's deepest secret. Through living with her, he had gradually learned to interpret the smallest nuances of her behavior, and he had long ago come to the conclusion that although she had married him, she still loved Henry Blake. But now, in her time of peril, Reed prayed he would have an opportunity to prove his devotion to her, to repay her for her unstinting duty toward him.

The first light of dawn touched the horizon behind the column, slowly dissolving the thick shadows along the road into gray twilight. Reed knew that Sandstone Butte would come into sight over the next rise, and he shouted a command to slow to a walk. As the noise of the column died down, he felt an immense sense of relief, for in the distance he could distinctly hear volleys of gunfire. Nolan and his men had held out through the night.

"Sergeant Murphy!" Reed called.

"Yes, sir!"

"When we breast the hill, we'll go straight in with a flank charge. Have the men ready for it."

The sergeant reined his horse around and shouted back to the column. "Lock and load! Check your sabers!"

A metallic rattle rose behind Reed. A minute later, the column was nearing the rise in the road, and he could see the top of Sandstone Butte in the dawn light. Loosening his saber in its scabbard, Reed urgently hoped that Nolan and his men would be able to hold out for a short time longer.

Dawn found Cindy preparing herself to face death with courage. The night had seemed endless, with sporadic gunfire claiming an occasional victim, and the comancheros had caught two soldiers who had tried to slip away to go for help. The screams of the men as they had been tortured to death still echoed in Cindy's mind.

Lying behind a wagon wheel and peering over the dead mules at the slope beyond, she flinched inwardly each time a bullet slammed into the wagon. Nolan and Hoskins were a few feet away, talking quietly, and as dawn brightened, Cindy could see for herself what they were discussing: The comancheros had moved closer during the night.

Puffs of gunpowder smoke were now rising from no

more than two hundred feet up the boulder-and-brush-strewn slope. At the closer, lower range, the rifle fire of the comancheros was much more accurate, and many of the bullets were coming under the wagons. A dozen soldiers were on the front line with Winchesters, trying to drive the comancheros back, but their fire was having no visible effect on the well-hidden renegades.

A few minutes before, Hoskins had ordered four soldiers to move the wounded from under the other wagon. The four, all of whom were wounded themselves, were dragging their comrades to near where Cindy was lying, and now she realized why they were being moved. Nolan intended to have the Winchesters stacked under the other wagon, which would be burned on top of the valuable weapons.

Cindy slid closer to Nolan and Hoskins, to hear what they were discussing. Hoskins was speaking.

". . . and from their rate of fire, the men think Calusa Jim is waiting for sunrise."

"That's my guess, too," Nolan agreed. "The only question now is whether he'll charge us or move in gradually. After what happened yesterday, I don't think he'll be foolish enough to rush us again. If I were in his position, I'd tried to get more men low enough on the hill to be able to fire clear under the wagons."

The sergeant nodded slowly. "We might want to pile some more brush under that other wagon, just in case, sir, so it'll go up quicker."

Nolan shook his head. "If they see what we're doing, it might just goad them on." He glanced over to the other wagon. "The men have almost finished moving the wounded. Have the Spencers loaded and on the firing line, ready to use. And post a couple of men to be ready to gather up the Winchesters and put them under the other wagon."

The sergeant's face was expressionless as he crawled away. The pistol with a single bullet in it seemed enormously heavy in Cindy's belt as she moved to a more protected position under the axle and peered out at the slope again. The light was brightening into full dawn, and she could now clearly see the bodies of many comancheros scattered on the slope. But scores of them remained, and their gunfire seemed to be increasing.

A soldier at the end of the firing line, only a few yards from Cindy, scowled and muttered an oath as a corporal crawled past and told him to load his Spencer and be ready to hand over the Winchester.

Suddenly the wagon was struck by a fusillade of bullets, as a volley rang out from higher on the slope. The soldiers aimed higher to return the fire, until the sergeant's voice rose over the gunfire: "That's covering fire for the closer ones! Keep your aim low, and watch for them moving up!"

The exchange of gunfire rapidly increased to a deafening roar, and Cindy knew that what Lieutenant Nolan had predicted was happening. Instead of charging toward the wagons, the comancheros farther up the slope were creeping closer and into position to fire volleys under the wagons at point-blank range.

Bullets were drumming into the wagon and ricocheting all around her, but Cindy lifted her head and peeked out cautiously. Some of the comancheros were much closer, and she saw brush moving within a hundred feet of the wagons.

A corporal crawled between her and the soldier in front of her, tapped the man's shoulder, and reached for his Winchester. The soldier swore but handed the rifle over and picked up his Spencer. The corporal moved on to the next soldier, and as he gathered up the small, light rifles, the slower rate of gunfire from the firing line was immediately apparent to Cindy.

With fewer bullets flying at them, the comancheros increased their own fire, and it also became more accurate. The soldier in front of Cindy jerked and rolled over, a bloodstain spreading on the side of his chest. She crawled toward the man to try to help him, then saw that he was beyond help, shot through the heart. She picked up his rifle and began firing it blindly into the brush.

When she ran out of bullets, she looked around for an ammunition box. The scene under the wagon was nightmarish, thick with sulfurous smoke and with wounded men everywhere, some of them dragging themselves to the firing line. Cindy knew that the last, desperate moments had come. Nolan, from his firing position, was looking at her, his eyes conveying the grim message that did not have to be put in words. Cindy slid back to the wagon wheel and pulled the pistol from under her belt.

During the long, terrifying hours of the night, she had managed to maintain control, but now she felt tears streaming down her cheeks. Burying her face against her arm to hide her weeping, she cocked the pistol and put the barrel to her temple. With her finger on the trigger, she waited for the final moment to come, waited to hear the howling of the comancheros in victory as they swarmed around the wagons.

The gunfire suddenly diminished, and Cindy realized that the soldiers had stopped shooting. At first she wondered if they were surrendering, but then, over the ringing in her ears, she thought she heard the pounding thunder of scores of horses in a headlong run, and the penetrating notes of a bugle sounding charge.

Cindy looked up, unable to believe what she was hearing, and at the same instant Sergeant Hoskins shouted exultantly, "It's a relief column from the fort! A whole damned company!"

He continued shouting, his voice drowned as the other soldiers began whooping in glee, and Cindy rose to her knees to see. A wide formation of cavalry was sweeping across the east side of the slope, bearing down on the comancheros. Even at a distance, Cindy recognized the tall, unmistakable figure of Reed leading the charge. The company guidon fluttered behind him, and dust boiled up in a dense cloud around the horses, the soldiers holding their rifles ready in bristling lines.

A few comancheros leaped up from the brush and began fleeing up the slope, then others joined them. The slope was suddenly alive with ragged, unkempt men fleeing for their lives. Reed lifted an arm and dropped it in a command, and gunpowder smoke billowed up along the wave of soldiers. A giant, invisible scythe seemed to sweep through the comancheros, the hail of lead mowing down a score or more of them.

Like a flock of sheep darting away from a threat, the comancheros began running to the west. Just at that moment, a small contingent of cavalry appeared on the road to the west of the wagons, riding up the slope at an angle. Cindy recognized the man leading them—Sergeant Burns, whose squad had escorted the telegraph-line repairmen and who had refused to take her to Fort Peck.

Burns's squad began firing, and the comancheros, caught in a cross fire, were forced to stand and fight or flee directly uphill. Most of them took the latter course, and a few of the nimblest disappeared over the top of the hill; but most were cut off or hit by the soldiers' fire. One group of comancheros, near the bottom of the slope, stubbornly held their ground and directed their fire at the main group of soldiers, and Cindy saw three troopers tumble from their saddles, their horses racing on. A moment later, she saw Reed weave as if hit, but he pulled himself back upright.

The soldiers returned the fire, and the outlaws who had stood their ground also began breaking and running, pursued by Reed and the soldiers, who were now exchanging gunfire with them at point-blank range. Sergeant Burns and his smaller group of men charged into the comancheros from the other side.

After the leading soldiers overran the comancheros, they turned and began using their sabers, to avoid shooting their comrades. The battle turned into a wild melee, with plunging horses wheeling from side to side and gleaming saber blades turning crimson with blood.

Lieutenant Nolan, his face smudged with burned powder and his uniform torn and bloodstained, had drawn his pistol and saber and crawled from under the wagon. His left arm was hanging uselessly, and he was limping, but he climbed over the dead mules and went to join the fray. Sergeant Hoskins followed his lead, along with a handful of others who could still fight on their feet.

Cindy scrambled from under the wagon, her eyes on Reed. Breathing a silent prayer, she wished his courage were tempered with caution. He had blood on one side of his face, and she could see two large, dark spots on the chest of his uniform tunic as he reined his horse about, in the thick of the dying battle.

As she watched, he ran down and sabered one of the fleeing bandits, then reined up, as if looking for someone higher on the slope. Cindy glimpsed the target of his attention only a moment after Reed spurred his horse up the slope, charging after a large, bearded man running through the brush. "It's Calusa Jim hisself!" a wounded man beside her observed.

Reed rode out of the battle and into the open, raising his saber to cut the outlaw leader down. The man, apparently hearing the horse on his heels, turned, lifted a pistol, and aimed. Running forward, Cindy shouted fruitlessly to Reed, willing him to duck or to veer aside. But he continued riding straight on, his saber lifted. Smoke spewed from Calusa Jim's pistol, and Reed swayed back in his saddle, almost falling. Somehow he kept his balance, however, and spurred his horse and swung his saber. Both the outlaw's pistol and severed right hand flew through the air, and Reed swung again, but Calusa Jim had staggered to one side, and Reed slipped from his saddle and fell to the ground, where he lay motionless.

Cindy was running up the slope, the brush dragging at her dress. The battle had died away into scattered, individual fights, and although soldiers shouted at her to get back, she had eyes only for the scene near the top of the hill. The bearded bandit, despite his missing hand, had grabbed the reins of Reed's horse and pulled himself into the saddle, and Cindy raised the pistol she suddenly realized was still in her hand and fired the bullet meant for herself, but the range was too far, and she missed. The rider disappeared over the top of the hill.

Breathless, she reached Reed. Helpless panic swelled within her as she knelt and took him into her arms. His tunic was blood-soaked, with three bullet holes in it. Under the dust and dried blood on his face, his features were deathly pale.

He smiled at her, the same boyish smile Cindy had always loved. "Our quarters are ready for you," he whispered. "I cleaned them—" A cough cut off his words, and Cindy was frantic, not knowing what to do.

"Please don't try to talk, Reed," she pleaded. "Just lie still and save your strength, and I'll see to your wounds."

"I love you, Cindy."

"Reed, please don't try to talk. Just lie still, and—"

Her voice broke, and she saw his eyes change. For the first time since she had known him, they no longer shone with his deep love for her. But Reed was no longer there. Clutching his body close, Cindy burst into tears, wailing in an agony of despair.

XIII

Every church bell in Madrid was ringing in celebration of the coronation of the new king of Spain, but their chiming was almost drowned by the joyous cheering of the crowd lining the procession route from the cathedral to the palace. Henry, riding with Gisela in a state coach near the front of the procession, looked out at the noisy, waving throng.

General Moncaldo and his plump wife were seated across from Henry and Gisela. The noise made conversation nearly impossible, but the two women, for their part, did not have a language in common, and the men did not feel like talking in any case, since both were extremely anxious, listening for any sign of trouble. Against all advice, the young Alphonse XII of Spain was riding in an open landau at the front of the procession, standing in the vehicle and waving to his subjects as he passed them.

From the size and enthusiasm of the crowd, it was obvious to Henry that the new king had correctly gauged the mood of his subjects; yet it would take only one anarchist or dedicated Carlist with a pistol to transform the celebration into confusion and terror, plunging the nation back into the turmoil that had plagued it for years.

The procession was drawing near the end of its route,

passing through the cordon of soldiers blocking off the broad square in front of the royal palace, and Henry and Moncaldo exchanged a glance of relief. The landau and the state coaches following it turned through a gate, departing from the rest of the long procession, and the high court-yard walls blocked the noise to an extent. As the carriages pulled to a halt, liveried servants filed up to each one. Henry stepped down from the coach and helped Gisela out; ahead in the line he could see Alphonse Ferdinand. The king's young face was red after his ride in the open vehicle on the cold, windy day, and he looked fatigued from the hours of the ceremony at the cathedral. Wearing his long robes and large, heavy crown, he was escorted up the steps by the palace chamberlain and servants.

Gisela, her normal formality overcome by her Teutonic love of order, helped Moncaldo's wife straighten her elaborate lace mantilla, and then Henry and Moncaldo, both in full-dress uniform, escorted their partners inside. In an anteroom they were joined by Willoughby and Anderson.

"Well, I am glad *that* is over," Moncaldo said. "And since there were no incidents, it is good that His Majesty chose to ride in an open landau. The people liked it, and perhaps even those who were against his becoming king are now resigned to his rule."

"Or perhaps," Willoughby suggested dryly, "none of them anticipated that he would be rash enough to risk his neck in public."

Moncaldo admitted that might have been the case. Soon the waiting company, including assembled royalty and cabinet ministers and their wives, were escorted up a broad, curving stairway to a lavishly decorated hallway that gave access to the royal balcony overlooking the square in front.

An echoing whisper of excited voices from the main reception hall downstairs, where the coronation ball would shortly begin, was abruptly drowned by the noise from the crowd outside as the balcony doors were swung open by servants. Alphonse Ferdinand emerged into the hallway,

227

and as he stepped onto the balcony, lifting his hands and waving, the roar that rose from the crowd below was almost like a physical force.

Glancing around at the others in the hallway, Henry noted that Moncaldo and the ministers were beaming with pleasure. However, the two great architects of the moment, Willoughby and Anderson, were expressionless, as if they were present only out of courtesy.

After the king stepped back inside, he took off his crown, handed it to a servant, and then, to the onlookers' amusement, scratched his head vigorously with a boyish grin of relief. The entire party proceeded to a suite of drawing rooms for refreshments, while the king went to the adjacent robing room to change out of the elaborate regalia he had worn for the coronation ceremony.

The drawing rooms, decorated in a Moorish style, were connected by wide, arched doorways. The party broke up into small groups while servants moved about with trays, and Henry could clearly observe Alphonse as two priests helped him take off his robes. Under them he was wearing the uniform of the commander-in-chief of the Spanish Army, and catching Henry's eye through the doorway, he pointed to the exalted insignia on his uniform and grinned. Henry laughed and lifted his glass in joking congratulations.

Willoughby and Anderson, who were standing nearby, turned to see what Henry was looking at.

"Captain Ferdinand has been promoted," Henry explained.

As a servant refilled their glasses, the three men began discussing their future plans. Neither Willoughby nor Anderson intended to remain for the ball, and they would take a train north that same evening.

"When we get back to London," Willoughby said, "I'll have my people examine the notebook you took from Krauss's body. Do you intend to be in England soon?"

"Yes, I've requested leave." Henry glanced across the room to Gisela, who was engrossed in a discussion with the new minister of trade. "Gisela and I plan to spend Christmas at Fenton, her estate near Bristol Bay. I can get in touch with you then. Clifford, do you plan to stay in England for a time?"

Anderson shook his head. "I must return to Washington to make a report on events here. But I've no doubt we'll meet again soon, Henry."

The two men shook hands with Henry, and after talking with Moncaldo for a few minutes, they left. When Henry looked around again for Gisela, he noticed someone present whom he had not expected to see among the royal party.

Doña Allegra Christina y Moreno was striding through the rooms purposefully, as if searching for someone. Observing her with curiosity, Henry watched as she waved away a servant with a tray and proceeded toward the robing room. The young king, now alone, was standing in front of a mirror and adjusting the tassels on his epaulets. Doña Allegra approached, curtsied deeply, and spoke to him.

Smiling cordially, Alphonse bowed and said something. Henry observed that the woman was wearing the same large, unusual-looking enamel ring he had noticed the other day, the one that had vaguely reminded him of another ring. He had thought about it several times since then, trying to remember when or where he had seen the other ring, and he felt increasingly uneasy as he watched the woman and the young king talking. Perhaps it was a certain glint in the woman's eye that sparked a memory, but suddenly Henry had a vision of another woman and another ring. It was a painting in the art collection at Grevenhof, a centuries-old portrait, he now recalled, by an Italian master.

The painting was a portrait of Lucrezia Borgia.

Placing his glass on a sideboard, Henry walked toward the other room. It might simply be a coincidence, he told himself as his troubled thoughts raced ahead of him, but by legend, the ring in the painting was the one

Lucrezia Borgia had used when she committed at least some of the murders in which she had conspired with her father and brother. A concealed needle was said to have injected snake venom into the victim, bringing on a fatal seizure.

Keenly aware of the need to prevent any disturbance that might encourage the young king's enemies or mar the joyful atmosphere of the coronation, Henry tried to appear casual as he approached the room, but his panic grew with every step.

Mercifully, no one attempted to stop him or engage him in conversation, and he reached the doorway just at Doña Allegra stepped closer to Alphonse to take her leave. Henry strode swiftly forward as she curtsied and offered her extended arm to the king. At her side, she flicked her thumb over the ring on her forefinger, but as she began moving the ring toward the young king's forearm, Henry reached out and gripped her wrist firmly.

An inch-long needle was jutting from the center of the ring, a drop of liquid dancing on its gleaming tip. The woman's ingratiating smile turned into an expression of savage, frustrated rage as she looked at Henry. For an instant Alphonse stood there in perplexed surprise; then his eyes opened wide as he glanced down and saw the ring.

Like an unleashed fury, Doña Allegra hissed and, trying to twist from Henry's grasp, threw her weight toward the king. The ring came very close to Alphonse, but Henry turned the needle aside as he countered the woman's frantic struggle. Doña Allegra's shoes must have slipped on the polished floor, for suddenly she lost her balance, stumbled forward, and fell on the needle. Henry had tried to turn it away from her, but in vain. The tip pierced her chest, just under the left breast.

Her anger abruptly replaced by terror, the woman screamed in despair at becoming her own victim. The conversation in the other rooms ceased. People turned to look, then started approaching the door. "Captain Ferdinand," Henry said quietly as he tightly held Doña Allegra, "word of this must not spread beyond this room."

Alphonse's deft reaction illustrated a presence of mind that surprised even Henry. The young king lifted a hand and stepped toward the door, and not a hint of agitation was in his voice as he spoke in Spanish and then in English: "Please remain outside. One of my guests has become ill and requires the assistance of the palace physician. General Moncaldo, please come in here."

The people obediently moved back from the door, and Henry walked Doña Allegra toward the couch. Either through fear or the rapid action of the poison near her heart, she was already slumping in unconsciousness, her eyes closing. Henry picked her up and put her on the couch, then carefully removed the ring from her finger.

Moncaldo was there, and Henry showed him the ring.

"Doña Allegra—I should have suspected," he said under his breath. "She has a son who could claim a right to the throne."

"The baroness told me that this woman was ambitious," Henry said, "but apparently that was an understatement. Luckily I noticed the ring."

Moncaldo looked increasingly worried. "Her son is an army officer," he said. "If word of this—"

He broke off as the palace physician rushed in. The small, graying man bowed quickly to Alphonse, then knelt beside the couch and opened his bag. He took out a brass tube with flared ends, placed one end of the instrument on the woman's chest, and put his ear to the other end.

He listened for a moment, then looked up at the king in consternation and said something in Spanish. Moncaldo went to the doorway and summoned servants, who came in and carried the woman out. The doctor followed them.

"He told me," Alphonse explained, "that Doña Allegra has suffered a heart seizure and is dying. She has been taken to a room upstairs. General Moncaldo, you were talking about Doña Allegra's son."

"Yes, Your Majesty," the general responded. "I know him well. He has been a loyal, dedicated officer, and I do not believe he had knowledge of what his mother intended to do. Still, there is always the possibility. . . ."

Alphonse shook his head. "If he has been loyal, he will not be punished for his mother's acts. Please arrange an appointment for him to call on me so I can express my condolences over his mother's untimely death. Then we shall consider this matter closed—with the exception, of course, of our deep gratitude to my good friend Captain Blake." He turned to Henry. "I am in your debt once again, it seems."

Henry shook his head. "As a representative of my nation, I am more than glad to be of service to you. Beyond that, you and I are friends, and I did no more than what one friend should do for another."

"Even so," Alphonse insisted, "I consider myself indebted to you. If there is ever anything you want that is within my power to provide, you need only ask, Captain Blake." He put a hand on the general's arm. "Perhaps we should join my guests now and let them know about Doña Allegra's unfortunate illness."

As Alphonse and Moncaldo walked to the door, Henry hung back and looked at the ring, wondering at the irony of how such a harmless-looking bauble could hide death. Then he thought of Josef Mueller, the mysterious man in Darmstadt. Mueller had been working for some unknown person or persons who might still be a threat, and Henry looked forward to hearing what Willoughby's associates might be able to determine from Krauss's notebook.

It was late afternoon on a cold winter day when Toby Holt rode around a curve in the road and Frenchman's Creek came into view. Large, feathery flakes were falling, adding another layer to the snow already on the ground and on the roofs of the single row of log buildings. The town was huddled on one side of the road, and the shallow stream that gave the settlement its name bordered the other side, coursing around large boulders that were rimmed with ice and capped with snow.

No one was in sight, and smoke rising from chimneys was the only sign of life. Driven by anxiety over Alexandra, Toby had left the Culley cabin against the advice of the entire family. His wounds had barely begun to heal, Eileen had chided him, and his head was still bandaged; but Toby had been as stubborn as she. Now, racked by a headache that the cold and the horseback ride had done nothing to improve, Toby passed a small building with bars on the windows—the sheriff's office. Perhaps because of the influence of the Culleys, Toby had become determined to deal with this situation himself, without interference. He reined up farther down the street, at a general store and tavern with a sign advertising meals and lodgings. He dismounted stiffly, tethered his horse, and went inside.

The small front room was homey and inviting after the cold outside, with a roaring fire in a stone fireplace. Two men were seated on a bench in front of the hearth, and one of them, his apron identifying him as the owner, stood up when Toby came in. "Howdy, friend," he said. "What can I do for you?"

"I could use a drink of whiskey."

"That don't surprise me," the man chuckled, going to the small bar at the side of the room. "It's a cold day for traveling, ain't it?"

Toby nodded, put money on the bar, and drank the liquor. It was bitter and harsh, though not as caustic as the whiskey at the Culley cabin, and its biting warmth helped dispel the chill gripping him. "Yes, that's good," he said as he put the glass down. "I'll have another one, please."

"You look like you can use it," the man said, refilling the glass and eyeing the bandage on Toby's head. "If you don't mind my saying so, you look a little puny, friend, and maybe you ought to settle in for a day or two. If the food makes you sick or you find nitties in your bed, you don't have to pay."

"No, I must be on my way," Toby replied. "Have you heard of some men who have been coming and going around here during the past months?" He added the local descriptive term: "They're city folk."

Both the tavern owner and the old man beside the fire eyed Toby warily. "Looking for some friends of yours, are you?" the owner asked quietly.

"They're not friends of mine."

The man seemed satisfied by the reply. "Some city fellers bought a farm a few miles from here, but they don't look or act like farmers. They've been coming and going, not causing no trouble that I've heard about, but everybody has been keeping their chickens cooped up."

"Where is the farm?"

"Take the turn away from the creek just north of here. The farm's in the second hollow you come to. The man who owned it died, and his widow went back to her people and turned it over to a man who deals in mules and such. He sold it to them city folk. Don't know if it's true, but folks around here think they might be hiding out from the law in Lexington or somewhere."

"That so?" Toby said noncommittally. He changed the subject to the weather, finished his drink, then left. Back outside, the warmth from the whiskey quickly faded, but Toby's discomfort from the cold and the pain of his wounds was slight compared to the uncertainty that tormented him. He had come to Frenchman's Creek on the basis of a vague memory of a conversation he had heard while verging on unconsciousness. He could have misunderstood, or the outlaws' plans could have changed, or innumerable other things could have happened. The life of the woman he loved was in peril, and he might be heading off on a wild-goose chase.

His horse plodded along at a walk, its steps silent in the new-fallen snow. When finally the trees opened out at the second hollow, as the tavern owner had described, Toby reined up.

The outlines of the wide valley were lost in the dim

light and snowfall, but a narrow trail to his left was indented with the hoofmarks of many horses, visible even through the layer of fresh snow. Keeping a sharp lookout, Toby followed the trail, and after a quarter mile or so he smelled wood smoke and reined up. The last thing he wanted was to happen upon the men unexpectedly, for he knew that in his condition he was no match to fight several well-armed outlaws. He turned off the trail and rode into the trees.

When he was well out of sight from the trail, he eased out of the saddle and tethered his horse in the shelter of evergreens. He took his rifle from its sheath and began making his way through the snow back toward the clearing. A few minutes later, he stopped behind a tree at the edge of a field.

The farm, some two hundred yards away, was a substantial one for the area. The dwelling house, facing the direction from which he had come, was built of split logs and had at least seven or eight rooms, with a second story. A barn and other outbuildings were clustered to one side. Nothing moved outside, but smoke rose from chimneys at the rear and side of the house.

Large snowflakes were drifting down, and Toby shivered as he studied the buildings for a minute or two. Deciding on a course of action, he skirted the edge of the forest until he had worked his way around to where the outbuildings concealed him from the house. He checked his rifle and crossed a crop field to the barn.

Like the house, the barn was relatively large, with a sizable hayloft over a workroom and ten stalls. Toby peered through a back door, but as he looked around, he frowned in puzzlement. Instead of sufficient horses for the large party of men that had ambushed him, only three animals were in the stalls.

Leaving the barn before he alarmed the horses, Toby circled the other outbuildings until he had a good view of the back of the house. What he saw made hope swell within him. One of the windows on the first floor was boarded up, with heavy planks nailed over it. If Alexandra was being held captive there, as he suspected, that would explain the small number of horses, for Sewell would no longer have needed most of his men. By now they were probably en route back to San Francisco.

Between him and the house lay more than thirty yards of open ground. The light of the dull winter day was only beginning to fade, and Toby knew that anyone who glanced out a window would immediately spot him once he broke from cover. But he was unable to wait. He held his rifle ready and hurried across the yard toward the house.

Still weak from his wounds, he was breathing heavily after running only the short distance, and pains shot through his side with each deep breath. He leaned against the house when he reached it, and as he held his side, waiting for the pain to subside, he could hear men talking in a front room. He stepped to the boarded-up window and peered through a crack between two of the boards.

The light in the room was dim, and the window under the boards was dirty. For an agonizingly long time, Toby was unable to discern anything more than formless shadows; then a movement caught his eye.

Despite his pain, Toby's spirits soared. Wearing her boots, trousers, and coat, Alexandra was sitting on a mattress in the cold, dingy room, a blanket pulled around her shoulders. She looked weary, Toby thought, but she was alive and seemingly unharmed. He ducked away from the window and, assuring himself that the coast was clear, followed his footprints back to the outbuildings. He knew now what had to be done.

As twilight settled, Toby sat waiting in the building that had once been used as a root cellar. At his feet was an iron crowbar he had found in another of the outbuildings, and a gap in the log walls afforded him a clear view of the back and side of the house. Several windows now glowed with light, and the smoke from the kitchen chimney had thickened. Toby could smell food cooking.

Ten minutes earlier, a man had come out the back door and gone to the barn to feed the horses. He had returned to the house, oblivious of Toby's already half-hidden footprints in the snow. Now, as Toby watched, a light appeared through a second-story window, indicating that someone had gone to a bedroom. Toby waited until full dark, then walked back to the house, with the crowbar dangling from his belt.

The light of a lantern now shone through the cracks of the boarded-up window. With sudden alarm, Toby realized that Sewell was inside the room, saying something in a threatening tone. Alexandra replied, her words defiant. They continued arguing for a few minutes—Toby was unable to make out the words—and then a door slammed. The muffled sound of sobbing assured Toby that Alexandra was alone again in the dark room.

He waited to make certain that Sewell would not return immediately, then began prying at a board with the crowbar. The nails squeaked, pulling out of the wood. A shadow moved on the other side of the cracks, and when the board came loose, Toby and Alexandra were looking at each other through the dingy pane.

Alexandra's face glistened with tears, but her apprehensive frown changed to wide-eyed astonishment when she recognized Toby. She had to put a hand over her mouth to stifle her involuntary outcry; then both hands fumbled with the window latch as her shoulders shook with sobs.

Three other boards came off, and Toby lowered them to the ground quietly. With tears streaming down her face, Alexandra raised the sash and scrambled out the window, falling into Toby's arms and hugging him frantically. "I thought you were dead!" she sobbed as she clutched him. "Sewell said he had killed you. He had your pistol."

"He didn't quite finish the job," Toby replied softly.

Alexandra released him, apologetic and concerned as

she eyed his bandage. "I'm sorry, Toby, but I've never been in such a state as I was when he said you were dead. Your head—are you hurt badly?"

"I'll tell you about it later. Right now I want to get you away from this house before Sewell checks and finds you're gone."

"He won't," Alexandra said. "They've all gone to bed, and he won't come back to the room until tomorrow."

"All right. Let's get to the barn. We can talk there."

Once inside the barn, Alexandra calmed the horses, which were snorting and pawing in their stalls, and when the animals were quiet, she and Toby went to the warmer hayloft to talk. At Toby's insistence, Alexandra first told him what had happened at Fair Oaks.

The second attack, more than a week after Toby had left, had been completely unexpected. Sewell and his men had rushed the house early one morning while Alexandra, her father, and Jonah were preparing breakfast. The attackers had burst through the kitchen door and seized Alexandra as Alex and Jonah reached for their guns, and she had been dragged out of the house in an exchange of gunfire.

"Dad was wounded again," she said sorrowfully. "I saw him fall as those men were carrying me away."

"Was it a bad wound?"

Alexandra shook her head. "I don't know—but Sewell must think so. He left a note for Dad, saying I would be killed if he didn't sell the farm. But now he must think that Dad is dying, because he's been trying to make *me* agree to sell it if I inherit it."

"Well, he might just be trying to cover all the possibilities. Have they been back to Fair Oaks?"

"No, but they've talked about returning to see if Dad is still alive and ready to sell. But first Sewell wants to get me to agree to sell. He's been trying to wear me down, keeping me locked in that room and coming in only once a day to bring some food and make threats. That's why I'm sure he won't check the room and know that I'm gone until tomorrow."

"He hasn't mistreated you physically, has he?"

"No, but he's made some horrible threats. Toby, I can't tell you how much I despise that man. But—what did he do to you?"

Toby briefly described the ambush and told her about his rescue by the Culley family. "But all that's not important now," he said. "I came here to free you, and to either bring in or kill Sewell and his men. That's what I intend to do, Alexandra."

"You've already done enough, Toby. There are still three armed men in that house, and I'm sure they're all killers. We can take horses, go to Frenchman's Creek, and be back with the sheriff before dawn. You're in no shape to fight them now."

Recognizing the logic of what she said, Toby was tempted to accept the suggestion. But then, feeling instinctively for the pistol that was no longer at his side, he recalled how Sewell's men had seized the weapon from his near-lifeless hand. He wanted to reclaim it himself, but more important still, he was driven by a principle that his parents had instilled in him since he was a child: Regardless of the difficulties, he had to finish what he had started.

The difficulties, he reflected, were great. But now the odds had been evened considerably, and he still had surprise on his side. Taking Alexandra's hands in his, he explained his plan. The farmhouse, he had observed, was built of seasoned pine, one of the most inflammable types of wood. And all around them was hay aplenty. As Toby went into details, Alexandra broke into a smile, for she, too, was eager to make Sewell pay for what he had done.

They waited about an hour, to make sure everyone was asleep, and then Toby climbed over the hay and opened the loft doors above the barn's back entrance, on the side away from the house. In less than a minute the two of them had pushed a large pile of hay to the ground below. They went back downstairs and, working as quietly as possible, began making trips back and forth between the barn and the house, piling hay under every window and against the back door. Alexandra was swift and nimble and made several more trips than Toby, and she also stuffed armfuls of hay through the window of the room where she had been held captive. Back in the barn Toby fashioned a torch from a broom and some oil-soaked rags, and as a last precaution he collected all the lamp oil he could find, put it in a bucket, and instructed Alexandra to empty it under the back door of the house.

When they were ready, he gave Alexandra the torch and matches and stationed himself behind an old stump about a dozen paces from the front door, which they had left unimpeded. At his signal, she lit the torch and began darting around the house, touching off each pile of hay in turn. As the first piles blazed up, Toby held his rifle to the light and checked the bullet in the firing chamber. He raised the weapon and readied himself.

The drifting snowflakes sparkled in the light as the flames leaped higher, and soon Alexandra came into view again, lighting the hay along the other side of the house.

When she had finished, she threw down the torch and ran back to join Toby. "The only way they can get out now is through the front door!" she said, panting from the excitement. "Your idea worked."

"We aren't finished yet," he warned her. "Get back out of the light of the flames, Alexandra."

She retreated to the edge of the trees, and a few seconds later Toby heard men's voices inside the house, calling out in alarm. He aimed the rifle, sighting high on the front door. By now the flames had climbed the sides of the house and were licking at the edge of the shingled roof. As he watched, the front door cracked open, and he squeezed the trigger.

The impact of the bullet knocked the door closed again, and an outburst of angry, surprised cursing came from the other side. Toby reloaded quickly and shouted:

"It's Holt, Sewell. Toby Holt. Throw out your guns and come out with your hands up!"

There was a moment of silence, followed by an unbelieving reply. "Holt is dead! Who are you, and what do you want?"

"You, Sewell. Don't you recognize my voice? Now throw out your guns and come on out."

Again there was silence, as the truth sank in. Sewell cursed in frustrated rage, and then another voice began arguing with him.

Glass suddenly burst from a front window, a shotgun barrel poking through the flames. Toby swung the rifle and snapped off a shot, aiming at the protruding barrel. The shotgun discharged into the porch roof, and the shadowy form just visible through the flames was knocked back into the room. Toby worked the bolt on the rifle, quickly reloading.

Again there was silence, except for the crackle of flames. Snow on the roof was melting, causing steam to mingle with the smoke rising into the night. Sewell shouted again: "I'll make a deal with you, Holt! I've got your woman in here!"

"I'm out here, Sewell!" Alexandra shouted back. "You'd better think of another deal, and you'd better think fast!"

There was more arguing inside, and then Sewell spoke again. "How much money would it be worth to you to let me go, Holt?"

"You're talking the wrong language, Sewell. Now throw out your guns and come out with your hands up."

Flames silhouetted the sides and rear of the house, and suddenly fire began racing across the porch roof. Toby knew that the smoke and heat inside were becoming unbearable, and he knew what would happen soon.

He didn't have long to wait. The front door flew open, and Sewell and the other man leaped out, both holding pistols. Toby had the rifle lined on Sewell's chest, and he squeezed the trigger before either of the men could fire. The bullet knocked Sewell back against the edge of the door, and he was dead as he fell on the porch.

The other man, half blinded by the heat and smoke, squeezed off a wild shot as Toby was working the bolt on the rifle, and fired again while Toby was aiming. The second shot was closer but not good enough, and Toby's bullet ripped through the man's chest and he fell down the steps, dead.

Toby ran toward the house as the porch roof sagged, spilling down burning shingles. Alexandra shouted in alarm, but he darted onto the porch and snatched up his pistol from Sewell's lifeless hand, then ran back. Behind him, the roof collapsed on the bodies in a roar of flames, and Toby slowed to a walk, putting his pistol back into its empty holster.

XIV

The desert wind pulled at her coat and fluttered the pages of the sketch pad under her arm as Cindy walked along the streets of Yuma to the Phelps's home. When she went inside, Anne Phelps met her in the hall with an envelope.

"I hope you enjoyed your walk, Mrs. Kerr," she said. "While you were out, one of my boys checked the mail at the fort, and this came in the last post for you." She handed the envelope to Cindy.

Cindy took it and glanced at the return address; it was from the lawyer who managed the estate Reed had inherited. "Thank you, Mrs. Phelps. You've been so kind, even after I've intruded upon you so much. I know it hasn't been pleasant for you to have me here—"

"Now, you hush up," the older woman interrupted, her tone stern but affectionate. "You have to stay someplace while you decide what you want to do, and we're more than glad to have you, my dear. There's fresh coffee in the kitchen, if you want some."

Cindy declined gratefully and went to her room. She had been in Yuma for nearly two weeks since Reed's death, and although she felt bored and dejected, she had no desire to be elsewhere. She tossed her sketch pad on the bed and hung up her coat and hat, then sat down and opened the letter. The lawyer had learned by telegraph report of Reed's death, and the letter concerned legal papers Cindy would have to sign in order to take full possession of the estate. The man wanted to confirm her address so he could mail the papers to her.

Uninterested in the letter, as she had been about everything during the past days, Cindy folded it and put it back into the envelope. Her glance fell upon the sketch pad she had tossed onto the bed, the pages open to the sketches of buildings and people she had done that morning. They were poor, reflecting no feeling, like all the sketches she had done since Reed's funeral.

Sighing heavily, Cindy stepped to a corner of the room to get a valise in which she kept books, letters, and other papers. In it was a letter that had arrived the week before from her mother, who had learned of Reed's death the day after it had happened, from the telegraphic dispatches at Fort Vancouver. Cindy also had a letter from Janessa, and both letters urged her to return to Portland immediately.

Cindy had written brief replies, stating that she was undecided as to what to do. More accurately, she was numb with grief and did not know where to turn. She had not admitted this, however, for although she was in an emotional turmoil and her life was in disarray, she was certain of one thing: She did not want to return to Portland right away. To seek the solace of loved ones was tempting, but what awaited her in Portland was her past and the danger of settling into a deadly, stifling routine built around that past.

As she opened the valise to put away the letter from the lawyer, a piece of paper fell out. Cindy picked it up and started to put it back, but then she froze, looking at it. It was the sheet of paper on which Marjorie had written the name and address of Gilbert Paige, the artist.

The paper had remained untouched in the valise since the night in her hotel room in San Francisco. Too occupied with other things even to think about it, Cindy had put the entire matter from her mind, intending to write to Paige after she was settled in at Fort Peck. Now, as she looked at the paper, an intriguing idea became planted in her mind, and she did not immediately dismiss it.

Along with an escape from indecision, it offered a new direction and an entirely new purpose in life. Cindy still felt some hesitancy about approaching a professional artist, for she wondered if he would consider her as talented as Marjorie had; but the way the paper had fallen from the valise seemed truly auspicious to her, and there was only one way for her to find out what Paige's response would be.

Coming to a decision, Cindy put away the valise and went into the kitchen. Over a cup of coffee, she told Anne Phelps her tentative plans, and the woman seemed genuinely enthusiastic. "I think that's a fine idea, Mrs. Kerr," she said. "You should have something to occupy your mind, and people get paid a lot of money for drawings that ain't half as good as yours. I'll hate to see you go, though, I will." The woman took out a handkerchief in preparation to cry.

"I'll certainly miss you as well, Mrs. Phelps," Cindy replied, patting her hand. "You've been a true friend to me at a time when I needed one. And I might be here for several more days—or at least until there's an opening on the westward stage. The one that leaves tomorrow is probably booked already." Cindy remembered how the paper had fallen from her valise. "But maybe I'll take a walk down to the stage office, just in case."

The further test of fortune appealed to Cindy, and in any event she was reluctant to impose even a day longer on the generous couple who had done so much for her. After she finished her coffee, therefore, she retrieved her coat and hat and walked to the stage office.

When she arrived and stated her request, the clerk behind the desk frowned doubtfully, checked in his fare book, then lifted his eyebrows in surprise. "You're mighty lucky, lady," he said. "A seat is still open, though usually they're all taken the day before. If you want the seat, be here with your bags at six o'clock. You can pay me then."

"I'll be here," Cindy assured him. She opened her reticule. "Please mark me down, and I'll pay now."

The clerk nodded, dipping a pen in an inkwell to write in the fare book. "What's the name, ma'am?"

Cindy hesitated. Then, with a pride she had never felt before, she answered, "Kerr. My name is Cindy Kerr."

Timmy Holt puffed breathlessly and shivered as he hurried up a road on the northern outskirts of Portland. When he reached the top of the hill, he looked down toward the Columbia River, and what he saw made him smile. The raw, gusty wind no longer seemed as cold to him, and the tools in the cloth satchel under his coat were no longer so heavy.

Hills dotted with houses rose to his right and behind him, but from where Timmy stood he had a full view of the river. So far December had been unusually cold and wet, and scattered ice floes carried downstream by early winter flooding were floating toward the sea in the vast expanse of the main ship channel beyond Tomahawk Island. But on the near side of the island, as he had heard from one of the ranch hands, the river was a solid mass of ice, choked closed by the floes.

Hitching up the satchel under his coat, Timmy trotted onward, heading down the hill toward the river. The temporary ice bridge was a golden opportunity for him to get to the island, where he had urgently wanted to go for months.

Since late autumn, the boiler on Timmy's road locomotive had been repaired and repainted, but Calvin Rogers, the man who often looked after Timmy, refused to bring it up to a full head of steam because the pressure relief valve was broken. A new valve was needed, but they were expensive, and Timmy had no money to buy one.

However, on Tomahawk Island there was a steam

launch that had run aground the previous summer and apparently been abandoned, for no one had attempted to salvage it. Timmy had never mentioned the wreck to Calvin or anyone else, for fear he would be ordered to stay away from the river, but he was sure that the wrecked launch's boiler had a pressure relief valve on it that was only going to waste.

Since it was Sunday afternoon, the streets were almost deserted as Timmy reached the waterfront. The strap of the satchel was cutting painfully into his shoulder, but he was too intent on what he was doing to stop and readjust it. He had put the tools under his coat so he could get away from the ranch without being questioned; it would be safe to take them out now, but—

"Timmy!"

The boy froze in apprehension as he recognized Janessa's voice. He tried to appear nonchalant as he turned to see his older sister riding her mare up the street from the direction of the ferry slip. She had left the ranch at noon to go across the river to visit with their grandmother, and Timmy had assumed she would afterward go to Dr. Martin's house. But she was heading back in the direction of the ranch, and it had been his bad luck to run into her.

Bundled in her heavy coat, muffler, and winter hat, Janessa gazed down at him suspiciously. "What are you doing here, Timmy?" she demanded.

"What are *you* doing here?" he countered, trying to hide his agitation. "I thought you were going to Dr. Martin's house."

"I have some homework to do," she said tersely. "Answer my question."

"Uh . . . I'm just going down to look at the ships," he lied. "Calvin isn't feeling well, and you told me not to pester him."

The latter statement at least was true. Calvin had a bad leg that bothered him in cold, damp weather, and he had been advised to stay off it as much as possible. Still,

Janessa looked skeptical. "You shouldn't be roaming around here by yourself," she said.

"I'm not doing anything I shouldn't," Timmy defended. "Did Grandmama have any news from Cindy?"

"No—she's still in Yuma. You're not going to sidetrack me that easily, Timmy. You don't have any business roaming around here." She leaned over and held out a hand. "Get up behind me, and we'll talk about Cindy on the way back to the ranch."

"No, I don't want to go to the ranch now," Timmy said, backing away. "The only thing I can do there is sit around. I've finished all of *my* homework. I'll be home before dark, honest."

The girl eyed him with undiminished suspicion. "All right—but you stay off the piers, and don't bother the sailors."

Timmy nodded eagerly. "I promise not to go on the piers."

Janessa still hesitated, her eyes seeming to bore through him, but finally she turned her horse and rode away. Timmy continued at a walk until she was out of sight, then began running again.

Once he was past the ferry slip and the piers where oceangoing ships tied up, the waterfront street grew narrower and the buildings along it fewer and shabbier. Eventually the street ended altogether and became a muddy track following the riverbank. Weathered shacks were scattered here and there on rises in the boggy wasteland, and the slabs of ice in the river became larger and thicker as Timmy approached the ice bridge.

The slabs gradually turned into a solid mass of floes that the current had driven together and piled atop one another in the narrows. Timmy was now abreast of Tomahawk Island, but he continued walking, searching for the best place to cross the ice. Every once in a while he glanced nervously ahead and to his left, away from the river, where a cart track led up to a low knoll overlooking the river. On top of the knoll was a cluster of shacks surrounded by a tall board fence. Timmy knew the place well, for it was the domain of Rufus Gooch, the strangest man in Portland. Some of Timmy's friends occasionally amused themselves by throwing rocks at the fence in the hopes of catching a glimpse of Gooch, and Timmy had joined them more than once, although he had quickly tired of the sport. A tall, lanky man with a crazed look in his eye, Gooch had long, tangled hair and an unkempt beard and dressed in old, soiled suits. Timmy had seen him once in the city, ambling about with a disjointed gait, muttering to himself in a loud voice and glaring at everyone he passed. He was regarded as somewhat deranged, but Timmy wondered. He had heard stories of how, years before, Gooch had built a large, low building with thick walls, half of it underground, and had hauled tons of sawdust to it from sawmills.

That winter, Gooch had cut chunks of ice from the river and hauled them to his building, and the following summer the people who had chuckled over his antics had paid well for the ice. But apparently Gooch had been a poor businessman, for he had sold his icehouse shortly thereafter.

Timmy had also heard that Gooch was an inventor and actually held patents on an adjustable wrench and other things. More important to Timmy at present, however, was the fact that Gooch owned the steam launch that had run aground on Tomahawk Island. It had occurred to the boy that perhaps the wreck had never been salvaged because Gooch was intending to do that at his leisure. The island was in full view from his knoll, and the man could be watching over it.

On the other hand, Timmy reflected, Gooch was rumored to be wealthy from his patents, and maybe salvaging the launch was more trouble than it was worth to him. Anyway, he would not have been able to see the island at night, when anyone could have gone there to take parts from the wreck.

The last thought disturbed Timmy, reminding him

that someone might have already removed the relief valve from the boiler. Without further delay, he slid down the riverbank and stepped out onto the ice.

The first twenty yards or so was no problem, for he simply scrambled over the tilting face of one huge floe. When he reached the far edge of the floe, however, he suddenly had worries other than Gooch to occupy his mind. From a distance, the bridge of ice had appeared to be a solid, corrugated surface. But from up close, he now saw, it was more like an irregular series of steep, slippery-looking ridges of up to ten feet in height, and it was far from solid. Between some of the ridges were open chasms that revealed the muddy water below, swirling with strong, erratic currents. And in spots the ice looked rotten, having partially thawed during its long journey downriver. Some of the larger floes were mixed with limbs, roots, and entire trees that had been caught up in the winter floods, and the tangles soon proved a nuisance to Timmy as he forged ahead.

It was slow going, and while trying to take a shortcut around one particularly thick mass of roots, Timmy lost his footing and began sliding down the icy slope of a floe toward a patch of open water. Clawing wildly at the ice, he caught hold of a gnarled root-end jutting from it, broke his slide, and managed to pull himself to safety. He sat there for a while, his heart pounding from his narrow escape, and when he continued on, it was with renewed caution.

He was about halfway to the island when he suddenly realized with a queasy feeling that the entire mass of ice was moving under him, bobbing slowly up and down. As he clambered over a ridge, the river upstream came into full view, not far to his right. The roiling brown surface was littered with small floes and waterlogged driftwood tumbling and sweeping rapidly along in the powerful current. His mouth dry, Timmy stared at the water and envisioned the vast river racing along beneath him and the shifting ice.

As he watched, a large tree trunk surfaced momentarily, then submerged again as it was forced under the leading edge of the floes. For the first time, Timmy thought seriously about turning back. But he summoned his courage and, keeping to the top of the ridges as much as possible, continued onward.

After a while, the mass of floes became more solid, and Timmy could relax to an extent. A large ridge was oriented in a straight line toward the island, and he followed its crest, the willows and brush on shore now looking invitingly close.

At last he stepped onto solid ground, and with his legs still shaking from his earlier close call, he walked along the beach to the upstream end of the island. The launch had run aground at night and at unusually high speed, Timmy had heard—although there was argument about the speed, some saying that a launch simply couldn't go that fast, even downstream. But everyone had been in agreement that only Rufus Gooch would be foolhardy enough to go steaming up and down the river in the dark at high speed.

When he rounded a curve of the island and saw the launch, Timmy was inclined to agree with those who had insisted on the higher speed. The vessel was some thirty feet long, but it had skidded all the way up the beach and nosed into the trees, where its bow had been stove in against the rocks. Timmy thought that the vessel looked old and badly neglected, certainly not worth salvaging.

He had heard it said that Gooch had survived the wreck only because of the good fortune that protected drunks and fools, but as he scanned the tilted deck he noticed that the chair in front of the helm was bolted down solidly and provided with wide leather safety straps. Gooch was no fool, it appeared.

A hole had been dug under the stern to gain access to the propeller screws, which had been removed, but Timmy was interested only in the engine. He pulled himself over the side and, with single-minded determination, made straight for the boiler. It took him only a few seconds to spot what he was searching for, and he grinned in delight. The fittings were intact, including the pressure relief valve, which looked just like the one on his road locomotive.

Timmy quickly shrugged out of his coat and slid the tool bag from his shoulder. As Calvin had instructed him, he tried wrenches until he found one that precisely fit the base of the brass fitting. He tugged counterclockwise on the wrench with increasing force until the valve began turning, and then he carefully unscrewed it.

As if it were a precious gem, Timmy wrapped the valve in a cloth he had brought along especially for the purpose and put it in the bag with his tools. He pulled his coat back on, reshouldered the bag, and lowered himself from the launch, deciding not to worry yet about how he would explain to Calvin where he got the valve.

Anxious now to get back to the ranch before dark, Timmy retraced his steps and set off along the long ridge on the ice bridge. He was cold, tired, and hungry, and he was not looking forward to the perilous journey back across the shifting ice.

Initially he made good progress, but after descending from the relatively safe first ridge, he lost the path he had taken on the way over. Suddenly confronted with a large patch of fragile-looking ice, he had to double back.

While he was carefully climbing down the end of a ridge and skirting a tangle of brush to get to the adjacent solid floe, Timmy heard steam whistles hooting upstream, in the vicinity of the docks. His attention was diverted from the sound, however, for suddenly the ice at the edge of the floe he was on sank beneath his feet, and water lapped around his boots. As the ice gave way under him, he jumped to the next floe and clambered up it as fast as he could, his heart pounding.

When he was safely atop another ridge, he looked upstream and saw the reason for the excitement. In the far distance, an enormous floe studded with uprooted trees was coming down the river, and two tugs were nudging it away from the piers. Paying little attention to it, Timmy continued on to the next flow.

Some minutes later, he was past the most dangerous sections of ice when, again looking upstream, he was astonished to see that the huge, tree-studded floe was now only fifty or so yards from the ice bridge behind him and approaching fast. Watching in fascinated terror, Timmy saw the floe collide with the stationary mass of ice, buckle, and crumble. Sheets of ice ten feet long shot into the air and then plummeted, and as he dropped to his knees, a wave of heaving, tossing motion passed sickeningly beneath him. Ice cracked on all sides, and the house-size floe he was on began rocking wildly, like a small boat on towering waves. Everywhere floes shifted and ground against each other, and Timmy fell flat down, holding on for his life.

Shouting in fear, he saw a giant trunk embedded in the tree-studded floe snap like a toothpick against the wall of ice. At almost the same instant, the ice under him turned almost ninety degrees, and with mounting horror he saw water opening all around him.

The entire ice bridge was cracking apart and shifting downstream, and on Timmy's left and right slabs of ice broke off and rolled into the water. The floe Timmy was on suddenly was an island in an expanse of other islands, all of them jostling and spinning slowly, but gradually picking up speed in the current. Even worse, an eddy was pulling Timmy's floe inexorably toward the part of the ice bridge that had remained intact, and the overhanging limb of a tree caught in the ice jutted toward him menacingly, threatening to sweep him off his floe as it passed. More with desperation than with courage, Timmy forced himself to stand up.

A limb on the tree crashed into his chest, and the impact almost bounced him back onto the floe, but he seized some smaller branches and hung on grimly as the floe passed from beneath him. He was left dangling several feet above the swirling water, the limb sagging under his weight, and the tool bag hanging across his shoulder was tangled in the branches, threatening to make him lose his grip.

For an instant he considered shrugging the bag loose and letting it drop into the water—and indeed, if the valve hadn't been among the tools, he might have done so. Instead, he gritted his teeth and swung one leg up over the limb, then pulled himself to a straddling position. The ice floe he had been on had already spun away and drifted well downstream, heading toward the open water.

After painstakingly working the satchel free, Timmy crawled along the limb and down the trunk of the tree to the ice in which it was embedded. By now the immediate effects of the cataclysm created by the huge floe were passing. The ice was bobbing about less, and Timmy set off again for the shore. To his dismay, however, he noticed that the shore itself was moving, even as he watched it.

Actually, he quickly realized, the entire remnant of the ice bridge was moving, in a gradual but no less perilous advance downstream. Timmy heard ice grinding near the shore, and he knew he didn't have much time left.

The last fifty yards was a nightmare. Timmy had started across the river a good distance upstream from Rufus Gooch's house, but now he was headed directly toward the knoll. With all caution forgotten, he hurried over the ice, falling more than once, and when he was only a few yards from the bank, a floe suddenly collapsed under him. Crying out in panic, he plunged into the water, but to his surprise, he felt something solid underfoot and realized it was the pier that Gooch had built, now collapsed under the ice.

In waist-deep water, Timmy carefully moved forward, feeling his way on the slippery wood underfoot. He finally reached the bank and scrambled up to the path, his wet clothes already stiff and icy against him. He was so grateful to have escaped his ordeal, however, that he scarcely felt the cold, and after trotting nearly all the way back to the ranch, he was actually sweating.

Timmy had enough presence of mind to replace the tool bag under his coat, but no one saw him approach down the front drive. He went straight to the barn where his road locomotive was kept, hid the precious valve, then took the tools from the bag and replaced them in the racks where they belonged.

He was putting the last wrench into place when the barn door opened. "Oh, there you are," Janessa said. "I've been looking all over for you. Dinner is almost ready, and—" She strode up to him and felt his pant legs. "You're all wet!" she exclaimed. "How on earth did you get your clothes wet?"

Timmy thought fast. "I—I got into the water at the edge of the river," he replied, deciding to tell the truth.

Janessa glared at him, then seized his ear between a thumb and forefinger. "You were walking on the ice, weren't you?" she demanded. "You were walking on the ice and it broke! Tell the truth!"

"Ouch! Stop that!" Timmy was lifting to his toes to ease the pain on his ear. "Yes, I was, I confess. But I won't do it again."

"The current could have pulled you under!" she shouted. "You could have drowned! Didn't you realize that?"

"I do now, Janessa, I do now," Timmy pleaded. "I'm sorry, really, and I won't do it again. Honest I won't, Janessa."

Releasing his ear, Janessa grabbed his arm instead and pulled him toward the door. "I knew I should have brought you home with me," she grumbled. "Now you get into that house and put on dry clothes! And be quick about it!"

She deposited him in his bedroom, slamming the door behind him. Timmy gladly followed her instructions, and once in dry clothes and feeling his normal self again, he went back outside by the front door, avoiding his sister.

After the terror he had endured on the ice, the normality of the ranch was almost jarring. The hands were in the bunkhouse, their voices and laughter faintly audible, and he could hear Clara and Janessa working in the kitchen. Feeling unexplainably cheerful, Timmy walked back to the barn, retrieved the valve he had hidden, and unwrapped and looked at it. Now, he reflected, his only problem was explaining to Calvin where he had got it.

XV

Alex Woodling died of his wounds a day before Toby and Alexandra returned to Fair Oaks. They learned the sad news from Colonel Basil Claibourne and Ezekiel Quint, whom they met on the road back, just outside the town of Richmond. Quint and the colonel had organized a dozen men into a posse to find Alexandra and Toby, but up until his final hours, Alex had insisted that they wait for Sewell's return or a ransom demand, and that they not endanger Alexandra's life. He had repeated over and over that he would gladly give up the farm in exchange for her safety.

The news was even harder on Alexandra than Toby had expected. She would not forgive herself for the two days they had spent in Frenchman's Creek, reporting the incident to the sheriff there and resting at the lodging house for the journey back. True, they had made all possible speed afterward, but it had not been enough. The final leg of the journey, with the colonel and Quint accompanying them, was made in almost total silence.

The funeral was well attended, for Alex had been a popular man, and the day afterward, while Jonah and some close friends tried to console Alexandra as best they could, Toby went into Lexington to see a doctor, for his wounds still pained him badly. The doctor did little more than put on fresh bandages and was of the opinion that the wounds had been skillfully treated and should heal in time, if Toby did not overexert himself.

When Toby returned to Fair Oaks, Jonah was working in the smithy, but Alexandra was nowhere to be seen. The old man shook his head and pointed to the outbuilding where bourbon was distilled and stored.

The building's stone-lined cellar had long been Alex's favorite retreat, the place where he went when he wanted to be alone. Toby found Alexandra at the bottom of the narrow flight of steps, sitting on a stool, with her face in her hands as she wept. She turned and wiped her eyes with a handkerchief as he came down to join her. "What did the doctor say?" she asked, a catch in her voice.

"That I'll heal up in time, which I could have told him. Would you rather be by yourself, Alexandra?"

"No—of course not," she replied quickly. "I'd much rather have your company."

He sat down on another stool and leaned back against the shelves, which were lined with five-gallon oaken kegs filled with bourbon. "Do you think it's best for you to stay down here?" he asked gently. "You might feel better if you took a ride."

Alexandra drew in a deep breath and released it in a sigh. "My dad made most of this bourbon, and his dad dug this cellar. I've always loved Fair Oaks, Toby, but now . . . now I detest the sight of it. This farm was what—" Her voice caught on a sob, but she controlled herself and continued. "This farm caused my dad to get killed, and now I hate it."

"Perhaps you'll feel differently about it as time goes by."

"No, never! That man Sewell changed this farm from my home into a place that I hate."

Toby thought a long while before he made the next suggestion. "If you want to, I'll take you away from here, Alexandra. I'll take you to where you'll have different surroundings and can make some new friends, or be alone if you want to."

She looked up at him, tears in her eyes. "Where, Toby?"

"To my logging camp in Wisconsin—at least for now. It's managed by a good friend of mine, Frank Woods. You could stay with him and his wife and their daughter, and I know you'll like them. You'll also like Wisconsin, because it's a beautiful place in any season."

"It sounds wonderful, Toby, but I can't walk off and leave the farm. And I have my horses."

"I suggest that you lease the farm to the Reverend Quint for a nominal fee; I'm sure he'll take good care of it. And you can take a few of your horses with you to Wisconsin and send the rest of them to my ranch in Oregon, if you like."

The unspoken promise in his words seemed to give her comfort, but still she hesitated. "How about my still and my bourbon? There are so many things to think about and to do, Toby."

"We'll see to all of them—don't worry. I'll talk to Jonah and find out if he'll hire on as one of my ranch hands, which will simplify matters, and I'll talk to Reverend Quint, too. There's no reason why you and I can't leave for Wisconsin in a couple of weeks." Toby stood up and offered a hand to Alexandra. "I'll talk to Jonah now. If things work out, I'll go to Lexington tomorrow to see to some details, and I can write to Frank and Bettina Woods in Wisconsin."

"Very well, Toby." She took his hand and and rose to her feet.

For the first time since Alexandra had heard about her father's death, she managed a wan smile. Toby put his arms around her and kissed her gently, and he knew that from this moment on, his life would never be the same.

Dusk was settling over Lexington when Jonah Venable stopped the buggy in front of the small, neat house where

Mabel Seeley lived. He spat out his chew of tobacco, climbed down from the buggy, and walked to the house with an unusually light step, smiling in anticipation of seeing Mabel again.

"Why, Jonah!" Mabel exclaimed when she opened the door to his knock. "What a pleasant surprise. Come on in—" Suddenly she lifted a hand, stopping him before he could advance another step. "Do you have a chew of tobacco in your mouth?"

"No, I spit it out," he said meekly.

Mabel beamed, let him kiss her on the cheek, then closed the door behind him and took his coat. "Luther is in the kitchen, having his supper," she said, noting Jonah's quick glance around. "Here, sit by the stove. Is Miss Alexandra holding up well these days?"

"Seems to be." Jonah sank into an old armchair, and Mabel picked up one of the rag dolls on which she had been working for the Christmas season. She sewed as they talked.

The parlor was comfortable and homey, with a small Christmas tree in the corner filling the room with its piny fragrance. Jonah always enjoyed his visits here—especially when Luther wasn't around—and his present happiness was marred only by his worry over whether Mabel would be willing to go with him to Oregon. Jonah had already talked with Toby about the move and given his preliminary agreement, on the condition that he could take Mabel with him.

After a few minutes, Jonah worked up the nerve to broach the subject, and to his dismay, Mabel's first reaction was unfavorable. "I don't see how I could," she said, glancing around at her dress forms and other belongings. "I've worked so hard for all this, and I have my customers to think of."

"We can pack up everything and ship it," Jonah said. "And you'll have even more customers in Oregon, because Mr. Holt told me that there ain't enough women there, never mind good seamstresses. Instead of working on dolls

260

and other oddments, you could just do coats, dresses, and such. I know that's what you'd rather do."

"Yes, but it would be very expensive to ship all my things to Portland. You know I don't have the money to do that."

"That's our least worry," Jonah scoffed. "Mr. Holt said he would be glad to pay the expenses." He lifted a hand, forestalling Mabel's objections. "I know what you're going to say—but look at it how he sees it. He wants me to take them horses, and he knows I want you to go, too. He sees it as something he ought to pay, and it'll only be pennies compared to what it'll cost to move them horses to Portland."

Mabel was silent for a moment, looking down at the doll. She had stopped sewing. "If Mr. Holt is sending Miss Alexandra's horses to his ranch," she said, "they must be intending to get married."

The analogy to their own situation was clear, and Jonah reddened visibly. "Well, to most people it's looked that way for a long time now. Dang it, you know that, Mabel! It—well, it ain't the kind of thing a body talks about at a time like this, is it? But it looks like I'll be spending the rest of my days in Portland, and I want you there, Mabel." He looked at her beseechingly. "I'll marry you, if you want me to."

It was Mabel's turn to blush, and she glanced toward the kitchen door. "I'd like to, Jonah, truly I would," she said in a soft voice. "But what can I do about Luther?"

"Pay the rent on this house through the end of the month," he replied promptly, "and let him worry about next month. Then he'd have to pull up his socks and shift for hisself."

"Oh, I couldn't do that," Mabel said. She sighed deeply. "He's in some kind of trouble."

"Trouble?" Jonah echoed. "With the police?"

"No, nothing like that," Mabel defended quickly. "It must have something to do with those . . . those bad men he knows. Either he owes them money or they're mad at him for other reasons, because someone has—" She broke off as the kitchen door opened.

Her half brother stepped into the doorway and leaned indolently against the jamb. He was disheveled, as always, and his unshaven face was splotched with dark bruises. "Well, I hear nothing but silence," he remarked sarcastically, "so I must have been the subject of conversation."

"Don't flatter yourself," Jonah growled. His expression became mischievous as he noted the bruises on the young man's face. "Looks like somebody gave you a right good knuckling, I'd say. We were wondering what you did to deserve it this time."

"Now, don't you two get into another argument," Mabel interrupted as Luther started to reply angrily. "Luther, Jonah intends to move to Oregon, and I've decided to move there, too."

"*Oregon?*" Luther exclaimed. "Why Oregon?"

Mabel briefly explained the situation and the arrangements she and Jonah had discussed. "So that's what we've decided to do," she concluded, with uncharacteristic firmness. "What do you want to do, Luther?"

The young man gently fingered a bruise on his chin, then shrugged. "I've often thought about going west, so I might as well go with you. I think I'd like it there."

"It ain't hard to figure out why," Jonah grumbled. "Whoever has been knuckling you is here, not there. But once you get there, it won't take you long to get crossways of some scalawags, like you have here."

Luther laughed sourly. "Jonah, the worse part of going to Oregon will be listening to you all the way there. It's a long journey, but I doubt if you'll run out of things to say."

"You ain't going to have time to listen to nobody," Jonah retorted. "You're going to be too busy helping with them horses."

"Helping with *horses?*" Luther exclaimed derisively. "You expect *me* to help you with—with animals?" I—"

"You'll help with the horses, Luther," Mabel interrupted, to Jonah's intense satisfaction. "As I said, Mr. Holt will be paying most of our moving expenses, so it's only right that we help on the way there."

Luther muttered something under his breath, stepped to his room, and slammed the door behind him. Mabel flinched visibly, then resumed her sewing and assured Jonah that Luther would do his share of the work. Jonah looked doubtful.

To change the subject, Mabel began talking about Oregon, recounting what she had heard about the place. Soon Jonah had regained his good spirits, for he was very pleased that Mabel would be going with him. He regretted that Luther would not be staying behind, for besides being a financial and an emotional burden for Mabel, Luther was a troubled young man, and it was always possible that he would cross the line from merely disreputable activities to serious crime.

The wagon jolted over a rut in the road beside the Columbia River, and Calvin Rogers winced from the pain in his bad leg. He shifted himself to a more comfortable position, then glanced out over the water toward Tomahawk Island. "I still don't see how you managed to do that," he said to Timmy, who was seated beside him.

"I just walked across the ice," Timmy replied sullenly.

"But the river wasn't frozen over," Calvin persisted. "That was just floating ice, and there must have been patches of open water between the floes."

"I just went around them." Timmy had been over this before, and he had a more urgent matter on his mind. "Calvin, why do I have to talk to Mr. Gooch?"

"Because that pressure relief valve came from his launch," Calvin answered firmly. "You must give it back to him, explain that you took it, and apologize."

"But that launch isn't even his anymore," Timmy grumbled. "It's up for grabs, because he just left it out there."

Calvin shook his head. "We've already discussed this several times, and talking about it doesn't change it. I don't know the law pertaining to wrecked vessels, but I do know right from wrong. You took something that doesn't belong to you, and you have to return it and apologize."

"Couldn't I just throw it over the fence and run?" Timmy asked hopefully.

Calvin suppressed a smile. "No, you can't. I know it's embarrassing for you, but it's something that must be faced. Besides, maybe he won't want it. He might tell you to keep it, and if he does, we can go ahead and use it."

"He won't do that," Timmy muttered. "And I'm not embarrassed—I'm just scared. He's crazy, and he might jump out of there and kill me."

Calvin smiled. "No, Mr. Gooch won't hurt you. And he isn't crazy. He's just different from other people."

Timmy grimaced skeptically. "You haven't seen how he acts when he's mad."

"No, I haven't," Calvin admitted. "But you and I aren't going there to throw rocks at his fence, are we?"

Timmy had confessed this last sin to Calvin, but to no avail. It had not gotten him off the hook. The wagon turned off the track near the river and drew closer to the knoll surmounted by a tall fence, and Timmy's fear intensified. He could hear the clank and rumble of machinery coming from the sheds beyond the fence, and he recognized the hissing sound of a steam engine. But there was something else—something that made a loud, steady popping noise.

"What's that funny sound, Calvin?" he asked.

Calvin looked puzzled. "I don't know."

As the wagon neared the top of the knoll, the horse balked, frightened by the loud noises. Calvin applied the brake, climbed down from the seat, and tethered the horse to a scraggly tree. "Come on, Timmy."

Reluctantly, Timmy jumped down and followed as Calvin limped to the fence and rapped on the gate. Steeling himself, Timmy stood there as Calvin knocked harder and then, getting no response, thumped on the boards with a fist.

The thumping drew a response from inside.

"Who is it, and what do you want?" an angry voice bellowed.

"My name is Calvin Rogers, Mr. Gooch," Calvin answered. "I would appreciate a moment of your time, please."

The rattling of a latch accompanied by mumbled curses caused Timmy's apprehension to increase by leaps and bounds. Abruptly the gate was jerked open, and Rufus Gooch, inches taller than Calvin and as thin as a rail, glared at them with piercing, bloodshot eyes. His clothes were wrinkled, and a wild tangle of gray-streaked hair and beard nearly obscured his flushed, craggy face.

Calvin cleared his throat and smiled amiably. "Uh, good day, Mr. Gooch," he said. "This is Timmy Holt, and—"

"I've seen him before!" Gooch snapped back, his unnerving gaze now fixed on Timmy. "It's been a while, but I've seen you here with other boys throwing rocks at my fence, haven't I?"

"Only once—or twice, sir," Timmy replied, quaking. "I'm sorry, sir."

"Saying you're sorry isn't enough!" Gooch shouted angrily, taking a step toward Timmy. "My work is too important to be interrupted by a bunch of hooligans throwing rocks! I won't have it!"

Calvin lifted a hand. "Now, just a moment, Mr. Gooch," he said. "If Timmy has thrown rocks at your fence, that was wrong, and he's apologized. But it's also wrong for you to browbeat him. I can't allow that, sir."

Gooch wheeled on Calvin. "What if boys came to your place throwing rocks at it?" he demanded. "Wouldn't it make you angry?"

"Of course it would," Calvin answered calmly. "And if it happened often enough, I'd take it up with their parents. However, as annoying as it may be, it's still a childish prank. For a grown man to browbeat a young lad is another thing altogether."

Gooch fumed, but he seemed to concede the point. "Well, what did you come here for?"

Calvin nodded encouragingly to Timmy.

His hand shaking from fear, Timmy took the valve from his coat pocket and gave it to Gooch. He explained that he had a road locomotive, that he needed a valve, and how he had got it. Then he apologized.

Surprisingly, the man's anger seemed to fade as he looked at the fitting and listened to Timmy. When the boy had finished, Gooch eyed his two visitors curiously. "Well, he certainly wanted it bad enough," he concluded, slipping the valve into his coat pocket. "Aren't you the two who burned down Horace Biddle's privy with a glider?"

He was referring to an experiment that had been the talk of Portland the previous summer. Calvin and Timmy had constructed a glider that had flown for several miles and finally crashed into an outhouse.

"Yes, that's right," Calvin admitted proudly. "But just between us, Mr. Gooch, it was Timmy who came up with the idea of attaching rockets to that glider."

Gooch took the brass valve from his pocket and looked at it again. For a moment Timmy thought he was going to give it back and tell him to keep it, but Gooch dropped it back into his pocket. "Well, come on in," he grumbled. "And you make that boy keep his hands off my things," he warned Calvin.

"Don't worry, Mr. Gooch," Calvin said reassuringly, nudging Timmy on ahead.

As they stepped through the gate, Timmy's eyes widened at what to him was a treasure trove of fascinating objects. Gooch's small house stood in the center of the enclosure, but Timmy's attention was directed to the sheds of various sizes scattered around the yard. One, with an open front, was filled with disassembled machinery, and adjacent to it was the shed in which the steam engine was running; the smoke from the firebox was venting through a pipe in the roof.

The noise that Timmy and Calvin had been unable to identify came from yet another shed, where bluish smoke with an acrid, penetrating odor puffed from a pipe in the wall. The rhythmic popping noise was so loud inside the fence that conversation became difficult. Gooch, frowning suspiciously, shouted at Calvin and Timmy to stay where they were, then crossed the yard in his awkward, ambling gait, slipped into the shed, and closed the door behind him. The noise stopped a moment later, the machine coughing and wheezing, then falling silent.

The smell of the lingering smoke reminded Timmy of the odor of the paints and solvents used at the ranch, and he recalled something Calvin had told him. "Calvin, do you think Mr. Gooch could have one of those engines that runs on petroleum in there?"

"I'll bet that's exactly what it is," Calvin replied, clearly pleased that Timmy had identified it. "And from the way it was running, he must have developed a better one than many experimenters have." Calvin turned his attention to the shed where the steam engine was chugging. "And he's using that steam engine to power machinery. It sounds like some sort of compressor."

"He has all kinds of things in here!" Timmy said excitedly, craning his neck and peering into the shed with an open front. "Maybe we could make friends with him, and he'd let us look around."

Calvin shook his head doubtfully. "That's extremely unlikely, Timmy. Inventors are very secretive about what they do, and Mr. Gooch appears to be no exception."

A moment later, Gooch emerged from the shed, locked the door behind him, and rejoined them. He looked no more friendly than before. "It's true then that this boy here has a road locomotive?" he challenged Calvin.

Calvin explained that Timmy's father had bought it for him. "It was collecting rust, and we've since repaired the boiler and plumbing, but I'm afraid to pressurize it.

The safety relief valve is broken, and I don't trust the pressure gauge. The glass on it is broken."

"Well, this valve wouldn't do you any good," Gooch said, again pulling it out of his pocket. "Your boiler would pop rivets before it released. This here's a high-pressure valve, and you need a low-pressure valve for a road locomotive."

"Yes, I know," Calvin replied. "If we were to use it, I would put a weaker spring in it. A spring should be easy enough to find."

Gooch grimaced. "Then you wouldn't know exactly what pressure it would release at, would you?" He shook his head sourly at the thought. "Maybe I can find what you need among my spare parts." He turned suddenly to Timmy and held the valve toward him accusingly. "Seeing as how you plundered my steam launch, that must be what you want!" he barked. "Is it, then? Speak up, boy!"

"Yes, sir," Timmy answered, shrinking back. "But somebody else stole the propellers, sir. I didn't touch them, honest."

"Nobody stole them," Gooch corrected him. "I took them myself. They were the only things I really wanted off that launch." He glanced around suspiciously, then set off toward one of the sheds, gesturing for his visitors to follow.

"They were the only things you wanted?" Calvin prompted, catching up.

Gooch nodded. "I guess it's all right to talk about them now, because I already have my patent filed. I had a pair of variable-pitch screws on that launch when I wrecked it."

"Variable-pitch screws?" Calvin mulled that over for a few seconds. "My word, that is something new. I did hear that the launch was traveling at a high speed when it went aground."

"I had her up to almost thirty knots," Gooch boasted. "I was testing them at night to keep anyone from seeing how fast I was going. That's why I got wrecked."

"Well, you obviously didn't suffer any lasting injury,"

Calvin said. "I'm sure plenty of shipbuilders will be interested in that invention." He glanced toward the shed with the steam engine in it. "I'm also sure it could be far more lucrative than that icehouse I hear you used to own."

Gooch paused at a shed door and stroked his tangled beard, smiling in secret satisfaction. "I might get back into that business sometime," he remarked enigmatically. His smile abruptly faded. "You and the boy wait right here."

Gooch went into the shed, opening the door only wide enough to slide through, then closing it. A moment later, he stepped back out with a pressure relief valve, as well as a pressure gauge. "These should do for what you need," he said, thrusting them at Calvin.

"They certainly will," Calvin agreed, holding them so that Timmy could look at them too. "But perhaps I should have told you that we don't have any money, Mr. Gooch."

"I don't want money," Gooch said. He eyed Timmy. "But I would like to know the names of them boys who've been throwing rocks at my fence."

Calvin shook his head. "No, I can't have Timmy tattling on his friends, Mr. Gooch. It's not fair."

"You don't have boys throwing rocks at your place!" Gooch barked heatedly. "If you did, you'd take a different attitude!"

"No, I would not," Calvin replied evenly. "It wouldn't be right for Timmy to tattle on his friends, and if that's the price for these fittings, then we'll have to do without them." He handed the valves back to Gooch.

Gooch fumed, and Timmy was about to protest, but before he could say anything, Gooch shoved the valves at him. "Go ahead and take them!" he snarled. "I don't need them. And I'd better not see you throwing rocks at my fence again!"

Timmy took the valves, his fear momentarily overcome by delight. "I won't, sir—I promise. Thank you very much!"

Gooch harrumphed, then strode to the gate and held it open for them. Timmy and Calvin followed, and Calvin paused long enough to express his thanks again, but Gooch's only reply was a surly nod. He closed the gate loudly behind them.

As Timmy and Calvin rode back toward the river, Timmy thought about what he had seen inside the fence. "I'd sure like to look around in there," he said wistfully. "Mr. Gooch has a lot of interesting things, Calvin."

"That he does," Calvin agreed. "And I'd bet that steam engine he has in there is powering a compressor. That's why I brought up the subject of ice. Do you remember what he said about it?"

"He said he might be in the ice business again sometime. What did he mean by that?"

"I don't know exactly," Calvin said, "but I'd bet that compressor is some kind of refrigeration machine. He's probably thinking about freezing water and making ice to sell."

"A refrigeration machine! I'd sure like to see that, and see how it works. But he's really unfriendly, isn't he? I don't guess we could ever make friends with him."

"No, I don't think that's likely, Timmy. But now we have the fittings we need to test the boiler on the road locomotive, don't we?"

Timmy grinned with glee as he took the brass valves out of his coat pocket, and Calvin, just as satisfied, patted the boy fondly on the shoulder.

XVI

Decorations in the stores and hotel in San Francisco reminded Cindy Kerr that Christmas was approaching. She spent the day in the city, sorting out her baggage and writing to her mother and Janessa to let them know where she was going, then set out on a train east. Her journey across the Sierra Nevada came to a standstill several times while snow was being cleared from the tracks, and a blizzard held the train up for a full day in Utah; but once they reached the plains east of the mountains, the miles passed more quickly.

Still, the winter days faded together, with gray dawns followed by long nights in stuffy, steam-heated cars, and the dim train stations filled with shivering passengers seemed much the same to Cindy. The nagging worry about how Gilbert Paige would receive her was always at the back of her mind, and although she knew that the long journey might be wasted, the promise of a new and rewarding purpose in life made it worth the risk.

When she finally arrived in Maine, it was near noon, and she was greeted by a fierce Atlantic storm sweeping up the coast. Few people were traveling, and the train was almost empty as it drew into the station at Belfast, the end of the line. Shivering and pulling her heavy cape tighter as she stepped onto the platform, Cindy looked around for another human soul. Seeing no one, she went into the waiting room, where a lone porter was standing near the baggage counter. He touched his cap politely as she nodded to him, but he made no move to retrieve her baggage.

Finally, Cindy spoke. "Will you get my bags from the train, please?"

"Ayuh," he replied.

Interpreting that as an affirmative, Cindy found that she was correct, for he disappeared with his handcart and reappeared with her luggage a short time later. Leading the way outside, Cindy pulled her cape closer still and ducked her head into the freezing snow and wind. Two carriages were parked nearby, but each driver silently shook his head when she said she wanted to go to Waverly.

Cindy turned back to the porter, who was waiting patiently behind her, apparently immune to the cold and the wind. "How can I get to Waverly?" she asked.

"You can go in the mail coach."

"Why didn't you tell me that?"

"You didn't ask me."

Cindy sighed in growing exasperation. "Will you tell me where the mail coach is?"

"Ayuh."

"Well, where is it?"

"At the post office."

Cindy looked along the street in both directions, then turned back to the porter. "Which direction is the post office?"

The man gestured with his head, then strolled along behind as Cindy trudged down the icy street, the wind whipping her cape. After a minute she saw the post office ahead and a coach parked at the snowbank in front. The horses were covered with blankets and huddled against the wind, but a man sat stoically in the covered box and smoked a pipe.

"Is this the mail coach that goes to Waverly?" Cindy asked him.

"Ayuh."

"What time do you leave?"

The man looked perplexed by the question. "After I get the mail and see if I have any fares from the train station."

"When will you get the mail?"

The man puffed on his pipe, then patted a canvas mail sack under the driver's seat. "I've already done that."

Feeling that she was missing some essential point in the conversation, Cindy thought a moment, then spoke again. "Well, it appears I'm the only one coming from the train station, and you have the mail, so when will you leave for Waverly?"

"When you give me thirty-five cents for your fare."

Concluding that the porter and the carriage driver were not on speaking terms, Cindy opened her reticule and hurriedly paid both of them. The driver got down and helped her into the coach, then helped the porter load the bags in the back. As they worked, there was a terse exchange between them, which Cindy overheard.

"Out-of-stater," the porter said.

"Ayuh," the driver agreed.

Grateful just to be on her way, Cindy pulled the rug on the seat over her legs and looked out the window as the carriage moved off. Through the haze of flying snow she caught a glimpse of the waterfront, where a forest of snow-and-ice-coated masts towered over the building roofs.

The town was soon left behind, and the coastal road wound through rocky hills dotted with gnarled pines. Although she could not see the ocean, it was always a presence, for the damp salt air and the pounding of distant surf both carried on the wind. Mulling over her experience with the porter and the driver, Cindy felt increasingly uneasy about intruding upon Gilbert Paige.

They reached Waverly well over an hour later. The coach rounded a curve, and the shoreline suddenly came into view; waves were bursting against a point of rock that protected a small cove where fishing boats tossed at their moorings. At the head of the cove clustered some two dozen houses and other buildings.

In front of a combination inn and general store, the driver stopped and climbed down with the mailbag, which was taken by a man waiting on the front steps. Cindy stepped down from the coach. "Sir, are you the innkeeper?"

"Ayuh."

Steeling herself, Cindy went inside as the driver unloaded her baggage. The front room of the inn was tiny but warm, with a door to the general store on one side and a small dining room on the other. The driver piled the baggage inside, and the innkeeper went behind a small counter and opened the registration book.

As Cindy signed the book, she noticed that no one else was registered. "You must not get many guests here," she remarked.

"Plenty. Vacationers."

"Well, there doesn't seem to be anyone else here now."

"Most people don't take vacations during winter."

Cindy made no reply, and the man took her hand luggage and showed her upstairs to a clean, cozy room. More hungry than eager to unpack, Cindy washed up and went back downstairs. It was well past midday, but the innkeeper didn't seem to mind when she asked if she could have lunch; he showed her to a table near the fireplace in the dining room, put a log on the fire, then disappeared into the kitchen.

To Cindy's relief, a matronly woman with rosy cheeks and a ready smile served her lunch, which consisted of spicy fish soup thick with vegetables, followed by a large, delicious fillet of fish that had been fried in butter until it was tender and flaky.

The woman proved more communicative than the men had been, and she paused to chat as she gathered up the dishes. Cindy took the opportunity to ask her where Gilbert Paige lived.

"In a red cottage about four miles from the village," was the reply. "If you turn right on the street outside, you'll come to a lane at the end of the houses. It leads along the shore to his cottage."

"Are there carriages for hire in the village?"

The woman seemed amused. "No, my dear. People here either have their own or walk."

Cindy's spirits, which had improved with the meal, fell again. Her uncertainty about her reception had become almost unbearable, and she wanted to put an end to her suspense. Four miles wasn't that far, but the weather outside was miserable, and there was no sign that the storm would abate anytime soon. Still, Cindy knew she wouldn't be able to rest until she talked with Gilbert Paige, so she went back upstairs, put on the heaviest clothes she had, and with her leather portfolio tucked under her arm, she went out into the storm.

The walk turned out to be even more of an ordeal than Cindy had expected. With the snow and wind driving straight at her, it was all she could do to hold on to her portfolio and keep to the road, and even then she twice lost her way at bends in the road and had to follow her tracks back to where she had gone wrong. With her face stinging painfully and her entire figure encrusted with snow, she had begun to fear she had passed her destination without seeing it or had taken the wrong turn when, just ahead, she spied a lighted window beside the road. Hurrying forward, she could make out the silhouette of a small house. Surf was crashing somewhere in the distance, and the storm was raging as fiercely as ever, and to Cindy's eyes the humble red cottage looked like a fortress of safety in the harsh, forbidding wilderness.

She rapped the knocker, and a middle-aged woman opened the door, gaped at her in astonishment, and ordered her to come in. "Young lady, whatever are you doing out in this storm?" she demanded. "You're freezing!"

Cindy realized that her teeth were chattering from the cold, and she shivered as she replied. "Yes, I certainly am . . . thank you. Is this where Mr. Gilbert Paige lives?"

"Yes, but he's working right now," the woman replied. "I can't disturb him when—"

"Who is that, Mrs. Carlson?" a man's voice carried from the back of the house. Before she could reply, Gilbert Paige himself appeared in a doorway.

He was wearing a white, paint-stained smock over an old shirt and trousers, and for some reason Cindy was surprised that he was a slim man of only medium height. About fifty years old, he had features that were unlined and almost youthful, even though the thick hair above his high forehead was snowy white. As he scrutinized Cindy, she stammeringly introduced herself.

"Yes, of course," he responded immediately. "You're Marjorie White's friend, the one who made those excellent sketches she brought to me. But a winter storm in Maine isn't exactly the ideal time for walking here, Mrs. Kerr."

"Well, I was anxious to see you."

"Yes, that's evident."

Suddenly aware of how she must appear, Cindy removed her ice-encrusted hat. A puddle of melted snow was collecting at her feet.

"You should have hired a boy in the village to bring a message," Paige said. "I would have sent the carriage for you. But never mind—it's done now. Mrs. Carlson, please take Mrs. Kerr's cloak and make her a hot drink. I'll clean my brushes and join you in a few minutes."

"Please don't let me interrupt your work," Cindy put in quickly. "I don't want to make a nuisance of myself, Mr. Paige."

"Nonsense." He smiled at her for the first time. "I'll be right back."

Mrs. Carlson took Cindy's cape, hat, and gloves, gave

her a dry pair of slippers, and seated her in front of the fire. The woman excused herself and returned a few minutes later with a steaming mug of hot buttered rum. Cindy took it gratefully and sipped it as she warmed her feet by the hearth.

The crackling fire and the steaming drink quickly dispelled her chill, and with the wind whistling and the snow still falling outside, she felt snug and comfortable. Yet that feeling was secondary to her excitement and anticipation over her imminent interview with Gilbert Paige, one of the premier artists in the United States.

He came in, having exchanged his smock for a coat, and was carrying the sketches Marjorie had brought to him. After taking the chair on the other side of the fireplace, he smilingly commented that Cindy appeared to have recovered from her exposure to the elements; then, falling silent, he reviewed the sketches.

"I read in the newspapers about your husband's death," he said after a while. "Your name was mentioned, and I immediately recognized it from what Marjorie had told me. You have my most sincere condolences."

Cindy thanked him, but what she most wanted to hear at the moment was his opinion of her sketches. "I—I came here partly because I was at a loss afterward as to where to go or what to do," she said.

"That's perfectly understandable." Paige was still looking at the sketches. "Quite frankly, when I first saw these, Mrs. Kerr, I knew you wouldn't be plagued by a young artist's usual problem—financial difficulties. Your work is already professional, and I think you could sell it quite easily."

"I'm very gratified to hear that," Cindy said, "but actually I wasn't thinking of selling my work—at least not now. My husband inherited a very substantial estate, Mr. Paige, and it was left to me. I don't need the money."

"Then you're fortunate indeed," Paige said. "You have an immense talent, Mrs. Kerr, and you are free to concentrate on your work—which I assume you intend to do, or you wouldn't have gone so far out of your way to visit me."

He looked at Cindy, and she answered him with a nod. "Good. Marjorie said you were interested in etching," he continued. "Have you decided how to get training in the rudiments of the craft?"

"No, I haven't."

"Well, I've given it some thought, anticipating that you might come here. There's a retired engraver in Waverly—a man named Ballard, who worked for many years for Boston newspapers and magazines. He also did bookplates, and I'm sure you could hire him to teach you the various mechanical processes and techniques."

Cindy needed no persuading, but one thing troubled her. "How did you know I'd be willing to move here, Mr. Paige?"

"You didn't walk four miles through a blizzard for a social visit, did you, Mrs. Kerr?" His smile abruptly faded. "Bear in mind, though, Mr. Ballard can teach you only the craft. Developing that into art is another thing entirely."

"Certainly. But I have to start somewhere," Cindy said.

Paige ran a hand through his thick white hair as he pursed his lips in thought. "It shouldn't take you long to learn the basics," he said. "Afterward . . . well, in Paris, there's an aged Russian émigré named Madame Kirovna, who once was one of the foremost etchers in the world. Her hands have been crippled by arthritis for years, and now she runs a large art gallery, not far from my studio in the city. She can be cantankerous, and as far as I know she's never worked with young artists. But you have exceptional talent, and she might agree to help you."

Cindy could hardly believe what she was hearing. "Paris!" she said in awe. "I've never even thought about leaving the United States!"

"Well, it wouldn't be forever," Paige said. "An American artist should stick to American subjects, in my opinion. But for now you must go where art leads you, Mrs.

Kerr, whether that means Maine or Europe. I'll be returning to Paris next spring, in any case—but we'll see what happens. This winter, you can learn the craft." He smiled encouragingly. "And study French, if you don't know it already."

The thought of going to Paris was almost too much for Cindy, and she rose to her feet, shook Paige's hand, and thanked him profusely. Then, her mind still in a whirl, she looked for her things, intending to leave. She had completely forgotten about the storm outside.

Paige called for Mrs. Carlson. "You can't go out into that weather again this evening," he said to Cindy as the older woman came into the room. "Why don't you have dinner here and spend the night in the guest room? Mrs. Carlson can see to your needs."

"That's very kind of you, but I don't want to intrude—"

"You won't be," Paige assured her. "I'll enjoy your company, and we have plenty to talk about—you did bring your portfolio, I noticed." He turned to the housekeeper. "Could you watch for Mr. Perkins when he comes back down the road, Mrs. Carlson, and tell him to alert them at the inn that Mrs. Kerr will be staying here tonight? We don't want them to get worried and start looking for her. And prepare the guest room and set another place at dinner, please."

Mr. Perkins was duly notified, and dinner, a little while later, consisted of thick, juicy slices of roast beef with carrots and potatoes. The food was simply prepared, but the conversation with Paige made it a memorable occasion for Cindy. She wanted to talk about nothing but art, but Paige also was curious about her reaction as a westerner to Maine.

"Well," Cindy offered, "the weather is certainly severe, and some of the people I've met here are almost as forbidding."

"Only at first," Paige chuckled. "Once you get accustomed to their ways, you'll find that they're the salt of the earth—industrious, thrifty, honest, and they don't put on airs. Others may be more outgoing, but no one is more dependable than a Maine down-easter."

Cindy jokingly agreed that they certainly could be depended on not to be outgoing. After dinner she and Paige returned to their seats beside the fireplace, and Paige lit a pipe and opened Cindy's portfolio. Included with her better drawings, as Cindy was painfully aware, were the few halfhearted sketches she had done in Yuma after Reed's death. They were on top, and Paige puffed on his pipe as he glanced over them, his face expressionless. He put them aside and began looking through the other sketches and discussing them with Cindy. She explained the circumstances and what her intentions had been in doing each one, and Paige listened attentively and occasionally pointed out other approaches she could have taken.

At length, he again looked at the sketches she had done in Yuma. "Something is bothering you," he said. "What is it?"

"The battle with the comancheros, in which Reed was killed," she answered. "Since then, it's been in front of my eyes every time I've done a sketch. But I believe if I concentrate hard enough and get completely involved in my work, I'll overcome that."

Paige closed the portfolio and handed it to Cindy. "No, you won't be able to overcome it that way," he said after a long pause. "I realize how painful that experience must have been for you, but you can't bury grief under art. Art is life itself, not an escape from life." He patted her hand sympathetically, then stood up. "It's late, and we can talk more in the morning."

Cindy said good night and, tucking the portfolio under her arm, went to the room that had been prepared for her. It was small but well furnished and had its own fireplace, in which Mrs. Carlson had built a fire. Cindy put on the flannel nightgown laid out for her, and although she was weary from the long, eventful day, sleep evaded her.

Gazing up at the ceiling in the flickering firelight, she

thought about Paige's last remarks. She knew there was only one way for her to come to grips with her grief, but she dreaded confronting the still-powerful images that she feared would haunt her for the rest of her life. Finally summoning up the resolve, she got out of bed, put a log on the fire, and opened her portfolio to take out a sketchbook and pencils.

Sitting in front of the fireplace, she began outlining the scenes of the first stages of the battle at the wagons. She lingered over her preliminary sketches, shrinking from the pain that would come when she started on those of Reed and his men. Hours passed, and the fire burned down as she filled pages in the sketchbook. She was wide awake now and no longer weary, she realized, and she put more logs on the fire and forced herself to begin on the final scenes.

They were ingrained in her memory in minute detail, every gesture, every expression, even every sound as sharp and clear as if it had all happened moments before. Tears streamed down Cindy's cheeks, and she sobbed softly as her pencil flew over the paper. Each line was drawn with absolute assurance, giving reality once again to the nightmare vision she knew she could no longer suppress.

Yet even in the midst of her grief, Cindy was aware that the sketches were the best she had ever done, for the figures seemed to come alive on the paper. She also knew that when she began making etchings, these scenes would be among the first she would do.

It had been an eventful two weeks for Henry. After the coronation, he and Gisela had hurried north to London, where they had attended the christening of the son of Henry's friend Randolph Churchill. Gisela had been impressed by the ornate, ancient abbey, where many of the kings of England had been baptized and buried, but after the ceremony she confided to Henry that the name chosen for the child—Winston—struck her as weak and undistinguished. Later that same day Henry had visited Sir Charles

Willoughby, but Krauss's journal, Willoughby had said had yielded little of value, and nothing at all about the mysterious Josef Mueller.

The following day Gisela and Henry had left London to spend a week at Fenton, Gisela's country estate near the Bristol Channel. Afterward they had taken a steamer back to the Continent and returned directly to Grevenhof where Gisela had immersed herself in the myriad business details that had been neglected in her absence, while Henry devoted all the time he could to little Peter, who was active and chubby. He had hardly had an opportunity to resume his normal liaison duties at the Mauser Arms Works in Frankfurt when he received first a telegram and then a visit from his former commanding officer, Andrew Brentwood, who had recently reported to his new post as military attaché in Bern, Switzerland.

Henry had been shocked to learn of Susanna Brentwood's death, but it was good to talk again with his old friend and fellow officer, and Gisela had responded generously to Andy's request for advice and assistance regarding his mother's business in Independence. Indeed, Gisela had taken charge of matters with her usual decisiveness, immediately dispatching one of her representatives to visit Independence and see what could be done.

And now, two days after Andy's visit, Henry was in Berlin. He had been summoned by an otherwise uninformative telegram from the American attaché, and upon arriving at the embassy he had been greeted by none other than the ambassador himself, along with General Moncaldo. Both the general and the ambassador had been all smiles but had told Henry nothing, and Moncaldo had hustled him into a carriage, which was ordered to proceed to the German government offices on the Wilhelmstrasse.

During the drive, General Moncaldo inquired solicitously after Gisela's health and discoursed upon the dampness of the German weather but would give no hint as to the nature of the business at hand. At the entrance to the government offices, guards saluted as the two officers went inside, and Moncaldo led Henry up a broad staircase and into the wing of the building where Henry knew Chancellor Bismarck's offices were located.

A guard passed them into an elaborately decorated anteroom, where Henry was astonished to see Captain Richard Koehler waiting for them. Richard, who was in his full-dress uniform, with his spiked, plumed helmet cradled in his left arm, looked just as surprised.

While he greeted Henry with his customary aplomb, Richard's expression and color betrayed a nervousness Henry had never before seen in his friend. Clearly the prospect of an interview with someone in the Chancellor's office upset him. From Moncaldo's and the ambassador's behavior, Henry was secretly confident that no one was in trouble, and deciding to play along with the game, he was determined to keep Richard in the dark for as long as possible.

"And what are you doing here, Heinrich?" Richard asked eagerly.

Henry shrugged and nodded toward Moncaldo, who was conferring with the uniformed receptionist. "I don't know. I was brought here by that Spanish general. What are you doing here?"

"I was ordered to come here," Richard replied, glancing uneasily in the direction of Moncaldo. "My colonel told me nothing. Who *is* that Spanish general?"

"Rafael Vincente Moncaldo."

The reply, not meant to ease Richard's bemusement, had precisely the desired effect. He began to ask another question but lapsed into silence as the general turned away from the desk and came to join them. "This must be Captain Koehler," Moncaldo said.

"Yes, sir." Henry introduced them, and the two men exchanged salutes and shook hands. "The Chancellor will see us next," Moncaldo said, "as soon as the visitor who is in his office comes out."

"The Chancellor himself will see us?" Richard paled visibly.

"Of course. This is his office, isn't it?" Moncaldo turned and walked back toward the aide's desk, and Richard gazed after him in stupefaction. After a moment he found his tongue and turned to Henry. "We are here to see Chancellor Bismarck?"

"It would appear so," Henry replied.

Richard pondered for a moment, then smiled weakly. "Heinrich, I am beginning to feel that I am the victim of a trick. I would be very grateful indeed if you would tell me why I am here."

"To see Chancellor Bismarck, apparently," Henry persisted. "How is Ulrica Fremmel? And I suppose I should ask about that maid of yours as well."

"Ulrica is fine," Richard said absently. "Like her father the general, she has the constitution and appearance of an ox. But Malwine . . ." He sighed regretfully. "My maid left me, Heinrich. I never before suspected Ulrica of having a jealous bone in her body, but I believe she was behind it. Perhaps a sum of money changed hands."

Henry smiled, but Richard's attention was now glued on the door to the Chancellor's office. The young aide who served as a receptionist had stepped inside, and a moment later he stepped back out and held the door open for the departing visitor.

Richard snapped to attention. "General Fremmel!"

Henry, who had also come to attention, realized with amusement that the man was none other than Richard's prospective father-in-law, and he did indeed resemble an ox. An archetypal Prussian general, he was a large, muscular man with powerful shoulders and a barrel chest and stomach. His gray hair was trimmed short, and his rugged features were dominated by an imperial nose and a deep saber scar on one cheek. His uniform was immaculate.

While talking to Henry, Richard had unconsciously pushed his saber around toward his back for comfort, thereby twisting his baldric out of alignment. The general's icy blue eyes immediately fixed on the offending article in silent annoyance.

Unhurriedly, Richard straightened his baldric and sa-ber, then snapped his heels together and bowed stiffly.

"Sir!" Richard pronounced. "Please allow me to pres-ent Captain Heinrich Blake of the United States Army. Heinrich, General Hans Fremmel."

The general's manner became distinctly more cordial as he exchanged greetings with Henry. Ignoring Richard, he asked a few questions about America and Henry's impression of Germany, then turned to leave. "And con-vey my best regards to the baroness," he said, pausing at the door.

"I will, sir. And my best regards to your daughter."

The general nodded and left.

"When he is out of his house," Richard explained in a low voice, "Ulrica prowls shamelessly through the papers in his study. She tells me that he is replacing General Reinfeldt as the head of military intelligence."

"Indeed?" Henry was keenly interested.

"Indeed," Richard said. "Now that I have told you something, Heinrich, please tell me something. What am I doing here?"

Henry felt sorry for his friend. "Oh, if you insist. It has to do with those Mausers you took from your armory."

Richard nodded, as if suspecting as much. "A man returned them, you know, and they're back in the armory. What did you do with them while you had them? Am I to be commended or reprimanded?"

"That depends on the Chancellor's attitude, doesn't it?" Henry replied. "Honestly, I don't know."

Richard sighed in resignation, rolling his eyes upward in a droll expression. "Well, if I am cashiered from the army," he said philosophically, "I shall have no means of livelihood, and my family will disown me. But I suppose every undesirable situation has its advantages, and so does this one."

"It does? What possible advantage do you see in being cashiered from the army?"

"For one, General Fremmel would not allow his daugh-

285

ter to marry me," Richard replied. "So perhaps I would b
able to find Malwine again and settle down to a happy lif
as a petty thief or vagabond."

Henry laughed heartily but quickly sobered as th
door to the inner office opened again. Moncaldo beckone
them in.

The inner office was spartan, the walls bare except fo
a large picture of the emperor. Beneath it, behind a wide
sturdy desk, sat the most powerful man in Germany.

Nearing sixty, Prince Otto Eduard Leopold von Bis
marck was a balding Prussian with a paunchy stomach an
slack frame from his fondness for good food and drink. Hi
face, wrinkled and pale, revealed both his full age and hi
periodic bouts of ill health. But his eyes reflected the keer
intelligence that had made him the master diplomati
strategist of his time, and his physical appearance wa
deceptive.

The Chancellor stood up and returned his visitors
bows, then stepped around his desk. Henry, having beer
introduced to Bismarck very briefly at two receptions, fel
certain that the occasions had faded from the man's mem
ory, but he was mistaken.

"I see you have been promoted since we last met,"
Bismarck said, shaking hands with Henry. "Congratula
tions, Captain Blake."

"Thank you, sir."

"General Moncaldo informs me that you have ren
dered invaluable service to the government of Spain. Tha
was highly commendable, Captain, and you are a credit t
your nation."

"It was my privilege and honor to serve my natior
through rendering assistance to a friendly nation."

Bismarck nodded and stepped to Richard. "Captair
Koehler, General Moncaldo informs me that you were als
of great assistance to the government of Spain. In recogni
tion of that, you are hereby promoted to major of dra
goons, which will be confirmed in orders issued today a
the Ministry of War. Congratulations, Major Koehler."

"Thank you, sir," Richard replied smoothly, shaking hands with Bismarck.

The Chancellor stepped back behind his desk, and Moncaldo, pulling up a chair, nodded to Henry and Richard that they could leave. Back in the anteroom, Richard breathed a sigh of relief. "Well, that went smoothly enough," he said. "By the way, what *was* done with those Mausers, Heinrich?" He lifted a hand and nodded knowingly as Henry started to evade the question. "Never mind—forget that I asked."

"You're a true gentleman, Richard," Henry said with a smile. "And now you're a major, too." He put out his hand. "Congratulations."

Richard beamed with pleasure as he shook hands. "Of course I have only you to thank, Heinrich," he said. "But remember—" He became suddenly serious. "There are sometimes disadvantages to even the most desirable of successes. And there is one in my being promoted."

"A disadvantage to being promoted?" Henry echoed. "What could that be?"

"Now that I am a major," Richard replied with a wink, "General Fremmel will regard me much more favorably, and I shall never be able to escape a sensible, practical marriage to Ulrica."

Henry smiled in appreciation of his friend's wit, but he did not say what he was thinking—that Ulrica sounded just fine, but that he, for one, would not be eager to have General Hans Fremmel for a father-in-law.

Late that same evening, Hermann Bluecher sat in his study, drumming pudgy fingers on his desk as he contemplated his recent failures. He had just come downstairs from his bedroom, where even Adela Ronsard's incomparable skills had been inadequate to the task of drawing his thoughts away from what he had learned that day. He had even lost his appetite for food, and a tray of pastries and a mug of cocoa sat in front of him, untouched.

On his desk was a message from an informant about a

Spanish general, an American captain, and a Prussian captain who had been to see Chancellor Bismarck that day. The message was fairly thorough, save for the names of the men and the actual words of the meeting, and it included detailed physical descriptions of the three visitors.

It was the description of the American captain, however, that had solved a puzzle. Bluecher's agent in Trier, whom he had ordered to investigate the arms dealer named Hoffmann, had reported there was no such man. That had puzzled Bluecher, until he had reread the description of the American captain in Bismarck's office and realized it was identical to the description Mueller had provided for Hoffmann.

Something about Hoffmann had always bothered him, and now that, too, made sense. The physical description in Mueller's report had also been identical to the description in the report prepared months earlier on the American officer at Mauser Arms Works.

Similarities did not end there. The American at Mauser had been an obvious danger to the nation because of the secrets he had access to, so Bluecher had sent two agents to dispose of him months ago. But instead the American had disposed of the agents—and in a manner similar to the way in which Hoffmann had dealt with Krauss and his employee. The incidents in Darmstadt that had led to the failure of the plot against Alphonse Ferdinand, and the American's part in them, were now completely clear to Bluecher.

"Heinrich Blake." Bluecher murmured the name to himself as he stared at the now-cold mug of cocoa, and then, with a savage swipe, he sent the mug and tray of pastries flying across the room.

XVII

The Saturday after Janessa received the letter Cindy had sent her from San Francisco, she received another letter, this one from her father. Standing beside the kitchen stove before the midday meal, she eagerly tore open the envelope, which contained several pages for her plus a letter for Stalking Horse, the ranch foreman. Janessa put Stalking Horse's letter in her pocket and read her own pages without sitting down.

"The man who owns that farm in Kentucky was killed," she announced to Clara, who was busy preparing dinner. "Dad doesn't say exactly how, but he's settled the trouble now and is taking the daughter to the logging camp in Wisconsin."

"Killed? How horrible!" Clara exclaimed in dismay. "I wonder what happened. That poor child doesn't have any other close relatives, does she? I wonder who will take care of the farm for her."

"Dad doesn't say. But he's sending her horses and other things here, so maybe she's selling it."

Clara turned from the sink. "Does your father say what she intends to do in the future?"

Janessa shook her head. Clara, she knew, had more than a passing interest in the subject, for she was seeing a man in Portland whom she wanted to marry; but she would never leave the ranch unless there was someone to take her place. It was clear that by sending the horses to the ranch, Toby was being far more than simply helpful to someone in need.

Janessa, however, did not speculate further. Of far more importance to her, her father had obviously been involved in a dangerous confrontation. The letter made no mention of whether he himself had been injured, but Janessa knew it would be uncharacteristic of him to admit as much. The fact that he had written the letter, however, proved he was in at least reasonably good health.

Certainly her grandmother would like to see the letter, if she hadn't already received one herself. Janessa pondered for a moment.

The coolness between the Blakes and Martins had shown no sign of abating, and Janessa remained fully aware that she had been the cause of the trouble. She had tried to smooth over hurt feelings, but so far she had failed. Looking at the letter, she thought of what her father might do in the same situation and became resolved on a course of action.

"Grandmama will want to know what Dad is doing," she said. "I think I'll go over to Fort Vancouver after dinner to see her. I can take the Christmas presents from Timmy and me."

"Just don't leave too late," Clara cautioned. "It gets dark early now, and you know how your grandmother feels about having you out after dark."

Janessa knew only too well. She was about to reassure Clara when they were distracted by a piercing noise from outside. It was the whistle Calvin Rogers had installed on the road locomotive boiler as a safety measure, in case Timmy tried to start up the machine by himself. As a further precaution, the whistle was installed so that if anyone removed it the boiler wouldn't hold pressure.

"Dad also sent a letter to Stalking Horse," Janessa said over the noise. "I'll take it out to him."

"Dinner is almost ready," Clara reminded her, "so fetch Timmy when you come back in."

It was cold outside, and Janessa buttoned her coat as she walked toward the barns. The road locomotive had been towed out of the barn where it was kept, and the whistle became deafening as she drew nearer. Calvin Rogers and Timmy were lying under the gigantic machine and looking up at something as a plume of steam rose high into the frigid air from the whistle. It was the third or fourth time the boiler had been pressurized since Calvin and Timmy had somehow procured a new steam valve.

Stalking Horse, his ward White Elk, and a few others were standing nearby, commenting in amusement and watching. Janessa gave the letter to the aged, wiry foreman, and Stalking Horse unfolded and read it.

Stroking his chin, he handed the letter to White Elk. "Well, it appears we will be getting some more horses," he said.

"Mr. Holt has bought more horses?" one of the other men asked.

"No, these are from the farm in Kentucky," Stalking Horse informed him. "They are going to need barns, and some fences will have to be rebuilt. It looks like we will be busy for a while."

White Elk lifted his eyebrows as he read. "This is all going to cost a lot of money."

Stalking Horse nodded. "If you read on, you will see that Toby says we will have all we need. And there will be a man coming here to take care of the new horses." His attention shifted to the road locomotive as Calvin opened a valve to vent the boiler, releasing a roaring billow of steam. "It looks to me like that machine is still nothing but a big, worthless wagon."

Calvin walked over to join the men. "Something is wrong with the gearbox and the drive shaft," he said to Stalking Horse. "We might as well tow it back into the barn."

"Whatever you say." Stalking Horse looked secretly

pleased. "Do you think that contraption will ever be repaired?"

"It'll take time," Calvin replied cautiously. "Getting that gearbox and drive shaft off will be a job."

Janessa corralled Timmy and walked toward the house with him, leaving the men discussing the road locomotive. The boy, his hands coated with grease, revealed more determination than disappointment, and he talked confidently about how he and Calvin were going to take the parts off the machine.

After dinner, Janessa collected the presents she and Timmy had made or bought for Eulalia and Lee Blake, then saddled her horse and rode into town to the Martins' house. She found Tonie and the doctor reading in the parlor.

"Yes, I'm sure Eulalia's curiosity will be piqued by that news," the doctor said after Janessa told him about the letter. "Give her and Lee my best."

"I will, sir. Mrs. Martin, I'm sure Grandmama would enjoy a jar of your marmalade for Christmas."

"You know, I'm sure she would," Tonie said, standing up from her chair. "Thank you for reminding me, Janessa. I'll get a jar and wrap it up."

As she left the room, Dr. Martin looked at Janessa over the top of his spectacles, his appreciative smile reflecting full awareness of her intentions.

It was late afternoon by the time Janessa boarded the Vancouver ferry. The crossing was rough, with a gusty wind whipping up, but Janessa was more concerned about her errand than her comfort. When the boat reached the other side of the river, she went below to collect her horse, then rode up to the general's quarters. To her dismay, it was already dusk by the time she arrived, and consequently the first words out of her grandmother's mouth did not surprise her.

"Janessa!" Eulalia exclaimed as she opened the door. "Whatever are you doing abroad at this hour?"

"I received a letter from Dad, and I thought you

might like to read it right away, Grandmama. And I brought Christmas presents."

"Presents? And a letter from Toby? Yes, well, I . . . Hang up your coat and come into the parlor, child. You must be freezing. Lee, look who's here."

The gray-haired general, sitting beside the fire, put down his newspaper and hugged Janessa as she bent to kiss his cheek. She turned to put her and Timmy's presents under the Christmas tree in the corner. "It's a beautiful tree," she offered. "Ours isn't nearly as pretty."

"Thank you, my dear," Eulalia said, sitting in her chair. "Please make yourself comfortable, and I'll have a look at your letter from Toby."

Janessa still had the wrapped jar of marmalade in her hand. "This," she said, holding it out, "is from Mrs. Martin."

The words came out like a formal pronouncement rather than the casual remark she had intended. There was a momentary awkward silence, during which Eulalia looked extremely uncomfortable. "Yes, well . . . that was kind of her, wasn't it? Put it under the tree, then, child."

Stifling a disappointed sigh, Janessa put the prettily wrapped package under the tree. She took out the letter, handed it to her grandmother, and asked if Eulalia had heard from Cindy yet. Eulalia nodded and said she would tell her all about it, then put on her spectacles to read the letter from Toby.

After scanning the first few lines, she frowned and shook her head. "Lee, my cousin Alex was killed in that trouble there."

"He was? Good God, I'm sorry, Eulalia. I assume Toby is all right?"

"Yes, apparently so." Eulalia read on, still frowning. "He's taking that girl Alexandra to his logging camp in Wisconsin. But he doesn't mention for how long, or what will be done with the farm and stock."

"Dad is sending the horses here," Janessa volunteered. "There was a letter to Stalking Horse, too, and it was about the horses. They must be a different kind, because they'll need their own barn."

"Yes, they're hunters and show horses," Lee explained. "They require much more care than quarter horses, and better fences. Well, that sheds a different light on things, Eulalia."

Eulalia finished reading the letter, refolded it carefully, and put it back into the envelope. "It certainly does," she agreed. "I can't imagine what possesses Toby. The very idea of that tomboy girl trying to keep Timmy in hand is so ridiculous—" Her words cut off and she glanced at Janessa, as if deciding she had already said too much. She handed the letter back. "Thank you, my dear."

"You're welcome, Grandmama. I suppose Cindy is in Maine by now."

"Yes, poor thing," Eulalia sighed. She described the contents of the letter she had received, which, like Janessa's, had been sent from San Francisco. "I do hope that man will help her and that she can keep her mind occupied."

Janessa glanced at Tonie Martin's present under the tree and knew it was only a matter of minutes before her grandmother gave her a cup of cocoa and sent her home. She also yearned for a cigarette, but her smoking still infuriated her grandmother. She realized it was now or never, and as Eulalia made a movement to get up from her chair, Janessa blurted out, "The present from Mrs. Martin is marmalade. It's very good, Grandmama."

"Yes, Tonie makes excellent marmalade," Eulalia said, settling back. "I'll have to send her a jar of my plum preserves."

"Don't you think it would be better if you took it to her personally?" Janessa suggested. "Christmas is a time for putting misunderstandings aside and renewing friendships, isn't it?"

With a sinking feeling, Janessa knew that her words had sounded much too awkward and harsh, almost accusing. Eulalia glared at her, clearly taken aback, then suddenly began laughing. "Janessa, Janessa," she said, shaking her head in amusement, "no one will ever be able to say you have a sly, oily manner. Lee, getting a hint from this girl is like having an anvil dropped on your foot."

Lee smiled in acknowledgment. "Yes, Janessa's strength is candor rather than tact—no doubt about that. But she's also correct in what she said."

Eulalia was silent for a moment. "Yes, she is," she admitted at last. "I suppose I was thinking that if I let Robert get away with taking her to Independence, he'd be dragging her off to Europe or somewhere like that next time. But that's silly, isn't it? Yes, we'll have to go see Robert and Tonie this week." She stood up and took Janessa's hand. "And you, young lady, will have to get home. I'll make you a cup of cocoa, and then I want you to get right on that ferry and back to the ranch."

Janessa accompanied her grandmother to the kitchen. Somehow, she reflected, she had blundered and fumbled her way to far greater success than she had dreamt possible, and it occurred to her that this holiday season, especially for the Blakes and the Martins, promised to be a keenly enjoyable one.

When the Culley cabin came into view, Toby Holt felt a sense of relief that his long journey was over. It was a scene of timeless rustic beauty, with the smoke curling from the cabin chimney, the snow-covered crop fields, and the deep, dark forest hills beyond.

The hounds began baying inside the cabin, and the door opened. The Culley men filed outside, followed by Eileen, her arms wrapped around herself in the cold. She shouted at the hounds to get back, and they slid to a stop, their tails wagging.

"Howdy, Toby," she called. "We didn't expect to ever see you again."

Toby slid off his horse and doffed his hat with a smile. "It's mighty good to be back, under better circumstances. How are you all?"

"We'll abide, I reckon." Eileen nodded toward the

packhorse Toby had brought along. "Have you taken up pack trading for a living now?"

"No," Toby answered, aware that the question had not been in jest. "I wanted to come see you all, so I brought along a few things for you."

A cloud of uncertainty seemed abruptly to settle over the family. The brothers had appeared keenly interested in the packs, from which several rifle stocks protruded, but glances toward their father evoked a black frown. Eileen, also uneasy, blushed as Toby advanced and shook her hand. The four brothers simply nodded when Toby shook hands with them in turn.

The old man shook hands readily enough, but his words were less than welcoming. "We don't take pay for help to them in need."

"I'm not attempting to pay you, Mr. Culley," Toby said. "You and your family saved my life, and it's impossible for me to pay for that. But I now consider all of you my friends, regardless of what you feel for me, and with all respect, sir, there's nothing wrong with giving a friend a present at Christmas."

The words were put more as a challenge than as an excuse, and the old man, stroking his gray beard, looked warily at Toby, then at the packhorse.

After a moment, Eileen broke the impasse. "Well, make up your mind, Pa. My moccasins is freezing to the ground."

He pursed his lips in disapproval, glared at her, then grudgingly nodded to Toby. "We're much obliged."

Toby smiled and beckoned Eileen's brothers over to the packhorse. They eagerly helped him untie the packs and lift them off the horse, and Zadoc, the youngest brother, led the animals to the barn.

Inside the cabin, Toby waited for Zadoc to return, then opened the packs. There was a case of traps, and he handed a new Sharps rifle to each of the men. He had also brought a bullet mold, gunpowder, and boxes of primers, and for Eileen there were bolts of calico and wool flannel, a large bag of assorted buttons, packages of needles, and spools of thread.

He also handed her an extra rifle and a box of traps. "These," he explained, "are for Clem Siler when you and he get married."

Eileen took them, awed by the abundance of things he had brought. "We didn't know you was rich, Toby," she said in amazement.

Toby glanced around the neat, homey cabin. A venison roast was sizzling on the spit in the fireplace, while pans of vegetables simmered on the coals, filling the cabin with an appetizing scent. In a corner stood a tree decorated with threaded popcorn and bright bits of cloth. "There are different ways to be wealthy, Eileen," he observed.

"Maybe so, but you're rich in the way that matters," she replied, practical as always. "We was just fixing to set down to supper. Zeb, pull Toby up a stool."

The men leaned their new rifles against a wall and were still eyeing them as Eileen dished up the food. The venison roast, which Eileen had larded with bacon, was tender and juicy, and the well-seasoned vegetables were delicious. As they ate, Eileen questioned Toby on the details of what had happened after he left the cabin; the family had already heard the rough outline of the story as it was known in Frenchman's Creek. Toby concluded with the death of Alexandra's father, which they did not know about.

Eileen and the men shook their heads regretfully, and there was an awkward silence. "You still seem to be a mite stiff in getting about, Toby," Eileen said at last. "Are you healing up all right?"

"I am, thanks to you. I went to a doctor in Lexington, and he said that you had done a very skillful job."

"I reckon it was good enough," Eileen said. "Women here have to know how to whittle bullets out of men just like they have to know how to cook. Anyhow, you saw to it that them varmints won't be causing any more mischief, so it's finished, ain't it?"

Toby had definite reservations on that point, but he made a noncommittal reply and let the comment pass. He strongly suspected that Sewell had been only a tool, sent to Kentucky by some criminal overlord in San Francisco. But it was only a suspicion, and he had no intention at present of going to San Francisco to try to track down whoever had been ultimately responsible for what had happened at Fair Oaks. Besides, Alexandra needed him with her now.

"Well, tomorrow is Christmas," Eileen said cheerfully. "Zadoc shot us two turkey birds for dinner tomorrow. You'll stay at least long enough to spend Chistmas with us, won't you, Toby?"

Toby hesitated, not having expected the invitation. More than anything, he wanted to be with Alexandra for Christmas, but that would be impossible. Both he and his horses needed rest, and it would take him several days to return to Fair Oaks.

While the Culleys were poor in some material things, they were humbly content and even rich in a way that meant much to Toby, especially during the holiday season, and he knew that sharing a Christmas with them would be something he would always remember. After glancing around the table, he accepted the invitation gratefully. Eileen smiled in reply, and the men grunted in satisfaction.

In San Francisco, the raucous revelry of a drunken celebration drifted up to the top-floor apartment where Carl Sykes lived and worked, ruling over the affairs of his criminal empire.

The noise was no more than a whisper of sound in the opulently furnished meeting room adjacent to Sykes's office, where he was presently seated at a long table with four other men. The meeting was an unusual one, and Sykes was in the grips of an unusual emotion. He was being humbled.

The four men at the table with him were his principal

underlings. Ordinarily they came to the meeting room to receive instructions, but today he was receiving instructions from them. Actually, their honeyed words, delivered with what appeared to be great deference, amounted to a reprimand, which he had no alternative but to accept. Individually, he could crush any one of them. But the four had been a part of the criminal organization for as long as he had, and acting together, as the entire first level of authority below him, they could remove and replace him.

In the past, Sykes's authority had always been absolute, because he had always been successful. Now that he had made a serious error, however, his authority was being challenged. Aware that a precedent might be set that would be dangerous to him in the future, he inwardly seethed, yet he was powerless to do anything about it at present.

"It was a good idea, Mr. Sykes," one of the men was saying. "It would have been good to set up an entirely new operation in Kentucky, because that's ripe territory. But things went wrong from the outset, didn't they? We believe you should have stopped it then."

"In light of what has happened," Sykes replied with icy calm, "I should have. But I didn't have the advantage of knowing the future."

One of the men shook his head and puffed on his cigar. "But Toby Holt was involved right from the beginning, Mr. Sykes," he said. "The way we see it, that should have tipped you off there would be trouble. You knew he was involved, didn't you?"

"Yes, of course. But if I had succeeded in getting rid of him, every organization in the country would have been grateful to us. And they would have feared us, and avoided trouble with us."

"But," one of the men objected, "if you had got rid of Holt and the evidence pointed to San Francisco, this place would have been swarming with federal marshals. That's the sort of attention we don't need, Mr. Sykes."

"The evidence wouldn't have pointed to San Francisco. I would have seen to that."

"Well, that's all water under the bridge," the first speaker put in. "Either Holt got Sewell to talk before he did him in, or he didn't. We'll never know." He looked directly at Sykes. "Unless Holt suddenly shows up here, that is."

The accusation was clear, and the other three murmured in agreement. One of them picked up a bottle and leaned over to refill their glasses. Sykes, who neither smoked nor drank alcoholic beverages, had a glass of water in front of him, which he had not touched.

"What happened was a mistake, Mr. Sykes," one of the men concluded. "We're all agreed on that, so there's no need for anything more to be said about it. But in the future, we believe it would be a good idea for you to discuss your plans with us. That would prevent something like this from happening again."

The four were looking at him intently, and Sykes nodded. "Very well. In the future, if I contemplate anything other than routine business, I'll consult with you."

The four men smiled, drained their glasses, and stood up. "None of us harbors any ill feelings over this, Mr. Sykes," one of them said. "We hope you don't either."

"Of course not. Business is business, gentlemen. I'll look forward to seeing you at our regular meeting day after tomorrow."

The men filed out the door. When it closed behind them, Sykes relaxed his rigid self control, no longer needing to conceal his anger. It swelled to a fury within him, causing him to tremble violently. He also felt nauseated, which was aggravated by the cigar smoke in the room. He went through a connecting door to his office and dropped into the chair behind his desk.

With his small, spare build, rimless glasses, and bookish manner, Sykes looked like a bank clerk, which he once had been, many years before. Indeed, if he had possessed a bit more patience or the slightest degree of moral judgment, his keen intelligence and driving energy would surely have advanced him to a place of leadership in the banking industry.

But Sykes had been ambitious, and he had been in a hurry. After skillfully embezzling a large amount of money from the bank where he had worked, he had contacted the four men who had just left the meeting room. At the time they had been leaders of small gangs of petty criminals, but with the money he had embezzled, Sykes had financed them and forged their gangs into an effective, tightly knit organization.

Over the years, with the help of his leadership, the organization had expanded into the largest one on the West Coast, with scores of lower-level bosses overseeing a wide range of lucrative criminal activities. But now Sykes's leadership had been successfully challenged. A precedent had been established that would leave all his decisions open to argument and discussion.

As his anger gradually cooled, Sykes pondered his best course of action. The next level of authority below the four consisted of sixteen men—fifteen, without Sewell—and Sykes had direct contact with many of them. He would, he reflected, have to strengthen those contacts without alerting the four. Through promises of promotion for some of the fifteen, he could arrange to have the four eliminated in one quick stroke, then replace them with others who would be more manageable.

Some temporary disruption of the organization would result, which Sykes deeply regretted. But he could not allow his absolute leadership to be questioned.

He opened a desk drawer and took out a clipping from a Lexington newspaper, which his private secretary had taken great pains to obtain. The clipping described what had happened at the horse farm. There was also a picture, and the caption under it stated that it was an engraving from a photograph made after the Great Chicago Fire. In the center of the group of subjects, flanked by a mayor and a governor, stood Toby Holt.

Reading the clipping and looking at the picture were galling for Sykes, but he wanted it to be thus, knowing it would spur him to greater effort to seek his revenge. It would also make his revenge more enjoyable. He picked up a pen, dipped it in ink, and drew a circle around the face of Toby Holt.

Anger made his hand tremble, and the pen traced a wavering line. Sykes had no specific plan in mind and was aware that he might have to wait for years for the right time to strike. But with the picture as a constant reminder, he would never lose sight of his goal. The opportunity would eventually come, and then he would crush Toby Holt.

Sykes put the clipping back into his desk drawer and closed it.

In the southern part of New Mexico Territory, the Whitman family sat working together during the early evening hours. At one side of the fireplace in the parlor of the small, comfortable ranch house, Tom Whitman's wife mended clothes, while her two teenage daughters knitted. Tom Whitman and his two young sons sat on the other side of the fireplace, oiling and mending a set of harnesses.

A sudden commotion from the corral outside carried into the parlor; the horses were whinnying and moving about, obviously upset. Tom Whitman put his work aside and told his family to be quiet. Mountain lions, bears, and other predators were a danger in this remote region, but far more menacing were recent rumors that comancheros had been moving into the area.

The family sat silent and motionless. The dog barked outside, then broke off with a yelp. Whitman frowned and got up quickly, moving for his rifle over the fireplace.

Before he could reach it, however, the door burst open and several ragged, filthy men rushed in. The women screamed, and as Whitman snatched for his rifle, a pistol fired with a roar and the bullet struck him in the shoulder, knocking him back against the stones of the fireplace.

Blood trickled between his fingers as he clutched his shoulder and leaned against the fireplace. The rest of the family cowered in fright as they looked at the intruders—six of them—both Indians and whites. Several wore bandages or bore other evidence of recent wounds; one had a half-healed scar on his face, and two were limping badly as they kicked open doors and looked into the other rooms.

Outside, men were shouting, rounding up stock and looting the smokehouse and other outbuildings. The Whitmans, frozen in fear and shock, waited to see what their fate would be. The noise outside began fading away, and then another man came into the room. From the manner in which the others made way for him, he clearly was their leader.

Tall and heavyset, he was wearing a strange-looking military tunic, a blue coat with red cuffs and collar. His dark eyes were savage, and he had the pale, drawn appearance of one who was still recovering from a serious illness or wound. In place of a hand, a gleaming steel hook jutted from his right coat sleeve.

Tom Whitman, his face blanched with fear and pain, found his voice: "Who are you? What do you want?"

The one-handed man's only reply was an evil smile.

"Have mercy on us!" Whitman's wife begged, bursting into tears. "Take our stock or whatever else you want, but leave us in peace! We've done you no wrong."

The plea was in vain, for there was no mercy in the leader's eyes. With his hook he reached out to one of the daughters, pushing her hair back from the side of her face and gazing at her lustfully as the girl shrank away and whimpered in terror. Then he turned back to the door.

"Kill the men," he said with a French accent. "And bring the women along."

NEW MEXICO!

by Dana Fuller Ross

Calusa Jim, the mysterious one-handed outlaw, resurfaces with his band of comancheros to despoil New Mexico Territory, and the U.S. Cavalry is powerless to strike at his refuge across the border.

Posing as a drifter, Toby Holt joins the cutthroat renegades in order to lead them into a trap, but exposure of his ruse will lead to certain death.

Marjorie White, photographing a whaling voyage, weathers stormy Cape Horn and sails across the vast Pacific, but a brief call in an exotic land results in tragedy as rampaging cannibals seize the ship.

Death stalks both Henry Blake and the baroness, while Andy Brentwood falls into a love trap from which there is no escape. And back in Portland, Timmy Holt tests the limits of speed, gravity, and authority.

Read **NEW MEXICO!**, wherever Bantam books are sold.

★ WAGONS WEST ★

A series of unforgettable books that trace the lives of a dauntless band of pioneering men, women, and children as they brave the hazards of an untamed land in their trek across America. This legendary caravan of people forge a new link in the wilderness. They are Americans from the North and the South, alongside immigrants, Blacks, and Indians, who wage fierce daily battles for survival on this uncompromising journey—each to their private destinies as they fulfill their greatest dreams.

☐	26822	**INDEPENDENCE! #1**	$4.50
☐	26162	**NEBRASKA! #2**	$4.50
☐	26242	**WYOMING! #3**	$4.50
☐	26072	**OREGON! #4**	$4.50
☐	26070	**TEXAS! #5**	$4.50
☐	26377	**CALIFORNIA! #6**	$4.50
☐	26546	**COLORADO! #7**	$4.50
☐	26069	**NEVADA! #8**	$4.50
☐	26163	**WASHINGTON! #9**	$4.50
☐	26073	**MONTANA! #10**	$4.50
☐	26183	**DAKOTA! #11**	$4.50
☐	26521	**UTAH! #12**	$4.50
☐	26071	**IDAHO! #13**	$4.50
☐	26367	**MISSOURI! #14**	$4.50
☐	27141	**MISSISSIPPI! #15**	$4.50
☐	25247	**LOUISIANA! #16**	$4.50
☐	25622	**TENNESSEE! #17**	$4.50
☐	26022	**ILLINOIS! #18**	$4.50
☐	26533	**WISCONSIN! #19**	$4.50
☐	26849	**KENTUCKY! #20**	$4.50

Prices and availability subject to change without notice.